THE UNTOUCHABLES

The tree's leaves were long, needlelike, and edged with sharp spines. Mahoney reached out a hand to touch.

"Don't," Sten snapped. Then he saw the puzzled look on Mahoney's face. "They don't like to be touched," he explained.

Sten picked out a low-hanging branch and inched forward, knife blade gleaming. The branch seemed to move ever so slightly toward him, the leaves rotating so the teeth were facing out.

Sten leaped forward and struck. Moisture boiled from the wound and the branch snapped forward, trying to curl around him, but he bounded back again. The liquid pouring out of the wound hissed and bubbled in the snow.

"That should make him nice and mad," was all Sten said.

By Allan Cole and Chris Bunch
Published by Ballantine Books:

The STEN Adventures:
   STEN
   THE WOLF WORLDS
   THE COURT OF A THOUSAND SUNS
   FLEET OF THE DAMNED
   REVENGE OF THE DAMNED
   THE RETURN OF THE EMPEROR

A RECKONING FOR KINGS

THE RETURN OF THE EMPEROR

ALLAN COLE
and CHRIS BUNCH

A Del Rey Book

BALLANTINE BOOKS • NEW YORK

A Del Rey Book
Published by Ballantine Books

Library of Congress Catalog Card Number: 90-91846

ISBN 0-345-36130-X

Manufactured in the United States of America

First Edition: November 1990

Cover Art by Michael Herring

To
Norman Spinrad
(Hippiecommiesymp - Active)
Who helped us walk into this drakh
and
Dennis Foley
(Green Hat - Retired)
Who keeps it from getting more than chin-high

Note

The titles of Books One, Two, and Three are the official ranks Augustus won from the Roman senate to become Emperor. *Princeps* means "Leading Man." *Imperator*, "Military Commander." This word is the Latin root for Emperor. *Pater Patriae* means "Father of the Fatherland."

The title of Book Four translates as "We About to Die Salute You." It was the famous cry of the gladiators as they paid respects to their emperor before engaging in the bloodbaths of the ancient circuses.

BOOK ONE

PRINCEPS

CHAPTER ONE

THE SHIP BULKED monstrous. Each of the decahedron's sides measured nearly a square kilometer.

There was but one man on board. He floated, motionless, in a shallow pool that curved in the center of one compartment. His eyes opened. Blue. Incurious, like a newly born child. Some time passed.

A valve activated, and the liquid drained out of the pool. One side dropped away. The man sat up and lowered his legs to the deck, moving slowly and carefully like an invalid testing himself after a long time bedridden. The deck was warm.

He might have sat there for a moment, an hour, or a day before a voice spoke. It came from everywhere.

"There is food and drink in the next chamber."

Obediently the man pushed himself to his feet. He swayed, then recovered. On a low stand beside the pool/bed was a blue coverall. He glanced at it briefly, then walked to a wall. It was smooth and blank except for a circular palmswitch. He touched the switch.

The wall became a screen. Vid? Imaging radar? Computer simulation?

Outside lay space/not space. It was black, and it was all colors. It hurt the man's eyes. He palmed the switch once more, and the screen became a wall.

Still naked, he padded through a doorway.

A table was set for one. The dishes were covered. The man lifted one cover and scooped food up with his fin-

gers. He chewed, then swallowed. His expression was
still unchanged.

He wiped his fingers on his thigh and walked into another compartment, where he saw a reclining chair with
a steel-gleaming helmet on it. Odd tendrils curled from
the helmet.

The man sat down and put the helmet on.

There were other people in the room. No. He was outside. He was wearing clothing—some kind of uniform.
The other people were all smiling and laughing and trying to touch him. He let them. He heard himself saying
words he did not yet understand.

He noted one person amid the throng. He had a very
pale face, and his eyes gleamed. The pale-faced man
stretched out his hand to shake. Suddenly he drew something metal-shining from his clothing.

The man felt blows in his stomach. Felt himself falling
backward. Felt pain. Pain rising until . . . until everything stopped.

The man took off the helmet. He was back in the compartment, back in the reclining chair.

The voice spoke again. "E-time since deactivation: six
years, three months, two days."

The man's expression changed slightly. A thought
drifted through his mind: Wrong. Five years late. Then
the thought was discarded as meaningless. What was
"late?" He rose.

"You have ten ship-days before departure."

The man nodded once. He returned to the mess compartment. He was hungry again.

CHAPTER TWO

IT WAS A quiet little planet in a nondescript system over-seen by a dying yellow star. The system had no particular history, was well off any major trade or tourist routes, and rarely had any visitors.

Many E-years before, an Imperial Survey Mission had made a desultory study and found little of interest. The science officer had duly noted that it was about .87 E-size, had commensurate gravity, E-normal atmosphere, and sat three AU from its sun. The climate was tropical to sub-arctic, and the planet supported any number of thriving life forms. The top predator on land was a shy, catlike creature that proved to be of no danger to anyone.

There were also "No beings of higher development observed."

The planet was dubbed Survey World XM-Y-1134. And for several hundred years, that was its sole name—although it was unlikely anyone ever asked.

It got a proper name of sorts from a restless entre-preneur who built a mansion in the temperate zone for himself and his hangers-on, then briefly toyed with the idea of turning it into a remote resort. To this end, he had constructed a state-of-the-art spaceport. Whether or not the idea had merit, no one would ever learn. The entrepreneur lost three or four fortunes and came to an obscure, rather sad end.

But the planet didn't mind. It hummed and wobbled busily about its orbit as it had done for several billion years, scratching its fur against a cosmic stump every few hundred millions of years or so—and wiping out any life-forms that had become too prolific and giving another group a start.

The planet's new name was Smallbridge. The source for that name was buried along with the entrepreneur and his conceit.

Sten liked it fine. He had spent more than five years exploring Smallbridge's beaches, marshes, broad plains and deserts, forests and ice floes, sometimes with eager companions, sometimes alone. There had been a few adventures—and more than a few trysts with lovely women. But nothing had stuck. He had encountered no one like the steel-willed Bet of his youth. Or the relentless Lisa Haines. Or the fiery gambler, St. Clair.

In the last year or so, he had found himself just going through the motions of living. He had fallen into a dark mood he couldn't shake.

During rational moments, he would rouse himself. Give himself a good talking to. Call himself all kinds of a rich fool of a clot.

He had everything any being could want, didn't he? Gypsy Ida, his old Mantis teammate, had seen to that. He and Alex Kilgour had exited the Tahn POW camp wealthy beyond their dreams. While they had languished in the Heath slammer, Ida had rolled their ever-growing back pay into one investment after another until the result was two not so smallish fortunes.

Besides the money, Kilgour wound up with the poshest estate on his heavy-world home of Edinburgh.

Sten got his own planet.

Thanks a clot of a lot, Ida. Now, what?

Come on, don't blame the Rom. As Mahoney would have said: "Don't be kicking over the milk the cow gave." Mahoney would have reminded Sten that he had plucked him off the factory world of Vulcan, a young Delinq half a breath from being brain-burned. Mahoney would sneer and point out that Sten had crawled through the mud and worse to rise from the ranks as an infantry grunt to a deadly Mantis operative to commander of the Emperor's personal bodyguard to hero of the Tahn wars— and finally to admiral. He would brush over the oceans of gore Sten was personally responsible for and tell him that he was still a young man and just needed to pluck his finger out and get back to business.

But Mahoney was dead.

Sten's old boss, the Eternal Emperor, would have laughed at him, poured a double shot of stregg to put blood in his eye, and sent him off to face a suitable enemy. It wouldn't matter much who the enemy might be. It would be enough that the beings were threatening the peace and security of an empire that had thrived for nearly three thousand years.

But the Emperor, too, was dead.

The last time Sten had seen the Emperor, he had sworn to the man that his career in the military was over. This despite promises of many honors and much important work to come in the aftermath of the Tahn conflict that had nearly bankrupted the Empire.

The Eternal Emperor had scoffed and said Sten was just weary, and understandably so. He said to look him up when he tired of the peaceful life. The Emperor had estimated it would take no longer than six months.

It was one of those rare times when the Eternal Emperor had been wrong. Almost six months to the day, Sten had looked up from blissful idleness in his mansion at Smallbridge, patted the curvaceous naked form nestled against the pillow next to him, and whispered ''no clottin' way'' to his absent boss.

A week later, the Eternal Emperor had been assassinated.

It had been one of those stupid things that Sten had dreaded when he commanded the Emperor's bodyguard. No matter what precautions were taken, there was no such thing as absolute safety for a man as public as the Eternal Emperor. Even the fierce loyalty of his Gurkha guards was not complete protection. The little men with the long, curving knives who had kept the Emperor's foes at bay for nearly thirty centuries were helpless under certain circumstances.

The Emperor had returned to Prime World the conquering hero. Billions upon billions of beings across his far-flung empire had watched on their livies as he stepped from his royal ship and advanced across the tarmac to the phalanx of waiting gravcars that would whisk him home to Arundel.

Tanz Sullamora, the great ship-building industrialist and most trusted member of his privy council, was at his side.

Sten remembered watching the screen in the mansion's vidroom. The newscaster's voice was hoarse from describing the triumphant return. The schedule, he said in a raspy whisper, called for no ceremonies at that moment. The Emperor would board the waiting craft and head for a well-earned rest. In a week or so, a grand celebration of the victory over the Tahn was planned. Beings from all over the Empire would gather to honor their leader. There would be no recriminations, it was said, even against the shakiest of the Emperor's allies.

Sten didn't believe a word of that. He knew his boss too well. There would be a purge. But it would be swift, sure, and hardly a bubble of interruption as the Emperor turned his attention away from war and back to the business of being the chieftain of the greatest capitalist system in history.

But it would still be a good show. The Emperor was master of dazzle and triple speak.

Idly, Sten noted the small group of spaceport employees gathered far to one side of the screen. They were drawn up in what was obviously a receiving line, waiting to shake the hand of the Emperor. Sten was glad his old boss was heading in the opposite direction. Not that there was any *real* danger. What would be the point of attacking the Emperor now that the war was over? Still . . . His instincts always fought his common sense in such situations. Once among the press of flesh, it would be impossible to totally protect the man.

Then he saw Sullamora catch the Emperor's attention and nod to the waiting line. Sten let out an automatic groan. Tanz would be pointing out, he knew, that the spaceport group had been waiting for hours to greet their ruler and should really not be disappointed.

Sure enough, after a moment's hesitation, the Emperor's party turned toward the assembled group. They were moving fast. The Emperor obviously wanted to get this bit of duty over with as quickly as possible. The Gurkhas hustled on stubby legs to keep the shield up.

Then the Emperor was going down the line in that smooth, graceful way he had among his people: the charming, fatherly smile fixed on his young features; the tall, muscular body bounding along from being to being; one hand coming out to shake, the other going for the elbow for a warm double-grip that also moved the greeter swiftly aside, so the next hand could be taken.

Sten had seen a blur of motion. What was happening? He heard the distinctive *crack crack crack* of pistol fire. And the Eternal Emperor was falling back. The camera swirled into mass confusion. Then it cleared—but just for a moment.

He saw the Emperor lying on the tarmac. Sten's heart was still. His breath caught somewhere in his chest. Was he . . . dead?

Then the screen turned to pure burning white, and Sten heard the beginnings of a mighty explosion.

Transmission was cut.

When it was finally restored, Sten had his answer.

The Eternal Emperor had been assassinated.

By a madman, it was said. Some malcontent named Chapelle, who had acted alone out of some insane motive—revenge for an imagined slight, or ambition for an odd sort of immortality.

Along with countless billions of other beings, Sten had been a numb witness to what followed.

It was inconceivable that the Emperor was gone. Although there were few who believed that any living thing could be immortal or even close to it. There were a few odd cells—usually particularly virulent things that destroyed their host, hence themselves—that could theoretically live forever, as well as a few dwellers of the seas and upper atmospheres. But that was nit-picking. For all things, to be alive meant eventual death.

For human beings, this was particularly so. And the Emperor *was* a human being. There was no dispute on that and never would be.

But as long as anyone could remember he had always been there. Whether one agreed or disagreed with his policies, the Emperor was a comforting and permanent presence. Even the most bitter and radical scholars gnashed their teeth as they tracked his reign back century after unbelievable century. It was no accident that the word *eternal* was the official preface to the Emperor's title.

It was also something one didn't dwell on. An ordinary human might live for two hundred years if he were lucky. To think of someone vastly older was frightening.

Sten had personally known the man a great deal of his own allotted span. In apparent age, the Emperor was no more than thirty-five or so. His eyes were youthfully bright. He even made occasional mocking references to his great age. But there was little the Eternal Emperor didn't mock. Nothing was holy to him, especially himself.

Sometimes, however, Sten had seen him overtaken by a great and terrible weariness. It had happened more often toward the end of the Tahn debacle. Deep lines would be etched on his features, and his eyes would suddenly grow so distant that anyone looking *believed* for a moment that the man had seen and been places far beyond any being who had ever lived. And somehow one was sure he would remain long after one's own memory was lost in distant time.

Two days after the assassination, the members of the Emperor's privy council had, one by one, mounted the stage hastily set up in the great grounds around the ruins of Arundel Castle. Only one member did not appear; Tanz Sullamora. Faithful servant to the last, he had died in the explosion that had also wiped out everyone within the one-eighth-of-a-kilometer kill zone. Why Chapelle had found it necessary to set off such an enormous explosion after he slew the Emperor, no one could say. Except that it was the act of an insane man. All else remained part of that mad puzzle, because Chapelle himself had been one of the first victims of his actions.

The five lords of industry stood before the vast throng assembled on the grounds. Prior to their entrance, it had been explained in great detail exactly who and what they were.

There was Kyes, a tall, slender, silver being, who controlled most things involving artificial intelligence. He was a Grb'chev, a vastly bright race, and appeared to be the chief spokesbeing of the privy council. Next was Malperin. She ruled a gargantuan conglomerate that included agriculture, chemical, and pharmaceuticals. Then there was Lovett, scion of a great banking family. Finally, the Kraa twins—one grossly fat, the other painfully thin—who controlled the major mines, mills, and foundries in the Empire. Besides Sullamora, there had once been another member of their group. But Volmer, a media baron, had died in some silly mishap just prior to the end of the war.

Kyes had a dry, light, pleasant voice. It was somber now as he explained that Parliament had cast a unanimous vote urging the five lords to rule in the Emperor's place during this terrible emergency. None of them had sought this awful burden, and none of them certainly felt worthy of the trust beings everywhere were placing in them at that very moment.

But they had been convinced that for the time being there was no other choice. Order must come out of this

awesome chaos, and they pledged to do their very best
to govern wisely and fairly until the proper moment
came—very soon, he hoped—when free elections could
be held to determine how exactly the Empire was to be
led without the presence of His Majesty, their martyred
ruler.

Kyes said he knew this was a weak solution at best,
but all of them had racked their brains for tortuous hours
and could find no other way out. A commission was being set up—as he spoke, in fact—to study the situation
and to make suggestions. He and the other members of
the council awaited word from this eminent body of
scholarly beings as eagerly as anyone watching and listening. But he had been told that what they were attempting to accomplish had never been done before and might
take a great deal of time and reasoned debate.

Kyes counseled patience, then pledged he would carry
on in the spirit of the great man who had rescued them
all from the threat of enslavement under the Tahn.

One by one the others stepped up to make similar re-
marks—and to add a bit of detail, such as the date of the
funeral, which would be vaster and richer than any funeral that had gone before. New honors were announced
to be posthumously bestowed on the Emperor, and a year
of mourning was declared. Sten palmed the button that
blanked the screen and sat back to reflect.

He did not need his Mantis psywar training to know
that he had just witnessed a power grab.

So. The privy council would *reluctantly* govern until
free elections could be held. Sten had propped up a few
despots in his time with similar empty pledges. He
wondered how long it would be before the first coup attempt. And which one would eventually be successful.
And then the one after that. And the other—on and on
until the entire system collapsed. He supposed there
would be constant warfare of greater and greater intensity
for the rest of his life.

Ultimate power was at stake. He who controlled the

Empire determined the flow of all the Anti-Matter Two—AM2—the fuel upon which civilization everywhere was based. It was the source of cheap power, the key to all major weaponry, and the sole practical means of interstellar travel. Without AM2, trade would be almost entirely reduced to intrasystem lumbering about on the infinitely practical but painfully slow Yukawa drive engines.

But there was nothing Sten could do about any of it.

The Eternal Emperor was dead. Long live the Emperor.

He would mourn him. Not as a friend. No one could call the Emperor friend. But, as—well, a comrade at arms, then. Sten got drunk and remained drunk for a month, switching from Scotch to stregg and back again—the Emperor's two favorite drinks.

Then he tried to get on with his life.

Sten didn't pay much mind to the chaos the Empire fell into. He only coppered his bets by purchasing all the AM2 he could lay his hands on, and it wasn't long before the shortages began and he was congratulating himself on his foresight. The why of the shortages didn't concern him. He assumed the privy council—in its infinite wisdom—had determined such a course to further line their already heavy pockets.

He dabbled a bit in business, found it far from his liking, then was reduced to an endless series of momentary enthusiasms. Not unlike the Emperor, who had a host of hobbies always in progress. He became a fair cook, although he knew he would never be the Emperor's match. He honed his skills with tools and building things. He took a fling at a few of the lusher fleshpots. When he wearied of that—a little too quickly for comfort, he sometimes thought—he explored and improved Smallbridge.

He and Alex corresponded, always swearing to get together soon, but soon never came. And as the controls on AM2 tightened, travel became more and more im-

practical, and before he knew it "soon" wasn't even
mentioned in any of their letters.

Ian Mahoney—his only other real friend—quietly retired to the life of a military historian, then died in some
silly accident. Sten had heard that he had drowned and
that the body had never been found. He supposed there
was some irony in such a meaningless death for a man
who had managed to survive against impossible odds so
many times before. But he didn't see it, or he was too
depressed to examine it.

The final year of his self-imposed exile was proving
the worst. His bleak moods were constantly on him, as
well as a gut-itching paranoia. Whom he should fear, he
had no idea. He had no suspects. But he became paranoid just the same. Every residence he set up on Smallbridge was enclosed with increasingly sophisticated
and—he had to admit it—eccentric security devices, including some nasty, being-devouring plants he imported
from some hellhole whose name he had easily forgotten.
They had taken off like mad in the nonthreatening environment of Smallbridge. Every once in a while he had to
set the perimeter on fire to keep the grove under control.

Lately, he had taken up residence in the northwestern
sector of the second largest land mass in the temperate
zone.

Temperate was a weak, nondescript word for this place
beside the chain of four mighty lakes. The winds always
blew fierce and cold there. The snow lay deep on the
ground and bowed the trees of the forest for many months
of the year. But for some reason it had a powerful attraction to him—just as it seemed to have for the being-
devouring plants, which thrived in the cold, wet climate.

Sten had built several frontier-style domes in the cluster by one of the lakes. One was devoted to a kitchen and
pantry where he prepared and stored food, butchered out
a little game, or cleaned the strange, bullet-shaped but
tasty dwellers of the lake. He grew vegetables in the hy-
droponic tubs that took up all of one side. The second

dome contained his workshop and was crammed with tools and building materials of every variety. He also kept and worked on his weapons there, as well as the snooping devices he was always toying with. The last dome held his living quarters and gymnasium. He spent hours in the gym and outside in the cold, endlessly practicing and honing his Mantis skills.

He lined the walls of his living quarters with real wood cut from his own forest. He built bunks and cabinets and all sorts of things from the same material. When he was done, it looked so homey that he was pleased with himself. Still, something seemed to be missing. He scratched his memory until he came up with an "aha." It wanted a fireplace. After several smoky and tortuous attempts, he finally had it. And it was huge, big enough to take a two-meter log. It drew like clot and gave off a wonderfully cheery glow.

A woman who had stayed with him a few months said it reminded her of something she had seen before but couldn't quite make out. Sten pressed her, but all she could remember was that it had involved some item at a shop where "less expensive things" were sold. From the tone in her voice, Sten got the drift she meant garish and sentimental.

He was so lonely, he let it pass.

A week or so later, he was returning from some errand in the forest. It was a beautiful, gray day, and a light snowfall was drifting down from the skies and through the trees.

Sten hailed the dome, and the woman opened the door to greet him. She was framed in the doorway, with the glowing fire lighting her from behind, and Sten knew then what she had been thinking of. Because now he remembered, as well.

A long time before, his mother had extended her contract for six months to buy a muraliv. A country girl completely lost and out of place in the workshops of Vulcan, she had deeded half a year more of her life for what she believed was a work of art.

It was of a snowy landscape on a frontier world. He remembered the snow drifting down on the little cluster of domes, and the door that always swung open to greet the returning workers from the forest and field—and the bright cheery fire the open door had revealed. It was his mother's dearest treasure. In eight months, it had gone quite still.

Sten had unconsciously recreated the mural.

He made some excuses and hustled the woman on her way. It was silly to blame her for a slight she couldn't know she was committing, but he couldn't bear to have her around anymore.

That was when the gloom reached its absolute bottom. Month after month, he pricked at the wound. He didn't need the walrus-psychologist Rykor to tell him what he was doing. Sten *knew*. But he did it just the same. He even named the four lakes after his long-dead family.

The largest lake, where the domes were clustered, he named Amos, for his father. The next in the chain became Freed, for his mother. Then Ahd and Johs, for his brother and sister.

When that was done, he sat and brooded, hoping his condition was no more than a lingering fever that had to be endured until the viral tide shifted and the fever broke.

Five hundred miles to the north, a bright light winked into being and arced down through the night skies. It steadied a moment above the frozen ground, then sped toward the lakes and Sten's retreat.

Then a globe appeared, hanging amid the stars. Powerful jamming devices hummed into life, bathing Smallbridge in an electronic blanket that comforted and coaxed Sten's alarm system into believing all was well.

A light very much like the first separated from the globe, then sped off in the same direction.

A few klicks from the domes, the battered little space-boat came to ground, a black splotch against the snow. The port groaned open, and a dark figure exited. After dragging on cold-weather gear and snapping snowshoes to his feet, the man straightened, then hesitated, scanning the skies, an immense, bulky figure, sniffing the air for danger very much like a big Kodiak from distant Earth. Suddenly he saw a light pop above the horizon. It was the other ship, coming fast.

The man turned and hurried across the snow, moving like a nullgrav dancer despite his bulk. He scanned the ground ahead with a practiced eye, setting a zigzag course and not bothering to obscure his tracks. There wasn't time.

Occasionally—for no apparent reason—he sidestepped little pimples in the snow.

Behind him, he heard the other ship settle down, the frozen crust shattering under the weight with little pops and cracks.

At the tree line, the man spotted an almost imperceptible ridge. He stopped. Moaning in frustration, he moved in first one direction, then the other. But the slight ridge seemed to stretch without relief all along the outer edge of the woods. For some reason, the man considered his path blocked.

The port of the other craft hissed open and seven black figures tumbled out. They were already garbed for the terrain. Fingers flew in silent code. Agreement was reached. And they sped off in the man's direction. They moved in a ragged vee, with the tallest being taking point. They skimmed effortlessly across the snow on gravskis, keeping a fast, measured pace.

If anyone had spotted them, there would be no mistake about their business. These were hunters—after very big game.

Their quarry was kneeling beside a drift, his gloves off, digging gently around the ridge. His fists felt like heavy, unwieldy things. He had to stop now and then to pound them back to life against his coat. Behind him, the figures moved on.

Finally there appeared a silver thread so slender that it would be the envy of an arachnid. Snow dust hung from it. The man blew on the thread, puffing out warm moisture that collected and froze. When he thought it was thick enough, he pulled out a tiny little device with just-visible claws. He flipped open the back with a fingernail, revealing little programming holes. He inserted a pin in several of the holes, until the device gave a chirp indicating that it was alive.

The man clicked it shut, breathed a prayer, and slowly . . . so slowly . . . stretched it toward the thread.

A laser blast cracked the frozen air with its heat and blazed a furrow in the snow millimeters from one knee. The man winced but fought back the urge to jerk away or hurry. He knew that if he was wrong, worse things than a charred hole in his corpse would occur.

He had to get to Sten, before Sten got him.

The little claws gripped the thread. The man held his breath, waiting. Another laser blast cracked. The heel of one snowshoe exploded as the lased AM2 round detonated. Finally a chirp from the tiny device said that all was well.

The man plunged across the wire into the woods just as the marksmen found their range. A hole boiled at the spot where he had knelt one breath before.

As he disappeared, the hunting team surged forward, faster. Skimming around the pimples their prey had avoided, they leapt the wire and landed silently on the other side. The leader motioned and the vee divided and the hunters scattered into the woods.

Sten paced the room. He was edgy. He picked up an antique, leather-bound book and he stared at the title, but it didn't register. He dropped it back on the table, strode over to the fire, and poked it up until the flames were hot and leaping. He still felt a little cold, so he tossed on another log.

There was something wrong, but he couldn't make it out. He kept glancing at the bank of security monitors, but all the lights were calming green. Why did he have this feeling that he was being lied to? The hackles were crawling at the back of his neck. One part of his mind said he was behaving like a whiny old being: afraid of the dark, jumping at every noise. Ignore it, that part ordered. But the tiny voice of survival kept up its keening.

Sten palmed the override on the monitors and went to manual scan. Still green. He flipped from sector to sector. Nothing. Disgusted with himself, he put it back on automatic. Just for one heartbeat, the lights seemed to blink yellow, then went to steady green. What was that? He switched back to manual again. Green, goddammit! Then to auto. This time there was no telltale yellow as the lights stayed steady emerald. He must have been imagining things.

He went to the front door, slipped to one side, edged it open and peered out. All he could see was the empty expanse of snow, bright under the hanging moon. He had reflecting devices hidden in several trees within easy view. Sten studied them. He could see his shadow peering out from the edge of the door. There was nothing lurking on either side of the dome.

Feeling like all kinds of a clotting fool, he slipped a miniwillygun from its hiding place in a slot by the door, flipped its safety off and stepped outside.

There was not a sight or a sound out of the ordinary. Sten scanned the area, millimeter by millimeter. Nothing seemed remotely awry. He snapped the safety back on, telling himself that if he was that edgy, he might drop the damned thing and blow off a knee. Still, old habits die hard—and, sometimes, not at all. He slipped the gun into his belt, backed into the dome, and swung the heavy door shut, turning to the fire as inertia carried the door on greased hinges.

He stopped.

Sten hadn't heard the lock click or the thud of the door closing. He probably hadn't pushed hard enough. Yeah. Probably.

He tensed the fingers of his right hand. The muscle sheath that held his surgically implanted knife contracted, and the slender, deadly blade slipped into its resting place in his palm. He curled his fingers around the haft.

Just to keep himself honest, and in tone, Sten sometimes played a game with himself. He would imagine there was someone behind him. A breath would give the lurker away—or a slight motion, a rustle of clothing. Failing that, his old Mantis instructors had pounded into him, any sort of presence added to a space, changed and warped that space. More heat. A shift in pressure. It didn't matter what the change was. One's senses just had to recognize it when it occurred.

Sten spun, dropping away to one side, to avoid any blow. At the same time, he slashed up with his knife. The knife blade was only fifteen molecules thick. It would cut through steel like ripened cheese. Flesh would be no contest at all. If there was an arm bearing a weapon, coming down at him, that arm—its hand still gripped around the weapon—would be neatly sliced off. It would plop to the floor while his enemy stared blankly at him, eyes widening in amazement and then dulling to instant shock as blood spurted from severed arteries. His enemy would be dead in seconds.

Meanwhile, as Sten fell, he would try to spot any other threatening presence. Which way he rolled when he hit the floor would be determined by the angle of the next attack, if any.

Sten slashed empty air. He continued the fall, imagining the first kill, concentrating on the second. More slashing at empty air. Panting, he stood with his feet splayed apart, staring at the almost-closed door. Of course, there was no one about. There never was any-more. The knife disappeared back into his arm.

Grinning and shaking his head, Sten walked to the door to push it the rest of the way shut, idly wondering what he ought to fix himself for dinner.

Just as he touched the knob, the door slammed back at him. The heavy wood caught him flat. He was hurled backward, clawing for balance and trying to twist as he hit the floor to free his knife-hand. He curled into a ball and let himself roll all the way. He rebounded off the wall, and using the force, was coming to his feet and slashing out before the knife had even cleared.

"Dammit, Sten!" the man shouted. "Stop!"

Sten froze, gaping. What the clot! It couldn't be. It was . . .

"Get your wits about you lad," ex-Fleet Marshall Ian Mahoney said. "There's a Mantis team right on my heels. And if I stand here explaining, we're both for the meat locker.

"Move. Now!"

Sten moved.

Sten and Mahoney quick-crawled through the tunnel that snaked from the hidey-hole behind the fireplace to-ward a small stand of trees about eighty meters from the main dome. It was dimly lit—on purpose. And it con-tained many bends—also on purpose. They could hear someone breaking away the stones of the fireplace to get at them. Sten tried not to think of the months he had worked on the beast, or of all the heavy rocks he had carried from the edge of the lake to build it.

He was only very thankful to the gods of paranoia that had commanded him to construct a bolt hole in the face of no apparent danger. When—not if—the hunters broke through, Sten and Mahoney would be dangerous game to follow. The lights would make aim difficult. The many twists and turns would make it even harder. They would also lessen the force of any explosions set off. And the narrowness took away any advantage in numbers.

Of course, there was always gas. But Sten was comforted by the howl of the powerful ventilators constantly pumping in fresh air. The atmosphere of the entire tunnel was recycled in seconds.

They finally reached a dead-end vault where they could stand. Emergency clothing, gear, and weapons were stacked on shelves to one side. The exit was just beyond. With a press of a switch, the port would lift silently away. The exterior was artfully camouflaged with brush, dirt, and rocks. The tunnel emptied into a thick clump of woods near the edge of the frozen lakes.

Sten quickly began donning his gear. He motioned for Mahoney to pick up a pair of gravskis like his. A small explosion rocked the tunnel as the hunters finally broke through the fireplace.

"They'll have this end covered, as well," Mahoney said.

"I know," Sten said. He palmed the switch, and cold fresh air flooded in as the port lifted aside. It would close automatically behind them. He pressed a marble-sized bit of impact-explosive under the edge of the switch, a down and dirty booby trap.

"They'll find it," Mahoney said.

"I know that, too," Sten said. "But it'll slow them down."

"Maybe we ought to—"

Sten raised a hand, cutting Mahoney off. "No offense," he said, "but there isn't a clottin' thing I don't know about tunnels. And exiting same. I had a little experience, if you recall."

Mahoney shut up. Sten had spent a small lifetime digging under the POW camp at Koldyeze. Actually, as Big X—commander of the escape committee—he had done a lot more than dig.

"Now, give me a hand," he said.

He pulled the cover off an elderly snowcat, which had

been converted to burn combustibles. Together they muscled it over to the exit. Sten flipped the various switches to the ''on'' position and set a meandering course on the navigator, then told Mahoney to stand back as he fired the engine.

A great blast and gout of smoke roiled out. Mahoney coughed and wheezed.

''So, we'll not be sneakin' up on them, then,'' Mahoney said, dry. Sten silenced him with a glare.

Then he jammed it into gear and leapt to the side. The snowcat jumped forward with a loud roar and in a flash boiled out of the tunnel. Sten peered after it. The tracks churned up huge clouds of snow as the cat plunged forward—straight for a tree. Sparks showered out of its engine ports, eerie against the night. The cat brodied to one side at the last minute. Laser fire smeared the darkness, and several holes appeared in the cat's body.

''Now!'' Sten shouted.

And he and Mahoney hurled themselves outside. Sten had just enough time to see one startled hunter whirl back from the cat and raise his weapon.

The hunter jerked, and a neat hole appeared in his forehead. As the hunter slumped down, Mahoney got another shot off at the man's companion, who dodged to one side. By the time she had recovered, Sten and Mahoney were gone. The Mantis operative moved forward, throat-miking hoarse instructions to the team inside the dome. She found the footprints leading deeper into the woods. They wouldn't be difficult to follow. They stood out starkly—almost deep blue—in the moonlight.

Then she sensed something behind her. She half straightened, bringing up her weapon and trying to spin to the side. Then she was lying in the snow, blood gushing from the red grin of her throat.

Sten wiped his blade on her tunic.

''Am I just getting old,'' he asked as Mahoney stepped out from behind a tree, ''or are the new kids really just not as good as they used to be?''

Mahoney looked at the corpse of the Mantis operative. As the former chief of Mercury Corps—meaning Mantis, as well—he had mixed feelings about seeing one of his own in such a state. Then he looked at Sten. He was a little older, and there were a few hard lines etched in his face, but he seemed tougher, somehow. Harder. His dark eyes were sunk deeper into his skull. They were a little bitter, but there was still that touch of cynical humor in them. Mahoney saw the slender dirk disappear back into Sten's arm.

As for Sten's question: No. They *weren't* slower.

Mahoney shrugged. "You've been practicing," was all he said. "There's five more. I doubt we'll be so lucky with them, lad," he said. "I hope you have a plan."

"I do," Sten told him. Without another word he stepped into the bindings of the gravskis, flipped them on, and adjusted the lift so that he hung bare centimeters above the snow. He poled off into the woods, digging the poles in hard just to make sure no one would lose the track.

Mahoney had seen a lot of strange things in his long life, but the thick grove that Sten was leading him through had to be up high on his personal list of the bizarre.

The trees weren't really trees at all, although they took that form. They towered over what, from a distance, appeared to be a gigantic root system at least three meters high before the main trunk started. Up close, the root systems were revealed to be more like immense tubers. They were so huge that Mahoney thought it must have taken centuries for so many leaves to form together to make such large bulbs for water and nutrients. Later he learned that it had only taken a few years.

The branches were furry and appeared almost muscular—if a plant could have muscles. And they looped about like tentacles, although they seemed stiff and relatively sturdy, like wood. The leaves were long, needlelike, and edged with sharp spines, and they were covered with a thin film of moisture. Extremely odd in this climate. Why didn't the moisture freeze?

He reached out a hand to touch.

"Don't," Sten snapped. Then he saw the puzzled look on Mahoney's face and took pity—but only a little. "They don't like to be touched," he said. He pushed on with no other explanation.

As far as Mahoney could tell, they were doing nothing more than traveling in a wide circle. Moving closer to the lake, he thought. With a shrill cry, a large, white bird with leathery wings suddenly bolted for the sky. It circled about in the moonlight, obviously angry.

"They're coming," Sten said. "Finally. I was afraid for a moment we'd lost them."

"Not likely," Mahoney said. "Probably talking to their mother." He pointed to the night sky beyond the bird. He was referring to the command ship, which he assumed was in a stationary orbit—very low, very close.

"We'll have to do something about that, too," Sten said.

Before Mahoney could ask exactly what, he saw the knife slip into Sten's hand again. Sten moved cautiously toward one of the odd trees. Picking out a low-hanging branch, he inched forward, knife blade gleaming. As his hand neared the branch, Mahoney swore he could see the branch ever so slightly move toward Sten. But the motion was so miniscule, he wasn't sure. The drops of moisture seemed to swell into larger beads, almost dripping like saliva, and the leaves seemed to be rotating so the teeth were facing out.

Sten leapt forward and struck. Moisture boiled from the wound and the branch snapped forward at Sten, trying to curl around him. But he bounded back again, just to the edge of safety. Mahoney felt his blood run cold. The liquid pouring out of the wound hissed and bubbled in the snow.

"That should make him nice and mad," was all Sten said.

He pressed on, Mahoney in his wake. Sten repeated his attack at least a dozen other times, each time with the same result: the tree lashing out in agony, just missing Sten. For a few moments, it was all painful motion. Limbs squirming, seeking justice; caustic moisture pouring out. But the wounds seemed to heal instantly, and in a few seconds the tree would fall still.

When Sten had first come upon the plants during his travels, he had been instantly repelled by their appearance and attracted by their nature. They possessed a defense system only an ex-Mantis kiddie could love. Something had once found them extremely delicious— hence the sharp leaves and caustic fluid. When attacked, the plant reacted by pouring even nastier fluids into the area where it was bitten. That took about fifteen minutes. Some creatures got around it by developing a tolerance to the normal fluid and just nibbling small areas at a time, moving on to a new section before the plant could react. The plants were a bit like cabbage or tomato.

But the plant species had not stopped there. A drastic change in climate, perhaps, had sent it in search of further means to feed. Why not the beings that ate it? With its superefficient tuber storage system as a base, it evolved into a carnivore. Oh, it would make do for years at a time on the nutrients in the soil and water, but the flesh and blood of any number of species were its particular dining pleasure.

And now that Sten had gotten their attention with his attacks, they would be laying for whoever or whatever followed. Such as the Mantis team.

Mahoney heard a terrible scream. It was not the kind that cut off abruptly. It went on and on, growing more horrible as long minutes passed. Laser fire cracked. Silence. Mahoney shuddered.

"Now there's four left," Sten said.

Mahoney didn't answer.

* * *

They knelt by the edge of the ice. Their cover was a small outcropping of rock. It was false dawn, and the light was tricky. But Mahoney could make out the tree line on the far side of the lake. It was little less than a kilometer, perhaps a two-minute crossing on their skis, if they didn't stumble.

He and Sten had led the surviving hunters on an all-night chase. Sometimes he thought Sten was trying to lose them. Then he would slow—purposely, he thought—and soon he could hear them on their heels again. By now, he thought they should be tiring. Clot! So was he.

The only good news he could think of was that the Mantis team had yet to be reinforced. There could only be one conclusion. There weren't any beings aboard the command ship to spare.

There had been no time for Mahoney to do more than hazily sketch in what was going on. Nothing about himself. Only the situation at hand.

The privy council was desperate. They had sent out similar teams all over the Empire. Their mission: Capture and return for questioning any being who had been close enough to the Emperor to know his deepest secrets.

Sten was amazed. "What the clot could I know? Sure, I commanded his bodyguard. And I had clearances up to my eyebrows during the Tahn business. But that's old news. Nothing worth ferreting about. You could stuff it in the small end of nothing and it would still rattle about. They should have saved themselves all the bother and just asked."

"It's the AM2," Mahoney said. "They can't find where our boss has it stashed."

Sten gobbled. "But, I thought—I mean, everybody assumes . . ."

"Too right, lad," Mahoney said. "And we all assumed wrong. Now the AM2 is running out."

Sten thought about that for a moment, munching on a dry nutra stick. Then, anxious, he said, "Alex! They'll be after him, too. We have to—"

"I already took care of that," Mahoney said. "I sent warning. Hope he got it. I didn't have much time."

He waved out at the darkness in the direction of the hunters. No further explanation was needed. Obviously Mahoney had only been half a step ahead when he reached Sten.

"We'll have to get word to Kilgour when we get free," Mahoney said. "Tell him where to meet us."

Sten laughed. "No need," he said. "Alex will know where to find us."

Mahoney started to ask how, but something cracked deep in the woods.

They moved on.

They were at the edge of Amos Lake, waiting to cross. Sten wanted just a bit more light. Mahoney cursed. The little clot *wanted* to be seen.

A hand gripped his wrist, then was gone.

It was time.

As they rose to make their dash, Mahoney saw a small, black orb in Sten's hand. There was a large red dot imbedded in the center—a pressure switch.

They soared out onto the ice, the wind at their backs so they barely had to pole to keep up the speed. The frigid air tugged at their garments, finding gaps where none in fact could exist. The cold nipped through those gaps with sharp, tiny teeth.

Mahoney thought his lungs were so brittle there was no way any self-respecting oxygen molecules could attach.

Ice gouted just in front of him, hurling up a thick cloud of particles that choked him as he sailed into it. The crack of the laser fire followed the shot. This was bad. The hunters had found them. It was also good. They were at a distance.

The far shore came crashing up at them. Mahoney could see the snow-choked trees just beyond. Without slowing, they plunged onto rocky ground. Mahoney felt the wind knocked from him, but he stayed low, hugging the frozen ground like a lover.

He saw Sten roll until he was lying on the ground, facing the enemy. Mahoney fought for air and dared a look, then ducked as an AM2 round powdered the rock in front of him. But he had just enough time to see the hunters advancing in a broken pattern so he couldn't get off a decent shot. Just to keep them honest, however, he raised his weapon.

The hand went on his wrist again.

"Not now," Sten whispered.

Mahoney found a safer angle to peer out.

The Mantis team was nearing the center of the lake. He heard motion beside him and looked over to see Sten holding the hard, black ball. His thumb rested on the red spot. The knuckle whitened as he pressed.

Instinctively Mahoney looked out on the lake. But all he saw was hunters coming on. Then there was an ungodly roar as the entire center of the lake lifted up. Sheets of ice the size of small buildings were hurled to the side.

A gleaming white ship arose straight through the center. He saw bodies—or what had to be bodies, from the way they were flailing—spin upward and then plunge into the frigid water.

He didn't know if death was instant, or long and agonizing. If anyone screamed, he wouldn't have been able to hear it over the noise of the rising spacecraft.

Then he saw Sten sitting up and fumbling another nutra stick out of his pack.

Mahoney groaned up himself. He looked worriedly up at the sky. "There won't be any question of capture, now," he said. "And they won't chance another team. If they've even got one. That command ship will just hunt us down and bomb the clot out of us. That's what I'd do, at least."

"I've been thinking the same thing," Sten said. "But we've got that—" He pointed at the white ship hovering obediently over the lake. "And we've got two spares.

Yours, and the team's. Should be enough for a diversion, don't you think?''

Mahoney caught his drift. It might work—just. He started to get up. Sten motioned him back.

"I'm starved," he said. "It might be a while before we get another chance. Let's eat."

Mahoney felt hunger pangs gnawing at his own guts. It was a comforting, being-alive kind of feeling. What the clot!

They ate.

CHAPTER THREE

LAIRD KILGOUR OF Kilgour, formerly Chief Warrant Officer Alex Kilgour (First Imperial Guards Division, Retired); formerly CWO A. Kilgour, Detached, Imperial Service, Special Duties; formerly Private-through-Sergeant Kilgour, Mantis Section Operational, various duties from demolitions expert to sniper to clandestine training, to include any duties the late Eternal Emperor wanted performed sub rosa with a maximum of lethality, was holding forth.

"... An' aye, th' rain's peltin' doon, f'r days an' days i' comes doon. An' her neighbors tell th' li'l old gran, 'Bes' y' flee t' high ground.'

" 'Nae,' she says. 'Ah hae faith. God will take care a' me. Th' Laird wi' provide.' "

It was a beautiful evening. The tubby man was sprawled on a settee, his feet on a hassock, his kilt tucked decorously between his legs. Conveniently to his right were his weapons of choice: a full pewter flagon of Old Sheepdip, imported at staggering—staggering to anyone not as rich as Kilgour—expense from Earth and a liter mug of lager.

The fire blazed in a fireplace that was tall enough for three men to stand in at their full height. Outside, a winter storm crashed against the walls of Deacon Brodie's Tavern with all the fury a polar frenzy could produce on the planet Edinburgh, Alex's three-gee home world.

A beautiful evening. Kilgour was on his fourth—no, fifth drink. There were good friends across from him, good friends who also had not yet suffered the complete repertoire of Kilgour's stories. The wee barmaid had shyly wondered if Laird Kilgour might not find the time—later—to escort her home through the muck an' mire.

It was safe and quiet and peaceable. It was just old habits that had Kilgour seated with his back to a wall, and his left hand, resting on his kneecap, was a few centimeters away from a miniwillygun holstered on his upper thigh.

"An th' rain comit doon an' comit doon, an' th' water's risin'. And her pigs are wash't away, squealin't. An' the' coo's swimmin't f'r shelter. An doon th' road comit ae gravcar.

" 'Mum,' comit th' shout. 'Thae's floodin't. Thae must leave!'

" 'Nae,' she shouts back. 'Ah'll noo leave. Th' Laird will provide.'

"An' th' water comit up, an' comit up, an' th' rain i' peltin' an comit doon. An' the chickens ae roostin' ae the roof. Floodin't her house t' ae th' first story. An' here comit ae boat. 'Missus, now thae *must* leave. We'll save y'!'

"An' agin comit her answer: 'Nae, nae. Th' Laird will provide.'

"But th' rain keep fallin't. An' th' water keep't risin't. An' coverin't th' second story. An' she's crouchin' ae th' roof, wi' th' chickens, an' here comit ae rescue gravlighter. It hover't o'er th' roof, an' a mon leans oot. 'Mum! We're here t'save y'.'

"But still she's steadfast. Once again, 'Nae, nae. Th' Laird will provide.'

"An' th' rain keep fallin't an' th' flood keep't risin't. An' she drowns. Dead an' a'.

"An' she goes oop t' Heaven. An' th' Laird's waitin'. An' th' wee gran lady, she's pissed!

"She gets right i' Th' Good Laird's face, an shouts, 'How c'd y', Laird! Th' one time Ah aski't frae help—an ye're nae there.' "

The com buzzed. The guvnor answered.

"Alex. F'r you. From your hotel."

"B'dam'," Alex swore. But he rose. "Hold m'point. 'Tis nae a good one, nae a long one, but be holdin't it anyway."

He went behind the bar. He recognized the face on-screen—one of the com operators at the hotel he stayed at when he came to the city.

"This is wee Alex," he said.

The operator was puzzled. "Laird Kilgour, this message wa' bounced frae y'r castle. A text transmission. But it seems a bit garbled."

"Gie it me, man. P'raps the twa ae us can decipher it."

The operator tapped keys. Across the centerscreen scrolled: XRME TRACD BYDG RRDG, and on for a full page.

Alex's face blanked.

"I'm sorry, Laird. But thae's all thae were."

"A garble, Ah ken. Ah'll be direct back ae th' hotel. Hae a call frae there." He forced a smile and cut the link. "Damned storm! Lost m'connection."

"They'll try again."

"Aye. That they shall," Alex agreed. "Tell 'em t' hold. Ah'm ta the recycler. Leith needs th' water. An' we'll be needin't another all round."

The smile fixed on his lips, Alex meandered toward the lavatory. His eyes skipped around the few people in the tavern. No. All known—unless this was a long-range setup. He thought to add an artistic, drunken stagger as he went into the bathroom.

Then he was moving. Foot braced on the washstand— it would hold his weight. Good. He pushed at the high, seemingly barred window. What looked to be rusted hinges swung smoothly open and the bars fell away. Kilgour wriggled headfirst onto the narrow ledge above the alley outside. He chose his pubs—or modified them—for more than cheery companionship, complaisant barmaids, and high-alk service.

He lay motionless for a moment. The ice-needled wind, the driven snow, and the below-zero cold did not exist in his mind. He was looking for movement. Nothing. Most of the message had, indeed, been a garble. Intentionally so, intended to bury the real message. The operative code groups were the second and third. They were old Mantis signals, and decoded as:

MISSION BLOWN. EXTRACT TO RV IMMEDIATELY.

Which posed some very interesting questions. Such as—Kilgour was out of the military. He certainly had no links with the Empire or with the supersecret Mantis Section since his hasty retirement after the assassination.

So: Who was trying to contact him?

Second: Why were they using a common, general code? One that was part of a standard SOI, had been around for many years, and almost certainly had been compromised?

Was Mantis looking for him? Did he want to be found?

Kilgour swore at himself. He was getting sloppy and careless in his declining years. For the past several days he had been feeling that skin-crawl between his shoulder blades that he should have listened to: You are being watched. You are being followed. There are beings about with bad intentions.

But nae, lad. Y'were bein't th' city cock ae th' walk. Doon frae thae aird mors an' coirs, thinkin't th' eyes on ye were naught but thae lassies admirin't ae man ae means.

Enough, Kilgour.

Y'r mither said years gone y'r nae better'n ae purblind ox. Noo, try t' find y'r way out off th' killin't floor.

He had a second for a final mourn. Nae m'friends'll nae hear the last line:

"An' th' Laird looki't ae her, an' he's sore puzzled. 'Gran, how can y' say Ah dinnae provide? Ah giv't ae car, ae boat, an ae gravlighter!' "

With a silent chuckle he slid down the alley to the High Street. He held close to the high gray wall next to him for a few meters, then stepped out suddenly, as if coming from a doorway—a man intent on late business, with nothing else on his mind but his destination and how clottin' miserable the weather was.

Movement. From the shadows across the street.

The first question was: Who was after him?

Kilgour was operating at an advantage and a disadvantage. On a normal E-world, his three-gee muscles might have provided an easy solution, either acrobatic or bloody. Here he was just another man. Of course, his pursuers would be under a disadvantage—unless they, also, came from a high-grav world.

He chanced a look back.

His tail had entered a commercial gravsled. The sled had lifted and was creeping down the street behind him. Kilgour grimaced. If this was a termination attempt, the sled would go to full power, lift over the sidewalk, and scrub him against the high stone wall beside him. An unfortunate accident. He listened, but the sled's McLean generators did not increase their pitch.

So let's see if we can find out who these lads are, he thought.

Three crossings down, he turned onto a narrow street. Very narrow. A close, actually—so steep it was not ramped but was instead a long stairway. Alex moved faster.

The close ended in a small courtyard. Four other lanes opened from it. Kilgour picked one, ducked into its shadows, and held for a moment.

Two figures moved down the stairs. The flurried storm broke, and Kilgour glimpsed them. Clot. He had no strength advantage at all. Either he was being chased by a pair of hyperthyroid Earth gorillas, or his pursuers were wearing fighting armor. Fighting suits were AM2-powered killing machines that turned the properly trained infantryman into something far more lethal than a conventional tracked assault vehicle. Amplified musculature gave the wearer many times the strength and endurance of an unsuited soldier. Their armor was impervious to conventional shoulder weapons and even medium-size shrapnel.

Against a suit, Kilgour was far more impotent than a man from a zero-gee environment would be against Alex.

Two of them. Just wonderful. Och well. *Th' Laird wi' provide* . . .

Kilgour was off, zigging through alleys at a dead run, his mind running at equal speed.

How were they tracking him? Had they planted anything on him? Was his kilt wired? Or that locator? He didn't think so but started to hurl the locator away, then considered.

He came out of the alley warren onto a street. It was very late and the streets were still. Ahead he saw a gravsled land and three other monsters lumber out and up the hill toward him. He went into another alleyway.

Who was after him? Occasionally fighting suits came into the hands of big-time private warlords, but these, Alex thought, appeared to be current Imperial issue. Which meant? That for some reason he had offended the powers that be. Not the planetary officials on Edinburgh—Alex had purchased far too many friends in high places not to have gotten a tip—but off-world.

Worst case? The Empire—or those clottin' imbecile thieves who'd taken it over after the Emperor's death. Assume that, Kilgour. For whatever the privy council's reason, assume that.

Now, he thought. What do they want of me? If they wanted me just dead they would've had plenty of opportunities over the past few days, weeks, or months. There's more'n enough lads still in service who remember how to plant a bomb or look through a crosshairs.

So it's alive, alive-o, then.

If they looked up m'wee record—th' honest one—then they'll noo send a boy for a man's work. So think those lads in thae braw suits are Mantis. They *are* lookin't f'r me. But nae quite the way I thought. An' they're nae suited up because th' grav pulls hard on their wee bones.

So it would be a simple snatch, wi' th' minimum of screekin' an' broken bones. Then off t' th' brainscan.

Ah think not. Ah'll nae hae some psych's slimy fingers pryin't ae m'soul. But I hae nae desire t' put m'back 'gainst a wall, spit on m'sword, an' go down yodelin' like ae Vikin' sarky, or whatever thae dubbed themselves.

The storm was lashing down harder.

Two back of me—driving. Three more backup. Plus there'll be another team in immediate reserve. Solution: drop all five of them before they hae a chance to gurgle f'r help.

Five men. Five of the Empire's best operatives, wearing suits that could have let them walk through the thickest walls of Alex's castle and emerge with their hair unmussed.

Nae problem, lad. Nae problem at all.

Kilgour stayed moving—just fast enough to keep the Mantis people after him, but not fast enough for them to blow the whistle and think he was on a full-tilt run.

His path wound through the back alleys of the city. His pursuers may have been in suits, but Alex had grown up familiar with the cobblestones that the idiotically tradition-minded builders of the city—God bless them to the twelfth generation—had installed when Edinburgh was first colonized.

First a wee rope . . .

He found it—a coil of 5-mm wire, hanging from a building site. Alex grabbed it and pulled. He had, he estimated, nearly sixty meters of wire. A bit too much.

His route became more direct, heading back toward the heart of the city. The cobbles were steep and the muck on either side of the road greasy. He led his pursuers back to the High Street, then went into the open. He doubled up the center of the street, stopped, and turned. Now his pursuers were in the open, as well.

They'll be thinkin' Ah'm armed. But noo wi' this. Imperial issue an' all. He knelt, pistol in right hand, left hand cupped around his right, left arm just behind the elbow on his knee . . . breathe in . . . out . . . hold . . . squeeze.

The willygun cracked. The bullet was a 1-mm ball of AM2, shielded by Imperium. AM2—spaceship power. The round struck one of the suited men in a leg—and the leg exploded. AM2 was not a conventional infantry round.

B'dam, Alex thought in some surprise. Moren' one hundred meters an' Ah hit somethin'. Sten'll nae believe it . . . Four left . . . Now the gloves were off. Return fire spattered around him. Kilgour assumed they were using more conventional weapons—and still trying to take him alive. One block up was his street.

The wire was knotted securely to a lamppost, half a meter off the ground. The Mantis operatives were bounding, ten meters to a leap, up the rise toward him. Alex went down "his" street at a run. At a skate, actually.

The narrow alley was at a fifty-degree angle—and icy. There was no way anyone could walk, let alone run down it. Kilgour could not—but he used that cable as a steadying ski tow in reverse, swearing as he felt the insulation sear his hands. He braked, stumbled, nearly skidded, and recovered.

Two Mantis operatives were leaping down the alley toward him. They touched down—on slippery, fifty-degree ice. Even as the pseudomusculature kicked in and they rebounded, their feet had gone out from underneath them. One man smashed into a wall, then skidded, motionless, toward Kilgour. The other man pinwheeled in midair, out of control.

Kilgour shot him through the faceplate as he tumbled past. Then Alex was going back up the way he came, hand-over-hand.

He heard a suitjet blast over the storm and went flat, rolling onto his back. One operative came over the rooftop. Y' panicked and let the power save you, lad. An' noo you're hangin' thae, like a braw cloud. Alex shot the cloud three times in its center. The suit's drive stayed on and rocketed the tiny near-spacecraft straight up and away into the sleet clouds.

One more. One more. Show yourself, lad.

Nothing.

Not knowing—or caring—if the final operative had cracked, had gone to aid his downed teammates, or had lost control of his suit, Alex went up the rest of the way to the High Street. Now all he had to do was get out of the city, offworld, and make his way to a very private rendezvous point, one known but to one other being in the universe.

Wi' m' left hand. Wi' m' left hand in m' sleep. Wi' m' left hand in m' sleep croonin't ae lullaby to a bairn.

And Alex Kilgour vanished from the planet of Edinburgh.

CHAPTER FOUR

THE GETTING OF power had always been a complex thing with complex motives. Socio-historians had written whole libraries on it, analyzing and reanalyzing the past, seeking the perfect formula, saying so and so was the right course to follow, and such and such was obvious folly.

Kin mated with kin to achieve power, producing gibbering heirs to their throne. The threat of such a succession sometimes assured the parents of very long and royal reigns.

Kin also murdered kin, or kept them in chains for decades.

Genocide was another favorite trick, one of the few foolproof methods of achieving majority. The difficulty with genocide, the socio-historians said, was that it needed to be constantly applied to keep the edge.

Politics without murder was also favored—under special circumstances. Power was won in such a case by constant and unceasing compromise. Many voices were heard and views taken into account. Only then would a decision be reached. A little artful lying, and everyone *believed* they had been satisfied. Everyone, in that case, was defined as beings of material importance. A leader only had to make sure those same beings had sufficient bones of imagined progress to toss to their mobs. The rule, there, was that if one had too little, the prospect of more was usually enough to satisfy.

There were other methods, but they tended to follow the same paths.

The most certain way, those historians agreed, was to possess a commodity that beings desired above all else. In ancient times it had been food or water. A well-placed road might accomplish the same end. Sex worked in any era, given the proper circumstances. Whatever the commodity, however, it had to be kept in a safe place and guarded against all possible comers.

The Eternal Emperor had had AM2. It was the ultimate fuel and the cornerstone of his vast Empire. In the past, he had merely to turn the tap one way or the other to maintain complete control. His policies had been supported by the largest military force of any known age. The Emperor had also kept the AM2 in a safe place.

More than six years after his assassination, his killers were unable to find it—and they were about to lose the power they had committed regicide to claim.

Even if they had possessed the key to the Emperor's AM2 treasure chest, it was likely the privy council was headed for disaster.

Times had not been kind.

In the aftermath of the Tahn wars—the largest and most costly conflict in history—the Empire was teetering on the edge of economic chaos. The Eternal Emperor's coffers were nearly bare. The deficit from the tremendous military spending was so enormous that even with the highly favorable interest rates the Emperor had bargained hard for, it would take a century to significantly reduce it, much less pay it off.

When the Emperor was still alive, Tanz Sullamora and the other members of the council had strongly proposed their own solution. It involved freezing wages below the pre-Tahn rate and creating deliberate scarcity of product, forcing sharp increases in the price of goods.

And a hefty surtax on AM2.

Through those means and others, the debt would be quickly paid, and corporate health assured for the ages.

The Emperor had rejected those proposals out of hand.

When the Emperor rejected a thing, it was law. With no appeal.

His Majesty's postwar plans called for a directly opposite approach.

The late, never lamented Sr. Sullamora had detailed the Emperor's views to his fellow conspirators without editorializing:

Wages would be allowed to rise to their natural levels. The war had been costly in beingpower—especially, skilled beingpower. This would result in immediate higher costs to business.

Prices, on the other hand, would be frozen, putting goods within easy reach of the newly prosperous populations.

Of course, the war had been a tremendous drain on supplies. To alleviate that, the Emperor fully intended to temporarily *reduce* taxes on AM2—immediately—making goods and transportation cheaper.

In time, he believed, a balance would be achieved.

Where the lords of industry had once seen a future of sudden and continuous windfalls, they now faced a long period of belt-tightening and careful management of their resources. Unearned perks and hefty bonuses would be a thing of the past. Business would be forced to compete equally and take a long-range view of profitability.

That was unacceptable to the privy council. They voted no—with a gun.

The vote had not been unanimous. Volmer, the young media baron, had been horrified by their plan. He wanted no part of it, despite the fact that he disagreed with the Emperor as much as anyone on the council. Although he had no talent for it, Volmer was a fervent believer in the art of persuasion. But he had always had whole battalions of reporters, political experts, and public relations scientists at his command, constantly feeding his enormous media empire. All that was inherited, so talent wasn't necessary.

Like most heirs, Volmer believed himself a genius. It

was his fatal flaw. Even such a dimwit as Volmer should have been able to cipher the precariousness of his situation when he broke with his peers. But the bright light of his own imagined intellect had kept that fact hidden.

The elaborate plot that ensued claimed Volmer as its first victim. The architect of the plot was the Emperor's favorite toady, Tanz Sullamora.

For most of his professional life, Sullamora had licked the Eternal Emperor's boots. For decades, he saw his ruler as a being without visible fault. Certainly, he didn't believe him to be a saint, with gooey feelings for his subjects. He viewed the Emperor as a cold and calculating giant of a CEO, who would use any means to achieve his ends. In that, Sr. Sullamora was absolutely correct.

He erred only by taking it to the extreme. Business was Sullamora's faith, with the Emperor as the high priest. He believed the Emperor infallible, a being who quickly calculated the odds and acted without hesitation. And the result was always the correct one. He also assumed that the Emperor's goals were the same as his own, and those of every other capitalist in the Empire.

To their complete dismay, many others had made the same assumption. But the Eternal Emperor's game was his own. It was his board. His rules. His victory. Alone.

As for infallibility, even the Emperor didn't think that. In fact, when he planned, he assumed error—his own, as well as others. That's why things mostly worked out in his favor. The Eternal Emperor was the master of the long view. "You tend to get that way," he used to joke to Mahoney, "after the first thousand years."

The Tahn war was the result of one of the Emperor's greatest errors. He knew that more than anyone. But the conflict had been so fierce that he had been forced to be candid—to Sullamora, as well as to others. He started thinking aloud, running the logic down to his trusted advisors. How else could he seek their opinions? He had also revealed self-doubt and admitted his many mistakes.

That was a terrible blow to Tanz Sullamora. His hero

was revealed to have feet of definite clay. The corporate halo was tarnished. Sullamora lost his faith.

Murder was his revenge.

To protect himself, he kept the actual details of the plot secret. He guarded his flanks by demanding that his fellow conspirators equally implicate themselves. They had all fixed their prints to documents admitting guilt. Each held a copy of the document, so that betrayal was unthinkable. But the particulars of Volmer's murder, the recruiting of Chapelle, and the subsequent death of the Emperor remained unknown to the other conspirators.

The members of the privy council watched the events at the spaceport unfold on their vidscreens along with the rest of the Empire. And there were no more fascinated viewers. They saw the royal party veer to the receiving line at Soward. They cheered Sullamora as their private hero. They waited in anticipation for the fatal shot. The tension was incredible. In a moment, they would be kings and queens. Then the Emperor died. Mission accomplished!

The explosion that followed surprised them as much as anyone else. The bomb might have been a nice touch. But it was inconceivable that Sullamora would commit suicide. The council members assumed the madman, Chapelle, was merely making sure of his target. Oh, well. Poor Sullamora. Drakh happens.

Although it meant there were more riches to divide, they honestly mourned the man. As the chief of all transport and most major ship building, Tanz Sullamora could not be replaced. They also badly needed his skills at subterfuge, as well as his knowledge of the inner workings of Imperial politics. His death meant that they had to learn on the job.

They didn't learn very well.

The Emperor had stored the AM2 in great depots strategically placed about his Empire. The depots fed great tankers that sped this way and that, depending upon the need and the orders of the Emperor. He alone controlled the amount and the regularity of the fuel.

Defy him, and he would beggar the rebel system or industry. Obey him, and he would see there was always a plentiful supply at a price he deemed fair for his own needs.

The privy council immediately saw the flaw in that system, as far as their own survival was concerned. Not one member would trust any other enough to give away such total control.

So they divided the AM2 up in equal shares, assuring each of their own industries had cheap fuel. They also used it to punish personal enemies and reward, or create, new allies. Power, in other words, was divided four ways.

Occasionally they would all agree that there was a single threat to their future. They would meet, consider, and act.

In the beginning, they went on a spending spree. With all that free fuel, they vastly expanded their holdings, building new factories, gobbling up competitors, or blindsiding corporations whose profits they desired.

The Emperor had priced AM2 on three levels: The cheapest went to developing systems. The next was for public use, so that governments could provide for the basic needs of their various populaces. The third, and highest, was purely commercial.

The privy council set one high price to be paid by everyone, except themselves and their friends. The result was riches beyond even their inflated dreams.

But there was one worm gnawing a great hole in their guts. It was a worm they chose too long to ignore.

The great depots they controlled had to be supplied. But by whom? Or what?

In the past, robot ships—tied together in trains so long they exceeded the imagination—had appeared at the depots filled to the brim with Anti-Matter Two. Many hundreds of years had passed since anyone had asked where they might come from. An assumption replaced the question. Important people knew—important people who followed the Emperor's orders.

Like all assumptions, it rose up and bit the privy council in their collective behinds.

When the Emperor died, the robot ships stopped. At that moment, the AM2 at hand was all they possessed. It would never increase.

It took a long while for that to sink in. The privy council was so busy dealing with the tidal wave of problems— as well as their own guilt—that they just assumed the situation to be temporary.

They sent their underlings to question the bureaucrats at the fuel office. Those poor beings puzzled at them. "Don't *you* know?" they asked. For a time, the privy council was afraid to admit they didn't.

More underlings were called. Every fiche, every document, every doodle the Emperor had scrawled was searched out and examined.

Nothing.

This was an alarming state of affairs, worthy of panic, or, at least, a little rationing. They only panicked a little—and rationed not at all.

They were secretive beings themselves, they reasoned. It was an art form each had mastered in his or her path to success. Therefore: An emperor had to be the most secretive creature of all. Proof: His long reign—and their momentary failure at figuring his system out.

Many other efforts were launched, each more serious and desperate than the last.

Real panic was beginning to set in.

Finally a study committee had been formed from among their most able executives. The committee's objectives were twofold. One: Find the AM2. Second: Determine exactly the supplies on hand and recommend their disposition until objective number one had been reached.

Unfortunately, the second objective obscured the first

for more than a year. If the Emperor had been alive, he would have howled over their folly.

"They tried that with the Seven Sisters," he would have hooted. "How much oil do you *really* have, please, sir? Don't lie, now. It isn't in the national interest."

The council would not have known what the Seven Sisters was all about, or the terrible need to know about something so useless and plentiful as oil. But they would have gotten the drift.

When asked, each member lied—poor-mouthed, as the old wildcatters would have said. The next time they were asked, they were just as likely to inflate the figures. It depended upon the political winds about the conference table.

What about the rest of the Empire? After they had been treated so niggardly, what would the truth gain the council?

Actually, the first outsider who had been questioned soon spread the word. Hoarding fever struck. There was less readily available AM2 than ever before.

Adding to the council's dilemma was a whole host of other problems.

During the Tahn wars, the Emperor constantly had been forced to deal with shaky allies and insistent fence sitters. When the tide turned, all of them swore long and lasting fealty. That, however, did not remove the cause for their previous discontent. The leaders of many of those systems had to deal with unruly populations, beings who had never been that thrilled with the Imperial system and became less so during the war.

Peace did not automatically solve such doubts. The Eternal Emperor had just been turning his attention to these matters when he was slain. The problems would have been exceedingly difficult to solve under any circumstances. It was especially so for his self-appointed heirs. If those allies of the moment had not trusted the Eternal Emperor to have their best interests at heart, than who the clot were these new guys? The council ruled by

Parliamentary decree, but most beings in the Empire were cynical about Parliament. They saw it as a mere rubber stamp for Imperial orders. The Eternal Emperor had never discouraged that view.

It was one of the keys to his mystique.

The Emperor had been a student and admirer of some of the ancient czarist policies. The czars were among the last Earth practitioners of rule by godhead. They had millions of peasants who were brutally treated. The czars used the members of their royal court as middle beings. It was they who wielded the lash and kept the rations to starvation level. The peasants did not always submit. History was full of their many violent uprisings. But the peasants always blamed the nobility for their troubles. It was the noble corpses they hung on posts, not the czar's.

He was a father figure. A kind of gentle man who thought only of his poor subjects. It was the nobility who always took advantage of his nature, hiding their evil deeds from him. And if only he *knew* how terrible was their suffering, he would end it instantly. There was not one scrap of truth to this—but it worked.

Except for the last czar, who was openly disdainful of his people.

"That's why he was the last," the Emperor once told Mahoney.

It was just one of those little lessons of history that the privy council was unaware of. Although if they had known of it, it was doubtful if they would have understood it. Very few business beings understood politics—which was why they made terrible rulers.

Another enormous, festering problem was how to deal with Tahn.

To Kyes, the Kraa twins, and the others, it was simple. The Tahn had been defeated. To the victors go the spoils, and so on.

To that end, the privy council had gutted all their systems. They had hauled off the factories for cannibalization or scrap, seized all resources, and beaten the various populations into submission and slave labor. They also spent a great deal of credits they didn't have to garrison their former enemy. The rape of the Tahn empire produced an instant windfall. But before they had time to congratulate themselves for their brilliance, the privy council saw all that gain going over the dike in an ever-growing flood.

The Eternal Emperor could have told them that tyranny was not cost efficient.

An economic miracle was what the Emperor had in mind. At least, that was how he would have portrayed it. Certainly he had reprisals in mind. The purge would have been massive and complete. He would have wiped out all traces of the culture that had bred the war-loving beings.

But he would have replaced it with something. The will to fight would have been harnessed to the will to compete. Aid every bit as massive as the purge would have been provided. In his thinking, such single-minded beings as the Tahn would eventually produce credits in such plenty that they would soon become one of the most important capitalist centers in his empire.

They would have made wonderful customers of AM2.

Which brought the dilemma of the privy council to full circle.

Where *was* the AM2?

CHAPTER FIVE

KYES SAW THE storm warnings before his ship touched down at Soward.

Prime World's main spaceport was nearly empty. A five-kilometer corner was a jumble of tugs, and from the pitting and streaks of rust on their bulky sides, they looked as if they had been idle for months.

The few liners he saw were pocked with the viral scale that attacked all deep-space ships and ate steadily away at them if left untended. He saw no work crews about. The once vital, bustling heart of the Empire looked like an ancient harridan who had lost even dim memories of lovers past.

A glistening phalanx of military vehicles was waiting for him. They were in stark contrast to the degeneration afflicting Soward. The tall, silvery being with the red mark of his kind throbbing angrily on his smooth skull slid into the seat of his official gravcar. He motioned the driver to proceed.

As the gravcar and its escorts hummed toward the entrance, they skirted the gaping black roped-off crater torn out by the bomb blast that had taken the Emperor. There had been a serious proposal to build a memorial to the Eternal Emperor at the site. Kyes himself had pressed the measure—as a gesture to the being whose memory he and his colleagues based their own authority upon. There had been no argument. Funds had immediately been approved and a designer set. That had been during his last visit, more than a year ago. As yet, not one iota of work had begun.

He was greeted by more squalor as they cleared the port gates. Empty warehouses. Closed businesses, boarding hanging from the vacant eyes of their windows, where gleaming goods had once enticed an affluent population. Unlicensed beggars and crowds of idle beings eyed him as he passed. A shambling tub of a lout, wearing the rags of a loader, glared at the flags of office fluttering on Kyes's transport. She looked him straight in the eye, then spat on the broken pavement.

Kyes leaned forward to his driver. ''What's happened?'' He waved at the desolation around them.

The driver needed no further explanation. ''Don't bother yourself with them, Sr. Kyes,'' she snarled. ''They're nothing but slackers. There's plenty of jobs, but they won't take 'em. Just want to suck on the public tit. Now they're whinin' and groanin' 'cause decent, hard-workin' folks are tellin' 'em: 'No work, no credits.' If the Eternal Emperor—bless him—were still around, he'd straighten 'em out fast.''

The driver stuttered to a stop as she realized that Kyes might take her comments as criticism of the privy council. Then she recovered. A toady's smile wreathed her broad face.

''Not that alla yuz ain't doin' best ya can. These'r terrible times. Terrible times. Wouldn't take on yer job for a fistful a credits. I was tellin' me hub just the other . . .'' The driver droned on. Condescension heaped upon forced humility. Kyes shut her out. He also made no objection to her talking, much less the language. It marked her as on the payroll of the Kraas. There were few things the twins even bothered being subtle about.

The reason Kyes was on Prime World after so long an absence was that he had been called to an emergency session of the privy council. The chief of the AM2 commission was scheduled to reveal the full details of his committee's study on the fuel situation. More to the point, he was to spell out exactly when the search for the Emperor's hidden resources was to be concluded.

Kyes hoped there would be better news here than the depressing report he had received shortly before he left for Prime World.

A crucial mission had been blown. That a number of military operatives had been killed in the process didn't concern Kyes. An important confidant of the Eternal Emperor's—one Admiral Sten—and his longtime aide, Alex Kilgour, had eluded the net spread for them.

The idea that had launched the hunt for all of the beings who had been close to the Emperor had not originated with Kyes. Possibly it had been the Kraa twins'. It didn't matter. Kyes had immediately seen that it could be a shortcut solution to his own dilemma. Round them all up, put them under the brainscan, and voila! All the Emperor's secrets would come tumbling out.

It had taken many, many months to lash that idea into action. Kyes had done the lashing. His plight was far more desperate than the others. It still amazed him how much inertia had to be overcome when dealing with a five-member ruling board. He and his colleagues were used to running their own shows, without compromise or consultation. But finally, the Mantis teams had gone out and quickly returned, prey kicking and mewling in their nets. The result: Zed. Zero. Not one tip or hint on the source of the AM2 . . . or anything else.

Kyes had analyzed the long list of suspects, and more and more he had come to admire just how close-mouthed the Emperor had been. Although his analysis came after the fact, it became apparent that only a very few beings might be able to help. None of those had been among the Mantis teams' catches. Two individuals stood out.

One was retired Fleet Marshal Ian Mahoney. He was officially listed as dead. Kyes had reason to doubt that. He had several reasons. The most important was the gut feeling he got studying the man.

The Mercury Corps files pertaining to Mahoney revealed an exceedingly canny individual who would have no difficulty at all in staging his own demise and remaining out of sight for as long as he thought necessary. The only flaw Kyes could find was his unwavering loyalty to the Emperor, a flaw that made Mahoney potentially dangerous—if he was alive. Assuming the death was a cover, that could suggest only one motive for Mahoney's actions: The fleet marshal suspected the privy council of assassinating his old employer.

The second most likely suspect was Admiral Sten, a man who had once commanded the Imperial bodyguard, the Gurkhas—who, oddly, had all resigned their positions immediately following the Emperor's death and returned to their homeland of Nepal on Earth. Sten had been an important but shadowy figure during the Tahn conflict. Kyes had also personally reviewed Sten's files. There were enormous gaps. Very strange. Especially since the gaps seemed to have been ordered by the Emperor himself. Adding to Kyes's suspicions was that the man had suddenly become enormously wealthy, as had his companion, Kilgour, although on a lesser scale. Where did all that money come from? Payoffs? From the Emperor, himself, perhaps? For what purpose?

Kyes added one and one and got an instant six: Sten must be among the very few that the Emperor had entrusted with his secrets. When the admiral had been located in his distant exile, Kyes had demanded that a crack team be sent to capture him. He had gotten gilt-edged assurances that only the very best would be sent. Obviously he had been fed a sop. After all, how good could those Mantis beings have actually been? Wiped out by one man? Clot!

Kyes had packed his steel teeth for this meeting. Some heavy ass-chewing was in order.

Out on the street, Kyes spotted three beings in dirty orange robes and bare feet. They were making their way through the motley crowd, handing out leaflets and proselytizing. He couldn't hear what they were saying from the soundproof comfort of his car, but he didn't need to. He knew who they were: members of the Cult of the Eternal Emperor.

All over the Empire, there were countless individuals who firmly believed that the Emperor had not died. A few thought it was a plot by his enemies: The Emperor had been kidnapped and was being kept under heavy guard. Others claimed it was a clever ploy by the Emperor himself: He had deliberately staged his death and was hiding out until his subjects realized just how terribly he was needed. Eventually, he would return to restore order.

The cultists were at the absolute extreme. They believed that the Emperor was truly immortal, that he was a holy emissary of the Holy Spheres, who wore a body for convenience to carry around his glowing soul. His death, they said, was self-martyrdom. An offering to the Supreme Ether for all the sins of his mortal subjects. They also firmly believed in his resurrection. The Eternal Emperor, they preached, would soon return to his benign reign, and all would be well again.

Kyes was a kindred spirit of the cultists. Because he, too, believed the Emperor was alive and would return. Kyes was a business being, who had once disdained all thinking based on wishes rather than reason as a weak prop for his mental and economic inferiors. But that was no longer so. If the Eternal Emperor were truly dead, then Kyes was lost. Therefore, he believed. To think otherwise was to risk madness.

There were ancient tales of his own kind that directly addressed the issue of immortality, or, at least, extremely long life. They were part of a Methuselah legend, based on the fatal flaw of his species.

Kyes—and all of the Grb'chev—were the result of the joining of two distinct life forms. One was the body that Kyes walked about in. It was a tall, handsome, silvery creature, whose chief assets were strength, almost miraculous health, and an ability to adapt to and absorb any life-threatening force. It also was as stupid as a tuber.

The second was visible only by the red splash throbbing at his skull. It once had been nothing more than a simple, hardy life form—which could be best compared to a virus. Calling it a virus, however, would not be accurate, only descriptive. Its strengths were extreme virulence, an ability to penetrate the defensive proteins of any cell it encountered, and the potential for developing intelligence. Its chief weakness was a genetic clock that ticked to a stop at the average age of one hundred and twenty-six years.

Kyes should have been "dead" already, that fine brain nothing more than a small, blackened ball of rotting cells. His body—the handsome frame that performed all the natural functions of the Grb'chev—might continue on for another century or so, but it would be nothing more than a gibbering, drooling shell.

When Kyes had thrown his lot in with the other members of the privy council, it was not power he sought—but rescue. Riches had no attraction to him. It was life he wanted. Intelligent life.

He cared nothing for the AM2, although he whispered not a hint of that to his colleagues. To reveal his weakness would bring his doom. When the Emperor had been slain and the desperate search launched for the source of the Emperor's never-diminishing fuel cache, Kyes had been looking equally as desperately for something else: What made the Eternal Emperor immortal?

At first he had been as sure of finding it in the Emperor's classified archives as the others were of locating the AM2. But it had proved to be equally as elusive.

When the murderous act had been committed, Kyes had been 121 years old. That meant he had just five years to live. Now a little more than six years had passed—and Kyes was still alive!

In the intervening years he had become a near-hysteric about his mental powers, constantly aware of the clock that was running out. Even the smallest lapse of memory sent him into a panic. A forgotten appointment plunged him into black moods difficult to hide from his peers. That was the chief reason he had stayed away from Prime World for so long.

He had no more notion why he continued to live than he had of the Emperor's greatest secret. No being of his species had ever survived beyond the 126-year natural border.

Well, that wasn't absolutely correct. There had been one, according to that myth—the myth of the Grb'chev Methuselah.

It was during the prehistory of the intertwined life-forms that the legend began. All was conflict and chaos during that long, dark era, the story went. Then along came an individual who was entirely different from the others. The being's name had been lost, which put the reality of his actual existence in extreme doubt but made the legend more compelling.

According to the myth, the being declared his immortality while still an adolescent. And in the hundred or more years that followed, he became noted as a wandering thinker and philosopher who confounded the greatest minds of his time. The year of his deathdate, the entire kingdom took up the watch, waiting daily for the heralds to announce his demise. The year passed. Then another. And another. Until his immortality became an accepted fact. That first—and only—long-lived Grb'chev became the ruler of the kingdom. An age of great enlightenment dawned, lasting for many centuries, perhaps a thousand years. From that time on the future of the race was ensured—at least that's what the tale-tellers said.

The last part of the legend was what interested Kyes the most: the prophesy that someday another Methuselah would be born, and that immortal Grb'chev would lead the species to even greater successes.

Lately Kyes wondered if he might be that chosen one. But this was only during his most hysterical fantasizing. More likely, the extra span he had been allotted was due to nothing more than a small genetic blip. In reality at any moment he would "die."

If he was to have any future, Kyes would have to seize it himself. He would find the secret and become the new savior of his kind.

Kyes looked out the window. The car was moving through a working-class neighborhood of tall, drab tenements facing across a broad avenue. The traffic was mostly on foot. The AM2 squeeze prohibited public transport, much less the boxy little flits favored by the lower middle class. Kyes saw a long line snaking out of a soya shop. A tattered sign overhead pegged the cost at ten credits an ounce. The condition of the sign mocked even that outrageous price.

Two armored cops were guarding the entrance of the shop. Kyes saw a woman exit with a bundle under her arms. The crowd immediately began hooting at her, clawing at the package. One big cop moved tentatively forward. Kyes's car glided on before he saw what happened next.

". . . been like that ever since the food riots," the driver was saying. "Course, security costs somethin' fierce, so the prices gotta go up, don't they? But you can't make folks understand that. I was tellin' my hub—"

"What food riots?" Kyes burst through.

"Dincha hear?" The driver craned her neck around, gaping in amazement that a member of the privy council was somehow not in the know.

"I was advised of disturbances," Kyes said. "But not . . . riots."

"Oh, *disturbances*," the driver said. "Much better'n riots. That's what they was, all right. Disturbances. Musta had twenty, thirty thousand lazy, filthy types disturbin' drakh all over the place. Cops went easy. Didn't kill more'n half a hundred or so. Course, three, four thousand was shot up some and . . ."

Furious, Kyes tuned out the rest. He had made his

views quite plain to his fellow council members. Prime
World and all the beings on it were to be handled like
gossamer. As the heart of the Empire, it was the last
place shortages of any kind should show up. When he
had learned of the "disturbances," he had made his
views even plainer. But the Kraas and the others assured
him that all was well. There had been a few small glitches
in the supply system, that was all. The supplies and the
peace had been restored. Right! It wasn't the lies that
disturbed Kyes so much—he was a master dissembler
himself. It was the plain wrongheadedness of the matter.

If the privy council could not keep matters under control a few kilometers from its own front door, how could
they possibly succeed in ruling a far-flung Empire? And
if they failed, Kyes was doomed to something far worse
than any hell they could imagine.

A second immensely irritating factor: If things were
really so awful that basic foods were out of the reach of
the local populace, then why were the members of the
council flaunting their own wealth?

He groaned aloud when he saw, ahead of him, the spire
needling up over the tall buildings of the financial district. It was the newly completed headquarters of the
privy council.

"Amazin' as clot, ain't it," his driver said, mistaking
the groan for a belch of admiration. "You fellas done
yourself proud with that buildin'. Nothin' like it on
Prime. Specially with the Emperor's old castle wrecked
by bombs and all.

"I know yuz ain't seen it yet, but wait'll ya get inside.
You got fountains and drakh. With real colored water.
And right in the middle they put in this great clottin'
tree. Called a rubiginosa, or somethin'. Probably sayin'
it wrong. Big mother fig. But the kind you can't eat."

"Who's idea was it?" Kyes asked—dry, noncommit-
tal.

"Dunno. Designer, I think. What was her name?
Uh . . . Ztivo, or somethin' like that. But, boy did she

charge an arm and two, three legs. The tree alone's gotta be fifteen, twenty meters tall. Dug it up from someplace on Earth. But they was scared it'ud shrivel up and blow away if they brought here direct, like. So they seasoned it. On three four different planets. Spent a big bundle of credits on it.

"Musta worked. It's goin' crazy in there! Picked up another two meters, I heard, in the last two-three months. Why, that clottin' tree's the pride and joy of Prime World, I tell you. Ask anybody."

As the gravcar slowed, Kyes saw a crowd of beggars push forward. A wedge of club-wielding cops beat them back. Certainly, he thought. Ask anybody. Go right ahead.

The AM2 secretary's report was a dry buzz against glass. On the table before him was a one-third-meter stack of readouts, the result of many months labor. He was reading—syllable by maddening syllable—from a précis not much slimmer. His name was Lagguth. But from the glares he was getting from the members of the privy council, it was likely to be changed to something far worse.

Kyes and the others had gathered eagerly around the table. This could possibly be the most important listening session of their lives. So no one objected a whit when Lagguth's aides hauled in the mass of papers. Nor did anyone raise a brow when the preamble went a full hour.

They were in the second hour—a second hour to a group of beings who habitually required their subordinates to sum up all thinking in three sentences or less. If they liked the three sentences, the subordinate could continue. If not, firing was a not indistinct possibility. After the first hour, the AM2 secretary had gone past firing. Executions were being weighed. Kyes had several nasty varieties in mind himself.

But he had caught a different tone than the rest. There was real fear beneath all that buzz. He caught it in the nervous shufflings and newly habitual tics in Lagguth's mannerisms. Kyes stopped listening for the bottom line and started paying attention to the words. They were meaningless. Deliberate bureaucratic nonsense. That added up to stall. Kyes kept his observation to himself. Instead, he began thinking how he might use it.

The Kraas broke first.

The fat one cleared her throat, sounding like distant thunder, loomed her gross bulk forward, and thrust out a chin that was like a heavy-worlder's fist.

"Yer a right bastard, mate," she said. "Makin' me piles bleed with all this yetcheta yetch. Me sis's arse bones'r pokin' holes in the sitter. Get to it. Or get summun else in to do the gig!"

Lagguth gleaped. But, it was a puzzled sort of a gleap. He knew he was in trouble. Just what not for.

Lovett translated. "Get to the clotting point, man. What's the prog?"

Lagguth took a deep and lonely breath. Then he painted a bright smile on his face. "I'm so sorry, gentle beings," he said. "The scientist in me . . . tsk . . . tsk . . . How thoughtless. In the future I shall endeavor—"

The skinny Kraa growled. It was a shrill sound—and not nice. It had the definite note of a committed carnivore.

"Thirteen months," Lagguth blurted. "And that's an outside estimate."

"So, you're telling us, that although your department has had no luck in locating the AM2, you *now* have an estimate of when you will find it. Is that right?" Lovett was a great one for summing up the obvious.

"Yes, Sr. Lovett," Lagguth said. "There can be no mistake. Within thirteen months we shall have it." He patted the thick stack of documentation.

"That certainly sounds promising, if true," Malperin broke in. She stopped Lagguth's instinctive defense of his work with a wave of her hand. Malperin ruled an immense, cobbled-together conglomerate. She did not rule it well. But she had more than enough steel in her to keep it as long as she liked.

"What is your opinion, Sr. Kyes?" she asked. Malperin dearly loved to shift discussions along, keeping her own views hidden as long as possible. It was Kyes's recent surmise that she actually had none and was waiting to see which way the wind blew before she alighted.

"First, I would like to ask Sr. Lagguth a question," Kyes said. "A critical one, I believe."

Lagguth motioned for him to please ask.

"How much AM2 do we have on hand right now?"

Lagguth sputtered, then began a long abstract discussion. Kyes cut him off before he even reached the pass.

"Let me rephrase," Kyes said. "Given current usage, current rationing—how long will the AM2 last?"

"Two years," Lagguth answered. "No more."

The answer jolted the room. Not because it was unexpected. But it was like having a death sentence set, knowing exactly at what moment one would cease to exist. Only Kyes was unaffected. This was a situation he was not unused to.

"Then, if you're wrong about the thirteen months . . ." Malperin began.

"Then it's bleedin' over, mate, less'n a year from then," the skinny Kraa broke in.

Lagguth could do no more than nod. Only Kyes knew why the man was so frightened. It was because he was lying.

No, not about the two-year supply of AM2. It was the first estimate that was completely fabricated. Thirteen months. Drakh! More like never. Lagguth and his department had no more idea where the Emperor had kept the AM2 than when they started more than six years before. Motive for lying? To keep his clotting head on his shoulders. Wasn't that motive enough?

"Stay with the first figure," Kyes purred to the skinny

Kraa. "It's pointless to contemplate the leap from the chasm when you have yet to reach the edge."

Both Kraas stared at him. Despite their brutal features, the stares were not unkind. They had learned to depend on Kyes. They had no way of knowing that from the start, his personal dilemma had forced him into the role of moderate.

"Sr. Lagguth believes it will take thirteen months to locate the AM2 source," Kyes said. "This may or may not be the case. But I know how we can be more certain."

"Yeah? How's that?" Lovett asked.

"I have a new mainframe about to go on-line. My scientists have been working on it for a number of years. We developed it specifically as a tool for archivists."

"So?" That was the fat Kraa, the blunter of the two—if that were possible.

"We plan to sell it to governments. It should reduce document search time by forty percent or more."

There were murmurs around the room. They were catching Kyes's drift, and all he was saying was true. If there was a lie, it was only in his real intentions.

"I propose that Sr. Lagguth and I join forces," Kyes said, "assuring us of meeting his stated goal. What do you think? I am quite open to any other suggestions."

There were none. The deal was done.

As for the other matters—the blown Mantis mission to capture the admiral, the terrible conditions Kyes had witnessed on the streets of Prime World—they were left untouched. Kyes had gotten what he wanted.

Only one other thing came up, and this fairly casually.

"About this clottin' two-year supply business," the skinny Kraa said.

"Yes?"

"Me 'n Sis, here, think we oughta try and stretch it."

"More rationing?" Lovett asked. "I think we've just about—"

"Naw. Don't be puttin' words in me mush. Drakh on that."

"What then?"

"We take it."

"From whom?" Kyes could not help but be drawn in by the fascinating discussion.

"Who gives a clot?" the fat Kraa said. "Somebody that's got a whole lot of it, that's who. Can't be that many."

"You mean steal it?" Malperin asked, also fascinated. "Just like that?"

"Why not?" the skinny Kraa said.

Yes. They all agreed. Why not, indeed?

CHAPTER SIX

STEN'S FIRST STEP, once clear of Smallbridge, was to go to ground. Mahoney had a planned refuge—which Sten rejected. Sten had his own very secure hideout. Where—he hoped—Kilgour, if he had been warned in time, would meet him.

The hideout was Farwestern, and there Sten saw firsthand the effect the dwindling of AM2 and the privy council's incompetence at managing what fuel there was.

Farwestern had been—and to a degree, still was—a shipping hub near the center of a galaxy. At one time it had provided everything a shipper could want—from shipyards to chandleries, recworlds to warehousing, hotels to emergency services, all cluttered in a system-wide assemblage of containers. "Containers" was about the most specific description that could be used, since the entrepreneurs who had gathered around Farwestern used everything from small asteroids to decommissioned and disarmed Imperial warships to house their businesses. Almost anything legal and absolutely anything illegal could be scored in and around Farwestern, including anonymity.

Years earlier Sten and Alex, on one of their Mantis team missions, had run through Farwestern. They found its cheerful anarchy to their liking. Most especially, they fell in love with a small planetoid named Poppajoe. Poppajoe was jointly owned by a pair of rogues named Moretti and Manetti. Having acquired fortunes elsewhere under almost certainly shadowy circumstances, they had discovered Farwestern and decided that there was their home. The question was: what service could they provide that wasn't available? The answer was luxury and invisibility.

They reasoned that there would be beings passing through who would want to be well taken care of and might prefer that their presence not be broadcast. This applied to criminals as well as to executives on their way to make a deal best kept secret until the stock manipulations were complete.

Moretti and Manetti had thrived in peace. In the recent war they had doubled their fortunes. Now times were a little hard. Not bad enough to drive them under, but ticklish. They survived because they were owed so many favors by so many beings, from magnates to tramp skippers.

There were still people who needed the shadows. Moretti and Manetti catered to them. All room entrances were individual. Guests could dine publicly, or remain in their suites. Privacy was guaranteed. Their food was still the finest to be found—fine and simple, from Earth-steak to jellied hypoornin served in its own atmosphere and gravity.

When Sten and Kilgour had run across Poppajoe, they had made a very quiet resolution that if things ever got Very Very Hairy, this would be their private rendezvous point.

As Sten's ship entered the Farwestern system, neither he nor Mahoney looked particularly military. As a matter of fact, neither looked particularly anything.

Beings frequently go to too much trouble when they decide, for whatever reason, that they would rather not be recognized as themselves. All that is necessary—unless the person is unfortunately gifted with the face of a matinee idol or an abnormal body—is to appear (A) unlike who they really are; and (B) like no one in particular. Dress neither poorly nor expensively. Eat what everyone else is eating. Travel neither first class nor steerage. Try to become that mythical entity, the average citizen. Mercury Corps called the tactic, for some unknown reason, a "Great Lorenzo."

Sten and Mahoney were now businessmen, successful enough for their corporation to have provided them with fuel and a ship, but not so successful that they had their own pilot, and the ship was a little rundown at the edges. Three days' work at a smuggler's conversion yard had turned Sten's gleaming white yacht into just another commercial/private—but only as long as no one looked at the engines or the com room, or figured out that some of the compartments were much tinier than they should have been, and that behind those bulkheads were enough arms to outfit a small army.

Mahoney had worried that the ship could be traced by its numbers. Sten was glad to find that his ex-boss did not know *everything*. The ship and every serial-numbered item on it was trebly sterile—another product of Sten's professional paranoia that was now paying off.

So they arrived on Poppajoe and were greeted by Messrs. Moretti and Manetti as if they were both long-lost cousins and complete but respected strangers.

Poppajoe may have been surviving, but Farwestern was not. Commercial travel was a trickle. Between the fuel shortages and the cutbacks in the military, even Imperial ships were a rarity. A lot of orbital stations had sealed their ports, and their people had gone dirtside to one of Farwestern's planets or moved on.

"But we will make it," Moretti explained. "We're like the old mining town that struck it rich. A group of emigrés moved in and discovered that no one likes to do his own washing. They were willing to provide the services. Eventually the minerals played out and the miners headed for the next strike. However, the laundrybeings stayed—and all became millionaires doing each other's laundry."

He found that quite funny. Sten did not. What he saw, and had seen from the time he and Mahoney had fled

Smallbridge, was the slow grinding down of the Empire. He had felt it going on even in his isolation on Smallbridge, but witnessing it was another thing. Beingkind was pulling in its horns—or was being forced to. Entropy was well and good as a thermodynamic principle. As a social phenomenon it was damned scary.

Mahoney gave him as big a picture as he could—which was hardly complete, he admitted. Worlds, systems, clusters, even some galaxies had slipped out of contact. By choice, rejecting the hamwitted leadership of the council? By war? By—barely conceivable—disease?

As Sten well knew, AM2 had been the skein holding the Empire together. Without the shattering energy release of Anti-Matter Two, star drives were almost impossible to power. And of course, since AM2 had been very inexpensive—price determined by the Emperor—and fairly available—depending on the Emperor, once more—it was easy to take the lazy way out and run anything and everything on the substance. Interstellar communications . . . weaponry . . . factories . . . manufacturing . . . the list ran on.

When the Emperor was murdered the supply of AM2 stopped. Sten had found that hard to swallow the first time Mahoney had said it. He was still having trouble. Back on Smallbridge, he had assumed that the privy council—for profiteering reasons of their own, as well as base incompetency—had merely been keeping the supply at a trickle.

"Not true," Mahoney had said. "They haven't a clue to where the goodies are. That's why the council wanted to pick you up—and anybody else who might've had a private beer with the Emperor—then gently loosen your toenails until you told them The Secret."

"They're clottin' mad."

"So they are. Consider this, boy. The *entire universe* is bonkers," Mahoney said. "Except for me and thee. Heh . . . heh . . . heh . . . and I'm slippin' away slowly if you don't find a bottle and uncap it."

Sten followed orders. He drank—heavily—from the bottle before handing it to Ian.

"Ring down for another one. If your prog circuits are DNCing now, it will get far worse."

Again, Sten followed orders.

"Okay, Mahoney. We are now on the thin edge."

Mahoney chortled. "Not even close yet, boy. But proceed."

There was a tap at the door. "Y'r order, sir."

Mahoney was on his feet, a pistol snaking out of his sleeve. "A little too efficient." He moved toward the door.

"Relax, Fleet Marshal," Sten said dryly. "It's open, Mr. Kilgour."

After a pause, the door came open, and Alex entered pushing a drink tray and wearing a disappointed expression.

"Did I noo hae y'goin't frae e'en a second?" he asked hopefully.

"You gotta do something about the way you talk, man."

"Thae's some think it charmin'," Alex said, mock-hurt.

Sten and Alex looked at one another.

"How close did they get to you?" Sten asked.

Kilgour told them of the near-ambush and the battle in the icy streets.

"Ah'm assum't," he said, "frae the fact th' warnin' wae in gen'ral code, nae whae Sten and I hae set up, y're responsible f'r tippin' me th' wink."

"I was," Mahoney said.

"Ah'm also assum't, sir, thae's reason beyon' y'r fas'nation wi' m' girlish legs an' giggle. Who d'ye want iced?"

"Quick thinking, Mr. Kilgour. But sit down. You too, Admiral. The debriefing—and the plan—will take awhile. You'll guess the target—correction, targets—as I go along. The suspense will be good for you."

Mahoney began with what had happened to him from the day of the Emperor's funeral, when he had looked at the Council of Five standing on the grassy knoll that was the Emperor's grave and knew that he was looking at five assassins.

He hesitated, then told them the impossible part. After the funeral, he had gone into the Emperor's study, dug out a bottle of the vile swill the Emperor called Scotch, and planned a quiet, private farewell toast. Stuck to the bottle was a handwritten note:

"Stick around, Ian. I'll be right back."

It was in the handwriting of the Eternal Emperor.

Mahoney stopped, expecting complete disbelief. He got it, masked on both men's faces by expressions of bright interest—and a slow shift by Sten toward Mahoney's gun-hand.

"That's—very interesting, Fleet Marshal. Sir. How do you suppose it got there? Are you saying the man who got assassinated was a double?"

"No. That was the Emperor."

"So he somehow survived getting shot a dozen or so times and then being blown up?"

"Don't clot around, Sten. He was dead."

"Ah. Soo he ris't oot'n th' grave t' leave ye a wee love note?"

"Again, no. He must've left instructions with one of the Gurkhas. Or a palace servant. I asked. Nobody knew anything."

"Let's ignore how the note got there for a sec, Ian. Are you listening to what you've just been saying? Either you're mad—or else you've joined up with that cult that goes around saying the Emperor has lived forever. And remembering six years plus is a long time for you just to be sticking around. Which is how long it's been."

"Neither one—or maybe I *am* bonkers. But will you keep listening?"

"Mought's well. Whae's time t' a clottin' hog?" Kilgour said. He poured himself a drink of quill—but still kept a wary eye on Mahoney.

Mahoney went on. He had made his own plans that day. He was going after the privy council.

"Did you consider maybe they'd think you were the type to carry a grudge?" Sten asked.

"I did—and covered my ass."

Mahoney put in for early retirement. The privy council, in the mad rush to get rid of the bloated and incredibly expensive military after the Tahn wars, was more than willing to let anyone and everyone out, few questions asked. Sten nodded—that was exactly how he and Kilgour had been able to slip into retirement and obscurity.

The council was especially happy to be rid of Mahoney, who was not only the Emperor's best-loved Fleet Marshal, architect of victory, but also once head of Mercury Corps—Imperial Intelligence—for many, many years.

"But I didn't want them to think I was going to create any mischief. I found a cover."

Mahoney's cover, loudly announced, was that he planned to do a complete biography of the Eternal Emperor, the greatest man who ever lived. That plan fit quite well into the council's martyr-building.

"What I was, of course, doing was building my stone bucket. Hell if I knew what I would do with it—but I had to do it."

Mahoney dived into the archives—he planned to spend a year or so researching The Early Years. By then he figured the council would have lost interest in him, and he could go for the real target. A little sheepishly, he told Sten and Alex that he had always loved raw research. Maybe—if things had been different, and he had not come from a military family—he would have ended up poking through archives trying to figure out The Compleat History of the Fork. Or something.

He was not the first, the hundredth, or the millionth person to bio the Emperor. But he discovered something interesting. All of the bios were crocks.

"So what?" Sten asked, disinterested. "If you were up there on the right hand of God, wouldn't you want everybody to make nice on you?"

"That is not what I meant." Mahoney said. He had seen a pattern. Biographers were encouraged to write about the Emperor. However, they were mostly of the type who would work hard to either find Deep-seated Humanity in Tamerlane, or else write a psychological biography of the poet Homer.

"Let's say there might have been a great number of sloppy historians. But somehow their work was still encouraged. They won the big contracts. Their fiche were picked up for the livies. And so on and so forth.

"I'm telling you, lads, no one was really encouraged to look at source material—what hasn't somehow, and I quote, vanished in the mists of time, end quote."

"So what was our late leader trying to hide?"

"Damned near everything, from where he came from to how he got where he is. You might spend a lifetime daring insanity trying to make sense out of the seventeen or eighteen thousand versions of events, each of them seemingly given the Emperor's imprimatur.

"I'll just mention two of the murkiest areas, besides where the clot the AM2 is. First is that the son of a bitch is—or was, anyway, immortal."

"Drakh. No such animal."

"Believe it. And the second thing is—he's been killed before."

"But you just said—"

"I know what I just said. He's died before. Been killed. Various ways. Several accidents. At least two assassinations."

"And you won't accept a double."

"I will not. But here is what happened, at least concerning the incidents I was able to document: First, the

Emperor dies. Second, there is, immediately afterward, a big goddamned explosion, destroying the body and anything around. Just like that bomb that went off after Chappelle killed the Emperor."

"*Every* time?"

"Every one I can find. And then—the AM2 stops. Wham. Just like that.

"Then the Emperor comes back. As does the AM2. And things start back to normal."

"Ian, now you've got me playing loony games on your turf," Sten said. "Okay. How long does he usually vanish? Not that I am believing one damned word of what you are saying."

Mahoney looked worried. "Accident—perhaps three or four months. Murder—as long as a year or two. Maybe time enough for people to realize how much they need him."

"Six years an' more hae gone noo," Alex pointed out.

"I know."

"But you still believe the Eternal Emperor is gonna appear in a pink cloud or some kind of clottin' seashell in the surf and the world will be happy and gay once more?" Sten scoffed.

"You don't believe me," Mahoney said, pouring himself a drink. "Would it help if I let you go through the files? I have them hidden away."

"No. I still wouldn't believe you. But set that aside. What else did you get?"

"I worked forward. And I got lucky, indeed. Remember your friend Haines?"

Sten did. She had been a homicide cop, and she and Sten had been up to their elbows unraveling the strange assassination plot that had inadvertently sparked the recent Tahn wars. She and Sten had also been lovers.

"She's still a cop. She's still on Prime. Homicide chief now," Mahoney told Sten.

He had gone to her for permission to access the files on Chapelle, the Emperor's assassin. He'd had the highest clearances—volume one of the biography had been published to great acclaim. ''Complete tissue, of course,'' he assured them.

''Anyway, your Haines. She's still as honest as ever, boy.''

Mahoney had asked some questions—and one day Haines had gotten the idea that the ex-Intelligence head was not in his dotage, indulging a private passion.

''She said the only reason she was doing it is because you'd spoken well of me. For a, ahem, clottin' general. You remember a young lad named Volmer?''

Sten did. Volmer was a publishing baron—or, more correctly, the waffling heir to a media empire. Part of the privy council. Murdered one night outside a tawdry ambisexual cruising bar in the port city of Soward. The released story was that he had been planning a series on the corruption around the war effort. A more cynical—and popular—version was that Volmer liked his sex rough and strange and had picked up the wrong hustler.

Haines had something different. She had been stalking a contract killer for about a year—a professional. She didn't give a damn about a triggerman, but wanted to know who had hired him. She got him—and with enough evidence concerning the disappearance of a gang boss to get at least an indictment.

The young man evidently agreed with Haines as to the worth of the evidence. He offered to make a deal. Haines thought that a wonderful idea. She might not care, particularly, if underworld types slaughtered each other on a daily basis. But when they kept leaving the bodies out on the street to worry the citizens—then action had to be taken.

The man offered her something better. He confessed that he had killed Volmer. The word had been that the freako was an undercover type. There had been an open contract. The killer had filled it—and then found out later whom he had touched.

Haines wanted to know who had paid. The man named

an underworld boss, now deceased. Haines punted him back to his cell, told him to think about corroborative evidence, and tried to figure out what it all meant. The assassin "suicided" in his cell that night.

"That's all she had?"

"That's all she had."

"So who terminated Volmer?"

"Perhaps his brothers on the privy council? Maybe Volmer wasn't going along with the program? I don't know—yet. But there was the first member of the council dead.

"Then Sullamora. Blown up with the Emperor.

"Something funny about that lone hit man, Chapelle. He came out of Spaceport Control. I did a little research on him, as well. Seems he felt the Emperor was after him personally."

"Yeah. I saw the livies, too. A head case."

"He was that. But he was set up to become one. Somebody—somebody who could have played with his career—arranged for him to get his face shoved in it every time he turned around. To this day nobody knows, for instance, why he suddenly lost his job and ended up on bum row.

"Spaceport Control. Ports, shipping—that was Sullamora's responsibility on the privy council. And now he's dead, too."

Sten started to pour himself another drink, then thought better of it and walked to the viewpanel and stared out.

"All right, Mahoney. You've got some interesting things. Maybe. And maybe you're a head case like this Chapelle. Maybe all you've got is that thieves fall out. A Mantis op on his second run could tell you that.

"Fill in the blanks. What happened next? And come to think about it, what *happens* next?"

Mahoney told them. About the time he had talked to Haines, he had started feeling a bit insecure. The council, he had realized, had not a clue as to the source of AM2. Mahoney thought it was a matter of time before they started rounding up the usual suspects and probing their brains for this had-to-be-somewhere secret.

"Brainscan's an uncomfortable feeling, I understand. Frequently fatal. So I died. Laundered my investments by somehow getting swindled. Paid the swindler ten percent of the money he stole. Then I drowned. A stupid boating accident. There were whispers that it was because I'd lost my entire fortune."

Dead and invisible, Mahoney went to work. Part and parcel of his research was looking up all his old service friends, anyone who might have had any knowledge of the Emperor.

"Many of them still serve. And most of them think we are heading for absolute chaos unless the council is removed."

Sten and Kilgour exchanged looks. Removed. Yes.

"Then . . . then we have access to everything the Emperor left on Prime. I know—knew—that man. He would have hidden the secret somewhere. Hell, for all I know, in one of those glue pots he used trying to make a gutter."

"Guitar," Sten corrected absently.

"Because that's the only chance we have," Mahoney said. "Probably you were right. Probably I am quite mad believing the Emperor will return. Maybe that he ever did. Indulge an old man's eccentricity.

"But if someone does not do something—this Empire, which maybe it's done things wrong, and even some evils, has still held civilization together for two millennia and longer.

"If nothing's done, it will all vanish in a few lifetimes."

Sten was looking closely at Mahoney—a not especially friendly look.

"So you get me out of harm's way, get word to Kilgour. And all you want in return is for us to kill the five beings who happen to rule the known universe."

Mahoney chose not to see the sarcasm. "Exactly. No

impeachments. No trials. No confusion. Which is why I
wanted you, Sten. This is the linchpin to the whole operation. You've done it before. In clean, out clean—with
five bodies behind you.''

Sten and Alex sat, wordless, staring out the plate into
deep space. They had told Mahoney they had to talk, then
thrown him out of their quarters. There had not been
much talk. They had capped the alk and called for caff.

Sten ordered his thoughts. Could he somehow take out
the privy council? Yes, his Mantis arrogance said.
Maybe. It was the "out clean" that bothered him. Sten
had always agreed with his first basic sergeant, who had
said he wanted soldiers who would "help the soldier on
the other side die for his country."

The privy council had tried to kill him—and probably
grabbed all of his wealth and pauperized him as well.
So? Credits were not important. They could be made as
well as lost. As far as the killing—once the shooting had
stopped, Sten, who prided himself as being a professional, had bought narcobeers for his ex-enemies on
many occasions.

Were the privy council members evil—which would
somehow justify their deaths? Define evil, he thought.
Evil is . . . what does not work.

Thus, another list:

Was the privy council incompetent? Certainly. Especially if one believed what Mahoney had said. Once
more, So? The worlds Sten had lived in, from Vulcan to
the Imperial Military itself, were more often than not
governed by incompetents.

The Empire was running down. For a third time, So?
Sten, veteran of a hundred battles and a thousand-plus
worlds, could not visualize that amorphous thing called
an Empire.

Another list. This time, a short one.

All Sten had known—like his father and his father before *him*—was The Eternal Emperor. That, in fact, was what Sten thought of when he considered the Empire.

He had sworn an oath. Sworn it twice, in fact. ". . . to defend the Eternal Emperor and the Empire with your life . . . to obey lawful orders given you and to honor and follow the traditions of the Imperial Guard as the Empire requires." The first had been administered after he had been cold-cocked by Mahoney, eons before, back on Vulcan. But he had retaken the oath when they had commissioned him.

And he had meant it.

If the council members had tried to kill the Emperor—and failed—would he have considered it his duty to hunt them down and, if necessary, kill them? Of course. And did he believe the privy council had killed the Emperor? Yes. Absolutely.

He thought of an old Tahn proverb: "Duty is heavier than lead, death lighter than a feather." It did not help.

That oath still stood, as did the duty. Sten felt somewhat embarrassed. He looked across at Kilgour and cleared his throat. Such were not things to be said aloud.

Kilgour was avoiding Sten's glance. "Ae course, thae's th' option ae findin't ae deep, rich hole, pullin' it in behind us, an' lettin' the universe swing," he said suddenly.

"I'd just as soon not spend the rest of my life looking over my shoulder."

"Y'lack confidence, lad. We c'd do't. Nae problem. But if we did, m'mither'd nae hae aught to brag on, come market day. So. Empire-topplin' it is? Sten?"

Sten managed a grin. Better this way. Let the real reasons stay inside. He stuck out his hand.

"Nae, we c'n gie lushed wi' a clear conscience," Kilgour sighed. He groped for a bottle.

"Ah noo ken whae Ah nae lik't thae livies. Here's a braw decision made. In ae hotel flat by a fat man dressed like ae commercial traveller an' a wee lad resemblin't ae

gig'lo. Nae a sword, gleamin't armor or wavin't banner
amongst us. Whae a world.''

He drank.

"Nae. How filthy d' we scrag thae' bastards?"

So Sten and Kilgour went into partnership with an ex–
Fleet Marshal who both of them considered, privately,
was a bit round the bend.

CHAPTER SEVEN

THE MAN STARED at the screen. His hands remained folded in his lap.

"You have not begun the test," the Voice—for he had begun to capitalize it in his mind—accused.

"What happens if I fail to obey?"

"Information will not be provided. Begin the test."

"I shall not."

"Do you have a reason?"

"I have already taken it. Three—no, four sleep periods ago."

"That is correct. Test complete."

The screen blanked.

"All test results have been assimilated. Subject determined within acceptable parameters," the Voice said. Very odd. It was the first time It had spoken as if to someone other than the man.

"You are ready for the next stage," It told him.

"I have some questions."

"You may ask. Answers may or may not be provided."

"I am on a ship. Is there anyone else on board?"

"No."

"You are a synthesized voice?"

"Self-evident."

"You said moments ago that I was . . . within acceptable parameters. What would have happened were I not?"

"Answer determined not to be in your best interests."

"I shall try another way. What constraints did your programmer limit you to?"

"Answers determined not to be in your best interests."

"Thank you. You answered, however. Another question. Who programmed you?"

Silence except for ship hum.

"Answer will become self-evident within a short period of time," the Voice said finally. "Those are questions enough."

A previously sealed panel opened.

"You will enter that passage. At its end will be a ship. You will board and prepare yourself for takeoff. You may issue two orders, if you feel you know the answers. If you do not, recommendations will be offered.

"First. Should the machines be reactivated?"

"What machines?"

"The recommendation is that they should—given recent circumstances."

"Recommendation accepted. I guess."

"Second. Should transshipment begin? The recommendation is it should not until you progress further."

"Accepted. Transshipment of what? And whatever it is, how do I communicate with you?"

"Both answers will become self-evident. Proceed to the ship now."

The man walked down the passageway. At the end, as promised, was the entryway to a small ship. He entered.

Again, the ship was constructed for one person.

He seated himself in a reclining couch. Behind him, the hatch slid shut. He felt motion: stardrive.

"This is a final communication," the Voice said suddenly. "There are four separate automated navigation systems on this ship. Each of them is preset for a different destination. On reaching each destination that system will self-destruct and the next system will activate.

"Do not be alarmed.

"Do not attempt to interfere with this system.

"Your final destination and debarkation point will be obvious.

"Good-bye. Good luck."

The man jolted. The fine hair at the back of his neck lifted.

Good luck? From a machine?

CHAPTER EIGHT

THE HONJO WERE a small but firmly committed culture of traders. Their antecedents went back to the early days of the Empire. They populated a system some light-years from Durer, the site of one of the famous Tahn war battles. Their home base was a less than desirable cluster of stars and planets with little in the way of commercially important resources.

This was no hindrance to the Honjo. Their distant, oceangoing ancestors had plied the island trades, and they were ancient masters at the art of playing middlebeing for any product. Their ships were of their own design, although constructed in the factories Sullamora had once owned. They were light, a bit boxy, and made up for lack of speed by being able to deal with just about any atmosphere where there might be goods to buy or sell.

The Honjo were also among the most frugal beings in the Empire. Since their resources were so few, they stockpiled and guarded them jealously. Especially AM2.

That had been a minor source of irritation to the Eternal Emperor from time to time. Since the price was pegged on supply—which he controlled—he was always just a bit touchy about the large amount they kept squirreled away. Whenever he let the price drop, the Honjo were the first in line to buy more. But it was only a petty irritation, and after wrangling with the thickheaded beings a few times, he let it slide. The Emperor had learned that it was usually best to ignore eccentrics. The Honjo performed well as traders, they were mostly honest, and their system was so small as to be nearly meaningless.

One other thing about the Honjo. They were always quite willing to take offense. Especially when it involved what they perceived as their own property. In short, if pressed, they would fight. They tended not to think about the odds.

When the privy council considered the Honjo, they were all in agreement: When it came to larceny, the Kraas had chosen well.

"Me'n Sis sussed it out," the fat Kraa said. "The stingy clots keep it stashed in one place. So, all we's gotta do is send in a fleet. Blow the drakh out of 'em. 'N it's home again, home again, with enough AM2 keep us goin' for more'n a bit."

"I don't think we ought to be that direct," Malperin objected.

"No? Why the clot not? Them Honjo's right bastards, and everyone knows it!"

"Good plan, just a touch short on diplomacy," Lovett chuckled.

Kyes noted that the energy level in the room was far higher than it had been the last time. Was it just because action—*any* kind of action at all—was contemplated? Or was it the thought of armed robbery that was so energizing? Kyes and his fellow businessbeings had participated in countless forms of theft in their long careers. But it was always on paper—kept at a distance, with at least a cloak of respectability thrown over it by their legions of legal experts. This was real! And, Kyes had to admit, extremely exciting. He was as susceptible to the excitement as the rest.

"Try it this way," he said. "We send enough ships to do the job, just as our colleagues proposed. Except, we send one small craft far out ahead. Something lightly armed. And not too expensive . . .

"Then, we have the ship deliberately violate the Honjo cluster's borders."

"That'll piss 'em, sure," the skinny Kraa said. She liked where he was going. "Then we just waggle our arses, make 'em shoot . . ."

"And we retaliate! And boom! It's ours!" Lovett finished.

Everyone was pleased with the plan. Oddly, the Kraas had an important caution.

"We need a bleedin' alibi," the fat one said. "So's it don't look too planned out, if yer get me drift."

They did indeed.

"Perhaps we should stage some kind of economic summit?" Malperin suggested. They had never had one before—there was not much economy to contemplate—but they understood the connection.

"Here's what we do," Malperin said. "And we can achieve two goals at once. It's about time for a little good news."

There were murmurs of agreement about the table. The situation was deteriorating so quickly they were all afraid to look it straight in the eye. But as system after system drifted away from their grasp, it always remained at the edge of their vision, like a recurrent nightmare.

Malperin proposed that they release a canned study, showing that the steadily dipping economic curve had bottomed out and was at last turning upward. Simultaneously, they would convene the privy council for the Economic Summit, a summit they would claim would set the course of the Empire for the next six or seven years.

They would play up the summit as the most important event since the death of the Emperor. Full media coverage. Pull out all stops. She also suggested where such a summit could be held, for maximum suspense.

It would be staged on Earth, in Tanz Sullamora's old fishing camp, now revitalized for the use of the council for their most private meetings.

There they would convene, innocently contemplating things of great and holy importance—the public good. At that moment, the Honjo would make their unprovoked attack on the defenseless Imperial ship.

The Kraas figured the booty would fill a spacetrain ten or fifteen kilometers long.

"That's a lot of clottin' AM2," the skinny one said.

Kyes agreed. It certainly was a clottin' lot of AM2.

Mahoney bounced into Sten's suite, happily singing/humming what he remembered of a medieval ballad: "Let me something my eyes . . . dah . . . dah . . . dah dah dah day, on the something green hills of Earth . . ."

He crossed to Sten's video display and booted up the news menu:

NEW COURSE FOR EMPIRE

The drop:

BIG 5 TO CONVENE
ECONOMIC SUMMIT
AT HISTORIC RETREAT

Sten read the story closely, Alex hanging over his shoulder.

"We would appear," Sten said, "to have acquired a Target Opportunity."

Mahoney beamed. "Never could figure why the black hats think there's safety out in the boonies. Maybe because they're usually ex-city punks?"

"Ah dinna ken either," Kilgour said. "But gie me a moor w' a wee rock to skulk behin', an' hae f'r a rest, an' Ah'm as happy ae a butcher wi' his mallet."

"That's it," Sten said. "Now . . . let's kill us some politicos!"

CHAPTER NINE

THE PRIVY COUNCIL'S announcement was the trigger for
the final meeting of Ian Mahoney's "conspirators." They
had a single target and a time to hit it.

The "conspiracy" had already gone on far too long
for Mahoney's comfort. As a rule of thumb the less time
passed and the less those involved had to meet in any
covert operation, the less likelihood that operation would
be blown or self-destruct. He mentally put both conspiracy and conspirators in quotes. Because while his plan
would ensure that anyone involved was for the high jump
if it was exposed, there really was not much to it.

Mahoney had, in his "research," looked up many of
his old compatriots, as he had told Sten. Once he was
conveniently deceased his secret wanderings from galaxy
to galaxy had increased. His purpose was simple. Once
contact was made with one of his old service acquaintances, the formal dance began. Mahoney set out trying
to lead each of them down the primrose path to murder.

Did they agree that things were going to hell in a hand-
basket? If so, did they think something could be done
about it? *Should* something be done about it? Should
something be done about it by the acquaintance? Would
he or she be willing to participate?

That leading took time—too much time. All too often
danger signals went off in Mahoney's spook-circuited
brain, and he broke contact.

What he wanted from each of those serving high-
ranking officers and/or civil officials was roughly the

same. If the privy council were to be rendered suddenly powerless, what would the officer do? Ideally, Mahoney wanted that officer to mobilize any forces under command to:

1. Maintain public order.
2. Disarm or otherwise deactivate any armed forces still loyal to the privy council, starting with the council's own security apparatus and private armies.
3. To control the media and prevent access to privy council loyalists.
4. To support the formation of an interim caretaker government. Mahoney was fairly vague on what that would be—he thought perhaps a loose federation headed by those members of Parliament who had not been corrupted by the privy council, representatives of dissident systems/galaxies, and others yet to be discovered. The federation could be headed up by the utterly incorruptible Manabi.

Possibly. Mahoney kept saying that "first we have to catch the rabbit." The conversation tended to stop there—very few wanted to know the exact mechanics of how the privy council was to be "rendered powerless." Knowing the bloody-handed intelligence chief in front of them, they had a fairly good idea it would not be something as civilized as house arrest.

Once—and if—the privy council was dealt with, whatever government replaced them would be operating under two very clear orders: first, to slow the Empire's slipping into chaos; and second, to find the AM2.

Mahoney had a single rule about what the caretaker government would *not* be: military. He didn't think, on reflection, that Ian Mahoney would make that bad a king, nor would some of his longtime friends. And that was exactly why the military would not be allowed near the government, not if he himself felt a bit of the slow crawl of power-madness in his own soul.

But all this took time. Not only because the solicitation toward what, after all, was high treason had to be done carefully, but also because of the incredible layers of bureaucracy between a leader and the people. Mahoney had always prided himself on his own lean and mean command. Anyone serving under him could have near access to the boss. Now he wondered, after having spent hours and days waiting in antechambers for an old friend to even be aware he was out there, if his own machine had been that lean and mean.

Time passing increased the dangers, as did Mahoney's failures. He tried not to blame anyone who wanted no part of the operation. There were those who simply felt the military had no place in politics. Others believed the problems were temporary—that eventually the privy council would improve. What was happening was merely the inevitable chaos of a war's end worsened by the death of the Emperor. Still others did not think the privy council was doing that bad a job—considering the circumstances. And still others had been coopted by the council. And, Mahoney grudged, there were those—even in his own profession of soldiery—who were moral or physical cowards.

Other than Sten and Kilgour, Mahoney told no one about his private belief that the Emperor would return. Their enterprise looked insane enough without adding proof of psychosis.

He ended with about a thousand beings he felt could be depended on. Now would be the final—and for most of them only—chance to gather for their final plans.

Such a meet was a terrible risk, but Mahoney knew he had to prove to his fellows that there was, in fact, a conspiracy beyond coded transmissions and one dangerous old man. He had reduced the threat of exposure—he hoped—by setting the meeting not only in plain sight, but also near the heart of the beast. It was in the system of Klisura, an entirely military group of worlds. Sten himself had gone through Guard training on the system's main world, years and years gone.

One smaller world had been set up for war games centuries earlier. War games without soldiers, without ships—what Mahoney had heard had been called in ancient times a "kriegsspiel." A map exercise, now played with computers and battle chambers. This particular game had been suggested by Fleet Marshal Wentworth, a longtime and completely trusted compatriot of Ian's.

Obviously, so that Mahoney's compatriots could assemble from their Empire-wide posts with as little suspicion as possible, the game had to be universal. It was that.

GIVEN: the current status of military forces (radical disarmament following the end of the Tahn wars); the current economic environment (lessened AM2 fuel availability); and the present political situation (worded more subtly, that a great percentage of the Empire felt the privy council were incapable of leading a goat to a garbage dump).

SITUATION: A sudden, large-scale threat to the Empire, up to and including full war.

REQUIRED: Possible military responses for the first two E-years of such an event.

In short, the game would refight the beginning of the Tahn wars, as if the Emperor were not present and AM2 was available only in limited quantities.

Such a large-scale exercise, even though it involved nothing but troop commanders, had come to the attention of the privy council. They thought the idea of a new, massive bogeyman coming out of nowhere slightly absurd, but there was merit in their military leaders accepting a far more limited future. At first they grudged that the game would be played with a realistic logistical scenario, but eventually they realized that their soldiery should know—even though it was uncomfortable—just how limited the AM2 actually was.

That did mean they required the assemblage and the

game itself to be held under the tightest security, which played exactly to Mahoney's desires. Kyes even thought there might be some interesting, if quite minor, concepts developed during the game.

Their hope was bolstered when they learned that Wentworth proposed to include civilians as well as military. The civilians—all of whom, of course, were properly clearanced—included retired military, experts in logistics, and even a handful of rather dreamy-eyed techno-prophets. Kyes was a bit surprised and pleased that the military, which he had always thought as rigid in its thought patterns as any computer, was capable of welcoming outside input.

So the admirals and generals, fleet marshals and intelligence specialists, with their aides and assistants gathered on Klisura XII. As did the civilians, including one elderly, cheerful human male who claimed to be a morale specialist. Mahoney chose the cover name of Stephen Potter.

The game *would* in fact be played out—and played again two or three more times, with different participants. This first game would be composed of Mahoney's conspirators, the following games played by the innocent, who would never know they were providing the most elaborate cover for Mahoney's schemes. It would have been more ideal if it could have been played just once, with the innocent sheep giving cover for the wolves. But too many people knew Ian Mahoney, and he understood there was no way he could keep those in the conspiracy who were inevitably hesitant, skeptical, or wavering in line if he were not there in person to share the risk.

Other arrivals trickled in, gray, quiet beings without faces. They were ex–Mercury Corps operatives, technicians, recruited by Mahoney. They were intended to secure the security.

Mahoney assumed that when the world had been screened by the privy council, part of that had included bugging everything. He was correct. But it was a simple matter for his own techs to find the bugs and key them. None were destroyed—although Mahoney thought it appropriate that some of them were reported to the proper authorities. The proper authorities expressed dismay and disconnected those bugs.

The rest were left in place and fed false information. Sometimes they were given blank time, as if nothing were happening in that particular chamber. Others were fed meetings that had been prescripted and then voice-synthesized, so that General X would be discussing with his staff whether or not transports would be available to move his units, and how much of their basic equipment load could be carried; whereas in fact General X was sitting with Ian Mahoney, talking about how many of his troops could be depended upon, once The Day was announced, to move out and seize barracks held by one of the Kraa twins' private thuggeries, and how many would have to be sent on leave or confined to barracks.

There were a few counterintelligence agents in attendance. They were quickly ID'd and beeped, their movements tracked constantly. Only one agent found anything suspicious, and he was skillfully terminated before he could either report or get offworld.

Mahoney was disappointed in his enemies—he had seen and run better CI when he was an assistant patrol leader in the Imperial Youth Corps.

Sten and Alex held well in the background. Both of them were quite hot—especially Sten.

All of the conspirators were told when the operation would be mounted. They were further instructed to have their troops on standby on that date, with those orders to be issued as unobstrusively as possible.

There were a few who wanted more. They had faith in Mahoney, to be sure, but they were beings who took very little just on faith. For them, Sten would be trotted onstage. To some, he was little more than a hero of the early stages of the Tahn wars. But the fact that an admiral would be willing to lead, in person, the raid on Earth seemed to satisfy them.

The most suspicious, generally, were those high-rankers with some intelligence background or training. For that reason, most of them had heard of Sten or known him—if not by fiche, then by reputation. In their eyes, he was a thoroughly acceptable head of the murder squad.

Near the end of the gaming Sten collected Mahoney and took him to an ultraclean room. Quite baldly he asked the fleet marshal if he really believed that all of these beings would swing into motion as ordered when ordered.

"Of course not," Mahoney snapped. "As your pet thug might say, I'm mad but I'm hardly daft.

"Assuming you carry out your end . . . prog: seventy-five percent follow their orders and we'll not only have the murderers dead, but the transition of power will be painless.

"Fifty percent . . . it'll be a little bloody. But I still think it'll come off. That's assuming those who get the collywobbles don't try to stop us.

"Less than that . . .

"Less than that, lad, and you'd best have the luck of the heavens and be in excellent running condition.

"Now, Admiral. You're in motion. Collect your assistants and start putting them through whatever rehearsals you need."

As he and Alex slipped offworld, Sten ran his own prognostication. He had even less faith than Mahoney that the conspiracy, in its entirety, would succeed. There were too many people involved, too much time had passed, and Sten had damn-all confidence in any conspiracy when the conspirators had a vested interest—no matter how loudly denied—in the state. Generals and admirals made lousy dissidents.

But as far as his and Alex's end . . . the murder in a ditch?

Just less, he calculated, than fifty-fifty.

Hell, for a Mantis operative, that was a sure thing. So very well. Eliminate the privy council, and what would happen, would happen. That was for others to decide—after the bodies stopped bouncing.

It was a pity Sten had never met Brigadier Mavis Sims—and never would.

CHAPTER TEN

STEN WAS IN a thoroughly crappy mood. He shut down PLAY function and removed the helmet. Repressing the urge to punt it across the room, he glowered out at the rain.

Clottin' poor mission briefing, he thought. Suicide run for sure. Sten *was* in a rotten mood—the intelligence data he had fed into the interactive livie machine gave him no more or less details than many, many missions he had already run and survived.

His mood may have been caused by the rain. Here in this forested province called Oregon, the sun seemed proscribed. The degrees of weather ranged from overcast threatening rain through drizzle to downpour to here comes another storm. He sort of wanted a drink. But he and the other team members were now temperance clots until they extracted.

Kilgour broke Sten's mood. Pushing the door to their rented A-frame—(a building Sten suspected had been made from real wood)—he said cheerily, "Oop an' away, boss. Y're gettin' fat an' sloppy sittin' here. Time f'r th' old pant-an-wheeze."

Sten pulled on running shoes, grabbed a rainproof, and they went out into the streets of Coos Bay. The village itself might have been the root of Sten's depression. Old—thousand-year-type old—ruins were one thing. But buildings only a couple of hundred years gone were different. People had lived there before it became a hamlet of rotting, collapsing buildings and shattered streets.

The city, Sten had been told, had once had nearly twenty-thousand inhabitants—farmers, loggers, sea-shippers. That must have been long ago. Now there were less than a thousand. A few fished, some were artists who made their credits off-Earth; there were a few tribal groups existing on their own, internal economy; and other residents catered to the sprinkling of tourists who arrived intent on the area's big game, a fish they called the salmon. They raved about its fighting qualities and wariness.

At first Sten thought they were talking about some woodsy predator before he realized. He found the salmon tasty, just as he did the area's crabs, oysters, bass, and a very ugly fish they called a sturgeon. Fishing could be worthwhile, he thought. Short-fuse an explosive charge, toss it in a pool, and you had dinner for a platoon. But these people used line as thin as a climbing thread, hand-constructed bits of plas supposed to resemble insects, and a casting rod. Often they merely had themselves photographed with their catch and then released it. Very odd.

"Which way today, boss?"

"Doesn't matter. Ruins, rocks, and trees in any direction."

Kilgour waved a direction arbitrarily and they ground into motion—starting up a hill, of course.

Run a klick, walk a half kilometer, run ten kilometers. A half hour of exercises, then run back. Standard Imperial dictates for combat troops.

Sten thought further on this depressed province of Oregon. Historically, he had read, it had always been an area of future dreams and present depression. But its current state of decline had three causes: the inhuman—to Sten, at least—climate; the constant drain offworld of its young people who couldn't find work at home; and finally The Eternal Emperor.

That last factor was only three hundred years old. About twenty-five kilometers north of Coos Bay was the mouth of the Umpqua River. The Emperor had decided he wanted to go salmon fishing. He put political influence to bear on the province's politicos. They granted him the river in perpetuity—from headwaters to where it rushed into the ocean. That had cost several fortunes in bribes and promises.

From there it got expensive. Little by little, the residents of all the towns along the river and its tributaries were cozened and bribed to move. They were compensated richly—but still . . .

Once there had been a small town—Redspurt, Reedsport, or some such—at the mouth of the Umpqua. Now it was a ghost town. There were other ruins along the river that had once been inhabited—Scottsburg, Umpqua, Roseburg, and so on.

The Emperor was the Emperor, Sten knew. But for some reason that demonstration of Byzantine power put his teeth on edge. But it was not his to question why, he thought as he crested the hill. More important—up the Umpqua river was the Emperor's old fishing retreat. And, kilometers beyond that, was Sten's target.

In the days when the late Tanz Sullamora had idolized the Eternal Emperor, he had aped everything about his ruler that he could. The Emperor fished . . . very well then, so would Tanz. But where the Emperor was happy with solitude, the redwoods, and a place to pitch a tent near salmon-fat rapids, Sullamora was miserable. His fishing camp became a lavish country estate, with every sophisticated convenience the plutocrat could afford. Sullamora could not chance the laughter that would come if he simply decided that Earth, fishing, and the wilderness was a busto idea. When the privy council's conspiracy began, Sullamora's estate was a perfect neutral ground/safe house to plot from.

Sullamora may have been splattered into molecular pulp but the validity of his estate continued. That was the target—and there were only a few days left before the privy council arrived. Sten was ready.

Knowing the target and area, he started putting his

team together. There was no problem with available, completely trustworthy Imperial gangsters. With the Tahn wars ended, the Mantis squadrons were far overstrength. And those soldiers had not chosen Mantis because of their pacifistic nature. They went looking for adventure. It was simple for Mahoney to sieve for availables. Those he chose were completely known quantities. If there would be betrayal, it would not come from any of them. All knew Mahoney's reputation as former head of Mercury/Mantis. As a good percentage had prewar service and had magically survived the decimation of the war against the Tahn, Sten was a known and near-legendary commander.

The first question he had for the purported Earth-specialist Mahoney assigned to him was who or what were the natives like? Earth-human. Any ETs? None to speak of. Sten grimaced. That would cut the available pool of talent way down.

He asked the specialist about local fauna and got a bland reply of the "usual oxygen-based food chain." Sten punted the "expert" into outer darkness and put Kilgour into research mode. Kilgour had talents beyond lethality. It did not hurt that he had once served with a Guards ceremonial detachment on Earth itself, before he had found a happy home in covert wet work.

While he waited for Kilgour, Sten began thinking of the Delicate Art of Murder, Multiple Variety. The easiest way to take care of the council would be a missile. Limited-yield nuclear or conventional—to him it didn't matter. Either way, it wouldn't work. First, the privy council would have the skies and space beyond saturated with warships. It was unlikely a missile would get through. Even if it did—Sullamora's retreat would almost certainly be shielded. And Mahoney had requested no survivors.

What about a ground-to-ground? Launch the missile from a safe range, infiltrate a controller to line-of-site of the lodge, and let him guide the bang on home. Unlikely.

It was doubtful the council would put on a public show without covering itself with every possible ECM device.

So it would have to be, Sten thought, the classic Four-H technique: Hit, Hatchet, Hand grenade, and Haul. Or as Kilgour somewhat indelicately dubbed the style: "Ambush, Axes, an' Arse'oles."

Then his Mantis conditioning cut in. Sten found himself running through fiche of *Antique Weapons and Tactics*. And, as so often before, he found his plan. A blast from the past—literally. His era's security specialists knew all of the sophisticated techniques going and guarded against them—and frequently forgot to wonder if someone might show up with a bow and arrow instead of a laser.

Kilgour reported, laden with fiche, tapes, and even a few antique natural-history books. They went to work. Within two days Sten had found enough Local Critters to enable him to start handpicking his team. Now they were in place, scattered up and down the coast of Oregon. Ten beings for the Kill Team, three on Intelligence & Recon.

Two of them had gone first—an E-type humanoid male and female. Claiming marriage, claiming retirement, they purchased a dockside café/bar. Cover names: Larry and Faye Archuler.

A third human, claiming to be a wandering artist, drifted into Coos Bay and took a casual labor job on one of the boat-hulled gravsleds used for sportfishing, when he wasn't wandering the hills with his tri-pad. He was actually a nearly competent sketch artist who was fascinated with river wildlife. Cover name: Havell.

Then Sten and Alex had arrived. Sten was now a hard-driving and -driven entrepreneur who had suffered a nervous breakdown. He was accompanied by a male nurse—Kilgour. The story Alex had told in the drinking houses—whining under his breath but sipping caff—was that his boss believed his ancestors came from this section of Old Earth. Kilgour added, however, that he personally considered this obsession just part of his breakdown. Sooner or later, he would decide that the ancestors had come from elsewhere, and they would move on.

Being the head of a successful corporation, even if on medical sabbatical, meant that Sten had to keep in contact with his company. That justified a rather elaborate com. Given the entrepreneur's secretiveness, it also justified his use of code. The code was a fairly available business encryption that Sten assumed the privy council's cryptographers had cracked. But the arrangement of the code groups, as well as the groups themselves, kept Sten in contact with Mahoney and Conspiracy Central. The com was poorly antennaed, and Sten's signals, fortunately brief, blanketed the area, to be received by his teammates.

That corporation really existed. Whatever Sten ordered would be done by the officers of the company. The code was also skillfully rewritten to be believable. Sten, like anyone else who had ever had cipher training, had heard the story of the code that had been blown when the criminal requested five and one half elephants.

Kilgour, while spreading the cover story through the village, had also ID'd the two men who were Imperial Security. One was a village constable, far too knowledgeable to be what he claimed to be. The other was a barkeep who was overly curious. Neither one warranted termination.

Four other men and women of the hit team were living in the ruins of that town at the mouth of the Umpqua. They were highly visible: Montoya, Valdiva, Corum, and Akashi. They claimed to be members of the Cult of the Emperor, making a pilgrimage to every place the Eternal Being had blessed with the presence of his glowing soul. So of course they had to journey upriver to his fishing camp. They did. Some days later, they were seen camping where the Eternal One had cast his fly rod, by one of the Imperial river wardens. They refused to leave. The warden brought in reinforcements. The robed cultists

smiled, bowed in surrender to the wardens, boarded the
gravsled, and were unceremoniously dumped in Reedsport.

A few days later they were back performing their ceremonies. The warden, a little worried, made some vid
calls. He discovered that the cult was completely harmless. The late Eternal Emperor had, in fact, considered
them beneficial if aberrant, since their beliefs encouraged charity and good works as well as the Emperor as
godhead. Just run them out, came the Warden's orders.
When they return, run them out again. You can jail them
if you want—if you find a jail in your part of the wilderness. I wouldn't bother, the advice from his superior
went. Eventually, from what I've read, they finish whatever rituals they're performing and move on. The warden, who hated the idea of being any kind of a policeman,
chose to ignore the cultists.

He had received an inquiry from the Imperial Security
station at Sullamora's retreat. Overhead surveillance had
seen the cultists. The Security officer heard the explanation, laughed, and disconnected.

The warden became used to the four. They would
wave at him in a cordial manner as he passed on patrol.
Once he saw a battered gravsled leaving the fishing
camp, but it was empty, and he could see no sign of the
gravsled having brought any supplies or building materials that would suggest the cultists were settling in for
a long stay.

Then they vanished. The warden found himself almost
missing the robed men and women, but he was more
interested in trying to photograph a pinniped he had never
seen before. Seal? Sea lion? He did not know, and the
few reference materials he could access gave him no
hints. He spent time trying—without success—to take a
picture that could be sent to a museum for identification.

The mammal, he assumed, seemed to range from the
mouth of the river all the way up to where that estate
began, and where he was forbidden entry. He hoped the

trigger-happy Security goons at the retreat would not shoot "her"—for so he romantically assumed the creature to be. He hoped she had brains enough to dive if she spotted any of them.

The multisexed creature, in fact, had approximately twice the intelligence of the warden. Cover name: F'lesa.

The warden had no interest in flying creatures, mammalian or avian. He paid no attention to the two batlike creatures flashing around close to Sullamora's estate. Nor did he spot the tiny vidcams hung around their necks. The two "bats" were beings that, though stupid, were found useful by Mantis for aerial intelligence, putting up with their stupidity. They could talk, but their language consisted of half-verbal, half-instinctual squeaks. Their names were, of course, a problem. On the Imperial payrolls they were carried by service numbers. Mantis troopers gave them paired nicknames—Frick and Frack, Gog and Magog, etc. Sten had worked with a pair of them before. These two: Dum and Dee.

Sten used their aerial intelligence to begin building the "model" of the target area. It would not, in fact, exist; it would be part of the interactive helmet system. Before shipping for Earth, he had already found every vid that was available of the estate. There was not much.

Kilgour managed to ferret out some old gillies who had worked for Sullamora back when he was convincing himself that fishing was fun. That gave them more data. Still not complete, but enough so each team member could put on a helmet, keyed to respond only to him, and "practice" the attack. Each being's moves were recorded, fed into Sten's central record, and cycled back out. Even though the helmets gave multisensory input, it was still strange. Charge a fence . . . feel the barbed wire in your hands. Climb it. Shoot a guard. Round a corner . . . and everything would go blank. NO RECORD AVAILABLE. A few meters farther on, the simulation would recommence. It was off-putting. Fortunately the combat-experienced Mantis operatives had learned to accept these partially complete rehearsal systems. It was the best they were likely to get, could well improve as more data became available from F'lesa, Dee, or Dum, and was far more secure than actually building a full-scale model for real physical practice.

The cultists, however, grew bored with the dry runs. But they had nothing else to do. They were, in fact invisible—invisible to any above-ground or aerial observer, scanning on any length known. The cultists ''ceremonies'' had been elaborate. They had dug a slant tunnel ten meters down, then built a large chamber. Into that had gone the weaponry and gear from the gravsled shipment. No one was happy that the sled had even been seen by the warden as it left, but accidents happened.

Now the four waited.

That underground chamber would be the assembly point for the assault.

There were two final members of the team: N'Ran, huge—three hundred kilos average—somewhat anthropoid beings who had become the Empire's best artillerymen. During the Tahn wars, inevitably some N'Ran became curious, adventuresome, and Mantis. Sten was delighted to have them along. Not only could they easily tote the Phase One elements of the attack in one hand, but they would be his weaponeers, as well.

Mahoney did a double take when Sten said he was using two N'Ran. ''Apes? No, lad. They'll not be taken for bears either.''

Sten pointed out their cover. Centuries before, there had been absurd legends of a creature called Big Foot. If spotted, they would be legendary creatures. Sten made sure, when he arrived in Coos Bay, that the legend was reactivated and told his two mythical monsters to lie low but leave chubby footprints if they must. The two N'Ran were waiting, living rough in the forested mountains near the Umpqua.

Sten panted back from his run in a different mood entirely. He considered his work and found it good—or at least acceptable. Privately he thought the odds might even be better than fifty-fifty. He was ready. Then he felt a crawl down his spine and shivered. The weather? Perhaps. But he instantly began a complete run-through of his plans for the nineteenth time.

Four days before The Day the rest of Sten's accomplices arrived—provided by the privy council itself.

Sten's accomplices were the Imperial media. The privy council wanted the maximum amount of publicity from their assemblage. The members handpicked the loudest, dumbest pseudojournalists they could find, journalists guaranteed to lap up every communique from the council as gospel. Legitimate reporters were not encouraged to apply to the press pool.

The council was pleased by the interest. The members thought it was because they were starting to turn the tide of public opinion. They did not realize that the interest was due to their seclusiveness. When a leader hid in what was dubbed by vid people "The Rose Garden," anything he said or did was of note and had nothing to do with whether the public thought him either an angel or an Attila.

The "press" streamed onto Earth. Immediately, they were disappointed. They would not be allowed inside the estate. They were given quarters in hastily thrown-up military campaign huts. Their superiors started snarling. Report. Report what? The council has not arrived yet. Report anything.

A real reporter or analyst might have filed "What Might This All Mean" pieces, or just filed background. Not the hacks on Earth. They surged out, looking for stories. Stories to them meant "color": the Benevolence of the Late Tanz Sullamora; the Little Known Estate he Kept on Earth Where he Communed with Nature and the Eternal Emperor; The Sadness of his Death.

That well soon ran dry, and the hacks became desperate. The Beauty of Oregon (tourist trade would be sure to go up). The Unusual Creatures of Earth. The Colorful Folk of the Rugged Seacoast. On and on. Some ass even wanted to interview Sten, without the foggiest as to a newspeg. He was declined, with a smile.

Every gravsled that could be rented was—from the shattered city of San Francisco north to the glacier regions. They dripped vidcams, engineers, and reporters, and were everywhere.

Imperial Security pulled in its horns and disregarded any satellite, aerial, or sensor intelligence from anywhere except the immediate compound. When the privy council arrived that would take care of things. They would have those damned people back in one place, being spoon-fed whatever the council wanted them to have. Certainly there was no particular reason to overload the sec-computers with meaningless data.

Thirty-six hours . . . Sten moved.

A single, completely meaningless code word was broadcast. Mahoney would receive it—and know the team was on its way in. From then on, until they accomplished the mission, there would be no contact possible. The signal was picked up in the hills and ruins, and his team was in motion. With one exception: Kilgour. That crawl up Sten's spine was still there. He gave orders.

Kilgour was detached from the hit team. Ten beings would go in instead of eleven.

Alex gave a good imitation of ground zero after a multi-KT warhead impacted. He slammed the table—and the two-inch-thick hardwood shattered. Kilgour recovered. His face went back down the spectrum from purple.

"Why?"

"I want you on the back door. That's an order."

"Y'no ken. Y'r no an' adm'ral, and Ah'm no a warrant. Nae more. Laird Kilgour ae Kilgour deman's—and will hae—an explanation."

Sten explained. He felt as if someone were watching over his shoulder.

"Best we abort," Kilgour suggested. "Ah'll no argue wi' invis'ble clottin' spirits. Or replan."

"No time for that," Sten said. "And I don't have any better ideas. I don't see what's wrong with what I've got—logically. Abort? When will we have another chance?"

"A' these years," Kilgour said, hurt. "An' y'll noo gie me th' chance t' keep you frae gettin' dead." Then he tried another approach: "M'gun'll do more i' th' fray than back i' th' clottin' RP."

Sten did not answer.

Alex stared at Sten for a long time. "Thae's the feelin'? Strong, is't?"

Sten nodded.

Kilgour sighed. "Best y'd be right, lad. I' you're wrong—you an' me'll hae a dustup a'ter th' extraction i' you're not."

He stamped out into the rain.

Sten and the others made their way to the bunker in the Emperor's camp. They left thin cover stories behind—they would be in, out, and gone within forty-eight hours, so an elaborate story was not needed. Or else . . .

A ship had entered Earth's atmosphere a day earlier, planetfall calculated to occur in one of the inevitable, momentary holes in the satellite coverage. "Ship" was not a correct description. Two tacships had been slaved together.

Just off the Oregon coast the ships were separated. One was allowed to rest on the bottom, fifty-plus fathoms down. Its controls were set to respond to a transponder in the hands of an angry, worried, and now-scared Kilgour, hidden near the beach.

The pilot of the second ship received a signal. He surfaced and opened a hatch. Dum and Dee darted in, and seconds later, F'lesa flopped into the ship. F'lesa had found all that could be discovered from the water, and Sten could not chance any transmission from Dum and

Dee's vidcams, no matter how useful they might be as aerial warning devices.

The tacship submerged. Some time that night, taking advantage of another hole, it would escape Earth's atmosphere.

The mission was hot and running . . .

CHAPTER ELEVEN

THE SENSOR/TRANSMITTER WAS the equivalent of a moron with a megaphone. It, and a power pack, were planted in an eons-old satellite in high orbit over Earth, part of the sky junk that made navigation on- and offworld so interesting. A tech had boarded the satellite just days after the summit had been announced. He positioned the bug, turned it on, took a moment to marvel at the primitive machines—clottin' light-optic computers—and was gone.

The transmitter waited, ignoring the flurry of ships approaching the planet. Too small. Too few.

Then it woke. *Ships . . . many ships . . . many big ships.*

It bleated twice on the assigned frequency, then fused into a solid lump of plas.

Sten shut the receiver down and tossed it into the pile in the center of the bunker. "Our customers are on the way. Shall we?"

The team grabbed packs and headed for the ramped tunnel. All of them wore phototropic uniforms that would also give some shielding against pickup by thermal sensors. They weaseled their gear, including the long, heavy cylinders in padded, shoulder-strapped cases, into the open.

Havell touched a button, and a dim light shone from his notepad as he checked the satellite sked. "Clean for an hour and a half. Then we've got an overhead and an Eye."

"Still—use overhead cover," Sten ordered.

Valdiva whispered a question: "These, umm, bears you mentioned? Are they nocturnal?"

One N'ran rumbled a laugh. "No . . . but hugging contest . . . interesting."

Hugging? The bear would place third. Not to mention, Sten thought, what other instruments of death they were carrying. The cylinders with their sights and mounts—plus each being carried a combat knife, a single-shot completely suppressed projectile weapon, three types of grenades, and heavy, short-barreled "shotguns," drumfed weapons that scattered highly explosive AM2 pellets as their charge. An excellent weapon for a barroom discussion.

Sten looked back at their hidey-hole and decided, not for the first time, that he was a perfectly lousy burrowing animal. If he had to buy it, he would prefer it be in the open.

They started off into the darkness.

In ten hours an incendiary charge in the pile of discarded gear, ration tins, and civilian clothing would go off. All of the team members, excepting the N'ran, had worn membrane gloves since they had arrived on Earth, so not even the primitive fingerprint system could ID them. Their quarters in Coos Bay had been swept Mantisclean. There could be no DNA or any other identification in the postbang investigation.

Each team member wore a vital-signs pack on his or her belt. Any change in the bearer—such as death—and the pack would detonate. There would not even be a corpse to autopsy.

With the exception of the cylinders, it was all perfectly normal gear for a Mantis mission.

Brigadier Mavis Sims had taken the same oath as Sten. But she chose to interpret it differently.

She could not remember having slept since she returned from the phony kriegsspiel and being recruited for the conspiracy.

There were five generations of Simses who had served the Empire. The family motto, just a touch embarrassing in its blatancy, was "Faithful unto Death." None of the Simses had abandoned that faith.

Now, deep in the heart of another sleepless, echoing night, Brigadier Sims decided she would not shirk it, either.

The atmosphere in the communication room of the main lodge had gone from high-pitched excitement to nervous boredom. Military techs had bustled about for hours as the Imperial fleet approached the Honjo system. The members of the council had literal front-row seats as the maneuvering commenced. A dazzling array of impressive commands were fired at the fleet commander. Responses, terse and warriorlike, crackled back. One entire com wall was ablaze with winking red and green lights marking the progress.

It was one helluva good show—to start with. But then the routine absolutely necessary for any large-scale action began to drag. And drag. And drag. There were endless countdowns at each stage. Then the clocks were reset again for another crucial juncture.

By the time the fleet had parked, pulled on its stealth cloak, and started baiting the hook for the Honjo, the privy council was considering canceling the whole thing for lack of interest.

Not for the first time in the past two hours, Kyes compared the action to the few combat livies he had seen. He could understand now why the livie makers steered well clear of any hint of reality. In a livie, all that was needed was a maximum three-minute conference of the warrior brass to set the target. That would be followed by a "what it all means to us" scene, in which each character mused on his or her lifelong goals and objectives. If he or she was warm and cuddly, the character was usually doomed. If cynical and bitter, that character was sure to see the light in the gore that followed. Then entire legions of fleets would be launched in blaze of fast-cutting action. The formula would require a momentary victory, followed by a setback in which all seemed lost. And finally the bravery and cunning of the heroes would conquer all.

Kyes did not like livies. But he liked this show less.

He stirred slightly as the little tacship crossed the invisible line that marked the beginning of Honjo territory. At any moment there would be a loud protest broadcast by the prey, backed up by a small, heavily armed patrol to warn the tacship away.

The plan was for the tacship to ignore the warning. If that went on long enough, the Honjo patrol would certainly fire. Then the wrath of the Imperial fleet would descend on the helpless Honjo to repay them for their temerity.

For a long time, there was nothing at all.

The Kraas sent out for more food. The big banquet table had already been emptied twice. Most of it had been drunk or devoured by the twins. They ate until even the skin of the fat one was stretched to bursting. Then they excused themselves, so that the obese one could help "Sis" into a lavatory. Loud sounds of vomiting followed. Then the two exited, the thin one flushed with effort and glowing with saintly joy at her after-the-fact temperance.

At first, Malperin, Kyes, and Lovett had been revolted. But the second time around, they became oddly fascinated. It was certainly more exciting than what was going on up on the big com board.

As the waiters were hauling in more supplies, a voice crackled out. A Honjo voice!

"This is Honjo Center to unknown tacship. Please identify yourself."

The tacship was silent, and the excitement in the com

room came sparking back. Each of the five leaned forward, waiting.

"Honjo Center, to unknown tacship. You are in violation of our borders. Turn back. I repeat, turn back!"

Still no response, just as according to plan. On the big screen, they could see the tacship moving inalterably on. Another flurry of warnings came from the Honjo, with similar negative results. They could see the small patrol now. A tech whispered to Kyes that the monitors showed that they had gone from alert to full armament. Any moment, a missile would be fired.

Then there was a loud, unconscious groan. Against all predictions, the Honjo patrol was retreating!

"Unknown tacship," came the voice of the Honjo commander. "Be warned! We are recording this violation of our sovereignty. And it shall be immediately reported to the proper authorities."

"Wot's bleedin' happening?" one Kraa burst out. "Why don't the bastards shoot?"

"Clottin' cowards," the other screamed. "Fight, you drakhs. Fight!"

Despite that odd cheering section, the Honjo did just the opposite. The patrol sensibly turned tail and ran.

The council members were mortified. Techs ducked their angry glares about the room, looking for someplace to set responsibility.

"What will we do?" Lovett hissed.

"Clot 'em. Let's go anyways!" the fat Kraa said.

"I don't know," Malperin said. "Are you sure we ought to? I mean, doesn't this change everything?"

Kyes thought it did—but he was not sure. They were so close. The patrol was tiny, the fleet waiting. All that AM2 just sitting there. Maybe . . .

At that moment, the com screen blanked. Then the startled council members found themselves staring at Poyndex, their chief of Mercury Corps.

The colonel made no excuses or apologies for the interruption. His face was pale. His manner, bloodless. "I have been notified that an assassination team is at this moment in place and prepared to strike.

"Gentlebeings, you will immediately put yourselves in the hands of your security personnel. There is no cause for extreme alarm. If you follow security procedures, all will be well."

The council members jolted around as the door burst open and grim-faced security beings pushed into the room. Then the five rulers of all the Eternal Emperor had once surveyed allowed themselves to be hustled away like little children astray in a wilderness.

Somewhere in the far-off Honjo system a fleet awaited orders.

The team closed in on the late Sullamora's estate. At first they had traveled fast. There were still gravsleds overhead that were clearly not Security vehicles.

At daybreak they had sheltered in a river cave that F'lesa had pinpointed. They had eaten a tasteless meal and tried to sleep, only to be awakened by earthquake rumbles. Quick hand signals were exchanged—reflexively, without orders, they had gone nonverbal, even for whispers. The signals gave redundant, obvious information, variations of "Target on ground," but they broke the silent isolation.

Now, any overhead had to be considered hostile.

Just at dusk, they moved again. Ten kilometers outside the estate, the first passive sensors were encountered. They were quickly given electronic "You don't see anything" signals, and the team moved on.

The sensors became closer together, and more sensitive. But again they were spoofed successfully. Then there was an old road, with a patrol, its time passage exactly what Dum and Dee had filmed. Routine and proper security are oxymoronic. Roving five-man patrols. Mantis, most likely. Again, evaded. A N'Ran crouched to Sten and signed scornfully: "I could dance."

They went on.

A kilometer or so outside the estate, Sten found a hill-top with a decent line of sight and fair overhead cover. "Here. Set up," he signed.

The cases were opened. Two missiles came out. They looked to be standard Imperial short-range, self-homing, fire-and-forget, ground-to-ground weapons. They were not. The propellant had been replaced by a reduced amount of a slow-burning solid fuel. The missiles would be fired from very short, closely estimated range. More explosive went in. The homing mechanisms also went into the trash. More bang went in their place. Space was left for a primitive guidance system near the missile's stern. A small pitot was welded into the base.

Telescoping rods were untelescoped, crossed, and pinned together into simple, X-shaped launching stands. The Archulers unshouldered their packs. Each pack contained a two-kilometer reel of chained molecular wire. One end of the wire connected to the missile, the other to a monopod-mounted passive light-intensification sight with a single, small joystick. The N'ran were ready.

The rest of the team stripped off the phototropic uniforms. Under them, they wore Imperial combat fatigues, exactly the same as those worn by the guard units inside the estate. Sten motioned them down the hill.

More sensors. Physical security barriers, including some archaic razor-wire. Booby traps, passive and active. Guards.

Easy. No problem. A little too easy?

Shut up. A hollow. Signal—flat of hand, going down. Needless. The team dropped. Just in front of them was the final wire—and the compound.

Now the bloodbath should begin—preferably on one side only.

Phase One, scheduled to begin when Sten keyed a tone-com, would be the firing of the first missile. The second would follow ten seconds later. Sten had felt—correctly—that any modern guidance system would be countermeasured or just blocked. So he went primitive.

The guidance system was via that wire the Archulars had lugged in.

Wire guidance had been discarded millennia earlier as an absurdity. Its faults were many: The operator was required to remain in one place and guide the missile to its target. He must have line of sight to the target. The target might also be looking his way and have some objection to being rocketed. Not a problem for Sten—he was back-stabbing, not playing Leonidas.

The wire could snag or break. Not this wire.

But the biggest problem had been the real catch-22. If the missile traveled at any kind of speed, it would take a guidance operator who could also dance on a rolling ball to hit the target rather than over- or under-shoot or, worse, send the missile into out-of-control yawing. They had to slow the missile down. That would give the target time to acquire and destroy the missile and most likely its operator, as well, but that was not a real factor. Luxury estates did not shoot back—Sten hoped.

First the missiles would sequentially impact on the target area, resulting in chaos, flames, and screams. Sten and his team would arrow into that chaos with "Rescue" in their shouts and murder in their hearts. They would terminate any surviving council members, then withdraw, break contact, and head for the pickup point.

The tone-com would also signal Kilgour to bring the tacship to the surface and low-fly upriver to a preset RP.

Then they could all go home and get drunk.

Stop hesitating. Go, lad.

Sten touched the button.

One . . .

The first missile was launched and nap-of-the-earth guided into the estate's main building.

Three seconds . . .

Faye Archuler pitched a sausage charge over the wire and pulled the fuse cord.

Six . . .

The first missile "crept" forward, at little more than 200 kph.

Eight . . .

The charge exploded, slicing the fence open like a gate.

Ten . . .

The second missile launched.

Eleven . . .

Sten shouted, "Grenades!" The team thumbed timers and hurled grenades into the compound.

Thirteen . . .

Sten was the first on his feet and charging through the hole in the wire. It may have saved his life.

Fifteen . . .

The grenades exploded, huge flares broadcasting confusion through visible-invisible spectrums.

Eighteen seconds . . .

Imperial Security sprang the trap.

Two armored gravsleds floated into sight, their multiple chainguns yammering. A missile launcher snapped up from its silo, tracking.

Twenty-one . . .

Sten's first missile was just four seconds from impact. The gravsled chainguns' sensors found the incoming missile. Solid collapsed-uranium slugs sheeted through the air—and the missile shattered!

Twenty-four . . .

The missile launcher acquired its target. Twenty counterbattery missiles spat into the night.

Twenty-eight seconds . . .

The missiles impacted on Sten's launch site. The two N'Ran disappeared in a howl of explosions.

The second missile, no longer under command, soared vertically.

Twenty-nine seconds . . .

Akashi's boot heel slammed down on a mine sowed less than an hour before. The charge took his legs off at the groin, and shrapnel scythed through Montoya.

The nearby blast caught Sten, flipping him up and back into the wire. He hung, limply.

Montoya's vital-signs pack blew, purple in the night.

Thirty-one . . .

High overhead, Sten's second missile exploded harmlessly.

Thirty-six . . .

The guns on the gravsleds tracked down . . . ammunition drums clanged as the loads automatically changed and the guns yammered on.

Larry and Faye Archuler were cut nearly in half.

Thirty-nine . . .

A sniper found the running Havell in his sights . . . lost him in a grenade blast . . . then touched the trigger. The AM2 round blew Havell's chest away.

Forty-two . . .

Corum and Valdiva zagging . . . rolling . . . firing . . . The chainguns found and smashed them.

Sten found himself flat. Stunned. Disoriented. He started to his feet—and the Mantis reflexes took over. He rolled, over and over, somehow keeping hold of his broken-stocked scattergun. Explosive rounds stitched centimeters over his head, and he was back in the hollow. Safety. Stay here, his mind said. They won't see you. They won't find you.

His body disobeyed. He ripped out of his combat harness, thumbed the switch on a grenade, and threw the vest back, into the wire.

The first grenade detonated—and the others went off in sympathetic explosions.

Sten was up, stumbling. Away. You're blown. Move! The others! Clot the others—they're dead! Follow the damned orders I'm issuing!

A five-man patrol came out of the smoke. Gun up, trigger held back—and red spray instead of men, AM2 bullets exploding the razor fence behind them and its sensors.

Through, skin ripping.

Water-sound. Run, damn you. It doesn't hurt.

A bank. Flat-dive over—fearing rocks, hoping water. Neither. Smash into the cushion . . . the ripping cushion of rusted high-piled concertina wire.

The knife out of your arm, man.

Slashing.

Nothing to slash. Somehow the knife was in its "sheath," and Sten was crashing forward, into the water and through the shallows.

Someone behind him was firing.

Bullet-splashes.

Deeper. Dive. Go under. Hold your clottin' breath. You don't need oxygen.

Now. Surface. One gasp—go under. Swim if you can. Let the current carry you. Away. Down the river.

One hand moved inside his uniform, found a tiny box, slid the cover back on the box, and pressed a stud.

Swim. You can.

Safety.

Downriver. Alex. The pickup.

Sten knew he would never make it.

Kilgour paced the control room of the tacship, waiting. It was not much of a pace—no more than four steps at the maximum before he would slam into something.

The ship was grounded on the river beach chosen for the pickup point. Alex had the hatch open. His orders were clear and exact: remain in place until one hour before daybreak or if discovered. If no one is at the pickup point, return to the ocean. Try to remain near mouth of the river. The team would try, if the pickup was blown, to E&E to the ruins of Reedsport. If no contact was made, he was to head offplanet and report.

In the not-very-distance, Alex could hear the sounds of hell. He hoped it was being given, not gotten. Once more he cursed Sten, then broke off in midobscenity as an ululation began from a com speaker.

One screen showed a projection of the target area. Just

outside it, a tiny red light blinked—from the river. Mid-river, the map told him.

"Clot!" The obscenity was heartfelt. The light—and signal—came from a standard search-and-rescue transmitter. Each member of the team had carried one, with orders to activate it *only* if they missed pickup. Certainly not anywhere close to the target zone.

An SAR light. One.

Kilgour zoomed the projection back, to see if there were others. Nothing.

His fingers found a mike. "This is pickup. Go."

Nothing but dead air. The light continued to blink.

Kilgour took about a nanosecond to decide that those clear and exact orders could get stuffed. Seconds later, he lifted the tacship, banged the drive selection into Yukawa power—and be damned who could see the torch—and drove forward, upriver.

A screen flashed at him. Six gravsleds.

Alex took one hand from the controls and slapped a switch. The tacship's chainguns blasted. The tacship yawed, ripping through the top of a redwood grove, and almost went in before Alex had control again. He shot through the falling debris of the gravsleds and a voice from a speaker smashed at him:

"Unidentified tacship! Ground, or we fire!"

Alex was forced to lift out of the gorge. He banked the ship into a tight spiral, took three steps away from the control board, and hit ALL LAUNCH on the long-activated weapons panel. Eight Goblin XIX's salvoed upward. He found time to hope the medium-range antiship missiles' brains were awake, and there he was back at the controls, diving down into the gorge; the cliffs dropped away, and Kilgour was almost overflying the blinking light—and into the alerted target zone.

He spun ship, still under power, his stabilizing and nav-gyros screaming, killed power, and went to McLean power.

Far overhead, a nuclear fire blossomed.

Kilgour splashed down and was at the hatch. Just upstream, a body floated down toward him, motionless. Then an arm lifted, trying to swim.

Kilgour stretched . . . almost fell in . . . then had the body by its ripped coveralls. He flipped the man into the ship and was back behind the controls and under full power, hands darting across the controls, barely finding time to cycle the lock closed as the tacship clawed for altitude, straight up, toward and through the nuclear blast that had formerly been an Imperial warship.

It may have been the instant fury of Kilgour's reactions, or just the luck of the Scots. But he cleared planet—and vanished into silence under full AM2 drive.

Behind him Sten lay unconscious. His mind concussed and his body, having done its duty and preserved the organism, shut down until repairs were made.

CHAPTER TWELVE

THE LIBRARIAN AND her staff were considering their futures when—or rather if—their boss ever departed. One thought fondly of suicide, another planned a complete breakdown. The librarian herself considered one of two new careers: as a staffer for an orgy livie production company, or, perhaps, as a serial murderer.

Her job had suddenly become a complete, dawn-to-dawn nightmare.

It had not begun like that, nor had it been like that for nearly five years. In fact, she had been enormously envied for getting the post.

Somewhat dissatisfied, certainly overqualified and without time to do her own research and publishing in her previous job as head librarian at a large university, she had been contacted, out of the blue, by an executive search service. She was offered what she thought was the ultimate job—at triple her present salary. Did she mind relocating to a different system? No. The headhunter seemed unsurprised, as if he knew everything about her. The position was as a private librarian. The woman demurred—she had no intention of burying herself in some recluse's dusty archives and letting the world pass.

Nothing like that at all, the man explained. He suggested she visit the planet of Yongjukl and investigate her new job. She would have a round-trip ticket. He offered to accompany her. She declined. The librarian was quite attractive—and the headhunter seemed disappointed.

The library was nearly mansion-size and was but one building on sprawling grounds. The main house dwarfed the library. It was secluded, with more than a thousand square kilometers of guarded, secure grounds. Her own quarters were lavish. There was a full staff: cooks, cleaners, gardeners.

Not that the librarian was imprisoned. She had her own gravcar, and a large, sophisticated city was no more than an hour or two away. She was allowed to keep her own hours—as long as the system remained current. If she ever needed help, she could hire as many day-workers as necessary.

Computers? Scanners? Filing robots? State of the art—and new models provided regularly.

She asked if she had permission to pursue her own studies and research. Certainly. Could she have visitors? If she chose. However, if she left the grounds, she was required to carry a remote. She must consider herself on call dawn-to-dawn. An unlikely possibility.

It seemed too good to be true. She felt like a character in one of the goth-livies she had supposedly given up when she was twelve but still ''lived,'' somewhat guiltily, in her occasional bubblebaths.

Especially since there was no one in the mansion. No one except the staff. And none of them had ever met the mansion's owner.

When she returned to her own world, her first question to the headhunter was: Who would I be working for?

The man explained. The mansion—and its grounds—were part of a family estate. Which one? I cannot tell you that. But the mansion must remain with the family, and be maintained. If not—it is a matter of a rather elaborate and eccentric trust, my dear—an entire commercial empire would be disassembled.

At the head of the family is the young heir, the man continued. You may never meet him. He is extremely busy and prefers living closer to the Empire's center. But he is an unusual man. He might well show up one day.

Alone or with an entourage—in which case he will require absolute privacy. The man shrugged. It must be nice to be so wealthy that you can order your life that precisely.

If I take this position, the woman asked—which you can accept on a weekly, monthly, or yearly contract, the headhunter interrupted—I must keep that a secret? No, not necessarily, the man said. It seems to be a favorite topic about once a year by the planet's newsvids. Say what you wish—it is not as if there's anything to hide.

Thinking dark thoughts of windswept castles and disguised, royal lovers, she accepted the position.

For eleven years, it was paradise. Staggering amounts of material churned in daily. It seemed the unknown heir subscribed to every scientific, military, or political journal in the Empire. The material was scanned, summarized, and mostly discarded by a computer/scanner who seemed to have completely elitist tastes. It was, the woman once thought, a machine that seemed programmed to provide an instant update for someone newly risen from the grave. The computer had two sysop stations. One was in a sealed room, the other belonged to the librarian. The sealed unit seemed to contain, she learned when she snooped in boredom, some files that were inaccessible to the rest of the system.

Annually the entire files for that year were deleted. Then the machine began all over, collecting, summarizing, and storing.

Until a little more than six years before.

At that time, the computer had switched modes and begun storing everything. The librarian did not notice until year's end. She panicked—just slightly. Had she done something wrong? She did not want to lose her position. Not only was she perfectly happy on this world, having met and loved a wonderful succession of mates, but she was publishing important analyses in a steady stream, the envy of her far-lesser-paid and, to their minds, overworked colleagues in the field. The man at the other end of the emergency contact number soothed her. Not to worry, he said. Just continue. So continue she did.

Now she was going quite insane. Because, to everyone's astonishment, the heir—a man she thought most likely a legal myth by now—arrived. A small ship set down on the small landing pad. One man got out, and the ship instantly lifted away.

Guards met him. "Sir, this is a private—"

The man said words—words everyone had been told would be uttered if their boss ever showed up.

No one knew what to do and cowered for their jobs.

The man asked to be taken to his room. He showered, changed, and asked for a simple meal. Then he buzzed and asked to be shown to the library.

In the huge hall he politely told the librarian that he would appreciate it if she remained on standby. He unlocked the door to the second sysop station, and the madness started.

He seemed to scan everything—and want more. She had to hire assistants. He appeared insatiably curious. Again, the librarian thought of someone raised from the dead. No, she corrected herself. Someone who had been in longsleep, like the starships in ancient times before AM2 drive.

It went on, the man ate sparingly, slept little, but soaked up information like a sponge. Once, when the door opened for a moment, she saw that he had five screens scrolling simultaneously and a synth-voice giving a sixth stream of data.

The librarian prayed for sleep.

Then it stopped. The man walked out of the room, leaving the door open.

He said he was sleepy.

The librarian agreed blearily.

He told her he would shut down the system.

Yes. The woman and her equally zombied assistants stumbled for their quarters. The librarian noticed—but it did not register until days later—as she passed the room where the second sysop station was, that the computer seemed to be punching up files and then deleting them en masse.

It did not matter.

All that mattered was sleep.

The man slipped out an ignored side gate to the mansion onto the road. He walked down the road, briskly. He wore nondescript clothes—just another of that world's blue-collar workers.

He stopped once. The walls of the mansion's grounds stretched solidly down the road.

He felt slight regret.

The computer had told him that when he left the staff would be paid off with handsome bonuses and encouraged with larger bonuses to relocate offworld. The mansion, the library, and the outbuildings would be razed within two weeks. Then the bare grounds would be donated to the planetary government for whatever purposes it saw fit.

A pity. It was beautiful.

The computer told him there were ten others like it scattered around the Empire.

He now knew six years of history. His plans—no. Not yet. But he had been given another destination.

Lights blazed behind him. A creaking gravsled lofted toward him, laden with farm produce for the early markets. The man extended his hand.

The gravsled hissed to a halt. The driver leaned across and opened the door.

The man climbed inside, and the gravsled lifted.

"Dam' early to be hitchin'," the driver offered.

The man smiled, but did not answer.

"You work for th' rich creech owns that palace?"

The man laughed. "No. Me an' the rich don't speak the same tongue. Just passin' through. Got stranded. Dam' glad for the lift."

"Where you headed?"

"The spaceport."

"You're light on luggage. For a travellin' man."

"I'm seekin' a job."

Snorted laughter came from the driver. "Golden luck to you, friend. But there's dam' little traffic comin' in or out. Times ain't good for spacecrew."

"I'll find something."

"Dam' confident, ain't you? Like a fellow who thinks like that. Name's Weenchlors." The driver stuck out a paw. The man touched thumbs with him. "You?"

"I use the name Raschid," the man said.

He leaned back against the raggedy plas seats and stared ahead toward the lightening sky—toward the spaceport.

BOOK TWO

IMPERATOR

CHAPTER THIRTEEN

AN HOUR AFTER dawn, Security let the five members of the privy council out of their shielded bunkers into the fog-hung compound. They looked at the craters where the assassins had exploded as they died, the two rows where the dead Security beings lay covered, the torn wire, and the shrapnel-ripped buildings. They could not see the hilltop, where smoke trailed up from the N'Ran's launch site, and the warship Alex's blind-launched Goblins had flambéed was a radioactive cloud, drifting and contaminating its way inland.

Four of them shared anger—how could this have happened? The other, Kyes, was trying to label what emotion he did feel. In all his years, no one had ever tried to harm him physically. Destroy his career and life—but that was in bloodless executive chambers.

All of them were outraged. Who and why?

The Kraas, hardly strangers to physical violence, were pure rage, but with something else behind it: the instinct of cunning.

"We want the bosses. This un's a conspiracy, not a buncha wildcats on a bust-out."

"I agree," Kyes put in.

"The *real* bosses c'n wait," the thin one said. She had understood exactly what her sister was hinting. "Till Monday, anyway. What we want are th' evil beings who planned this atrocity. Nobody else but th' Honjo."

"Clot that clottin' tacship," the fat one said. "We got us some *real* bodies now."

Lovett, as always, reached the bottom line. "Conspiracy. Indeed. Far superior to any violation of territorial limits by a tacship."

"I will issue the orders to the fleet," Malperin snapped, and was inside.

"Righto," one Kraa said. "First we snag the AM2. Then we kill—slow—whoever actually come a'ter us.

"Them," her sister agreed, "an' some others. We've been needin' an excuse for some housecleanin'."

It was a peculiar curiosity that social entities could take on a personality of their own—a personality that remained the same for many years, even though the beings who first established the entity's policies which had given it that personality were long dead and forgotten. To psycho-historians, such an organization was an "Iisner." The same could be applied, on occasion, to military formations. One of the most famous examples was a tiny unit called the Seventh Cavalry. The unit, from inception, was fairly poorly led and suffered enormous casualties in combat, culminating in one entire element being wiped out to the last man. Over the next hundred E-years, in three successive wars, even though they had been modernized with wheeled or in-atmosphere transport, they were still abysmally generaled and regularly decimated.

A more modern example was the Imperial 23rd Fleet, now ordered to attack the Honjo worlds and seize their AM2 caches. When the Tahn wars had begun, the 23rd had been obliterated, mostly due to the incompetence of its admiral, who had had the good grace to be killed during that obliteration.

A new fleet was formed. It fought through the rest of the war, officered indifferently at best and known throughout the Imperial Services as a good outfit for anyone curious about reincarnation.

For some completely unknown reason, the 23rd was kept on the rolls when the war ended, when far superior, more famous, and "luckier" formations were broken up and their cased colors returned to depot.

Its admiral—until recently the fleet's vice-admiral—was one Gregor. He had replaced his CO, Mason, when Mason refused to follow the privy council's orders and requested relief.

Oddly enough, both the relieved and reliever had crossed Sten's orbit. Mason had been Sten's brutal nemesis during flight school and a particularly lethal destroyer commander in the Tahn wars. He was a man without pity or bowels for his own sailors or the enemy, but he was one of the best leaders the Empire had.

Gregor, on the other hand, had begun his military career as a failure. He had been in Sten's Imperial Guards' Basic Company and had been washed out for slavishly ordering, as trainee company commander, a by-the-book attack that was obvious suicide. He had returned to the tourist world where his father was a muckety—not as much of one as Gregor bragged, but still one with clout. The old man had sighed, put another tick mark in Gregor's failure list, and put him to work in an area where he could screw nothing up. Gregor's father was an optimist. By the time the Tahn wars began, Gregor wanted out—out of the division he had bankrupted, out of the relationship he had ruined, and away.

The Empire took almost anyone in wartime. They took Gregor—and commissioned him. This time Gregor discovered the path to success: Think about your orders first. If they aren't obvious booby traps, follow them slavishly. Develop a reputation for being hard. No one, during time of war, will be that curious about things like prisoner policy or retaliation. Gregor got promoted.

He decided that Imperial Service—particularly with the political connections he had been careful to make—was his forte. Particularly with the AM2 shortage. Tourist worlds without tourists were not, to him, the pattern of the future.

He had arrived with his reputation in front of him.

Mason, a *real* hard man, had taken two weeks to decide that Gregor was not only an incompetent but someone destined to preside over a future version of Cortés's obliteration of the Aztecs.

He was correct. Unfortunately, Mason ran out of time.

The privy council had looked carefully for exactly the right admiral to head the attack on the Honjo system. In a way, they chose correctly. Mason would have followed orders and used just enough surgical force to convince the Honjo they were outgunned and outnumbered.

But they went too far. The Kraa twins had decided that, in addition to their other talents, they had a freshly discovered talent for military tactics. Their concept of "good tactics" was as subtle as the way they handled labor disputes in the mines.

Mason asked to be relieved. He was. Disgusted, he decided to disappear for a long vacation, helping some retired friends restore old combat spacecraft for a museum. It saved his life.

Seconds after the change in orders from the privy council, Gregor ordered the 23rd Fleet into action. His fleet still looked impressive, even though some of the weapons systems were off-line, waiting for replacement parts that would never arrive; the ships themselves were at seventy percent or less of full complement, and the command "Full emergency power" from any powerplant engineer would have been regarded as an order for "Full public sodomy."

Peace had struck hard at the Imperial Military, especially in personnel. The privy council had offered nothing but encouragement to anyone who wanted to leave the service. Many did. There was still a scattering of the dedicated in the fleet. And hard times on civvy street had provided other qualified sailors. But more than not, the 23rd's personnel were what should be expected: those who fell, dropped, or were pushed out of civilian life.

Still worse, most of them knew themselves to be marginal. Pay was sporadic, punishments arbitrary, and privileges awarded and withdrawn haphazardly. Morale was just a word in the dictionary between mildew and mud.

Ten worlds were chosen for the first attack—as an "example in frightfulness." Two were the AM2 "warehouse" worlds. The other eight were system capitals. For both targets, the weapons and their deployment were the same.

Neutron bombs were carpet-sewn across city centers and the warehouse worlds' control areas. Instantly, no life—and the blasts did not set off any of the stored AM2. Neither Gregor nor the privy council had thought warnings or declarations necessary preludes to war.

Gregor then made a broadbeam cast for the Honjo to surrender. First mistake: he had vaporized all the Honjo leaders who had the power to negotiate with the Empire. Second mistake: he had scared the Honjo into, he thought at first, paralysis.

Berserker rage can sometimes, on initiation, be mistaken for terror.

Gregor's fleet took up parking orbits and set patrols around the AM2 worlds. Then they brought in the slaved transports that would make up the "spacetrain."

The council had underestimated the supply. The convoy would be at least twenty kilometers from leadship to drag.

And the nightmare began as the Honjo exploded.

There seemed to be no leaders, nor generals. Just—resistance. The workers imported to load the AM2 were as likely to club a guard down and smile in the dying as work. They sabotaged any crane or beltway they got near. Robot systems and computers were crashed.

Gregor tried hostages, reprisals.

None of it seemed to matter to the Honjo.

The Emperor might have been able to tell the privy council that. The Honjo were hardheaded traders, and before they had learned that a contract was sharper than a sword, they had been excessively fond of sharp objects and private settlements of disputes.

The Honjo slave laborers—those who survived—were returned to their home worlds. Fleet sailors were on-planeted and used for the work force.

The situation got worse.

Small strike forces—squads, platoons, companies, ir-regulars—were landed. A one-sided guerrilla war began. Imperial soldiers and sailors could not open fire in the maze of buildings, each building a monstrous bomb. The Honjo had no such compunctions.

The fleet itself was attacked by such patrolcraft as the Honjo had, those light, boxy transports with three brave men or women at the controls and a bomb in the cargo hold. Kamikaze—the divine wind—worked.

It seemed as if the entire Honjo culture had held its breath for a moment and then heard, whispering from the dim past, a war leader's words: "You can always take one with you . . ."

It was a siege, but not a siege. The besiegers arrived—and died. A battle, but not a battle. A perpetual series of alley murders. There seemed to be no way of stopping them. Put out destroyer screens to shield the big boys? Fine. The Honjo would attack the destroyers. Even a spaceyacht with a cabin full of explosives was enough to take a destroyer out of combat. Three . . . or six . . . or ten such spitkits . . . and then survivors went on for the battlewagons.

Gregor bleated for reinforcements.

There were none that could be sent.

There *were* ships—and men—standing by on the depot world of Al-Sufi. All they needed was fuel. Once fueled, they could support Gregor. But Gregor had the fuel . . .

Men—and ships—died.

Gregor knew better than to abort. The fleet *must* return with the AM2.

Gregor's officers and long-termers started hearing ru-mors then. Rumors from the Empire itself. Something was happening. People—leaders—they knew were being relieved and brought to trial. There were whispers of executions. All the deck sailors of the 23rd could do was work in a frenzy and pray that the final cargoes would be loaded before they all died. No one was willing to give odds, either way . . .

Mavis Sims did not expect a reward for betraying her fellow officers as part of her sworn duty to the Empire.

At best, she knew that her career would be over and her friends would send her to Coventry.

It was worse.

She should have known better. Regicide, even attempted regicide, has its own laws from investigation to punishment, laws limited only by whatever humanity the king chose to allow. Robert François Damiens, tortured and torn into four parts by horses, could have shown her that. The Eternal Emperor himself had paid little attention to the statutes in his cleanup after the Hakone plot failed. And the privy councillors were far less saintlike than the Eternal Emperor—or that declining monarch Louis XV either, for that matter.

When Sims had decided she must expose Mahoney's conspiracy she alerted the highest-ranking Intelligence officer she knew and told him of the assassination plan, when and where. No more.

What would happen next . . . she would not think.

What *did* happen was that Sims was arrested and her mind systematically ripped apart on the brainscan. The expert "interrogators" had no interest in Sims's survival, either as an alert human or as a brainburn.

Yes . . . ten other officers at the table. Record faces. Does Sims know their names? Record them. Next meeting. Yes. Here. The amphitheater. Single-vision for this. Who is speaking?

One of the interrogators knew.

"Clottin' Mahoney! But he's dead!"

Continue scan . . . we'll report as necessary. Now. A

party. Dammit . . . that group in the corner never looked at her. Never mind. They're most likely duped elsewhere.

"Dammit-to-hell! There's Mahoney again."

"Who's that smaller guy in mufti beside him?"

"Dunno. Look. He's talking—and Mahoney's listening."

"Do we have an audio?"

"Negative. Sims was just passing that room when somebody came out and shut the door behind them."

"Get a make on the little one. Anybody your Mahoney shuts up and listens to is somebody the council's gonna want bad."

When it was over, nearly eight hundred of the nearly one thousand conspirators and their aides present for the kriegsspiel had been positively identified. Among them—Mahoney and Sten.

And when it was over, Sims's body was cremated. Her fiche vanished from Imperial records. Five generations of Imperial service ended—in night and fog.

That was the cover name for the roundup operation: Nightfog. Target lists were made and sent out. They were to be implemented not only by Mercury and Mantis operatives, but by the council's private armies as well.

Some of the conspirators were arrested and tried publicly. Some of them, prodded by threats to their families, or more often just drug-programmed, confessed that the Honjo had indeed organized the conspiracy, through an outlaw general named Mahoney. Then they were permitted to die.

Others just vanished.

Innocent or guilty, the Imperial Officer Corps was shattered—shattered in self-image, shattered in fear, shattered in paranoia. All of them knew that Nightfog II . . . or III . . . or ? could happen.

There were eight hundred names from Sims's brainscan, and eight hundred names on the original list.

Later estimates varied, but at least seven thousand beings were killed.

People had personal enemies. Each of the privy councillors, except Kyes, cleared up some of their own problems as the list was passed around—and as it grew.

When the deathlists arrived on the desks of the Security people chosen to make the pickups, it was simple for the officer or thug in charge to make an addition. Or two. Or six.

There were, of course, mistakes.

A writer of children's fiche named White, much loved and respected, was unfortunate to live in the same suburb as a retired major general named Whytte. The writer's house was broken into in the middle of the night. The writer was dragged to the center of his living room and shot. The writer's wife tried to stop the killers. She was shot, as well.

When the mistake was revealed, the head of the murder unit, a Mercury Corps operative named Clein, thought the matter an excellent joke.

CHAPTER FOURTEEN

ALEX SAW THE beast raise its head from the trencher of
meat and fix bloodshot eyes on Sten. The huge brows
beetled into a murderous frown. The being wiped the
gore from its lips with the long brush-tail beard and grimaced at some foul thought, exposing thick, yellow teeth.

The creature lumbered to its feet, harness creaking under the weight of many weapons. It came forward three
steps, knobbed, hairy paws brushing briefly on the floor.
It was a meter wide from the neck down and weighed in
at a fearful 130 kilograms. Although only 150 centimeters high, it was massive power in a smallish package.
Muscle cells were easily as dense as Kilgour's, despite
his heavy-worlder's genes. Its spine was curved, and its
great trunk was supported on legs like bowed tree trunks.

The being raised itself to its full height, brandishing
an enormous stregghorn. His shout filled the big hall like
a large explosion in a small cylinder at depth.

"By my mother's beard!" it bellowed at Sten. "This
is unbearable."

The being waddled to the table and loomed over Sten.
Drunken tears welled out of the gaping holes the Bhor
called eyes. Blubbering like a hairy infant, Otho collapsed next to Sten, his breath laced with enough stregg
to peel the hide off a deep-space freighter.

"I love you like a brother," Otho wept.

The Bhor chieftain turned to his feasting subjects. He
gestured with his stregghorn, spilling a pool that could
drown a small human.

"We all love you like a brother!" he roared. "Tell him, brothers and sisters. Are we not Bhor? Do we hide honest feelings?"

"*No!*" came the shout from the more than a hundred assembled warriors.

"Swear it, brothers and sisters." Otho shouted the order. "By our fathers' frozen buttocks—we love you Sten!"

"By our fathers' frozen buttocks . . ." came the return shout, amplified by a more than a hundred Bhor maws. Otho flung himself on Sten and sobbed.

Alex shuddered. He did not envy his friend's popularity with these beings.

Across the great hall there were a few human warriors sprinkled among the Bhor. Of all the admiring eyes watching Sten—the returning hero—one pair viewed him with special interest. Her name was Cind. She was very, very young and very, very lovely. It was that special kind of beauty that grabbed at the heart through the loins. Cind was also one of the most highly regarded practitioners of that supremely lethal art—sniping.

Her own personal weapon had started life as an already-exotic Imperial-issue sniper weapon. It fired the normal Imperial AM2-charged, Imperium-shielded round, but instead of using a laser as propellant it used a linear accelerator. A variable power automatic-estimate scope gave the range to target. The scope could then be adjusted laterally on its mount—in the event the nominated target was sheltered behind something. It was a weapon that could shoot around corners. The rifle was never offered on the open market, not even to Imperially equipped allies. Cind had acquired hers on the black market and then further modified it for her own tastes— thumbhole stock built for her, increased barrel weight for better balance and less "recoil" flip, double-set trigger, bipod, and so forth. As issued, the rifle was heavy. Cind's modifications made it still heavier. But despite her slender form, she could lug it hour after hour over the hilliest

terrain with little effort. So much for the alleged inability
of female humans to possess upper body strength without
hormone implants.

The problem with the rifle was that its ammunition,
like every other form of AM2, was currently very scarce.
So Cind had trained on every other weapon she could
find that could reach out and tweep someone long distance, from crossbows to projectile weapons.

Like most of the Bhor warriors she was cross-trained
in all fighting skills. On a ship, for instance, she was a
boarding specialist and had proved herself on several
hairy engagements.

The young woman was a Jann, or perhaps more correctly an ex-Jann. The Jann had been a suicidally dedicated military order, the striking arm for the Talamein
theocracy that had once ruled the Lupus Cluster with
genocidal hands. The Wolf Worlds, as the systems now
controlled by the Bhor were dubbed, had long been a
minor thorn in the Eternal Emperor's side. It was minor
only because the cluster was on the outskirts of the Empire. It was not so minor in the view of the Bhor. The
warrior trading culture was quickly being killed off by
the xenophobic Jann. They had become very nearly ex-
tinct.

But many years before Cind was born, an important
discovery was made well beyond even the Wolf Worlds.
It was new deposits of Imperium X, the substance used
to shield, and therefore control, AM2. The people of
Talamein and the killer Jannissars, however, lay at the
crossroads where the shipments of Imperium X had to
pass. Flailed on by their homicidal religion—the worship
of Talamein—the Jann became a cork in an extremely
important bottle.

Sten and Alex had headed a Mantis team sent in to
pull the cork. In the bloody sorting out that followed,
Sten eventually had taken advantage of a deep gulf in
Talameic theo-politics, placing two competing pontiffs in
bloody competition with one another. They both died.

To Sten's dismay, the immediate result produced a third religious leader, as powerful as he was traitorous. He was also a handsome hero—the proverbial "Man On A Horse"—that attracted the fanatics even more than his passion for Talamein. But suddenly that final leader decided he was Talamein himself, denounced his own faith as being sinfully misguided, called for peace, and then suicided. It was a lucky turn. Luck, in that case, was provided by a brutal assault on the prophet's stronghold, followed by Sten's carefully thought-out hand-to-hand reasoning with the man and an injection of a hypnotic into his veins, followed by the Programming, The Speech, and The Self-Martyrdom.

With the reluctant blessings of the Eternal Emperor, Otho and his Bhor subjects were raised up as the new rulers of the Wolf Worlds.

Most historians agreed that thus far it had worked out fairly well. The Bhor tended to let other beings think and do as they please, so long as they did not interfere with the operations of the Lupus Cluster, or trigger new quarrels.

Oddly, the Faith of Talamein collapsed along with its power. Despite ancient roots, it had become so repressive that the surviving believers were delighted that their noses were no longer pressed against the rough stone wheel of Talamein. It helped that the sight of the two competing pontiffs had become so ridiculous that even peasants tilling distant soil had become embarrassed.

The Jannisars themselves became crusaders without a cross, ultimate ronin. They found other, peaceful lives but remained both ashamed and proud of their heritage.

Cind had grown up in such a household. The stories of the past were told to her, privately, around the family hearth with the old weapons hanging above it, or sometimes loudly at family/clan reunions held in very secret places.

Cind had grown up as a throwback—she was one of the former Jann who had the old love of battle. Since

childhood she had disdained the ordinary playthings of
other young Jann. Toy weapons were her favorite. Vid-
books on great battles and heroic deeds stirred her more
than any fairy tales. So it was only natural that when she
came of age she volunteered for the Bhor military. Her
culture's old enemies—but the only game in town.

Her instinctual ability with the rifle quickly won her
favor among the Bhor. Now, whenever there was conflict
requiring arms, Cind was among the first to volunteer for
action and also among the first to be accepted. Her youth
was no handicap at all. In fact, it was most probably a
plus, since the Bhor loved a fight almost more than
stregg, that powerful and evil potion Sten had first become addicted to and then passed on to the Eternal Emperor. The Bhor encouraged instincts like Cind's in their
own young and boasted of them in their huge feasts and
drinking bouts.

As Otho drunkenly blubbered and patted his clearly
embarrassed friend, Cind gazed with adoring eyes at the
great Sten. This was the being whose exploits were
boasted of more than any other in the Bhor drinking halls.
No Bhor who had been even vaguely involved in those
exploits could walk down a public byway without drawing admiring looks and comments. Over and over again
the tale was told, and each time Sten and Alex shone in
greater and greater glory. Especially Sten. He was
younger than she imagined. She had been expecting a
hoary graybeard filled with stiff dignity. She also found
him most handsome.

Otho had drawn away and was conversing with Alex
Kilgour. Cind saw Sten look absently around the room.
She thought she had never seen a being so lonely. Her
heart went out to all the imagined horrors the great Sten
must conceal in his breast. She ached to coax them out,
to comfort him. Sten's eyes swept over her . . . then . . .
Ohmigod . . . He's looking back! At me! She grew un-
comfortably warm, and then his eyes moved on. Oh, dear,
oh, me, if only they had lingered. Would he see her

worth? Understand her passion for her only true friend—the long-range rifle? Of course he would. A great warrior like Sten would immediately know her feelings about such matters. Cind determined that somehow, some way, they would meet.

She turned back to her meal, unaware of how nasty an affliction youth could be.

Alex drained the horn and let Otho refill it. The Bhor chieftain had pulled him aside and was drunkenly quizzing him. Sten's manner was greatly troubling him, Otho said. His mood was so dark, and Otho was at a loss to dispel it. He told Alex he had only gotten a thin smile when he had reminded Sten of their first meetings, back when the Bhor had been handing out Jann captives to all the ships and bloodily executing them in the ancient, joyful Bhor rite of The Blessing.

"Remember that clottin' Jann's face as we stuffed him in the lock?" Otho said. Alex remembered. "By my mother's gnarly beard, was that a funny sight. He was so scared his face was screwed up like we'd given his nose a dozen twirls.

"It was only two or three—and we'd hardly tortured him at all. Then we fired him out to ice up his guts and drank his soul to hell! Ah, those were the days."

He clapped Alex on the back with a paw like a half-ton club. Even Kilgour was ruffed a mite by that. "Aye," was all he said. But before Otho could think that he shared Sten's glum disease, Alex remembered to roar with laughter at the thought of those gory times.

"What's wrong with our Sten?" Otho asked. "There's no fire to him. Point out the being who has wronged our brother and I vow we will slay him now!"

Alex would have been delighted if the matter were so simple and Sten's dilemma could be cured with an old-fashioned Bhor Blessing. Right now, the thought of guts in space was far more cheery than any Sten had entertained since they had fled Earth.

* * *

Kilgour had run like the gates of hell had been un-locked and all the demons in it were at his heels. This was not much of an exaggeration. If Kilgour had not acted so quickly, not only would they have been pursued, but they would have been caught. Alex threw caution and the laws of physics to the wind. He jinked and jolted and veered the little tacship about until every joint pairing gave a tortured scream of pain. He used every trick he had been taught and invented a few, besides, to elude detection. Once clear, he transmitted a fast "run like bleedin' drakh" to Mahoney, then shut down and made like a ghost.

Mahoney would have to take care of himself. Th' braw gr't clot's used t' it, Alex thought, although not unfondly. Kilgour *liked* Mahoney. Considered him a Gaelic kin. Alex hoped Ian made it intact. But there was little else he could do about it. If they all survived—and that was certainly an immeasurable "if"—they had a fallback, emergency rendezvous point. Not Poppajoe's. They had agreed, if the mission went awry, not to test their luck twice there. But all that would be in the very doubtful future.

Kilgour assumed the wrath of the privy council would be so great that they would go to any and all means to bring them to bay. He was correct. So—where to hide? Where could they go to ground? There were two crucial elements the hiding place would require. The first was that no one was likely to look for them there. The sec-ond—and far more important—was that if anyone *did* look, he and Sten would not be betrayed.

It took awhile to figure it out. Sten was no help. How could he be? The lad was definitely bad off. Alex had strapped Sten to the medtable in the tacship's tiny treat-ment center and punched in a trauma program. He could hear the little hisses and tricklings of the medic bots at work. The sounds were far too busy for comfort. Even-tually, as he dodged in and out of warp to throw off pur-suit, they calmed a bit. He looked into the small cabin and saw Sten lying on the medtable. A little less pale. But still out—puir, wee lad.

The perfect hideout finally dawned on him. It involved calling in a debt, but there were few beings who owed Sten more. He punched in a course for the Lupus Cluster—and the Bhor.

They were a bit more than halfway through the journey when Sten was finally able to get about feebly. As company, he was clottin' awful. Stone face. Absolute silence. He conversed rarely, and then it was confined to a few grunts. At first Alex thought it because he was still on the road to recovery. Then the trauma-center computer informed him that no further treatment was necessary and gave Sten a clean bill of health. At last, Kilgour had to admit that his friend had suffered a far greater wound than the physical ones that had temporarily incapacitated him.

He hadn't the faintest idea how to deal with it, or even how to bring the topic up. So he gritted his teeth and left it alone.

Then one day Sten broached the matter himself. They were eating dinner—in total silence. Sten had lately formed the habit of staring straight into his dish while he ate. Never speaking, never looking to one side or another. And certainly never raising his eyes as he shoveled in food—more as if it were fuel than anything potentially flavorful. Kilgour watched him out of the corner of his eye.

Sten popped in a hunk of something. Chewed. Swallowed. Another hunk. Another mechanical repetition. Suddenly he stopped midchew. His face grew dark with inner fury. Then he spat the food out as if it were poison, slammed to his feet, and slammed just as loudly out. That time, Alex decided not to ignore the incident. He waited a few moments and then went to Sten's quarters. The door was open, and Sten was pacing back and forth, working off the angry energy. Alex waited at the door until he was noticed. Sten saw him, stopped, then shook his head.

"I'm sorry, Alex," he said. Kilgour determined to bite the bullet and shake Sten up if he could.

"Y' aught t'be," he said, forcing irritation in his tone. "Y' clottin' aught t'be."

He went on, reaming Sten's butt. Sten was told that once again, he had spoiled Alex's dinner. And he was such terrible company that he had driven Kilgour to thoughts of murder, or suicide. He had been behaving like an adolescent, Alex said, and it was time he grabbed himself by whatever pride he had left and started thinking about how he was affecting others, such as his longest and dearest friend, one Alex Kilgour.

Alex felt like drakh when he started—hitting the lad while he was down. But as he went on he warmed to the task. Sten *had* been getting to him, dammit! And he needed to be told. Then he saw that Sten was not listening—or was only partly listening. His head was down and his fists were clenched until the knuckles were white.

"I blew it!" Sten hissed. "I clottin' blew it!"

"Aye," Alex said. "*We* did thae, lad. I' spades. But y'ken, 'tis nae th' first time. Nae wil't be th' last."

He had known all along what was haunting Sten. And with the opening he had just achieved, he tried to put it in perspective. He talked about all the other missions that had gone awry, the heaps of corpses left behind. They had suffered far worse things in the past, had witnessed and been partly responsible for far more dead. Alex knew he was pissing in the wind. But he had to try, just the same.

This was not just a sudden case of the guilts. It went back to Sten's reasons for abandoning his career more than six years before. The Tahn conflict certainly had been the costliest in terms of lives, as well as credits, of any war ever. Even on their own infinitely unimportant level, Sten and Alex had been forced to sacrifice so many lives that the foul taste of blood could never be washed out.

Sten had grown sick of playing butcher—which was why he had not only resigned but had turned his back on the only family he knew. Living family, at least.

Some of that also had to do with Kilgour's own decision to quit. But he had Edinburgh, with family and ancestral friends.

This time, what made it harder for Sten to pay the butcher's price was his long self-imposed exile. There was no way, no matter how hard he had continued to train, that he would not blame the blowup of the mission on his own rusty skills. Morally, if he felt that way, he should have turned down Mahoney's urging to lead the mission and helped Ian find someone else—someone fresher, someone not so tired and bitter.

Alex laid all of this out for Sten. He cajoled him. He cursed him. But nothing did any good. How could it? In the same position, Alex knew he would probably feel the same way.

The silence resumed. It lasted the remainder of the trip. And beyond.

Cind faithfully attended every one of the numerous feasts the Bohr had laid on to honor the returning heroes of the Jann war. She couldn't know that one of the key reasons for the banquets was Otho's clumsy attempts to break Sten out of his gloom and self-blame. But she couldn't help but notice how drawn Sten seemed, how oblivious he appeared to his surroundings, as if he were lost in some torment that no normal being could imagine. It seemed terribly tragic to her—and romantic.

She had finally gotten up the nerve to enter Sten's exalted presence. After considering how best to present herself, she had bought a costume so daring that she blushed even to think of it dangling in her locker. When she put it on and looked herself over in the mirror, she had almost pulled a sheet in front of herself so she would not have to look. Cind smoothed her already blemishless features with the most expensive and exotic makeup she

could find, then dotted herself with a perfume guaranteed
by the salesbeing to make strong human males fall at the
feet of the woman wise enough to seek out this particular
musk.

Cind dared the mirror again. She thought she looked
like a clotting joygirl. If this is what men wanted, they
could . . . she couldn't think of what they ought to do,
but she was sure that with thought she would come up
with something suitably nasty. That even included Sten.
Clot it! He would have to take her as she was.

She showered and scrubbed off all the offending stuff,
then threw away the bitty thing that had disgraced her
closet. Instead she chose one of her best uniforms. It was
made of a fine leatherlike cloth and fit as if the beast who
had borne the skin had been genetically bred just for
Cind's fine young body. Her face was fresh and glowing
from the scouring, her cheeks rosy from the bold thoughts
she entertained.

Cind looked herself over in the mirror again. Oh, well.
It would have to do.

She could not have picked more wisely. Sten had once
had a lover from this part of the Empire. Her name was
Sofia. Lady Sofia was a woman who entertained ambi-
tions for the Imperial Court. Sten had helped her achieve
them. A long time passed until he and Sofia had met
again. It was at a Function, thrown by those greatest of
all Imperial hosts, Marr and Senn.

The makeup and perfume Sofia had worn were not
much different than Cind's—although vastly more expensive. And as for her dress—Sofia had worn nothing at all
except some scattered glitter dust.

Faced with all that pulchritude, Sten had done what
Sofia had least expected. He had run like the wind—into
the arms of a homicide lieutenant, one Lisa Haines, a
woman who was much more Sten's style.

Cind knew that this particular feast was going to be
semiformal—for the Bhor, at least. Preceding the usual
gluttony, there would be a receiving line to greet the

honored guests. She called in a heavy favor with a Bhor friend and found a place at the end of the line.

Otho paraded Kilgour and Sten into the hall and past the line. After his stint as chief of the Emperor's palace guard, there was little Sten did not know about such polite entries. He shook the hand of each being, looked them in the eye, and smiled. It was not a great smile, but it would have to do. Then he passed on to the next. Still, by the time he reached Cind he was anxious to hie himself to the safety of his table. He gave her a perfunctory handclasp, smiled, and started to move on.

Cind held the hand tight. It was just for a moment, but it was enough to make Sten hesitate, so as not to be rude. Then he found himself looking at an absolutely lovely young woman with a stunning uniformed figure, face as fresh as nature itself, eyes clear and innocent, and the sober serious look that only the young could adopt and still be charming.

Cind spoke in a rush, to get it all out before Sten moved on. "Admiral Sten, I want you to know this is the greatest honor in my life. I've studied all the details of your actions during the Jann conflict, and I'd like you to know just how much of an inspiration you've been to me."

Sten couldn't help himself. He had to laugh. But it was not the kind of laughter anyone—especially Cind—would take offense to, or think she was the object of.

"Thank you," he said. He meant it. He started to move on. But Cind wasn't through.

"If ever you have a free moment," she continued, "I would very much appreciate if I could steal a little of it. There are so many questions I'd like to ask. Any warrior would. Although, I'm sure I'd bore you."

Then she turned on her best smile. It was far from shabby. It was the kind that lit up whole rooms. One did not have to look too closely to realize there were all sorts of other invitations implied.

Sten would have had to be a dead man not to have

understood that this young lady thought him very attractive and would be delighted to share his bunk. This time,
he didn't laugh. Instead, he gave her his most sincere
thanks and asked her name. Receiving it, he promised
he would certainly remember her and would be delighted
with her company—if he ever had the time. He gave her
a sad little smile at this last bit. He meant it to say, of
course, that he unfortunately never would. But, ah,
well . . .

Only then did he move on. By the time he reached his
table he had all but forgotten her—but not entirely. Although she was very young, Sten was not made of ice.
He was flattered. His steps were just a bit lighter as he
walked.

Cind watched him go. As far as she was concerned the
meeting had gone perfectly. She was so pleased that she
wanted to hug herself. She thought that close up, Sten
was even more handsome. Mission accomplished. Invitation made. Invitation accepted.

Now it was up to her to make sure Sten had the time.

Sten tossed in his sleep, the thin covering knotted
around his legs. He was back on Vulcan, a seventeen-year-
old Delinq hiding from Baron Thoresen's Sociopatrolmen.
Sten had taken refuge with Oron, the brainburned king
of the Delinqs. He was weary from running so long and
hard. Sten felt a slender body slide onto the soft mattress. It was Bet. Seventeen, as well. Naked and lovely.
Eager for him. Lovely. So lovely.

He gasped out of the depths of the dream and found
a willing, wriggling form in his arms. What the clot?
Gently he pried the lady away. It certainly wasn't Bet!
But she *was* lovely. The young lady moaned and grabbed
for him again. For a moment, Sten almost went for it.
He was still so far gone into the dream—which had
proved to be very real—that he had almost no resistance.

Then he thought: who was this woman, anyway?

Mmmm. More kissing and stuff. Then he remembered the sincere young lady in the receiving line. What was her . . . Cind. Ooohh boy! Careful, Admiral. This is not a lady one screwed and forgot. Once bedded, she would be his responsibility. Mmmmm. More stuff. More kissing. Yeah, but . . . But me no buts, you clot! This is serious business. How'd you like someone as nice as this on your conscience? Aww . . . Come on. What's a little . . .

Sten plucked Cind away again. She started to protest, but he gently covered her mouth with a hand. He tried to explain to her that this was definitely not a good idea. He was flattered and all, he said, and he was sure she was the most wonderful human-type female in the Empire, but he was in no position to start up any kind of a relationship. So, although he would regret this moment the rest of his life, would Cind please, please, get her clothes on and go?

It took awhile. But Cind did as she was told. When she was gone, Sten punched the drakh out of his pillow. He did not sleep again that night. For once, it had nothing to do with nightmares of a blown mission.

As for Cind, she was hurt, to be sure. She was also more in love than ever. By thinking so much of her that he was willing to forget her attentions, Sten was promoted from hero to godhood.

Cind consoled herself. There would be another time, with a far different result.

S'be't!

Kilgour was not present at the meeting, but he had arranged the entire thing. Otho was primed and almost sober.

The Bhor chieftain had asked Sten to go for a walk with him beside the little lake in a glen not far from his headquarters. It was no accident that the lake he chose was a memorial to the Bhor casualties suffered during the Jann war.

As they strolled around it, Otho pretended to seek Sten's advice on his plans for the Lupus Cluster. It was also no accident that all those plans assumed a future laden with a plenitude of AM2. Otho laid it on thick, just as Alex had coached him to. It was his own idea to mention also—in unsparing detail—the hardships the people of the Wolf Worlds had suffered during the reign of "those privy council clots." Not only had extreme deprivation been caused by the shortages of AM2— which Otho assumed was intentional on the part of the council—but all business involving the mining and export of Imperium X had also ceased. He also did not exaggerate when he said he saw a time, a year or so away but no more, when the Lupus Cluster would cease to exist as an entity. One planetary system at a time would be lost, until all were as alone as they had been in the primitive days, when no being had known for certain that other living things existed beyond the upper atmosphere.

Sten listened and not just politely. All that Otho said was true. Although what he could do about it, he didn't know. At least he could listen. As they strolled around the small lake, he began to notice that its surface shimmered like no other he had seen before. He realized it was because the bottom consisted of an immense black slab, polished to mirror-brightness. There were little imperfections pocking the slab. At first he could not make them out. He thought it might be algae. Then he realized that they were names, the names of the Bhor dead, honored there by their brothers and sisters, mothers and fathers, lovers, and friends.

He found himself near tears when he understood the meaning of the lake. Otho pretended not to notice.

"I must speak to you frankly, my friend," the Bhor chieftain said. Without waiting for a response, he went on. "It is no secret that you are suffering. To tell you it is only the affliction of an old soldier will not help. This I understand. To say it is no more than the swollen joints a farmer earns from long years behind a plow is equally as useless.

"Another foolish comparison. This one involves a confession. You understand that not *all* Bhor choose the, ahem, Way of a Warrior."

Sten raised an eyebrow but kept his thoughts to himself.

"I had an uncle—who was a tailor. Do not laugh! By my father's frozen buttocks, there has never been a living thing who loved to work with cloth like this uncle I am speaking to you about. Many years passed. Pleasurable and rewarding years. And then his hands began to ache. His knuckles grew great knots. So thick and painful he could barely manipulate them. You understand what a tragedy this was to my uncle?"

Sten nodded. He did.

"Did he give up? Did he cease the toil that gave him so much pleasure? Or did he damn the eyes of the streggan ghost that afflicted him and drink until he could feel no more pain? And then—and only then—continue his work?"

Sten said he assumed the latter. He believed stregg, named for the ancient nemesis of the Bhor, to be a powerful reliever of pain.

"Then you would be wrong!" Otho bellowed. "He did not. He gave up. He died a bitter and broken being. And this is the shame of my family, which I swear to you I have told no other. Except, perhaps, when I was drunk. But, I swear, I have never revealed it sober. Never!"

Sten was beginning to feel a little stupid. His friends were treating him as if he were some helpless child. Well, perhaps they were right. Maybe he did need a swift, hard kick. Poor Otho was trying so hard.

"What is it you want?" Otho shot at him.

"What?"

"What do you want? These . . . things, who rule in the place of the Emperor. You owe them a debt. Are they not your enemy? Do they not deserve your hate? Why do you treat them so shabbily? Make them happy. Kill them!''

''I tried,'' Sten said weakly.

''So try again. Don't be my uncle with the cloth.''

Sten wanted to say that killing them would satisfy nothing. At least not in himself. But he didn't know how to explain it to his rude, rough friend.

''You want more than death? Is that it?'' his rude, rough friend asked.

Sten thought about it. The deeper his thoughts swam, the angrier he became.

''They are assassins,'' he hissed. ''Worse than that. When they killed the Emperor, they might as well have killed us all. Soon we'll all be living like animals. Sitting in front of caves. Knocking rocks together to get a bit of fire.''

''Good. You are mad,'' Otho boomed. ''Now think about how to get even.''

''Getting even isn't what I want,'' Sten said.

''By my mother's beard. We're back to that again. What do you want? Say it. Then we'll board my ships and see all their souls burning in hell.''

''I want . . . justice,'' Sten finally said. ''Dammit. I want every being in the Empire to know the council's crime. Their hands are bloody. Justice, dammit. Justice!''

''I don't believe in justice, myself,'' Otho said gently. ''No true Bhor does. It is a fairy story created by other, weaker species who look for higher truths because their own lot is so miserable.

''But I am a tolerant being. If justice is your meat, load up my plate, my friend. We both shall eat.

''Now. Decide. What form do you wish this justice to take? And by my father's frozen buttocks, if you retreat to that pool of emotional muck again, I shall personally remove your limbs. One by one.''

Sten didn't need that kind of coaxing. It suddenly came to him exactly what kind of justice would do.

"Load the ships, my friend," Sten said.

Otho bellowed with delight. "By my mother's great, gnarly beard, there's a Blessing upon us. We'll drink all their souls to hell!"

CHAPTER FIFTEEN

THE COMPUTER WAS a bureaucrat's dream. As a pure storage center, it had few equals on the civilian market. But the key to its beauty was its method of retrieval.

The R&D team leader had come to Kyes with the design proposal ten years before. Kyes had spent four months with the group, firing every thinkable objection and whole flurries of "supposes" to test the theoretical limits. He had not found one hole that could not be plugged with a few symbols added to the design equation.

He had ordered the project launched. It was so costly that in another era Kyes would have automatically sought financial partners to spread the risk. Certainly he had briefly toyed with the idea. But the computer—if it could be brought on-line—would reap such enormous profits that he had dismissed the thought.

More important than the profits was the potential influence.

The computer was a one-of-a-kind device, with patents so basic that no other corporate being could even contemplate a copy without risking loss of fortune, family, reputation, and well-being to Kyes's battalions of attorneys. From the moment it was first proposed, he knew it would replace every system used by every government in the Empire. And the terms of its sale would be set by him and him alone.

Once installed, his influence would grow as quickly as the newly created wealth. After all, only one firm—his—

would be permitted to perform maintenance and periodic upgrading. In short, mess with Kyes and your bureaucracy would collapse. The state itself would quickly follow.

Almost every action of any social being created a record. The first problem was what to do with that record so that others could view it. If there was only one, no problem. It could be put under a rock, the spot marked, and someone with directions could retrieve it at his leisure. But records bred more quickly than cockroaches. Hunter-gatherers rapidly ran out of space on cave walls; scribes filled libraries with parchment; clerks jammed filing cabinets until the drawers warped; and even at the height of the Empire, it was possible for data to swamp the biggest computers.

But that was no longer so severe a problem. More banks or linkups could always be added. Modern systems had gone so far beyond light optics that speed was also no encumbrance.

There was one threshold, however, that no one had ever broken through: How to find one small byte of information hidden in such a great mass. The great library of legend at Alexandria reputedly employed several hundred clerks to search the shelves for the scrolls their scholarly clients requested. Days and weeks might pass before a certain scroll was located. That did not please the scholars, who were usually visiting on a beggar's budget. Their many bitter complaints survived the fire that destroyed the library. And that was in the long time past, when there was not much to know.

In Sten's time, the problem had grown to proportions that would stagger a theoretical mathematician contemplating the navel of the Universe.

Consider this small example: A much-maligned commissary sergeant has been ordered to improve the fare at the enlisted being's club. Morale is sadly sagging to the point that the commander herself is under the scrutiny of *her* superiors. Suggestions are made—many, many suggestions—that *will* be carried out. One of the suggestions concerns narcobeer. But not any old narcobeer. The commander recalls one brand—whose name she disremembers—that she shared with the troops on some long-forgotten battleground a century or more ago.

That is the only hint. Nothing more.

The commissary sergeant swings into action. Fires up his trusty computer. And the computer is asked to find that clottin' beer. The list he receives will almost certainly include the brand favored by his commander. But it just as certainly will be buried in a million or more possibilities, with no means of narrowing the search—short of ordering every one and spending several lifetimes letting the commander taste-test each one. Although enjoyable, this solution has obvious flaws.

With Kyes's computer it would be no trouble at all. Because it had been designed to understand that living minds had definite limits. The computer worked in twisted paths and big and little leaps of logic. Any simple explanation of this computer would be in serious error.

However, it was basically taught to think of itself as a chess master, engaged in a game with a talented inferior. The chess master knows she can conceive of many moves, with any number of combinations, well ahead of her opponent. But, in a single game, the amateur is quite likely to win. His limited ability may become a plus under such circumstances. The chess master might as well roll dice, trying to figure out which stupid ploy the dimwit has in mind.

Kyes's brainchild would summon the commander—or at least call up the commander's records. A series of questions would be asked: a short biography, a few details of that long-ago drinking session, for example, and certainly a medical examination to determine the reaction of the being's tastebuds. Voila! The narcobeer would be located and morale boosted. The sergeant and commander would return to good graces. Happy ending through better electronic living.

When Kyes introduced Sr. Lagguth, the chief of the AM2 commission, to his baby, the being instantly fell in love. With such a machine, he could track the path of an errant electron on a flight through a star storm.

The next bit of information, however, made him fall just as quickly out of love.

"Forget the AM2," Kyes said. "It's not important."

Lagguth stuttered that that was the task set for him by the privy council—that the whole future of the Empire rested on locating the Eternal Emperor's golden AM2 fleece. Even when the raid on the Honjo was completed, the resulting AM2 bonus would only stave off the inevitable for another seven months at most—not counting the terrible cost in fuel the Empire was expending to finish the theft.

"Haven't you learned your lesson, yet?" Kyes said. "The Emperor's secret died with him. We're never going to find it. At least, not the way we've been going about it."

Then he told Lagguth what he had mind.

Sr. Lagguth violently protested. He did not say he thought Kyes was mad—although that certainly might have been hinted at. But he did say he would immediately have to report the matter to the rest of the council, and he would have to get their permission to abandon his search and to take up the new one.

Kyes did not explode, or threaten, or call the being all kinds of a fool. Instead, he rang for a clerk, and in a moment or two she appeared, wheeling in a great stack of readouts on a cart. The readouts were copies of the report Lagguth had delivered not too long before to the privy council, the one in which he said that the AM2 would be located within thirteen months.

Kyes strolled about the room while Lagguth stared at the report, considering his many sins.

"Would you like to change your conclusions in that report?" Kyes asked finally.

Lagguth remained silent.

"I had a team of my own people go over it. They found it . . . interesting," Kyes added.

Lagguth's mouth gaped—he wanted to speak—then snapped shut again. What could he say? Every page of the report was fiction. He might as well have said two months, or six months, or—never.

"Shall we try it my way?" Kyes purred.

The logic was impeccable. Sr. Lagguth was convinced.

The old woman was a delight. She wore her gray hair long and tumbling down to her waist. It glowed with health. She had a high-pitched giggle that charmed Kyes, especially since she let it ring out at his weakest jests. Even then, there was no falseness in it. Despite her age, which the investigators estimated at 155, her figure was good and she filled her orange robes in a pleasing manner. From what he knew about such things—if he had been human, Kyes assumed he would have found her still attractive. Her name was Zoran. She was the elected leader of the Cult Of Eternal Emperor, insofar as they had real leadership.

Zoran and her group had been shadowed by his investigators for some time. They were a puzzling lot. Most of them lived ordinary lives and were employed at ordinary jobs. During that time they dressed and mostly behaved like everyone else. The only main difference was their attitude. They were absolutely cheerful beings. There seemed to be no setbacks or disappointments that disturbed them. His chief detective swore that if the immediate demise of Prime World were announced, they would giggle wildly and then go on about their duties. They would probably only add a "Last chance for the word" when they donned their robes, kicked off their shoes, and wandered the streets preaching their peculiar beliefs.

Zoran explained away some of the misconceptions about their thinking to Kyes, giggling all the while.

"Oh, we *certainly* don't think of the Eternal Emperor as a god." Giggle. "Or, at least a god, per se." More giggling. "He's more like an emissary—you know—" giggle—"a representative of the Holy Spheres."

Kyes wanted to know what a Holy Sphere might be.

"Very good question," she said. "They're, well, round, I suppose. (giggle) And holy. (Thirty seconds of sustained giggling) Actually, it's just concept. One you accept, or don't. If you accept it—you can see it. In your mind. But, if you don't (massive giggling) . . . well, of course you won't see it at all."

Kyes laughed himself—the first real laughter from him in ages. "I suppose I'm one of the blind," he said.

"Oh, no. Not at all. At least, not completely," Zoran said. "Otherwise I wouldn't be here talking to you."

Kyes puzzled at that. How could she be so trusting? His motives were far from pure. In a mad moment—the giggling got to a being after a while—he almost confessed this. But he didn't.

"Of course, there might be some who would say that you were thinking of using us," the old woman said. This time, when the giggle came, Kyes jumped. "But how could you? All I have is this poor vessel." She dramatically drew her hands down her robes, outlining her body. "And it is filled with the joy of the Holy Spheres. (small giggle) Use us if you wish. (bigger giggle) There's more than enough joy for everyone."

"But wouldn't the joy be even greater," Kyes answered, trying to avoid being *too* smooth, "if more beings believed as you?"

That time, there was no giggle from Zoran. She studied him, her eyes sharp and clear. Kyes could feel himself being measured.

"You were correct in your assumption that my feelings are not far apart from yours," he continued. "I know nothing about Holy Spheres. Or gods. Or godly representatives. But I do believe one thing. Very firmly. And that is the Eternal Emperor is still with us."

Zoran was silent. Then, she said quickly, "Why is it necessary for you to believe this?"

Kyes did not answer—at least not directly. He was starting to come up to speed with the woman.

"You've stopped laughing," was all he said.

"What do you have in mind to help others hear our thoughts?" the old woman asked. "Money?" Kyes said there would be money for her order. "Temporal support?" Kyes said that as a member of the privy council, his support could hardly be thought of as anything else.

"What do you want in return, then?" she asked.

"Only what you would give me, even without my support, " Kyes said. "I want information. I'd like to be notified when any of your members—no matter where they reside in the Empire—report a sighting of the Emperor."

"You're right," Zoran said. "None of us would withhold that kind of information. It's what we're trying to convince others of, isn't it?"

It wasn't necessary for Kyes to answer.

"You'll be deluged," she said after a while. "Our religion—if it can be called that—tends to attract many individuals with, shall we say, frantic minds."

"I'm aware of that," Kyes said.

Zoran stared at him for a long time. Then she let loose with one of her wild, ringing giggles.

The bargain was set.

Kyes continued to extend his net across the dark waters. As he did so, he could not help but keep peering into the murk hoping to catch sight of the great, silver shadow of the Eternal Emperor lurking in the depths. The exercise was pointless and agonizing. He was very much like a starving being who had bought a lottery ticket. The hope the action generated seemed harmless enough. At least there was something to dream about for a while. But the hope was just a thin coating on a tragic pill.

But Kyes was an old master of self-control. He recognized the glooming for what it was and continued apace. As his colleagues scrambled frantically about with their bloodletting at home and in the Honjo worlds, he put all of his marks into secret play.

How there was only one mark left, one key being to suborn. Potentially, the most difficult and dangerous of all: Colonel Poyndex, the chief of Mercury Corps. But when he finally determined what the cost would be, Kyes did not hesitate for a moment.

The colonel was as chilling in person as he had been on the screen when the assassination plot had been announced. Poyndex listened intently to every word Kyes had to say. He never blinked or smiled or even shifted in his seat once he had settled.

Kyes carefully skated around his own beliefs and merely restated the logic. The Emperor had reportedly disappeared—he didn't say "died"—before. And he had always returned. Also, the supply of AM2 always followed the same course: diminished during the alleged absence, plentiful when he came back. That part could be charted—and had been by Lagguth's staff and Kyes's computer. The great historical shifts in the AM2 supply appeared to match the times when rumor and myth held that the Emperor was gone.

Finally, Kyes was done. He eased back in his seat, keeping his own expression as blank as the spy master's.

"I wondered why you met with that Zoran woman," Poyndex said. "Now it makes sense. It didn't when my operatives first reported it."

Kyes clawed back his instinct to gape, to be shocked that Poyndex apparently routinely shadowed any member of the ruling council. He had been advised that such comments were one of the colonel's favorite ploys—to win the upper hand with a seemingly casual verbal blow.

"I thought you might be puzzled," Kyes shot back. "That's why I thought we should talk."

He was hinting that the shadowers had shadows of their

own, operating at his behest. It was a lie, but a good one. Poyndex allowed an appreciative nod.

"Regretfully . . ." Poyndex deliberately let this trail. "I don't see how I can help. My department's resources . . ." Again, a deliberate trailing off to indicate lack of same. "Also, I fear I would be exceeding my authority."

It was not necessary for Poyndex to detail his agency's awesome responsibilities and the additional burdens it now bore as a result of such things as the disaster in predicting the Honjo as a relatively soft target.

Lovett would have bottom-lined Poyndex's statement immediately. The deal—if there was to be one—would begin with increased resources and more authority. Kyes was no slower. He had come prepared to make one offer and one alone. He believed the price was set so high, that no one—especially a spy master—could resist.

"My colleagues and I have been considering a matter for some time," Kyes said. "All of us are concerned that certain views—important views—never come to our attention. In short, we feel a lack of depth on the privy council."

Poyndex raised an eyebrow. The first show of emotion! Especially since the spy master had no idea where Kyes was going. He saw the eyebrow forced into place—a bit irritably, like a cat angrily coaxing back an unruly tuft of fur. Kyes was pleased. Poyndex could be handled. No trouble at all.

"What would you say," Kyes said, "if I proposed that you join us? As the sixth member of the privy council?"

Kyes was absolutely delighted when the spy master gaped like a freshly landed fish!

CHAPTER SIXTEEN

SR. ECU HOVERED at the edge of the lake. The sun was warm, and the rising moist air from the Bhor memorial allowed him to float without effort: a tic of a winglet for steadiness; a flick of the tip of the three-meter tail to keep his eyes on the small being walking toward him across the grass.

In most other circumstances, the Manabi would be enjoying this moment. The warm air and sun were pleasurable, the setting perfect. He appreciated—as only the Manabi could—the contrast of his dark body, with its red-tipped wings and pure white sensing whiskers, against the mirroring lake with its small, rocky beach, and the deep blue-green of the healthy lawn.

He had reluctantly agreed to the meeting. To him, further involvement with any of the surviving conspirators was not only pointless—witness Fleet Marshal Mahoney's dismal failure—but extremely dangerous. Ignoring the invitation, however, might create equal, or greater, peril.

One stray word from the conspirators—deliberate, or otherwise—would implicate the Manabi no matter how tentative their previous role. It took no imagination to know what form the privy council's reaction would take. Imagination was one thing the Manabi were more than blessed—or cursed—with.

Sten did his best to appear casual as he approached. He wanted no hint of self-doubt, although he had a clot of a lot of it. He had already invested a week of preliminary discussions with Sr. Ecu. Diplomacy was a maddening art. Still, he threw everything he had been taught and learned into the effort. There were the circlings to begin with, as each being measured, tested, and got to know the other. Then there was a host of initial discussions—never once hitting, or even coming near, the point.

It did not help his confidence to know he was dealing with the most skilled diplomat from a race of ethereal beings who were individual experts before they had left their childhood behind along with their milk sting.

He had consulted heavily with Kilgour and Mahoney well before Sr. Ecu's arrival. Even now, his two friends were ablaze with the effort of launching the main body of his plan. Weapons, ammunition, fuel, and supplies were being gathered. The Bhor were already rehearsing, and Otho's patience was wearing thin. When Sten had said "load the ships," he was being symbolic. By the time he explained that to the literal-minded Bhor chieftain, Otho was ready to blast off with a ragged crew aboard an iffy warship. Suicide was *not* painless, Sten kept telling Otho. Eventually, he made his point.

Sten was vastly relieved when he and Kilgour had finally reached Mahoney. After seventy-five years as chief of Mercury Corps, Ian had found little difficulty in staying many steps ahead of his pursuers.

Mahoney had just kept moving. He would go to ground for a few days in a well-chosen hidey-hole, then pop up to see what was going on about him, moving on again before suspicions were aroused. By the time Sten and Alex had contacted him through Jon Wild, their old smuggler friend, he had already hidden in a dozen wildly disparate spots, using an equal number of identities. The faster and more often one moved, Ian always said, the less perfection was required when it came to forged paperwork. The role was the thing, he said. The whole thing. That, and being able to think on one's feet and shed the role like old, itchy skin.

Sten's former commander had instantly seen the value

in his plan, and they had put it into motion. The key was the Manabi and their spotless reputations for honesty. Without their agreement, the plan had far less of a chance. However, considering his recent, explosive failure, Mahoney urged Sten to take point in the discussions. He would come in later, if needed. Sten agreed. But he was far from sure. One thing was certain, however: whatever the outcome, Sten was determined to proceed. Still, he wanted Sr. Ecu. He wanted him bad.

Today was the day. It was all or nothing. His goal was simple and did not require total victory. He only had to drive in a big enough wedge to get a glimpse of sunlight.

Sten could only see one way to go about his task. He had to hard-ass the Manabi. But first, as his father used to say, he had to get Sr. Ecu's attention. In this case, however, his father's suggested club would not do.

He waved a greeting when he was a few meters away, then knelt on the grass. He placed a small black cube on the ground, gently pinched the sides, and stepped back. The cube began to unfold. As it did so, Sten sensed a slight flutter in the air and Sr. Ecu floated closer. He could also sense the being's curiosity. Sten did not turn. Instead, he kept his rapt attention on the unfolding cube. It was show time, folks.

The cube became a base for a little holographic display: a moving, almost-living art form that Sten had wiled away the time with most of his life. The one he had picked as a gift for the Manabi diplomat was not all that elaborate. Sten had built replicas of entire ancient mills and factories and towns, all with active workers and residents going about their programmed daily lives. This hologram was an off-the-shelf kit that took him no more than six hours to complete. Of course, by now he was highly skilled at his hobby.

But it was not the difficulty of a display that necessarily attracted him. Sometimes it was just nice to look at, or it was oddly moving, or it had something to say. The gift for Sr. Ecu had a little of all of these.

The cube was gone, and in its place was a meadow converted into some sort of arena surrounded by makeshift wooden bleachers, which were filled with a cheering crowd of humans. Their costumes were early twentieth-century Earth, and if one listened extra closely, so were their comments. Hawkers moved in and out of the crowd, selling all kinds of odd foods and trinkets. Gangs of tiny wild boys ran about, getting into minor mischief. After all that sank in, the observer started looking at the strange little object in the center.

Suddenly the object shuddered and belched a miniburst of smoke. Followed by a sharp *kaaaklacka*. Sten could feel the Manabi move in even closer. Sensing whiskers brushed his shoulders as Sr. Ecu jockeyed for a better view. At the sound, the gangs of wild boys abandoned mischief and ran for the fence that enclosed the field.

Another *kaaaklacka*, and it became a bit more obvious. What they were both looking at was an ancient flying machine. Twin wings joined by struts. Stubby. A strong little propeller in front. A tiny pilot was in the cockpit. An equally small coveralled ground-crew member was turning the prop. He leapt away as the explosive sound came again. Except this time the prop kept turning, stuttering at first, with small pops of engine smoke—warranted by the model manufacturer to smell like castor oil. Then the engine sounds smoothed out, the crewman was kicking away the blocks at the wheels, and the little plane was moving down the field.

A sudden roar, and it surged forward. There was no way it had enough runway to clear the stadium. Sten could feel the tension in the winged being by his side. The pilot hauled his stick back, and the plane abruptly rose into the air. The crowd gasped. Sten thought he could hear something similar beside him.

Stick around, Sr. Ecu, he thought. You ain't seen nothin' yet.

The biplane pilot opened his act with a daredevil series of turns and flips and barrel rolls.

"That's not possible for such a machine," Sten heard Sr. Ecu whisper. He said nothing in return.

Then the plane went into a long dive—straight for the ground. The crowd shrieked in terror. Sr. Ecu, who knew all about gravity, could not help but flip a winglet in reaction. It jolted his body upward a few centimeters. Still the biplane came on and on. At the last instant, when Sr. Ecu could no longer stand the suspense, the pilot pulled away—almost brushing the ground and holographic disaster. The crowd shouted in relief, then rose for loud applause.

"Remarkable," Sten's companion muttered.

The pilot saluted his admirers with another long series of rolls and dives and turns. Then he steadied out, and the engine sound shifted. The plane arced gracefully through the sky. White smoke streamed out behind. Gradually, that trail of smoke made the pattern clear.

Skywriting!

"What's he saying?" Sr. Ecu had become Sten's emotional captive—at least through the end of the show. Again, Sten said nothing.

Finally, the pilot was done. The smoke lettering hung over the field like a high-flying banner. And this is what it said:

Anyone Can Fly
At. . . . . .
THE AIR CIRCUS

Sten stepped quickly forward and pinched the sides of the display; it became a small black cube again. He picked it up and offered it to Sr. Ecu. "What do you think?"

"Did they really do that?" Sr. Ecu asked. He did not wait for the answer. It was obvious. "You know, I've never really appreciated before what it was like to be permanently grounded by an accident of genes. My God, how desperately they wanted to fly."

"Beings will risk a great deal," Sten said, "for a little freedom."

There was a long silence from the Manabi. A flip of a wing took Sr. Ecu into a long, slow glide over the lake. Sten knew he was pondering the names on the slate bottom, the names of the permanently grounded Bhor. Another flip, and he came gliding back.

"Where did you get it?" the Manabi asked.

"I made it," Sten said. "Just a kit, really. But it was fun."

"When?"

"Last night."

"Then you really did make it for me." It was a statement of realization, not a question.

"Yes."

The Manabi remained quiet still.

"Ah . . ." he said at last. "Now we begin . . . A very good opening, Admiral."

"Thanks. And you're right. Now, we begin. But first, I have a little preamble. I had it all worked out in the best diplomatic form I could imagine, and then I thought, to hell with it! I should just speak my mind. Say how it is."

"Go on."

"There's a lot of doublethink between us. After a week I'm still trying to figure out how to put my case to you. And you're still trying to figure the best way to say no and be done with me. In other words, we're both grounded. Neither of us can get any forward motion, much less clear the stadium."

"Fairly accurate."

"The thing is," Sten said, "you're more earthbound than I."

The Manabi stirred, surprised.

Sten filled in a few more blanks. "You see, from my point of view, you're still stuck with a previous action. One you now think was not that wise. Trouble being, you can't take it back. Not completely. You have to wonder if we have blackmail in mind. Are we going to hold the club of betrayal over you to force your continued support?''

"Well? Are you?"

Sten let Sr. Ecu's anxious question hang for a while.

"No. We're not," he said finally, firmly—a promise.

"You can speak for everyone?"

"Yes."

"Why are you being so . . . magnanimous? Or is it temporary?"

"If we fail, everyone is in the same drakh. That includes the supporters of the privy council. When this is over, if there are any pieces to pick up it might make me rest easier in my grave to think a few Manabi might be about to help. And, no. The decision isn't temporary. For the same reason.

"But my real reason is loyalty. You once left your neutral corner to support the Emperor. This is why you even spoke to Mahoney when he came to you. Out of that same loyalty. Actually, logic is a better word for it just now. The same logic that once brought you to the Emperor's side—meaning prog zero for any kind of future without him—allowed you to be swayed by Ian. Isn't that so?''

"Again . . . yes."

"Now you've seen Mahoney's plan fail. Dismally. Meanwhile, all over the Empire beings are being rounded up for the brainscan—and then the slaughterhouse. No wonder you're shy of us. I would be, too."

"You make a better argument for my case than yours," Sr. Ecu said. "In my sphere, this means there's a great deal more to come."

"You got it," Sten said. "To begin with, what happened was my fault. Not Mahoney's. He was in command—but I was there, in person, and I sure as clot didn't pull out in time. I crashed that plane, not Mahoney."

"Admirable that you should shoulder the blame, but it only underscores my uncertainty—in even meeting with you. Do you have some—what is the phrase your kind favors—ace up your sleeve?''

"Maybe. Maybe not. Right now, what I *do* have is your attention. Let me tell you what is going to happen next. If you return to your fence sitting.

"We'll ignore it. But will the privy council? How long before their paranoia reaches out to the Manabi? Failing that, as this AM2 situation gets worse, they're going to be looking for repeated opportunities. The Honjo are only the first. There'll be others.

"How much AM2 does your cluster have in its storehouses? Enough to tempt them?''

It was not necessary for Sr. Ecu to answer. They both knew the Manabi had more than enough.

"And can you stop them? Do you have the means, much less the spirit? I'm not talking about bravery now. I'm speaking of pure meanness. Digging in like the Honjo. Willing to die for every square centimeter of turf. Can you do that? Are you willing?''

Again, there could be no answer but one. The Manabi were diplomats, not warriors.

"What do you propose?" Sr. Ecu asked. That did not mean he was going for it, only that he was willing to listen. But now that Sten had the Manabi going for the bait, he wanted to dangle it awhile. No way would he let this big flying fish off the hook.

"I only want you to watch and wait," Sten said. "I have something I need to accomplish. To show you *we* have the will and means. In return . . .''

"Yes." Real abrupt. Sr. Ecu was going for it.

"In return . . . I want the opportunity to speak with you again. Or Mahoney, if that's how it ends up working best. Probably I'll be busy. So Ian it will be. If you agree. Will you at least do that?''

How could Sr. Ecu reject him? He did not. Instead he asked to see his gift again. He wanted to visit the air circus—where anyone could fly.

* * *

It worked out exactly as Sten had predicted. No sooner had Sr. Ecu returned home than he found a request for him to meet with a member of the privy council. Actually, it was no request at all. It was a summons.

The council members had discussed at length how to handle the Manabi. They as yet had no suspicion of them. But their purge, and especially the long, drawn-out invasion of Honjo sovereign territory, had produced howls all over the Empire. They badly needed to keep things glued together, at least for a while. To do that they needed the support of the Manabi. Badly.

There was some discussion of whom to send. Malperin was mostly favored, because she had the best diplomatic skills, at least as far as a businessbeing could go. But even she saw drawbacks in that. If Sr. Ecu sensed the slightest opening, they were lost, she said. They had to act from strength. What they needed was a master of the bottom line.

They sent Lovett.

That meant there was no foreplay.

Lovett deliberately chose a small, shabby park for the meeting. There was little room for the graceful Manabi to maneuver, and he had barely cleared the fence when dirt and dust particles began clogging his delicate sensing whiskers. Lovett waited just long enough for Sr. Ecu to get really uncomfortable. The healthy black sheen of the Manabi's body turned to gray. The lovely red tinge shaded to a sickly orange. Then he let him have it.

"We want a statement from you," he said. "I've got a copy of what we have in mind with me. Okay it now. You can read it later. At your leisure."

"How very thoughtful of you," Sr. Ecu said. "But first, perhaps I should know what exactly we're to agree to say. The topic . . . would be especially enlightening."

"It's about the assassination business," Lovett snapped. "You know . . . you say you deplore it—etcetera, etcetera."

"We certainly do deplore it," Sr. Ecu agreed. "It's the etcetera I'm worried about."

"Oh . . . no big thing. It lists those responsible. Calls for their punishment. That sort of thing. Oh . . . and yeah. The Honjo. We figure any right-thinking being will back us on liberating all that AM2. Can't let wild types like that have all that fuel. Do what they please. When they please.

"I mean . . . it's legal as drakh. Our actions, that is. We license the AM2. Therefore we have the right to see that it's used properly."

"I see," the Manabi said. And he certainly meant it.

"So that spells it out. Got a problem with any of it?" Lovett spoke as belligerently as possible. He wanted there to be no mistake about what would happen if Sr. Ecu did object. So he continued just a touch longer. "See, if you do, we've all got problems. My friends on the council have to be sure whose side everyone is on. Times are tough. Tough actions are required. You're either with us— or the Honjo. Okay?"

Sr. Ecu did not think it was okay. However, there was no way he was fool enough to say so. Instead, he explained that he had rushed to the meeting so quickly that he had failed to get any kind of blanket approval from his own government. This was a terrible oversight on his part, he apologized. But it was a necessary formality. Otherwise, he could not legally speak for all the Manabi. And was this not what Lovett wanted?

"No. I want it settled. I want no loopholes some sneaky legal types can slip through later. Okay. Get whatever approval you need. Make it good. Make it soon. Do I make myself clear?"

Sr. Ecu said that Lovett spoke with impeccable clarity.

The privy council's ultimatum put Mahoney in what Kilgour called the catbird's seat. Ian only vaguely understood what a catbird might be, but he hadn't the foggiest what kind of a seat the being might prefer. Something lofty, he assumed. Mahoney knew he had assumed correctly when he was spared the long dance Sten had suffered through in the initial negotiations with the Manabi.

Sr. Ecu got directly to the point. Without preamble, he described the spot between the rock and the hard surface in which Lovett had placed him. Both options were intolerable.

Ian didn't say "We told you so." Nor did he waste Sr. Ecu's time by making appropriate soothing noises. Instead, he was as direct as the Manabi. He sketched out Sten's main plan.

What the young admiral had in mind, he said, was a murder trial. The trial would be conducted by an independent tribunal, composed of the most prestigious beings in the Empire. The previous loyalty of each representative had to be beyond question. To ensure that the proceedings were impeccable, Sten proposed that Sr. Ecu act as a neutral referee. He alone would be granted the authority to see that all evidence and testimony were handled with complete fairness.

During the tribunal's proceedings, Sten and Mahoney would do their absolute best to guarantee the security and safety of each member.

"How possible can that be?" Sr. Ecu asked.

"It isn't—totally. That's why I said we'd do our best. No more."

"Quite understandable," Sr. Ecu said. "And fair."

Mahoney was not surprised at the answer. It was a far better pledge than any offered by the privy council. He went on to say that he and Sten would make sure that every moment of the trial would be broadcast as widely as possible. It was Sten's intent that every being—no matter how distant or lowly—would have the opportunity to learn the impartial details of the proceedings. He did not have to point out that the privy council would also do everything possible to prevent such publicity.

"Will you invite them to defend themselves?" Sr. Ecu asked.

"Of course."

"They will refuse."

"So?"

Sr. Ecu mused a moment. "So, indeed."

It was not necessary to explain that if the tribunal came in with a guilty verdict, it did not mean that the members of the privy council would meekly turn themselves in to their jailers. It was moral weight Sten was after, enough to tip the balance. Handled correctly, the decision would punch so many holes in the privy council's power bucket that all their allies would leak away. What else did they have to offer, besides AM2? And that they had found impossible to deliver.

"Who will choose the members?" Sr. Ecu asked next.

Mahoney said that only a Manabi could be trusted enough to do such a thing. The same went for the mechanics of meeting with potential appointees. Sr. Ecu would have to launch a supersecret effort, shuttling from one system to another, all the while making sure that no tracks of any kind were left behind. He was to have complete freedom in this, not only for reasons of trust and secrecy, but for practical ones, as well. Without the Eternal Emperor, who else had those kinds of skills?

Sr. Ecu had some thoughts of his own about the Emperor, but he did not share them with Mahoney. He would have been surprised that Ian's thoughts ran along similar lines. And Mahoney would have been equally surprised that the being's thinking added a great deal of weight to his decision.

As the Manabi was drifting toward agreement, Mahoney flashthought about the second part of Sten's plan. He had revealed not one detail of the reasons for Sten's absence. It was not lack of trust that kept him silent, but the old inviolate Mercury Corps rule of "Need to Know." Besides, if he had told about the mission, he was not sure which way Sr. Ecu would decide. If Sten failed this time, all bets were off. The independent tribunal would be an empty exercise.

"One final question," Sr. Ecu said. "What is the legal basis for this tribunal? What's the point, if we do not have the force of law?"

"There'd be none," Mahoney said. "Sten thought you'd ask that, however. And he said to tell you he hadn't a clot of an idea. We don't exactly have regiments of Imperial legal scholars at our command."

"No, you don't," Sr. Ecu said. "My problem is that I can't imagine a circumstance where the Emperor would have ever allowed such a thing. He wouldn't have permitted anybody that kind of power. Not over him. And the problem we have now is that the council is acting in his name. With the same precedents and force of law."

"Oh, I don't know about that," Mahoney said. "As old as this empire is, something like this must have occurred at least once."

"I think you are right," Sr. Ecu said. "And once is all we need . . . Very well. I'll do it."

Fleet Marshal Ian Mahoney was very relieved. He and the Manabi hammered out a few more details, and then it was time to go. Sr. Ecu had one parting comment that Mahoney puzzled over for some time.

"Oh . . . yes . . . I have a message for our young admiral," Sr. Ecu said.

"Yes?"

"Tell him whatever the mission he's on now—if it should fail . . ."

"Yes?" There was a bit more tension in Mahoney's voice.

"Tell him I still expect to meet with him again. No matter the outcome. And I only hope it's someplace where *all* beings can fly."

"He'll understand this?" Mahoney asked.

"Oh, yes . . . he'll understand."

CHAPTER SEVENTEEN

THE MAN WHO called himself Raschid looked at the sign: EXPERIENCED COOK WANTED. LONG HOURS, LOW PAY, FEW BENEFITS, HARD WORK, FREE FOOD. The man smiled slightly. It was honest, at the very least.

Above the ramshackle building a sign blinked in several colors, all of which hurt the eye: LAST BLAST TEAROOM AND DINER. Below that: PROP.: DINGISWAYO PATTIPONG.

A knot of three very primed sailors lurched out of the barroom next door and down the cracked plas sidewalk. Raschid smiled politely and stepped out of their way. One of the sailors looked regretful but passed on.

Again, Raschid smiled, his smile broadening as he heard the Yukawa-whine of a ship lifting off from the field just beyond a blastfence. The produce-sled driver had been correct—the spaceport was full of ships that had not lifted for some time and would likely never lift again. But there was traffic.

Raschid entered the diner.

The man who greeted him was very small and very dark. There were about ten tables and a counter in the diner. The small man was the only other person inside.

"Sr. Pattipong?"

"You police?"

"No. I want a job."

"You cook?"

"Yes."

"No. Not cook. Maybe cook where people not use knife if order wrong. Too pretty be cook down here."

Raschid did not answer.

"Where you cook last?"

Raschid muttered something inaudible.

Pattipong nodded once. "Maybe you cook. Cook never say where last. Too many wives . . . alks . . . children . . . police. Come. We see."

Pattipong led Raschid through the door into the kitchen, watching his expression closely. Pattipong nodded when that gawp of surprise came.

"Yes. Not good. I build station for gooood cook. Cnidarians. Stay two, almost three years. Then . . . go. Leave me with bathtub for cook station."

The cnidarians were intelligent aquatic corallike polyps that grew together as they matured . . . into mutual hatred. They . . . it must have been very, very good. Because Pattipong had specially built the kitchen. It was a now-drained tub, with all the necessary appliances and counters built circularly around it.

"Not good. Take gooood cook know how to use."

Raschid climbed into the pool.

"Couple eyes. Over easy," Pattipong ordered.

Raschid turned the heat on and put a pan on the fire. He brushed clarified butter from a nearby bowl on it, picked up—one-handed—two eggs from another bowl, and in a single motion cracked them both into the pan and disposed of the shells. Pattipong nodded involuntarily. Raschid chopped the heat down and waited as the eggs sizzled in the pan. Pattipong was watching his wrist closely. At just the right moment, Raschid flipped the eggs. They slid smoothly onto their blind sides.

Pattipong smiled. "You cook. No one else do that right."

"You want anything with your eggs?"

"No. Not want eggs. Hate eggs. Eggs make me . . ." Pattipong waved his hand across his buttocks. "Every-

body else like eggs. I serve eggs. You have job. You cook
now.''

Raschid looked around the rather filthy kitchen. "Cook
later. Lunch is an hour away. Clean now." Pattipong's
speech patterns seemed habit-forming.

Pattipong considered, then bobbed his head. "Clean
now. Cook later. I help."

And so began the Legend of the Eggs of Pattipong.

Pattipong described them on the menu as Imperial
Eggs Benedict. For some reason, the name bothered Raschid. He argued—mildly. Pattipong told him to get back
to the kitchen. "Imperial good name. Thailand . . . best
elephants Royal Elephants. Or so I hear."

It started from boredom. The lunch crowd had been
nearly nonexistent, and it was hours until dinner. Raschid wasn't sleepy enough to walk back to the tiny room
he rented for a nap, didn't feel like drinking, and had no
desire for a walk. It started with baking. Raschid felt
about baking, mostly at least, the same way Pattipong
did about eggs. It was too damned unpredictable, and he
never understood exactly what ingredients should be
changed to match the temperature, the humidity, the ba-
rometer, or whatever made his loaves look suddenly un-
leavened. But there were exceptions and this was one of
them.

He had made sourdough starter a week or so before—
warm water, equal amount of flour, a bit of sugar, and
yeast. Cover in a nonmetallic dish and leave until it
stinks.

He used that as a base for what were still called En-
glish muffins. They were equally easy to make. For about
eight muffins, he brought a cup of milk to a boil, then
took it off the stove and dumped in a little salt, a tea-
spoon of sugar, and two cupfuls of premixed biscuit flour.
After he beat it all up, he let it rise until double size;
then he beat in another cup of flour and let the dough
rise once more.

The open-ended cylinders were half filled with the dough. Raschid did not mention that the short cylinders had been pet food containers with both ends cut off. Even in this district, somebody might get squeamish.

He brushed butter on his medium-hot grill and put the cylinders down. Once the open end had browned for a few seconds, he flipped the cylinder, browned the other side, and lifted the cylinder away, burning fingers in the process.

He added more butter and let the muffins get nearly black before putting them on a rack to cool. For use—within no more than four hours—he would split them with a fork and toast them.

He next found the best smoked ham he—or rather Pattipong—could afford. It was thin-sliced and browned in a wine-butter-cumin mixture.

"Best, it should be Earth ham. From Virginia. Or Kerry."

Pattipong goggled. "I didn't know you had ever been to Earth!" Raschid looked perplexed. "I—haven't. I think."

Then it was Raschid's turn to goggle. "Dingiswayo—the way you just talked."

"Normally, you mean? I slipped. Normal too much trouble. Talk too much trouble. Like eggs. Just hot air. Besides . . . talk short, people think you not understand. They more careful in asking what they want. Not careful in saying what they think you not understand.

"And around here," Pattipong said, lapsing into a full speech pattern, "you need all the edge you can get."

That was true. The spaceport's traffic may have been light, but there were still stevedores, sailors, whores, and everyday villains looking for amusement—which was often defined as laying odds on how long it would take someone to bleed to death in a gutter. Pattipong kept a long, unsheathed knife hidden under the pay counter.

Raschid went back to his recipe. The browned ham was put in a warming oven. He had lemon juice, red pepper, a touch of salt, and three egg yolks waiting in a blender. He melted butter in a small pan. Then his mental timer went on. Muffins toasted . . . eggs went into boiling water to poach . . . the muffins were ready . . . ham went on top of the muffins . . . two and a half minutes exactly, and the eggs were plopped on top of the ham.

He flipped the blender on and poured molten butter into the mixture. After the count of twenty, he turned the blender off and poured the hollandaise sauce over the eggs.

"Voila, Sr. Pattipong."

Pattipong gingerly sampled.

"Not bad," he said grudgingly. "But eggs."

Raschid tried them on a customer, a sailor drunk enough to be experimental. The man sampled, looked surprised, and inhaled the plate, then ordered a second plate. He swore it sobered him up—now he was ready to start all over again.

"Like sobriety pill? Maybe great invention. Cure diseases. Sell through mail."

"Clot off," Raschid snorted.

The sailor came back the next day—with six friends.

The port police started dropping by around lunchtime. For some reason, Raschid felt uncomfortable—with no idea why. They ate, of course, on the cuff. Lunch was no longer slow.

Raschid came up with other dishes: something he called chili, and something he called "nuked hen." He convinced Pattipong that the customers wanted something more than the bland, airport/diner standard dishes Pattipong had previously featured on the menu.

"You talk. I listen. I do. Make curry. Curry like mother made. Customers try—I laugh. Get revenge for all yata-yata-yata talk all time."

Pattipong's curry may not have been quite that lethal—but it was nominated.

"Know why I listen to you?" Pattipong asked.

He waved an arm out of the serving window. Raschid looked out at the dining area. It was packed. Pattipong had even put tables and chairs out on the sidewalk. Raschid knew that they had been getting busier, but he really hadn't realized just how much. The crowd was different. There were still the bruisers and brawlers, but Raschid saw suits and some uniformed port authorities, as well. There were even two orange-robed members of the Cult of the Eternal Emperor. For some reason, they made him just as uncomfortable as the policemen did—also for equally unknown reasons.

"Last Blast now hot place to go. Walk wild side . . . eat good. It last for while. Then they find new place. Happen before. Happen again. Hard thing to remember. Not expand. Not drive old customers away.

"These people like . . . like insect that buzz . . . buzz . . . flower to flower. Then vanish."

"Butterflies?"

"Butter not fly, Raschid. Work. No more jokes."

Raschid went back to his stove. Another damned order for Imperial Damned Eggs. He was starting to share Pattipong's hatred for eggs.

Raschid was glad Pattipong was making money. But it meant nothing to him.

He felt . . . as if he were waiting. For someone? For something? He did not know.

Others noticed prosperity, as well.

It was very late. The Last Blast opened early and closed late—but this was getting absurd. Around midnight they had a gaggle of guests, all caped in formal wear. The thea-tah crowd.

Raschid was exhausted. As soon as he finished stoning and oiling the grill he was for his room, the fresher, one drink, and unconsciousness. They had a new hire—a baker, one of Pattipong's innumerable relatives—coming in. Raschid was supposed to train him—a clear case of a double amputee teaching ballet.

He heard the scuffle and argument from the front. An-other damned robbery. Pattipong had a dump near the pay counter—almost all money went into a sealed, time-locked safe. Since they would lose only a few dollars in a heist, it was easier just to give the robbers the till than fight back. Safer, as well. The next morning Pattipong would tip the port police, who would find the thief and either have him make restitution or, if he had spent the money, just break his thumbs for an hour or so.

This sounded different.

Raschid picked up a heavy cleaver and went to the kitchen doorway. Then he set the cleaver down on a shelf and looked out. He instantly knew—but did not know how he knew—what was going on. Four heavysets. Flash expense. False smiles and real menace. He walked over to Pattipong.

"G'wan back, cookie. This don't pertain," one of the thugs said.

"Protection?" Raschid asked, ignoring the man.

Pattipong nodded. "We pay. No stinks. Furniture not busted. Customers protected."

"Are they connected?"

"Hey. We told you get out of it."

"I not see before. New. Not connected. No connec-tions now. Old boss go hoosegow. Baby new bosses still fighting."

"Knock off the drakh. We made our offer. Polite folk respond."

Pattipong looked at Raschid. "You think we pay?"

Raschid shook his head slowly—and spun the heavy glass match bowl on the counter into one man's face.

Pattipong snapkicked the second—a man nearly two meters tall—under the chin. The man stumbled back and went flat.

A third man grabbed a chair. The chair came up . . . Raschid went under it, head-butting. The man dropped the chair and sagged. Raschid double-fisted him on the back of the neck, and the man was out.

Pattipong had his long knife about halfway out, and the rules changed. The last man's hand slid toward his belt. A gun.

Raschid, having all the time in the world, spun right . . . two steps back toward the kitchen, hand reaching inside. Whirl . . . the gun was coming up. Finger touching the trigger stud. Raschid overhanded the cleaver. It smacked into the tough's skull with a dull sound not unlike an ax striking rotten wood.

Pattipong hurried to the door. "No cops."

He came back inside and shook his head at the carnage and the scatter. "This not good."

"Sorry. But he was—"

"You misunderstand. Not bad he dead. Bad he dead not neat. Messy. Take two, maybe three hours to clean up. Long day. I was sleepy." He started for the com. "I call cousin. He pick up bodies. Leave maybe in front of police station. Let three explain one, when they wake."

He touched buttons.

"You not bad fighter. For cook."

Raschid was looking at the moaning or unconscious human and formerly human debris. Feeling . . . feeling as if there were a curious observer behind him. He felt . . . he felt . . . push it away . . . nothing in particular. A necessary act.

He went to work helping Pattipong.

Two men sat at Pattipong's counter. Both wore what might appear to be—after suitable degreasing, cleaning, pressing, and sewing—uniforms.

Beside one man was a captain's cover, with formerly gold braid on its bill. Raschid had seen braid go green, even black, with age, but this was the first he had ever seen what looked as if it were infested with barnacles. The cap may have suggested the man's position—little else did. It was not merely the grime: he was a tiny little rabbity person, with the twitching mannerisms of that creature, as well.

The other man, a hulk, had the peeling braid of a ship's officer on his sleeve and on his breast a COMMAND-QUALIFIED ribbon. On the man's shoulder, Raschid could make out a round patch: PEASE SHIPPING.

Both men were drinking caff and arguing. The "captain"—if that was what he was—looked fondly at the lined bottles of alk behind the counter. The other man—mate?—shook his head. The rabbit sighed and whined on. Raschid could make out bits of what he was saying.

"Undercrewed . . . clottin' agent . . . converter leakin' . . . bonded freight . . . sealed destination . . . client I never heard of neither. Not good, Mister Mate. Not good at all."

Raschid, pretending to wipe the counter, came closer.

"The contract good?" the mate asked.

"Cashed it this morning," the rabbit said grudgingly.

"Then what'a you care? Damn few cargoes come wi' a fuel guarantee, Captain. What's to worry what we're carryin'?"

"I'd hate like hell to finish my career gettin' taken off as a smuggler."

The mate looked the little man up and down. "Career? Pattipong, more caff."

Pattipong, unsmiling, refilled the mugs.

"Where's the best place to sign on some casuals?" the mate asked.

"For you? For Pease Lines? Maybe try port jail."

"Thanks, Patty. I love you, too."

Raschid spoke. "What slots you got open?"

The mate evaluated Raschid carefully. "Greaser. Cook/com. Second engineer. If you got papers."

"What's your com rig?"

"World's oldest VX-314. Your grampa could'a known it. We call it Stutterin' Susie."

"What's the pay?"

"Standard. Three hundred a month. Found. Got a sealed destination. You can pay off there, or stay on when we pick up a cargo and transship to a new port."

"Three hundred's cherry-boy pay."

"That's the offer."

Pattipong was signaling from the kitchen.

"Sorry," Raschid said. For some reason he thought he was supposed to say yes.

The captain was about to bleat something. The mate stopped him.

"How good a cook are you?"

"Order something."

"What about the com?"

"Bet the check whoever your last idiot was didn't triple-ground the box," Raschid said. "That'll give a Vexie hiccups all the time." He went back into the kitchen.

"You drunk? Drugs? What wrong with job?" Pattipong asked him.

"Nothing, Dingiswayo. It's just . . . time to go."

"Look. I give you better pay. Give you . . . quarter business. No, eighth. You stay."

The two merchant officers were arguing inaudibly.

"Those two . . . Jarvis, Moran. Bad. He weak. Drinker. Moran . . . busted down from skipper. Killed men. Ship . . . *Santana*. Boneyard. Recycled. All Pease ships same. Junk. Certificates forged. Out of date. Line pick cargo where can. Not care where go. Not care kill crew, lose ship. Insurance always paid prompt."

"Sounds like an adventure."

"You full hop. Adventure someone else, in livie. You watch—adventure. You do—deep, deep drakh."

"You. Cook," Moran growled. "We'll go 450."

"And slops?" Raschid pressed. "M'gear got left aboard m'last."

"Happens when you jump ship. But yeah. We'll go it."

The wait was over.

CHAPTER EIGHTEEN

ALL NIGHTMARES END. Eventually the last of the pirated AM2 was loaded onto the transports, and the 23rd Fleet could lift for Al-Sufi and then home base.

But even escaping, men died. A Honjo had positioned a booby trap, fused with a pressure-release device under one freighter. It went off when the freighter lifted, and the blast took out two more cargo ships and one of the destroyers providing overhead cover.

Just out-atmosphere an Imperial corvette was sniped. An offplanet Honjo lighter had mounted a single missile on its cargo deck, managed to infiltrate through the fleet cover, and waited. The missile killed the corvette, and one of Gregor's cruisers blew the lighter and crew into nothingness. But by that time killing Honjo—in greater or lesser quantities—was no longer thought a victory. It was merely a duty that might—but probably would not— stave off one's own death for a few hours.

Admiral Gregor ordered the fleet into a standard convoy formation. It was by-the-book but not tactically bad. It looked like a three-dimensional mushroom with a base. The mushroom's "stem" was the transport train, with light cover outside the main formation. The mushroom's "cap" was his heavies, with destroyers and cruisers screening to the front. The base was two heavy-cruiser squadrons with their screens, giving rear security. They should have been unnecessary—but they were potentially vital.

That was just part of the bad news Gregor gloomed

over at his battle computer. The only data he had was bad, with one exception: fuel.

His fleet AM2 chambers were at full battle load—probably the only ships in space these days that were, Gregor thought. In theory that should have meant he could have ignored the council's economy dictum and ordered full battle speed toward Al-Sufi. Well, if not full battle, then at least to whatever max drivespeed the transports were capable of.

He could not. His fleet had taken too much damage in the Honjo's guerrilla raids. Damage ranged from hull integrity to warped drive chambers to blown tubes to almost anything the Honjo's ingenuity had come up with to destroy or cripple the Imperials. Two cruisers had even been slaved together and given external emergency drive from one of Gregor's tenders.

His fleet was limping—limping at many multiples of lightspeed, but still limping. Which meant that the 23rd Fleet was vulnerable to a stern attack. Gregor considered abandoning any units that could not hold top transport speed. Then he shuddered and decided against that course. He would face enough flak as it was.

He decided that the only salvation his career had was returning to Al-Sufi with the AM2—all the AM2. That might keep him his flag. Maybe.

Scowling, he scrolled on. The siege-that-was-not had been incredibly expensive:

Crew casualties, all categories: twenty-seven percent.

Ship casualties, all categories: thirty-five percent.

That, factored into his already-dismal combat-readiness factor before invading . . .

Gregor did not want to run the figures.

A second admiral was no happier with the state of the universe.

Fleet Admiral Fraser sat grounded, along with her command, on three of the Al-Sufi worlds. Her orders were clear: Hold in place until the 23rd Fleet arrives.

Fuel from the AM2 transports. Combine forces with the 23rd, yourself to assume command as CINCCON. Continue mission to Prime World sector. Further orders will be given at that time.

She had a fairly good idea of what shape the 23rd was in. Gregor had tried to make his reports sound as favorable as possible. But since complete lies were not permissible, Fraser expected a ragtag collection of limpers.

Fraser, an aggressive leader, believed the Nelsonian dictum that no one can find himself in too much trouble if he steers toward the sound of the guns. She would have cheerfully modified her orders, lifted, and gone to immediate support of Gregor's wounded fleet.

But she could not. Combined AM2 available: not more than one half an E-day cruising range—for *all* her ships.

Fraser was not a happy admiral.

The 23rd was coming home. Gregor's navigational section had suggested a circuitous plot from the Honjo Sector to Al-Sufi. Gregor had rejected it.

He had some good reasons: the status of his ships, the poor skill-levels of too many nav-decks in following the proposed multiple-point plot, and finally his fear of inexperienced deck officers having to maintain convoy position. No, he thought. He did not need the added calumny that would come, for instance, if two of his battleships suddenly set collision courses.

Besides, Gregor was starting to regain some of his customary poise. He called it confidence; his staff preferred "arrogance."

Who, in these times, could challenge an Imperial fleet? Even in its present state of combat semireadiness? Almost no one. Who had the fuel to chance battle? It took power to steal power. The course would be linear—or as "linear" as navigational trajectories could be under AM2 drive.

Watches passed. Gregor felt himself proven right.

Negative contacts. Except for two.

One was reported as a small squadron of light attack craft. System patrol? Raiders? Gregor neither knew nor cared. The 23rd was far too strong for them to attack.

The second contact was laughable.

A trading ship blundered across the 23rd's path. A destroyer matched orbits with the ship. Nothing to worry about—just a trader, from some unknown culture called the Bhor. The ship's intelligence—also mail, censorship, sports, and recreational fund—officer took the time to check a fiche. Bhor? He whistled to himself. They were a very, very long way from home looking for business.

Sten looked at the projection of the based mushroom. He spun it through a couple of 360s, muttered, then brought the focus in to as tight as his "trading" spy ship had managed to get. He ignored the immediate breakdown of estimated forces on another screen. He had it memorized already.

A third screen lit: BATTLE ANALYSIS READY.

Sten ignored that screen, too.

He got up and started pacing back and forth. He had an estimated four E-days, given the Imperial fleet's current speed, to come up with a Plan, position his troops, and attack.

Kilgour and Otho sat nearby. Alex was busy at his own computer; Otho was stroking his beard and looking at that mushroom.

"Straight in, straight on. They won't expect that," the Bhor chieftain said.

"No," Sten agreed. "Neither would I. But I'll bet I could figure out a response before we got in range."

"It was a suggestion."

"Accepted as such, rejected as such."

He looked at Kilgour's screen. Kilgour was scrolling the hourly update from Sten's fleet.

Fleet. Eighty-three ships. Most of them warships, but none of them lighter than an equivalent Imperial cruiser-class, and all of them intended for cluster security/interdiction missions. Others were armed traders and armed auxiliaries. Weapons, electronics, and countermeasure suites would be at least one and more likely five full generations behind the Imperial warships. Not good.

Worse: FUEL STATUS. Maximum range, at full drive: eleven E-days. Getting fuel for the raid had stripped the Lupus Cluster nearly dry. At present the fleet was "parked," with all nonessential systems off. They were masked from the projected trajectory of the Imperials behind a collapsed star.

The status screen cleared, then added a needless worry: MAXIMUM TIME REQUIRED TO ABORT . . . UNDER PRESENT CONDITIONS . . . Meaning that if they stayed parked, they had the equivalent of two E-centuries. UNDER NORMAL DRIVE . . . eleven ship-hours . . . UNDER BATTLE DRIVE . . .

Sten did not look at that figure. He concentrated on the mushroom. It would not have been his choice for a convoy formation—the heavies were concentrated at the front. Better to carry them outside the formation near the center, for ready response in any direction if an attacker feinted. Feinted. Hmm. Yes, Admiral. With what are you going to pull your ruse? Eighty-three ships, remember? Against . . . against too many.

On-screen, the mushroom's cap started sliding back and forth on the fleet's "stem," like a winding-down toy gyro. Kilgour was beaming at him.

"Dammit, Alex! Quit gamin'!"

"Thae gamin', ae y'put it, i' another suggestion, Boss. Or hae Ah noo leave t' suggest?"

Otho rose. "By my mother's insect-infested beard, we must cure this bickering disease." He owled a prox screen. "Nearest contact . . . we have lifetimes. Time for stregg, time even for the hangover. I'll get the horns." He palmed a bulkhead door and slid out.

"Sorry, Alex," Sten said.

"Dinnae fash. Y' want t' hear what I was thinkin't? 'Tis jus' a wee thought, Boss. Ah nae hae a scheme."

The mushroom's gyroing, Alex went on, came as he projected near-simultaneous attacks from various directions at the Imperials. "Slide aroun', slide aroun', an' sooner come later, thae'll lose comman' cohesion. All Ah need f'r't t' be a plan is, p'raps, anoth'r two, three hundred ships."

Otho came back with the stregg. Sten had something wandering in his backbrain. He put the horn in its stand untouched.

"My turn," Sten said. "First, I know where to hit them." He touched a point on the fleet's projected overall passage. "Here."

"Good. Thae'll be sloppy then."

"Maybe even how. Clot the ships. Clot the weapons. Clot that they've got all the damned AM2 in the universe. Think about the troopies. Who we going against?"

"Your mind has fled," Otho said. "We are fighting the Empire, and you are lacking stregg. Drink, my Sten."

Sten ignored him and went on. What kind of Imperials were they facing? This was hardtimes and peacetimes. The ships would most likely be officered and crewed by an odd mixture—experienced war veterans/careerists and new, or fairly new, volunteers.

"Thae hae th' facts ae history arguin' wi' you," Alex agreed slowly.

"Second. Their Admiral Whoever. Rules and regulations. Right way, wrong way, navy way."

"Frae one formation? Estimate frae insufficient data. Theory only."

Sten grinned at his stocky friend, who seemed to have found a new avocation as a strange-talking battle computer.

"Formation, yes. Also the response to the trading ship. Destroyer screens shifted . . . like so. Heavies closed toward area of threat . . . so. Reaction—one ship to close with unknown, two detached in front of the screen for backup. Just like the fiche tell you in Staff School."

"Still theory."

It was.

"Second. Alex, if I give you . . . four ships, can you rig two spoofs?"

Alex thought. "Ah kin. But thae'll noo be world-class. No' enow time, no' enow gear f'r a good 'llusion."

"One more time. Think about the troopies."

"Ah."

"Now, won't that get your mushroom slippin' an' slidin'?"

"Might." Kilgour sank his horn and got up. "But we'll hae t' hit 'em hard an' fast. Ah hae a sudden date wi' a tech. If y'll excuse me?" And he was gone.

Otho winced. Hard and fast. That meant full power and being marooned in space if they did not capture the freighters.

Sten caught his expression. "Don't worry. If we lose—and are still alive but out of power—we'll have Kilgour knock out the ports, issue oars, and we'll row home."

Otho laughed and smacked his lips. The upcoming battle promised to be fast and nasty. He had an addition to the unformulated plan. Would this fleet have a common com-link frequency to the admiral? Very probably. Could it be detected quickly? Almost certainly. Could it be analyzed, pirated into, and blanketed? Given a com with enough power . . . yes.

"Four of my ships, at the least, have links strong enough to shout from here to Hades in a whisper. That is not a factor," Otho said.

Shout . . . whisper? Sten put aside Otho's idea of analogies and asked what he had in mind. Otho continued. When he was finished, Sten sat down, drank stregg, and ran the idea through. It was brutal. Bloody. Practical. About what one would expect from a Bhor warrior—or a Mantis operative.

"Service soldiers," Sten thought aloud, "would want revenge. Conscripts . . . particularly if these people have seen hard times on Honjo, as we've heard. Yes.

"Refill the horn, my friend. My mind is starting to

work. One slight modification to your idea, however. We'll need six, maybe eight, of your best and bloodiest . . .''

Cind went ballistic one nanosecond after getting the orders from her section officer. She was detached for special duties and ordered to turn in her weaponry except for her pistol and combat knife. Then she drew her weapon for this battle—a battle that would be led by Admiral Sten himself. A battle that would win glory for all.

Her weapon was a small camera with a transmitter attached. A joke? No. Because she was human, and those clottin' Bhor never really . . . No. She was the only human. The other seven beings in this special detachment were Bhor—all of them just as homicidally angry as Cind.

She refused the order. The officer shrugged and ordered her confined to quarters. She relented but wanted to protest the assignment.

" 'Twill do you no good, woman."

"Why not? I've got rights!"

"So file a protest if you like. I was ordered to pick eight of my best shipboard fighters. Eight who were most likely to find themselves in the heart of battle. And eight who might survive the fray. I chose accordingly."

"Clot the compliments! I want to protest."

"As I said, protest as you like. The orders came directly from the Great Otho and Admiral Sten himself."

Cind recovered her chin from where it sat on her collarbone. Sten? Why this shaming?

No. Stop being a child. Sten was Sten.

There must be a reason.

If you can understand Sten's thinking, she told herself, then you may truly be on the Way of the Warrior.

CHAPTER NINETEEN

THE 23RD IMPERIAL Fleet was attacked less than one ship's day from safety.

Once contact was made with Al-Sufi and the waiting reinforcements, Gregor relaxed. He ordered stand down from General Quarters. Modified Readiness—one third at combat stations—was the new status. The rest of the Imperial sailors were ordered to clean ship and themselves.

Gregor thought himself a humane commander and knew his troops would not want to port looking like tramps. Also, if there were livie cameras there, a formation of slobs would reflect poorly on Gregor himself.

The first attack came as Gregor was luxuriating in the fresher: *"All Hands . . . Battle Stations . . . Raiders Attacking!"*

Gregor found himself on the bridge wearing the full-dress white mess jacket he had laid out—and briefs. He quickly analyzed the screens.

"Sir, I've already ordered the formation shift toward the enemy's angle of attack as per your standing instructions."

Gregor swore at the Officer of the Deck and then punched up the ECM officer.

"Screen the attackers."

The man seemed puzzled, then touched keys slowly, as if he did not have his signal orders memorized as reflexes. Nothing happened. The attackers continued in, coming from the high forward port quadrant. He ran another program . . . the raiders vanished! Only two ships remained on-screen.

Gregor was about to scream at his flag officer and break the ECM officer when another alarm shrilled. Another formation was coming low forward center—the real attack. Gregor took command and ordered the battle formation shifted down toward the foe.

The mushroom cap seemed to spin as the battleships changed formation and their cruiser and destroyer screens followed. There were two collisions—a cruiser physically "brushed" a destroyer, and two destroyers slammed into one another. The cruiser had some survivors.

In the ECM center, the officer was still following orders and screening the attackers. On his fourth try, just as he was convinced that these were for real, the second set of raiders disappeared. Once more, two ships—the spoofers—remained.

There was a stunned silence on the bridge. Then alarms once more, and a third, larger, near-fleet-size attack began.

"Flag!"

"Sir."

"I want you in ECM. Make damned sure we aren't being fooled again."

The officer ran. Gregor determined to wait for a few seconds before he ordered more changes. Meanwhile, his twin set of orders and their countermands continued wiggling the mushroom's cap as ship captains and squadron commanders tried to reformulate the dome of attack.

The third attack was most real.

Sten shut the chatter of battle commands out of his mind and focused on the bridge's main battle screen.

He was attacking in a crescent formation. He would dearly have loved to have several hundred more units—the halfmoon was very thin. Necessarily so—Sten, hoping the Imperials would be stupid enough to think he was planning an envelopment, wanted the tips of the crescent spread beyond the Imperial defense dome's area.

The Imperial mushroom was looking a little ragged. Part of its cap was shifting toward the attackers. But a segment appeared not to have gotten the word and was restabilizing into normal convoy formation.

At the rear of the stem, the cruisers were deploying fairly efficiently, the base swinging up to cover the transports.

"Com! Are we linked?" Sten asked.

"All ships receiving."

"Sten to all ships. Standby on Longlance launch—as ordered."

"Waiting . . . waiting . . . all ships ready, sir."

"Countermeasures," he said to another officer. "What're they doing?"

"Their detectors have us . . . two . . . six launches made. Five ineffective . . . one acquired."

"Kilgour. Talk to me."

"Range closin't . . . seven seconds . . . three . . . mark!"

"All ships. Launch!"

Missiles spat from the Bhor fleet—but not at the same time. Sten had ordered a ripple fire from the rearmost ships forward. As the missiles cleared the forwardmost Bhor ships, weapons officers armed and aimed the ship-killers. There were not that many missiles launched—at least for a major battle—but all were meant to arrive on target at the same moment.

"Alex. I want that wedge between the heavies exploited. First section . . . individual control . . . acquire and launch when ready.

"Countermeasures! What're they doing?"

"'B' Kholoric . . . not much!"

"Report, dammit!"

The Bhor tried his best to assume the role of an efficient, toneless Imperial officer. "Minor launches . . .

most directed at incoming missiles. Correction. I have a mass launch. Central control is on overload.''

On-screen, there were sparkles between the two closing fleets: operator-guided antiship missiles, Kali II's, most likely. They would be taken out—or they would hit. That was not part of what Sten should be thinking about.

He turned off the ''but what if we're one of the unlucky ones'' part of his mind and looked beyond the sparkles. He grinned suddenly and made a comment frowned on in Basic Admiral School.

''Kilgour! You owe me a stregg! The bastard's by-the-book!''

Gregor was, indeed. There were many possible responses to an envelopment. The best response would have been for Gregor to break the dome into a spearhead or even line formation and attack the center of Sten's fleet, break through the crescent—which was no more than two ships deep—circle, and destroy Sten's fleet in detail.

But that would have meant leaving his transports unguarded except by the cruiser force. No doubt this Imperial admiral had read of Cannae. But there was a big difference: Sten was not Hannibal, nor did he have any heavy infantry to slam the horns of the crescent shut and trap the attacker.

Instead, the admiral was putting his fleet on-line. It was counterenvelopment evidently, such as the Turks should have used at Lepanto. Not bad. It would, in time, destroy the Bhor fleet. In time.

The gap that formed when the Imperial formation was still in its dome remained as ships clouded toward the new formation, ready for Sten to exploit.

''All ships,'' Sten ordered. He was broadcasting in clear, having no time for codes or the polyglot spoken on the Bhor bridges. He hoped that the Imperial admiral's response time would continue as laggardly as it had so far.

''Standing by, sir.''

''I want a blink on that hole in the Imperial formation," he ordered another com officer. "To all ship screens. Now."

"Transmitted, sir."

"Good. All ships . . . maneuver point as indicated . . . X-Ray Yaphet . . . signal when ready."

"All units ready, sir."

"Maneuver . . . now!"

The Bhor captains, any of whom could maneuver a single-tube transport sideways up a cobblestone alley, snapped their orders. Sten's crescent folded over on itself and became a wedge. It was just like an acrobatic squadron—but on-screen he could see the big difference. His fleet was taking hits. Lights indicating individual ships changed colors—*Hit . . . Lost Nav . . . Hit . . . Drive Damage*—or just vanished.

He ignored them. He also ignored the low murmur of a low-ranking weapons officer at the ship's own board. "We are acquired . . . homing . . . impact nine seconds . . . I have counterlaunched . . ."

But he was damned relieved when he heard, "Hit! Incoming destroyed."

The Imperial formation was a real shambles, spitting missiles in all directions. Sten would not have liked to be in the center of that kaleidoscope as it changed shapes and then fragmented further.

"Fleet status," he snapped.

"Fifty-one units still report full—"

"That's enough." Later—maybe—there would be time to worry about casualties and pickup.

"Otho. Do you have their command frequency?"

"On-screen. Ready to pirate."

There was a large screen, set away from the main control area. On it was an Imperial admiral, giving orders. Otho had the audio blanked. Sten thought he recognized the admiral . . . no. Impossible.

"Team Sarla . . . go!" he ordered.

"Acknowledged."

"Team Janchydd . . . go!"

"Janchydd . . . attacking."

"All fleet units. Individual control. Acquire targets and exploit. Command, out."

The real battle began. The Bhor swirled into the melee like so many piratical Drakes against an armada. This was the best possible use of their talents. Most of the traders had vast experience at going one-on-three against raiders. Going against—and winning—by always doing the unexpected, lashing out in all directions and with missiles and electronics, every bit as berserk as their ancestors.

Between Gregor's standing orders and battle experience from the Tahn wars, most of the Imperial ships were expecting to fight a conventional battle against conventionally arrayed enemies.

This main battle had all of the symmetry, logic, and clarity of a feeding frenzy. Sten turned his attention away. The Bhor could not win—sooner or later numbers would out—but they were not supposed to.

His two combat teams were: Sarla, two cruisers that had been hurriedly converted to assault transports; Janchydd, eleven light escorts—corvettes and patrol craft. Just as many ships as Sten had calculated to be controlling the slaved transports. He knew how the Empire ran its convoys, so all of the escorts had been given the electronics and sensors of deep-space tugs.

Sten had named his teams after old, barely worshiped Bhor gods for morale reasons. If there could be Victory, these two teams would gain it.

Now he waited—if waiting could be defined as hanging on to an upright on a chaotic ship's bridge while the ship itself was in the middle of a Kilkenny cats' brawl.

Team Sarla: The two assault ships closed on an already-damaged battleship, well inside the BB's minimum safety launch range. A Bhor missile blew most of the ship's stern away, and the assault ships' ports yawned. Lines were jetted across by scouts, and the three ships were linked.

Armored Bhor went across the lines—and they boarded the Imperial warship.

"First wave across," came the broadcast.

"Otho!"

The Imperial admiral's on-screen image blanked and was replaced by a blinding succession of visuals that would have gagged the biggest splatter-hound director of livies.

The Imperial battleship was already a slaughterhouse from missile hits. More Imperials died when the assault transport's missile dumped the ship's atmosphere. They may have been suited, but many of them had not closed their faceplates or pulled on gauntlets. It was hard to fight a ship wearing armor.

Then the Bhor ravaged through the ship. They had explicit orders: no prisoners. Play to the cameras.

The Imperial officers and crew died to the last being. The deaths were filmed by Cind and the other camera operators, their images selected for maximum effect at a mix panel in Sten's control room and then rebroadcast on the Imperial command link.

It did little for a young sailor's morale when a ship-screen showed a CIC with beings just like himself standing with their hands raised in surrender being butchered like so many hogs. Some ships blanked that frequency—and lost any link to command for many seconds while a secure link was being established. Other ships left the screen on, allowing every slaughter to burn into the minds of their crew members.

Team Janchydd: The control ships for the transports were lightly armed and armored. They could offer little resistance against the weapons of the Bhor escorts. Six of the eleven stopped firing after taking hits. Two plugged on, still fighting with what armament they had. Three more blew into debris. One Bhor ship was lost.

Techs boarded the six control ships and took over the navboards for the AM2 transports. Their escorts closed, slaving to those ships. That was not enough. If more transports—and AM2—couldn't be "stolen," Sten's mission would be very close to a failure. But Team Janchydd's sailors had initiative.

The two still-firing command ships were battered into surrender. They also were boarded and seized. Somehow the Bhor electronics wizards also picked up control frequencies for two of the destroyed Imperial command ships.

Team Janchydd's commander gave the word. Slowly the convoy—the mushroom's stem—broke apart as the Bhor ships diverted the transports, just as a tug would take over a liner's controls while docking.

The heavy cruiser squadrons reacted late to the attack—but reacted. They formed for a counterattack.

Sten saw the counterattack on-screen, put another indicator on the formation, and sent it out.

"All fleet units," he ordered then. "Targets indicated. Priority target. Individual control. Go!"

He did not wait for an acknowledgement.

"Otho. Phase Two," he said.

Otho triggered a switch. A prerecorded disc started broadcasting on the pirated command frequency. It showed a grim, heavily armed Otho looming into the camera, flanked by Sten and another lethal-looking Bhor. It may have been Sten's show, but he knew he did not look nearly as horrid as Otho.

The Bhor chieftain's voice boomed: "All Imperial units! It is useless to continue the resistance. You are ordered to surrender. Fire yellow-blue-yellow flares to save your lives. Ships surrendering will remain unharmed."

Sten had not been stupid enough to think that cheap ploy would get him an entire Imperial fleet to white-flag. All he was after was further confusion.

He got it. A few ships obeyed. Some of them were fired on by other Imperial ships. On other ships, panicked sailors minimutinied, which gave their officers problems more immediate than what was happening outside.

Thirty-nine Bhor ships slammed into the cruiser formation, and another confusion began. The stolen transports broke away from the battle area. Their controllers put them on full drive.

Now, Sten thought. "All units. Break contact!"

This is the turning point. I've stolen their clottin' gold. The Imperials have two options. Please—what the hell were the names of those damn Bhor gods—hell, any god paying attention right now . . . let me be lucky. Let that clottin' admiral be consistent.

Gregor was. Finally having patched a second secure com link to his fleet, he should have ordered a general pursuit of the raiders, under individual or squadron control. He didn't. Perhaps he had heard of Hattin, where Saladin had decoyed a crusading army into the desert and then slaughtered them piecemeal. For all he knew there could be an ambush element lurking out there somewhere.

He ordered all fleet elements to regroup—by elements, by squadrons, and then into main fleet formation. Regrouping, at the very least, requires a visible standard for soldiers to head toward. This battleground was a little short of signposts. Ships hunted for their leaders. Com links were a bleat of confusion. None of it was helped by Gregor's own stream of impossible-to-obey commands.

Sten's forces pulled away.

Team Sarla, with no one left to kill, had already pulled back onto their assault ships. Cind stood to one side of the assembly deck, the normal silence/battle of post combat letdown unheard. She had learned something that day indeed from Sten. From then on, she resolved to dance close attendance on him. To learn, and to . . . She smiled to herself.

Sten's getaway appeared to be working. He chanced a bit of humanity and ordered ten ships to pick up survivors from the crippled Bhor ships. As they could . . . if they could. They were to try to get the ships under power, but abandon any ship not capable of full drive.

It would get ticklish now. At full drive, his units would soon start running out of power.

He gave more orders. Bhor ships closed on the stolen convoy. On each, their best fueling techs were waiting. Only two Bhor craft ran dry—and Sten had full-powered ships ready to slave to them and transfer energy.

"Y' jus' might hae pulled th' biggest heist a' all, Admiral."

Sten managed a grin, then forced himself to another station. "Casualties?"

There was not much joy in this victory. He had lost almost half of his force. Otho walked up beside him and looked at the same figures. "Better than I had expected. Worse than I had hoped. But the gods decide."

Sten nodded. Perhaps. But why the hell did they have to be so murderous?

"Remember that pool, Sten."

Sten remembered. And now he had fuel to fight his war.

BOOK THREE

PATER PATRIAE

CHAPTER TWENTY

FIVE MINUTES AFTER boarding the *Santana*, Raschid decided that Pattipong could have added several more deep deeps to his description of the drakh he was stepping into. Then he wondered why it had taken him so long to realize it.

It had probably been the mad scurry. Both Captain Jarvis and Mate Moran seemed to go into Overdrive Decision Time as soon as they hit the field. It could have been, Raschid thought, that if they hesitated to consider anything other than immediate lift, unpleasant alternatives would come into play.

The *Santana* was several generations beyond qualifying as a tramp. It must have been marked for salvage several times before its owner decided there was still life and profit in the hulk.

Beauty there had never been. As the port gravsled deposited Jarvis, Moran, and their new cook at the ship's boarding ramp, Raschid had tried to figure what the *Santana* had been designed for. He was blank. The ship consisted of three elongated acorns, X-braced together fore and aft. In the middle, between the acorns, a long cylinder stretched above the main hulls. Engines and drive area, Raschid guessed. But why in front? Could the tub have been originally built for some other drive than AM2? Impossible. No one would have bothered converting such a dinosaur. Nor would they have kept it in commission. Would they?

One acorn contained control rooms and crew quarters,

the other two cargo. The crewpod was as puzzling inside as the *Santana*'s exterior. Raschid got lost several times before he found the galley and his quarters. Passageways had been sealed off, then cut open at a new owner's whims. He passed compartments filled with long-abandoned machinery that must have been cheaper to chop from a system than rip out for scrap. Raschid was expecting the worst when he reached his kingdom. He was an optimist. The twin stoves were so old that they were probably wood-fueled. Later for that problem. He found his compartment and was grateful. It was pig-filthy, of course. But at least cook's hours and cook's privileges gave him his own quarters.

The bunk—if the sagging pallet against one wall deserved the title—had safety straps. Raschid seriously, if illogically, considered strapping himself in before lift. That way, if the *Santana* disassembled, as it seemed to have every intention of doing, there might be a recognizable corpse for the pauper's field burial.

Raschid wryly thought that this, indeed, was going to be every bit the adventure Pattipong had promised and waited for the ship to lift off Yongjukl.

Ships did not "scream" into space, except perhaps in stone-age film documentaries or in embarrassingly amateurish livies. But the *Santana* did just that—or perhaps he was anthropomorphizing. He felt a little like screaming himself. The McLean generators told him that "down" was half a dozen different directions before the Yukawa drive went on. The bridge held the ship on Yukawa until the *Santana* was out-atmosphere. A gawd-awful waste of energy—but most likely shifting to AM2 drive in-atmosphere with this scow was an invitation to demolition.

A com buzzed.

"Cookie. Stop arsin' about. Officers' mess, one hour. Crew to follow."

Raschid went back to the galley where he was met by Moran. Raschid noted that the mate was carrying a side arm. Moran took Raschid to a storeroom, unlocked it, and told him to select whatever he needed.

"How many bodies am I cooking for?"

"From these supplies—me, the skipper, first engineer. Crew's supplies are off the galley. You'll be sloppin' twelve of them."

Raschid was not surprised to find that the supplies in the locked room were not the same as in the crew larder. Officers' rations were standard ship-issue, but the crew's victuals appeared to be long-stored military-type goods— issued to a military that would have mutinied itself into oblivion generations earlier. Yes. Mutiny.

Raschid planned menus with what he had. He was a genius, he felt, at being able to cordon-bleu any drakh given him. Genius, yes, but not a god. Spices? Some sweet syrupy-tasting synthetic. Salt . . . and those old military rations appeared to have been salt-cured. What other condiments were in the larder had long since passed into tastelessness.

He combined foodstuffs into a concoction he hoped would be taken for a stew, put that on the heating range, and made dinner for the officers.

He need not have worked too hard. Jarvis had retired to his quarters to reward his abilities at getting the *Santana* once more outward bound. Moran ate—if a conveyor-belt blur of consumption was eating—whatever was in front of him and made a valiant try at his napkin. The first engineer, a morose woman named D'veen, con- sumed half of what was in front of her and disappeared into the engine spaces. She, like Moran, was armed.

Then he had to deal with the crew. He was in for it.

He was not—at least not for six watches, while the sailors sobered enough to appear at the table and hold down what he put in front of them.

Raschid spent the time cleaning his galley and think- ing. What was he doing there? More importantly, why did he feel he was in the right place? Unanswerable. Clean the galley. Moran turned down Raschid's request that he be allowed to suit up, seal the galley, dump the atmosphere, and let the grease boil into a residue.

"First . . . I don't know if the bleed valve works. Second, I ain't chancin' hull integrity. Third, there ain't no guarantee we can reseal after you get done. Fourth, ain't no pig down there'd appreciate the work. Fifth, I got drakh on my mind. Get your butt off my bridge. Next time you won't walk off."

Raschid got.

That night, Moran grudged a compliment. The mess in front of him was better than usual. Raschid blandly explained that he had used some new seasonings. Glucose, acetone bodies, minerals, fats, creatine . . . Moran told him to shut up before Raschid reached uric acid.

The crew had sobered enough to concentrate on their new enemy: Raschid. There was nothing that could be done about the ship, except pray it made it to a landing where one could desert. That sealed cargo—it would prove trouble in its own time. Their still-unknown next port? It would be another sinkhole—the *Santana* took only those cargoes that nobody would handle for worlds that no one but the desperate would land on.

The officers? Jarvis was either drunk and invisible, drunk and visible, or a sober, ghostlike image, huddling on his own bridge.

Moran? Bitch to the mate and hope there's still some med supplies left in what was called sick bay. Raschid admired—intellectually—Moran's lethality. The man seemed unable to give a command without a blow, and the blow *always* hurt, just enough for an instant, an hour, or a day's agony, but never badly enough to take a man off watch.

D'veen? Why bother? She kept the *Santana*'s drive working. 'Sides, she's no different 'n any of us. Took any slot offered to get away from dirtside. Times're tough f'r any deep-space sailor. Take it out on the cook. Somehow he's responsible for the slop. Don't matter if he come on on'y an hour b'fore lift.

Raschid ignored the complaints, insults, and then threats for a while. Then the following sequence of events occurred: A tureen went against a bulkhead. The thrower went after it. Someone came out with a knife. The knife became two pieces, and Raschid attempted to duplicate the effect on its wielder. Two other crewmen jumped Raschid and went against the tureen-bulkhead.

This crew was exceptionally thick, Raschid decided, deep in the dogwatches, when he heard the fumbling at his door. After the flurry subsided, he rousted out the off-watch and had them carry the avengers to the sick bay. He bandaged as best he could. He did not have the supplies or knowledge to straighten the second man's nose, but he consoled himself that he was not the first or even, most likely, the tenth to smash it. He set the third man's leg and the next day, when Moran threatened to brig the now-useless sailor, convinced the mate he could use some help in the galley.

Not that there was much to do between planetfalls. On a normal ship there would be maintenance, cargo handling, and so forth. On the *Santana*, why bother? Scrape rust . . . and one could well go right through the hull.

That added to the mutterings—the crew had little to do when they were off watch. Moran was even a lousy bully mate—as long as crewmen stayed out of his sight and showed up for their watch, he didn't care.

Very, very stupid, Raschid thought. Matters were getting tense. The crew had gone beyond complaints into sullenness. They were beginning to talk once more, some of them, two, sometimes three at a time, talking very quietly in corridors or unused compartments. The talk could be of only two things: murder or mutiny. Or both.

Raschid watched closely and listened where he could. There were three sailors he thought would be ringleaders. He used his new potwalloper to background the three.

Then he sought them out. One had been part of the off-watch ambush party. All T'Orsten wanted was trou-

ble, and promised that part of that trouble would be thin-
slicing Raschid at the first possible moment.

The second was a basic bully. Cady. All she was un-
happy about was that Moran was a more successful, more
dangerous bully.

The third, however, was a bit more complex. Engine
Artificer Pitcairn. She tried to sound no different than the
others and mostly succeeded. But Raschid heard the echoes of some kind of education in her speech. He paid
close attention to the woman—and his attention was
noted.

She sought him out in his quarters.

"Wanted to ask you something about dinner," she began, and pointed to the com.

"It's clean," Raschid said. "Moran or somebody had
an induction pickup inside. It don't work no more."

"Pretty sophisticated for a hash slinger."

"Not sophisticated. Just careful."

"You SDT?"

Raschid shook his head.

"Didn't think so. Pease Lines don't hire nobody but
scabs. Or those who don't claim a union card."

"Like you?"

"Hard stayin' militant when you been beached for a
couple of years. Plus where I boarded, union organizin'
was a bit risky."

Raschid's curiosity about Pitcairn was satisfied. The
Ship, Dockside, & Transport Union was on hard times.
It was famed as a militant and understandably aggressive
organization; the Empire's down economy made it easy
for bosses not only to force yellow-dog contracts on any
spaceport workers, but to blacklist any union official or
organizer.

"Reason I wanted to talk . . . this drakh can't keep on
the way it has been," Pitcairn said. "If Moran don't beat
somebody to death, Jarvis'll get blistered an' navigate us
into a collapsar."

"Mutiny's a hard way to go."

"Nobody said nothing about that. Yet."

"What other options do you—do we have? I don't see any grievance committees lurkin' out the porthole."

"You're quick," Pitcairn said. "Course th' others ain't figured that out yet."

"How many are in on it?"

"Ten. You'll make eleven."

"That's a start. But we don't have enough goin' for us. Run up the black flag—that closes out the options. Especially if an officer gets dead or marooned to death in the process. Bosses get hostile, somethin' like that happens. They'll hunt us all down, however long it takes, and we'll be dancin' Danny Deever."

"You talk like you've got some experience."

Raschid started to answer by saying "Not for a couple of thousand years or so," then stopped. Where the hell did *that* come from? He wasn't Methuselah.

"I read," he said instead. "But let's say nobody feels real logical and the drakh comes down. What then? We got ourselves a ship. Maybe half a fuel load. With a cargo. Which gives us what? This scow ain't suited for smuggling, and the on'y place people go piratin' is in the livies.

"Say we head for whatever Smuggler's Roost we can find. What are we gonna get for what's in the hold?

"Somethin' better. Where we headed? What kinda armpit? Desert with cannibals, or someplace where we klonk Moran over the head, jump ship, and live with what we got?"

"Good questions," Pitcairn said after thinking. "We need more skinny. Can't compute with what we got. Problem's gonna be keepin' somebody from gettin' assed, goin' berserk, and we got blood on the bulkheads."

"You rabble-roused for the union. With only twelve goons to worry about, you oughta have no trouble keepin' 'em under your thumb," Raschid said.

"For a while," Pitcairn said, "I can do it. But they

ain't gonna stay in a holdin' pattern forever. We better get more info quick."

Four ship-days later, they did. Their destination was the Cairenes—specifically, the capital world of Dusable.

"That ain't good," Pitcairn observed. "I organized there for about twenty minutes. If there was an honest being in the whole damn system, I never met him, her, or whatever. Plus they got a righteous depression goin'. We jump ship there, we'll be on the beach a long, long time.

"You know anything about Dusable?"

Raschid was about to say no, but didn't. Because he suddenly realized he knew a whole hell of a lot about the system and the way it worked. But he could not remember ever having visited or read anything about the Cairenes.

"A little," he lied. "That's one piece. Now, it'd be real nice to know what's the cargo."

"I asked Moran. Got my chops slapped for doin' it."

"Hercules helps those who help themselves."

"You pray to your gods. I'll stick to Jack London. We decide to tippy-toe out th' lock, Moran sees the lock alarm go off, an' you an' me'll be out there till we figure a way to breathe space."

"The lock alarm's been disconnected for a week. I made sure at least one suit ain't leaky. I'll check another one right now."

"Well, well. First the bug, now the alarm. For a cook, you'd make a fair spy. All right. First watch. Moran sleeps like a corpse, long as you don't try to go in his compartment."

They went out the air lock as quietly as they could. Raschid winced at the air-hiss and the whine of the lock mechanism. Both of them pulled themselves out of the open lock, making sure the attractors on their boot soles had no chance to clang against the hull. Pitcairn aimed a line-thrower and fired, and the grapnel at the end of the line snagged through an X-beam.

They hand-over-handed their way across to the cargo hold and inside, then opened their faceplates, found prybars, and went to work.

"Bless m' clottin' sainted mother," Pitcairn swore after a while. "There's at least *one* somebody on Dusable ain't in no depression."

The cargo was entirely luxury goods. Exotic foods. Liquors. Wines. One case held jewelry.

"We been livin' on swill, an' all this was just across the way. I'm tryin' not to lose it, tear Moran's face off and order a hog-out. What next?"

"Interestin'," Raschid observed. "You note there ain't no customer ID on any of the packing lists. Just: *As Per Instructions To Captain.*"

"Okay. I say again my last. What next?"

"I think . . . maybe a mutiny."

"That sets real easy. Then what do we do with all these goodies? Smugglers'll pay heavy credits for what's here."

"Maybe that's the option. Mutiny first, questions later."

The mutiny came off painlessly, to use the term broadly. Raschid had given explicit orders, so only four of the twelve conspirators were used—those Raschid thought would not go berserk.

Jarvis was easy. Cady, on bridge watch, waited until the captain got tired of wearing his gun-heavy uniform coat and hung it up. The next time Jarvis paced by, a bar of soap in a stocking was applied with some firmness to his medulla oblongata. He was carried to his cabin and, after the cabin was searched for more weapons and the sealed shipping instructions taken, locked in.

Moran took a bit more skill. One sailor, selected for her slenderness, draped herself on an overhead conduit running past Moran's compartment door. Moran was buzzed for his watch. He came out, and the sailor prayed and dropped.

The flurry before Moran pitched her the length of the corridor gave Raschid, Pitcairn, and T'Orsten time enough to rat-pack him. Eventually Moran was hammered into unconsciousness.

They knew he had to have weapons stashed in his compartment, so they locked him in a bare and disused room. The fresher worked, and they could slide meals through a narrow slit cut in the door's base.

Raschid fingered his split lip, then went for the engine spaces and D'veen. He carried Moran's gun as a completely empty threat. D'veen took no threatening whatever. All she asked was that when the mutineers were caught and tried, they would testify that she had put up a magnificent battle.

"We have no intentions of being in front of a court," Raschid said. "But if so, we'll save your ticket."

The mutineers held their council of war in the officers' wardroom—after Raschid and Pitcairn had made a careful selection of goodies for a victory feast. They allowed one half bottle of alk per sailor—and Raschid thought that was too much.

He was right, but Pitcairn had made sure that only she and the cook were the ones with guns. T'Orsten bellowed rage at being informed that he *could not* toss Moran out the lock. He *could not* orgy out on the luxury cargo. And he *could not* revenge himself on D'veen.

Raschid let him bellow, saw that T'Orsten wasn't letting steam but building for a berserker, and blindsided him. They tucked him away next to Moran and went back to the wardroom.

Raschid opened, read the sealed shipping instructions, lifted an eyebrow, and passed the sheets across to Pitcairn.

"I guess that settles what's next," she said. She was a little pale. "We look for some smugglers, dump the cargo and the ship, and do our damndest to vanish."

She quoted from the instructions: " 'Land bleat-bleah

section, transmit blurt-blurt signal. Cargo will be off-loaded by personnel bearing authorization personally signed by Tyrenne Yelad, duplicate signature below.'

"Just the whole goddamned system's MaxMoFo, is all. And we just took his toys away. Nice going."

There was something moving in the back of Raschid's mind. Yelad . . . Yelad . . .

"Workers of the *Santana*, haul ass! You have everything to lose including your chains," Pitcairn finished.

"No," Raschid said. "No," he went on. "I think we make delivery."

Ignoring the gape, he fielded a bottle and poured himself a celebratory drink. Things were going very well, indeed.

CHAPTER TWENTY-ONE

THE PRIVY COUNCIL reacted in confused fury to the raid on the AM2 convoy. The crime against the Empire—*their* Empire—seemed an even greater felony because they had stolen it themselves. Add to that the tremendous cost in blood and credits, the enormous hopes they had placed on the many extra months the AM2 shipment would have provided, and, finally, the humiliation that a wild gang of pirates had bested Imperial forces.

Plots within plots were hinted at within the fabric of the raid. Were the Honjo themselves involved? No one knew. The Kraas suggested that perhaps they had not been too far off the mark when they made up the accusation of Honjo culpability in the conspiracy to kill them. The makeup of raiders was equally as puzzling. What were the Bhor doing so far from home? Malperin believed they were just mercenaries. Adding weight to her argument was that the human on-screen during the Bhor's terrorcast had been identified: Sten. Kyes's target earlier, who had been identified as that smaller man in civilian clothes at the conspirators' kriegsspiel. Ex-Mantis, and a longtime associate and probable friend of the man they had once believed dead: Fleet Marshal Ian Mahoney, the man who had plotted their assassination on Earth. As soon as Sten and Mahoney had been connected, most of the council members were sure that Mahoney was the man behind all their troubles.

They were careful in not stating their exact reasons— such as the very good possibility that Mahoney suspected them of slaying the Eternal Emperor. So they took a care when maligning him, especially in front of the newest member of their body, Colonel Poyndex.

If Poyndex wondered at the extreme paranoia of his new colleagues, he kept it to himself. He had joined them prepared to expand his influence to the fullest. With that in mind, he made no attempt to soothe their anger.

The privy council wanted heads—and they wanted them now.

Poyndex offered up all his skills in helping them to widen the continuing purge. A new and vastly greater list of suspects was devised. Hunters were sent to track them down and bring them to swift justice. Poyndex was careful that his signature rarely appeared on any of those orders, and when it did, it was always following everyone else's.

The purge was not setting well with the council's dwindling allies. Many of the victims had friends or relations in those crucial areas. Poyndex knew that could not be helped. He reasoned that the council would be satisfied long before they drowned in the very blood they were spilling—and he was doing his best to pad the list of suspects with beings of little importance to anyone.

In only one area did he subtly rein them in. When they started looking for new targets from which to steal AM2, he drew the line.

"I think we should delay on this matter awhile," he said.

"Give us one reason why," Lovett snapped.

"After the incident with the Honjo," Poyndex said, "even a fool would suspect that your real reason for the attack was the AM2. And that they were innocent of any conspiracy."

"I see your point," Malperin said.

"Bloody hell!" one of the Kraa twins exploded. "Wot's an Honjo or twelve to any fella? Bunch a shutfists, that's wot they be. 'N everyone clottin' knows it! They'll get little sympathy."

"Possibly," Poyndex said. "But if we immediately attack another AM2-rich system—no matter what the excuse—then all our allies will feel as if they were potential targets, as well."

"Too right," the fat Kraa said. "Me 'n Sis got some good candidates."

"I'm sure you do," Poyndex said. "And I think all these things should be taken into consideration. But not now. Not just yet. Or else we'll lose too many of our supporters."

They saw the wisdom in his advice. But just to make sure, Poyndex suggested some particularly bloody actions that could be taken as part of the purge. It helped a great deal to keep them all relatively calm. He also helped them launch a massive effort to bring the beings responsible for the AM2 theft to justice. Poyndex had sniffed the rotten fish the council was attempting to hide: Ian Mahoney, former chief of the same intelligence department Poyndex commanded. How very interesting. Was Mahoney just a rogue? Possibly. Possibly not. Why were his colleagues so afraid of the man?

Poyndex was sure that one way or another, he would soon learn the reasons behind all of it, and that the answer would be useful to him. Meanwhile, as the junior member of the privy council, he would do his best to satisfy.

Besides Poyndex, there was one other relatively pleased member of the council.

Kyes had found it difficult to hide his boredom. He cared not a whit what the outcome was of all this. He did his best to appear interested and to add his opinion to the debate when warranted. But on this particular day of fury, Kyes had received extremely good news.

The data banks of his one-of-a-kind computer were now full to the brim, thanks to the assistance of Lagguth, Poyndex, and a whole host of historical ferrets. The computer had been crunching all the data for weeks, and at last it possessed all of the facts, rumors, and half rumors they could find on the Eternal Emperor.

Kyes had almost dreaded asking the question. It was all very well for him to believe as he did, but believing did not make a thing so. As a scientist/inventor, Kyes knew that better than anyone. Was he mad to think the Eternal Emperor was not dead? Despite all the evidence? The witnesses? The filmed assassination itself?

Only the computer could answer that. It had been fed every detail of previous reported attempts on the Emperor. But what if he asked and the prog was unacceptably low? Kyes was certain that if he were not already mad, such an answer would drive him over that final brink. But if he did not ask, he would never know. Kyes was literally in the position of a being who has been told that whether he would live or die was a known quantity. All he had to do was look in the crystal ball to find out. It was just as hard to look as it was to ignore it.

Finally, he looked.

The prog was ninety percent plus that the Eternal Emperor was alive.

With that news, Kyes was ready to move.

Far away from that debate, there was another extremely happy being.

Sr. Ecu had labored hard since his meeting with Mahoney. As his assistants pored over legal tracts, ancient and modern, he had put out careful feelers on Sten's proposal that an impartial tribunal be formed to try the privy council for the assassination of the Eternal Emperor.

Of course, such a question had not been asked outright. But, working from a narrow list of systems that were guaranteed not to leak even a hint of his disloyalty, much less run shouting panic-stricken from his presence, he had felt his way around the edges of his goal.

He knew now that if such a tribunal were proposed, there were beings he could convince to join the panel. It would be very difficult, but far from impossible. Before he could ask, however, the Manabi needed a legal basis for such a body. Else, the whole exercise was pointless.

Sr. Ecu found his precedent.

As he suspected it might, the answer came from the early days of the Empire. It was during the time—well over two thousand years before—that most of what was now the Empire did not exist. In fact, places that were currently heavily populated and considered the very heart of the Empire had then been wild frontier regions, where there was little law and equally little order. It was a time when six years or more could pass before an Imperial circuit judge visited any of those regions to settle local disputes.

The Eternal Emperor had been well aware that many things could go very wrong if left to fester. So he encouraged the creation of local magisterial panels, empowered to settle nearly all civil claims. Their decisions could be appealed to the region's Imperial governor, but the length of time to get a hearing, much less a presence, was so formidable that few took advantage of that option.

In the matter of major, life-threatening felonies, the Emperor had been far more cautious. Sr. Ecu could read his concerns between the lines. Jailings and executions could easily become a tool of vengeance. It was unlikely that the Eternal Emperor was concerned as much about the morality of such actions as he was that unsettled crimes would create further instability, blood feuds, and spreading wars.

So in those cases, the magisterial panels were slightly limited in their authority. If a suspected violent felon were hailed before them, the panels were only to determine if there was a great likelihood that a crime had actually taken place, what manner of crime it might have been, and whether the being(s) before them was probably responsible. To determine the evidence, they were empowered to subpoena witnesses—bringing them to the bench by force, if necessary—to arrest all suspects, and to hold in contempt of court any being who opposed them.

If the evidence pointed to the suspect before the bench, they could indict him for the crime. If he were considered extremely dangerous, they could back up the indictment by imprisoning him until an Imperial judge arrived to try the case.

The system worked so well that the Emperor had kept it alive for many hundreds of years. So Sr. Ecu had not one case to back his claims, but millions upon millions of them.

He had found the means of justice. Now, all he needed were the judges.

CHAPTER TWENTY-TWO

THE BIG COP was in a surly mood as she paced the dock. The gnarly *Santana* sat silent at its berth. The ports remained firmly closed despite repeated efforts to get someone—*anyone*—to respond.

Lieutenant Skinner muttered obscenities under her breath, casting dark looks at the idle workers who were grinning at her difficulties. Her scab crew remained silent. If the crowd's humor turned to violence they were too far from their home ward to expect any assistance. There would be no reprisals. The SDT Union was too strong and its pockets too deep, even in this time of awful unemployment.

Skinner could not figure out what had gone wrong. Her ward captain had said this was a plum job. A little favor for Tyrenne Yelad that'd go into Skinner's merit book.

All she had to do was retrieve the *Santana*'s cargo. A few personal and *private* things for the Tyrenne. It was a job to be handled with Skinner's usual discretion.

Skinner's use of scabs was hardly unusual, or even provoking. In such cases one approached the appropriate union steward who would estimate the number of beings required for the job. The mordida would be set at double their prospective wages—then scabs would be allowed to unload the cargo, while the steward spread the money around to those who normally would have toted those bales. Keeping a nice taste for himself, of course. That was only right. Skinner had picked up more than a few

226

earners of that type herself as a Dusable officer of the law.

Okay, so what had gone clottin' wrong? They had trundled up to the freighter, but no one had come out. Impatient, Skinner had gotten on the horn to see what was the hang up. No response. She tried again. Still no answer. What kind of game was this? She had sufficient mordida in her pocket to pay off anyone, from the captain of the *Santana* down, if necessary.

The steward exited his office. From his look deep drakh was about. "Get your butt outta here," he snarled.

"What the clot for? We got a deal. *Remember?*"

"The deal's off. Only reason I'm tellin' you, 'stead of sendin' a couple of guys to thump you first, is we done business afore. So I owe you a warnin'. Now, get!"

Skinner blew herself out to her most coplike proportions—which were considerable. But before she could deliver her full wrath at this scrote, she heard cheering. She whirled to confront the new threat—and gaped.

It was Solon Kenna! Advancing with a phalanx of aides, a big crowd of SDT workers, and a livie news crew. Ohmigod. Skinner knew it was time to make herself scarce. She should have known. This was an election year. In fact, the election was only two weeks away, which made things even stickier. Especially since Tyrenne Yelad's challenger was Kenna himself. Clot the ward captain! She was gettin' out.

Solon Kenna took position in front of the ship. He was an immense, elderly man who bore his girth like the seasoned pol he was. His nose was bulbous from many hours and many bottles, but his eyes and instincts were sharp. And he had a smile that would swallow a swamp beast. He turned the full force of that smile on his pet newscaster.

"I will speak no further on the perfidy of my opponent," Solon Kenna said. "Instead, I will let the facts speak for themselves. They will soon reveal themselves when I assure the poor mistreated and honest laborers inside that they are among friends—and they exit with the awful evidence of Tyrenne Kenna's greed.''

"Hang on a sec, boss," the newscaster said. "You sure you wanna say perfidy? I mean, callin' the butt-wipe a lyin' sack might be going too far. But—I don't know. The word's kinda thick. Might make folks think you're stuck up."

"No problem," Kenna answered. "Fix it any way you like. I trust your professional judgment."

"Second question, what do we call these guys?" the newscaster asked. "We don't wanna say they're mutineers, right? I mean, that's not the drift of this bit, is it?"

"Absolutely not," Solon Kenna said. "What we have here is an injustice of enormous proportions."

Before he could continue, there was a cheer from the dockworkers as the main cargo port of the freighter creaked open and the ragged crew members stepped out.

Raschid kept to the sidelines, watching with oddly professional interest as the events unfolded. Pitcairn proved to be a great interview subject. The other mutineers took their hints from her and Raschid thought they all did a credible job. But the illicit cargo would have won the day, regardless. Kenna handled it like a seasoned pro. His expression shifted from sadness, to anger, to outrage at the greed of Tyrenne Yelad, expending dwindling AM2 credits for luxury items while his own people starved.

Not bad, Raschid thought. Although the guy had an unfortunate habit of tossing off fancy words when they weren't called for. It didn't matter that he misused them. The people he was aiming them at wouldn't know. They would possibly take offense only because he might be coming across too pompous. Still, he was mostly getting in all his shots.

Once again he puzzled at why he knew so much about this sort of thing. But he pressed the question away, along with that odd feeling he had of being watched by something or someone just out of view.

He saw Pitcairn pointing in his direction. Kenna looked over and smiled a big wolfish grin. Raschid did not know what that meant, but he would soon find out. Solon Kenna was motioning the livie crew to keep back and was coming his way. Raschid decided to stay put and play the cards as they were dealt.

Kenna planted himself in front of Raschid, lighting half the dock with his grin.

"How you doing, friend?" he said. "I'm Solon Kenna. The humble representative of these poor working beings."

Then as Raschid took his hand to shake, Kenna leaned closer and whispered. "I got word you were coming," he said. "We need to talk—later."

Raschid hesitated, then nodded. "You're right," he said. "We need to talk."

The Cairene System was a dozen or so lightly populated agro-worlds and the big, dense port planet of Dusable. This is where the late Tanz Sullamora had made his second fortune—in shipbuilding. The factories, which had groaned under triple shifts during the war, were now desolate. The AM2 crisis had struck nearly every part of Dusable.

That would be bad for any planet. But on Dusable, it was disaster. Because the Cairene System was a political throwback. On Dusable there was really only one industry: politics. There was barely a being on the planet who did not owe his or her existence to patronage, from pot scourer, to sewer worker, to cop, to business owner, to joygirl, to ward boss, to the Tyrenne Yelad himself.

It was an unwieldy system, and corrupt to the core, but it had worked for centuries, and worked very well, For thirty years Tyrenne Yelad had ruled. His patronage was so vast there was little hope he would ever be defeated. Still, just because he won with ease every four years did not mean that his opponents were in any way helpless.

There were checks and balances in this system. No matter that they were equally as corrupt. Under the Tyrenne was the Council of Solons. Each member ran a group of wards, whose voters he rewarded with jobs, advice, and influence. A perfect Solon made sure no one went without. If one had trouble with the grocery money, one went to the ward captain. Same for a spouse with a brutal or drunken other. Paid hospital stays were assured. Fines were leavened, or even dismissed.

Bribe money flowed in and out of all this. Joygirls paid their pimps, who paid the cops. The cops themselves paid for prized beats such as vice, or traffic in the rich resort areas. They also paid for rank, which placed them higher on the mordida ladder. Mob bosses paid both ways: cops on one end, pols on the other. And all those people paid the ward captains—who, in turn, poured all the credits into the coffers of the Solon controlling their district.

The Solons, in turn, shared the mordida with the key leaders who actually ran the whole thing. Tyrenne Yelad was a good example of one such leader. He had come to power as a reformer, as had the Tyrenne before him. This election, the new hopeful reformer was Solon Kenna, president of the Council of Solons and Yelad's worst enemy. Kenna's power came from the unions, particularly the SDT, which was why, after three tries and three defeats, Kenna was convinced that this year was his best chance. The hordes of unemployed beings had put big brass knuckles on his fists. He had been slugging it out with Yelad for more than six months. But now, two weeks before the election, he had not been able to deliver a knockout. If he couldn't, Kenna's long run was over—unless there was a miracle. He was hoping that Raschid was that miracle. The more they talked, the surer he became.

At one point Raschid had quizzed him about the credit situation. How full were Kenna's campaign coffers? Kenna said he had sufficient. Raschid shook his head and advised him to get more, much more. Kenna asked why.

"Unruh's First Law," Raschid said. "Money is the mother's milk of politics."

The answer spoke volumes. This man was no dry political-science scholar. Kenna had seen too many elections lost with that type. Raschid was obviously an expert street politician who knew how to play the game from the top right down to the gutter.

Kenna found it easy to be candid with Raschid, because . . . he *knew*, dammit. The guy *knew*! The next question, however, threw him into temporary orbit.

"Why are you telling me all this?" Raschid asked. "What do you expect me to do about it? I'm just a ship's cook. A mutinous one in some lights."

"Come on," Kenna sputtered. "You can drop that. You're among friends, here. Besides, I've already been filled in. I knew you were on your way."

"Who told you?" Raschid asked.

Kenna figured it was a try on—so he bit. "It wasn't anyone I could name right out," he said. "You know that as well as I do. I got it from . . . back channels. We were advised the *Santana* was inbound. With a cargo I'd be a fool not to inspect. More importantly, I was told there would be a man on board posing as the ship's cook. And that he was the absolute best there was in political strategy.

"I can't tell you how we all reacted here. To know that some very important outsiders were with us. And that rescue was on its way."

Raschid considered. For some reason, it all made sense to him. Although he wondered why those outsiders had not informed him as well. He buried that. It was another test, maybe the final one.

"Okay," Raschid said. "You got your boy. I'm on board."

Kenna breathed a heavy sigh of relief.

"Who else is in the race?" Raschid asked.

"Only one other," Kenna said. "Solon Walsh. And he doesn't have a chance. Although the guy's as handsome a pol as has come along for three forevers. But he's young. And he's stupid.''

"What's his bit?"

"Reform," Kenna said dryly. "He's trying to steal the march from me, I guess. Because that's my main platform. Walsh can't seem to get any ideas of his own."

"He's probably got Yelad behind him," Raschid said. "But real quiet. Walsh is intended to bleed off support from you."

Kenna was startled, then comforted again. It was just the way he had seen it.

"All right . . . here's how we go," Raschid said. "We need three things.

"First, we need a Dummy. Second, an Issue."

He took a long swallow from the brandy glass Kenna had been constantly filling since the meeting began.

"What's the third?" Kenna asked.

"Easy," Raschid said. "Then we steal the election."

CHAPTER TWENTY-THREE

THE TINY AND the meek may never inherit the earth—
but they can sometimes rock it worse than the most cat-
astrophic earthquake.

Napoleon's hemorrhoids. He'd slept poorly the night
before a battle, and napped the next day. Twenty-five
thousand of his soldiers died, and he was no longer an
Emperor.

Three woman cipher clerks conspired. The secrets of
Earth's Third Reich were revealed. At least ten million
Germans died.

And Zoran mentioned, with giggles, what one of her
"frantic minds" had reported. There was a new shrine,
she said, shaking her head at the credulity of some of her
followers. Not a mountaintop where the Eternal Emperor
had appeared to the faithful, nor a large pile of crutches,
abandoned after he had worked miracles.

"Loaves and fishes"—giggle—"might be the comparison," she said. Kyes was blank. "Oh. My apologies,"
she said. "There was an ancient cult on Earth. Called
Christers. That was one of their miracles.

"My frantic mind has less than that.

"Eggs"—large giggle—"for pity's sakes. Not millions
of them, and not used to feed the starving. But sold."

There was a small spaceport restaurant, on a world
called Yongjukl. "I could not find it in my atlas, but I
suppose it is out there somewhere." According to Zoran's acolyte, it served food exactly like that the Eternal
Emperor favored. Using his exact recipes, "Or at least,"

Zoran added, "those that were reported before the Eternal One chose to absent himself for a period.

"A minor . . . fetish"—giggle—"of ours? I have cooked and enjoyed some of those recipes myself."

Kyes interest was sparked—the Eternal Emperor, indeed, fancied himself a gourmet chef. But if Zoran had cooked some of his recipes . . . that did not compute. Had to be a restaurateur with a new gimmick.

Ah, but no, Zoran continued. These recipes had been taught to the owner by a mysterious chef who had appeared, worked for a few periods, then disappeared.

"My frantic one takes this as a precursor. Of course, he swears the descriptions of this mysterious man in the white apron are exactly what you would expect a man seeking miracles to say. Oh, well. When the Emperor does choose to return from his time with the Holy Spheres, I question whether it would be in a greasy spoon."

Kyes was in contact with Yongjukl. He ordered its most skilled and subtle psychologists to talk to the cult member—and to any other customers of that restaurant who might have seen the cook.

The descriptions varied, of course, but overall they fit the Eternal Emperor exactly. Kyes had the restaurant's owner questioned.

The owner refused to cooperate. Instead, he threw the investigators out of his dive—named, Kyes noted, the Last Blast.

Kyes ordered the owner, a human male named Pattipong, followed. He could not be. He changed clothes and washed before shutting down, so electronic tracers did not work. Surveillance experts, singly and teamed, tried to track him. Pattipong lost them all, every time, and reappeared the next morning to reopen the Last Blast, smiling as if nothing had happened and he was completely oblivious to the attentions.

Kyes started to order Pattipong's arrest but stopped

himself. You are on to something. Finally: Do not panic. Do not rush to judgment.

He told Lagguth and the computer team to load and analyze *all* events occurring on that world within the last six years, concentrating on the last few months. If the mysterious cook was the Emperor, he would not have used Yongjukl as a base for very long. Or so Kyes thought—with no logic behind him.

The computer found a mansion, or the remains of a mansion. It had been, for some generations, among the holdings of a very rich, very mysterious offworld family who never visited their estate. Recently, however, a ship had landed on the grounds and one man had gotten off. The ship had immediately lifted. The man was the family's heir apparent. He had stayed in seclusion for a brief period of time and then disappeared. The mansion's staff had been paid off, the mansion torn down, and the grounds donated to the government. The mansion—and who owned it—had already been a favorite mystery story for the local media. Its destruction created a one-day wonder. But there was no more information, and the story disappeared.

A mansion, Kyes thought excitedly. Equipped with the most elaborate library and computer. That was enough. He ordered Pattipong's arrest. Two of Yongjukl's most skilled operatives went out to seize the tiny man. Dingiswayo Pattipong killed both of them and vanished once more, this time for good.

Kyes held in red, red rage. He forced himself to re-think. No. This was not a disaster. Analyze it. HUMINT has failed—not surprisingly. But artificial intelligence . . .

He ran Yongjukl, the worlds around it, and the galactic cluster it was in through every analysis possible. He found what he was looking for.

Kyes's quest was almost over.

CHAPTER TWENTY-FOUR

HE STARTED WITH the Dummy.

Raschid stayed in the background for an hour or so while Kenna laid the groundwork with Solon Walsh. Even Walsh's keen-eyed aide, Avri, started ignoring him after a while as her boss played the political mating game with Kenna.

It was Raschid's professional opinion Walsh had most of the makings of an ideal candidate. He was young and sleekly handsome. He spoke without stuttering. He had a steady, clear gaze. There were no food spots on his clothing, and his carefully arranged coif had a charming habit of going slightly out of kilter after a few minutes of conversation. It made him seem more relaxed and genuine. In some areas Walsh had received some expert advice.

The man exuded honesty. That had everything to do with lack of IQ. That open, wide-eyed look was there because there was nothing behind the optic system. But stupidity could be a candidate's greatest asset—as long as he listened to the right people. Raschid figured the right people in this case was Avri.

"I'm surprised to learn there's so much common ground between us," Walsh said as the political dance wound down. "I mean, I had no idea you felt that way about taxes, for instance. Wow! After all this time our whole argument with one another disappeared, just like that." He snapped his fingers by way of illustration.

Solon Kenna made with a gentle, fatherly smile. "A

misunderstanding, that's all," he said. "See what happens when two honest beings speak frankly?"

"That's real good drakh, and all," Avri interrupted. Walsh shot his aide a nervous look, ready to fold if Avri gave the word. Good. He could be handled. "But where are we at? What's the deal? There's gotta be a deal, else you wouldn't be blowin' all this smoke.

"Now, if you think Solon Walsh is gonna take a little earner and fold his tent . . . I don't know . . . Whatcha got in mind?"

Kenna handled it without a blink. More points for him. Raschid was feeling better and better about his plan.

"Right on the mark as always, young Avri," Kenna smoothed. "I'll let Sr. Raschid help me with this. I really can't stress too hard that this being's credentials go far deeper than I can say. Far deeper."

Avri's eyes narrowed as Raschid joined the game.

"Solon Kenna and I have run through this every which way we can," Raschid said. "Thing is, everybody agrees we have to have a change. Tyrenne Yelad just isn't making it anymore. Trouble is, any way you cut the deck, Yelad keeps coming up on top. Because Walsh and Kenna cancel each other out. Am I right?"

Avri nodded firmly. She had a hint of a smile at her lips, which Raschid knew meant he had to beat Yelad's mordida, plus the after-election promises.

"So. What Solon Kenna proposes to do is pull out. And throw his support to you." He nodded in the direction of the stunned Walsh.

There was much surprised babbling. But Raschid got the meeting back on track and spelled out the details. Kenna would slip a hefty wad of credits to Walsh, who would put his campaign into high gear, splashing his name all over and hitting the stump hard. That would be just the outward display, however. The real money would be aimed at those few mighty wards with a big number of independent voters, folks who held out to the last so they could get the biggest payoffs.

Meanwhile, Kenna would run a lackluster campaign, letting some of his support bleed off.

"Two nights before the election," Raschid said, "Kenna pulls out. Says he's seen the light, and all. Credits it to the persuasive words of his worthy opponent—one Solon Walsh. Then throws his support to you."

They did not go for it right off. Nobody ever does. There had to be bullet-proof assurances that there would be no last-minute betrayal. These were made. And the rest of the terms were set. Walsh would be Tyrenne. In return, Kenna would wield even more clout than before. Avri did not give a clot about the giveaways. She was more interested in being the power behind a Tyrenne's throne.

"It still ain't enough," Avri said. "Even if we join forces, Yelad's still got the vote edge. Too many independents. Maybe we can squeak through on that.

"But he's the man with the pad. He can always top whatever we got by voting the graves."

What Avri was referring to was that delightfully old-fashioned system still in play on Dusable. There was a joke that no one ever really died. The death certificate got dumped into Yelad's computer banks and that person's name remained on the voting rolls. When Yelad's people saw the count going against them, they voted the dead. Or the living, in the case of people who had emigrated from the Cairenes but were still there on the voting rolls.

Of course, Yelad could not be too blatant about it. Millions and millions of nonexistent voters would be too much even for the corrupt people of Dusable. Appearances were important. So Yelad's staff kept careful watch on the real voting, an easy task because of the deliberately out-of-date method of vote-casting. First off, every adult being was required by law to vote. The ward/mordida system could not work unless everybody was in the game, physically and psychologically. Second, each person registered with the solon of his or her choice. An ID card was presented at the polls, and the vote cast was registered upon it for a ward captain to examine later. So much for the secret ballot. Finally voters were physically required to go to the polls, rather than voting by computer at home, unlike most citizens of the Empire. This gave a master thief like Yelad all kinds of interesting ways to cheat.

"How do we get away from *that*," Avri asked.

"We got it covered," Raschid said. "It'll be tricky, but that's what makes the game fun. But we'd like to keep all that to ourselves awhile. If you don't mind."

No one did. Kenna was taking all the risks. Avri knew nobody would be mad at Walsh. He was just the Dummy.

The deal was done. Then Raschid tackled the next part: the Issue. Yelad represented the status quo. Kenna, labor. But Walsh had nothing but empty words. He needed a target. Raschid had the gringo ploy in mind. Nobody in the room knew the term's origins except Raschid, and he wasn't saying, but they knew what it meant. Attack the outsider, somebody big and far off you could blame all troubles on.

So Walsh's issue was the privy council. It was their fault things had been bungled since the death of the Emperor. It was their fault there was no AM2, creating such bleak times. Yelad would be forced to defend them. If he did not, he was doomed with the all-powerful Imperial council.

When Raschid had brought it up prior to this meeting, Kenna had been so excited he contemplated forgetting the whole deal with Walsh and keeping his own campaign running. Raschid doused that idea. He pointed out since Kenna was already President of the Council of Solons, the privy council would be highly annoyed at this attack. Kenna did not want or need that kind of attention, Raschid strongly advised. The thought also made him feel personally uncomfortable, although once again, he did not know why.

"Let the Dummy do it," Raschid said. "They'll figure

he's just grabbing for straws because there's no way he can win. They won't care one way or another what a Dummy says, and they'll ignore the whole thing.''

It was not necessary to spell that out to Walsh. Avri knew what it meant, which was more than enough.

Kenna was in high spirits as they exited the bar. Everything was on track. Raschid wanted him to stay happy, so he praised his performance.

''The trick you just pulled was invented by a master,'' Raschid said. ''It's called a rossthomas.''

''Which means?'' Kenna asked with lifted eyebrows.

''It means that now the fools in this town are on our side,'' Raschid said.

Kenna laughed all the way back to headquarters.

There were other meetings with key beings who had to be bribed, clued in, brought into line, or a combination of the three. The results were happily similar.

One meeting, however, Raschid thought best to handle alone.

The mob boss's name was Pavy. She was known as the hardest, canniest, and most unforgiving of all Dusable's crime royalty. Her turf was a dozen of the biggest independent wards. Not one coin came through any of them that did not have its edges well skinned. She ran all vice— from joygirls and joyboys to the most addictive narcotics. Her loan sharks were the toughest and most knowledgeable. Her thieves the wiliest. Pavy was also stone gorgeous.

She was of average height, but in the clinging body suit she wore when she greeted Raschid her legs climbed into the upper atmosphere. Her hair was a dark, close-cropped skullcap, and her eyes were as black as any he had ever seen—with hard, gleaming, diamond points of crafty intelligence. They met in a cozy little room deep inside the one-square-kilometer warren of vice she called The Club.

Pavy ordered her thug assistants out of the room after

the preliminaries. Raschid had already been fine-toothed for weapons in the bombproof room just inside the entrance. Not that Raschid could not have snapped that long slender neck with one hand—which Pavy knew as well as he. Still, she had dismissed her bodyguards. From the look in her eyes, Raschid knew that the woman had already taken his measure. He was there for a deal, not to kill.

After they left, she refilled their glasses with the aromatic liquor she favored, dropped the jeweled slippers from her feet, and settled back on the soft settee, her legs tucked up under her. She gave Raschid a silent toast with her glass and sipped. He followed her lead.

"Now tell me what you have in mind," she purred. Raschid did not make the mistake of thinking the purr was anything other than that of a very deadly tiger.

He spelled out the program. The fix was in, he said, although he couldn't tell her exactly how it was going to come off. Pavy nodded. That groundwork had been more than satisfactorily settled by Kenna's people. Then he told her what he wanted her to do, just sketching the main points; the little details could be spelled out later. Pavy's smile grew as he talked. She liked this. It was going to be very expensive for someone. She laughed a couple of times, then told him what she wanted in return, a sum that would keep a small planet happy for a year. Raschid shaded the price by one fourth, but only because he sensed she would distrust him if he didn't try. Then Pavy surprised him.

"What's your end?" she asked. "What did you tell Kenna you wanted?"

"I didn't say," Raschid answered.

"That's wise," Pavy said, nodding. "If you win you can probably get at least as much as he's giving me."

Raschid figured she was right. In fact, Kenna had asked him the same question. What did Raschid want in return? He knew it disturbed Kenna to be told he would find out when it was over. Why had he done that? Raschid was not sure. All he knew was that the price would come at the proper time.

Pavy asked him about other political battles he had been involved in, as one criminal to another, giving him the out of dodging anything that might be incriminating. But that was no problem. As far as Raschid could figure, this was the first election he had ever worked, so he lied. Political events came tumbling out of him, complete with victories and desperate setbacks and stunning reversals. Oddly enough, as he told the stories and she kept their glasses full, he realized that he was not lying at all.

Finally, it was getting late. Time to go. Pavy's hand hovered over the button to call for her thugs to escort him out. Then she flashed him a most peculiar smile. It was glowing, and her lips were soft, her eyes wide and wanting.

"You could stay longer if you liked," she whispered very softly. Long nails brushing the microthin body suit. The rasping sound gave Raschid the shivers.

He considered her request—because that was what it was. Why was this woman so suddenly attracted to him? He saw the reason. It was from being so close to power— real power. But he was just Raschid. Wasn't he? Where was the power? Then he knew it was there. Inside him. But not why. Nor who. Yet.

Raschid stayed the night.

The 45th Ward was one of Tyrenne Yelad's lesser bailiwicks. It had not always been so. The chief occupation of the sprawling neighborhood involved the plasfill contracts for the Tyrenne's massive public-works programs. Before the AM2 crunch, all of Dusable had been busy one way or another in these projects. Bridges were built duplicating perfectly good arcs a few klicks away. As were unnecessary roads. Or tall, gleaming public offices that were always in short supply. The reason for this was that each time the public payroll was padded, new offices were required for patronage. Departments continuously warred with other departments for more employees, thus increasing their power, and posh offices to house them in, thus increasing their prestige.

So there was always a tremendous need for plasfill. The 45th had always prided itself on supplying the thinnest gruel at the highest price possible. These big profits made the world go around.

Then came hard times. Yelad had to throw one of his wards off the plasfill sleigh—the 45th. Now people were beginning to hurt in the 45th. Long lines lined up daily before the ward captain's door. By day's end, the captain had barely whittled into the line.

So when the official gravcar hummed into the neighborhood, it was greeted with quiet but keen interest. The windows were shut and darkened, but it was no mystery who was inside. The car flew the tiny flag of Tyrenne Yelad.

It cruised slowly through the neighborhoods, as if inspecting the shuttered shops and "For Sale" signs on the businesses. The people of the 45th who were about that day—and there were many, since jobs were scarce—wondered about its purpose. Was the great Tyrenne Yelad there with some great surprise? A bonus contract for plasfill? A few shabby vehicles chose to follow at a discreet distance.

The Tyrenne's car made the turn that led to the ward captain's house. Aha! Good news.

Suddenly, the gravcar sped up. As if harsh orders had been given and the driver was heading back.

At that moment, a small, tubby, darling child of a boy darted into the street after an errant ball. The gravcar sped on. The child looked up with wide, innocent, and oh, so frightened eyes, frozen. But there was still plenty of time for the car to stop. On it came. People screamed warnings. Mothers wailed in empathy. The child turned and half stumbled toward escape. Then the gravcar accelerated. Almost as if it had been done on *purpose*. The car clipped the child, and, to loud shrieks of horror, the boy was hurled into the air. He crashed to the ground, blood spurting. The gravcar came to a fast stop. A uniformed driver leapt out. People ran toward the accident. The driver drew a pistol and shouted for them to stay back. They did.

Then he marched to the corpse of the boy and stood over it. He looked back at the gravcar. A window hissed open, and people thought they could see someone motioning an order. The driver scooped up the body and dumped it in the gravcar as if it were trash. Someone shouted a protest. The driver snarled an oath and waved the gun. But the crowd was furious. Beings started running for the gravcar. The driver leapt inside and sped away, leaving angry voters behind. Voters who now cursed the very name of Tyrenne Yelad—a being who scorned them so much that he killed their children.

Inside the car Raschid flung the driver's cap into the back. Beside him, the corpse stirred, then sat up.

"Gimme a clottin' rag," the boy's corpse said.

"Pretty good first act," Raschid said as he handed a cloth to the boy, who began wiping away the fake blood.

One close look at the "boy" would reveal the lines in his face and the cynical twist around his eyes. He lit up a giant tabac, inhaled deeply, and blew out, filling the car with the cloud. This was a boy who had been in the acting business for fifty years or more.

"Think you can do it again?" Raschid asked.

"No problem," the boy said. "I could do it three, maybe four more times before I get too tired. And careless, if you know what I mean." Raschid said he did.

"How about a little drink break?" the boy asked.

"Nope. The thirty-sixth first. Then you get that drink."

The boy cursed, but Raschid did not mind. Raschid could tell the actor was very happy with the work.

Lieutenant Skinner was one pissed off cop. It was collection day, and the first stop had put her in a foul mood.

She always started her rounds with a tidy little joyshop. It was a private deal, so she didn't have to share the earner. She also had a cute little joyboy she had been diddling every collection day for the past few months. That morning, however, there was no earner—and no joyboy.

The frightened and confused manager burbled out that the earner had already been picked up. He said a couple of real scary cop thugs had dropped by an hour before. They were there for the juice—said from now on Skinner was out. It had not taken much in the way of heavy leaning—the manager's face was bruised, and he walked with a limp—to make the message stick. They had also picked up the joyboy and said he would be working at another house.

Skinner was damn sure the toady manager was not lying, especially after she administered a professional beating of her own. Afterward, she stormed out of the joyshop, vowing revenge. Then it sank in. It would not be that easy. Her captain didn't know about this little caper. Frustrated, pissed, and confused about who the cop interlopers might have been, Skinner continued her rounds. Each place she went, the story was the same. Skinner began to realize that the beat she had spent so much money in payoffs to acquire had been turned upside down.

Steaming through her big beak like an ancient engine, Skinner headed for the cop shop to clue her captain in. An interdepartmental turf fight had just been launched.

Skinner had one more large jolt awaiting her. It was no mere fight, nor was it over a single piece of turf. Somehow or other, outright war had been declared. But by whom, no one would know until it was too late.

Kym was young and blond with innocent eyes and a not-so innocent body. She was also a wicked little number who haunted pickup spots outside her home ward. A Lolita lick of her lips, a hip thrown just so, a jut of milky breasts, and the mark was soon in her clutches—thanks to the knockout gas and sharp knife she kept tucked away in her skimpy costume.

Kym was also the apple of her daddy's eye and a minor hero in her neighborhood. Well-raised child that she was, Kym always brought all her loot home to Poppa. Since he was a sewer superintendent on Yelad's pad, that equalled large local clout.

But there had been a wee misunderstanding one night. Kym got picked up by cops who were too stoned out on narcobeer to check her out, so they hauled her to the slammer and booked her. To everyone's dismay, there was no choice but for Kym to go on trial. Nobody liked that, even Tyrenne Yelad's enemies. After all, juice on Dusable had to stay universally sweet, or the whole jug would go sour.

But such slips had been made before. The procedure was to have a little trial. The cops would get a minor scolding for busting somebody so obviously innocent, and Kym would be home again in her daddy's loving care and back out on the streets pursuing marks.

That was not what happened. The judge convicted the child of all charges—and threw the book at her.

In the howl of outrage that followed—picked up and played for all it was worth by Kenna's pet livie casters—the judge slipped out of town to retire to a life of newly wealthy ease, leaving Tyrenne Yelad holding the bag.

Avri praised Raschid to the heavens for the inspired dirty work. "Stick around," Raschid said. "I got a new twist on that new twist."

The juice went so sour in a score of key wards that it consisted almost entirely of solid matter.

Cops went after cops. The mobs went after everybody. Shops were bombed out, joyhouses raided, and gambling dens ripped off. Muscle banged muscle, and the innocent got in between—assuming that anyone on Dusable fit that description. The capper was the Mother's March for Kym.

Two thousand angry women from her ward hit the streets. Huge banners bore the innocent profile of the dear child. There was wailing and weeping and much colorful tearing of hair. Kenna's livie crews were out in force to cover it for the home folks, running down the dreaded incident for the thousandth time for their viewers. There were lots of close shots of her stunned daddy, who wobbled along at the head of the parade. Pop looked great, blasted on narcobeer, with eyes red-rimmed from cavorting on the cuff at a joyshop Raschid's people had steered him to. He was the portrait of stunned sorrow.

Screaming oaths, the women converged on the Tyrenne's headquarters, where a phalanx of cops waited. The lawbeings were in full riot drag—helmets and shields and clubs and gas and blister guns.

The women drew up before the line of cops. There was more shouting and screaming. Livie crews recorded the standoff.

Suddenly a big gravtruck burst out of a side street. Cops identically clad to the Tyrenne's guards boiled off, kicking and punching and flailing about with clubs. The women howled in agony as the stunned *real* cops gaped on. Who were those guys? The phony cops ducked out of sight as the women recovered and went for blood. The battle would go down in Dusable history. Hundreds of mothers were injured in a scene witnessed by the entire planet.

Yelad's good name was quickly being reduced to a synonym for drakh.

The Dummy performed like a champ.

The best researchers and speech writers mordida could buy spilled out a tsunami of attacks on the privy council. Ad spots that would stop an overheated ox in its tracks were created. Raschid was all motion, ripping and tearing and putting the whole back together.

Solon Walsh delivered. In spades.

He started with a rather sad talk on the hardships of

the beings of Dusable, leaving open the question of who was to blame for the troubles. But at his next appearance, he struck the pose of an outraged and betrayed citizen. He was aboil with facts that had just come to his attention. AM2 was being deliberately withheld from the Cairenes. Prize contracts had been wrested away. Solon Walsh bellowed for justice in speech after fiery speech. Dusable needed a strong hand now, he preached. One who owed nothing to those devil rulers on the privy council.

Tyrenne Yelad reacted mildly at first. He was surprised at the slickness of Walsh's campaign. But Avri assured Yelad that it was all part of the plan to leech off reform support from Kenna. Since Yelad was personally handing over mordida for Walsh's campaign kitty, he was reassured. As for the attacks on the privy council, what did he care? Those exalted beings certainly didn't, since the attacks came from a noncandidate like Solon Walsh.

Just to keep things square, however, he had his own speech writers make some minor course corrections. He delivered a few mild speeches defending the privy council.

Raschid made sure that each and every one of them was exploded out of proportion. He turned Yelad's mild defense into gigantic ad spots in the skies, complete with thundering volume, which warped every word Yelad spoke.

Then the other drakh started hitting the fan: The curdled juice. The internecine cop warfare. The mob attacks. Et cetera, et cetera. Yelad was so busy rushing about trying to plug the spurting leaks that he did not notice that Solon Kenna—his archenemy—was barely running a campaign at all.

Three nights before the election, the Tyrenne called an emergency meeting. His confidence was shaken.

Yelad looked like a ball top—skinny bottom and skinnier uppers, with a big round bulge in the middle. He chose his tailors so that those defects were emphasized rather than lessened. The clothes themselves were of materials just above middle class. Yelad lived in the same small ward home he had grown up in. He was nice to his mother, spoke well of his wife, and was understanding about the mishaps his brat children got themselves into. All of those artifices he had developed over many decades of campaigning. The message was: As a man of the people, Yelad possessed many of the people's flaws—but also many homespun strengths. It was one of the many reasons he had won term after term.

Not counting his vast patronage, of course, or his giant, smooth machine. On that night, however, nothing was smooth. Yelad was half drunk, one of many bad habits he had slipped into after years of easy victories.

"Whaddya mean, ya don't know what's behind it? What am I payin' ya clots for? Clottin' lazy bastards, that's what ya all clottin' are. Drakh under my feet."

He stormed and raged, and his aides cowered, waiting for the awful storm to break. It didn't.

"I'll tell ya what's goin' on. It's that clottin' Kenna. Pullin' a sly one. Yeah, well . . . we'll see what's what, we will. I'm pullin' out all stops. Ya hear! Dumb clottin' low-down piece of drakh bastards . . . s'what I got."

Many, many yessirs later, he was soothed enough to grit out orders. With times so tight, he needed a mandate. A mandate of historic proportions.

Teams of thugs and poll riders were doubled, the hired phony voters nearly tripled. Waiting in the wings were those grave vaults to be voted when the final count came in.

Tyrenne Yelad had plenty of funds. What he lacked was organization. After so many years of constant victories, he required a far smaller team to administer the elections. Now he ordered heavies hired by the hundreds. They all hit the ground running—and instantly stumbled into each other and crashed to the ground. But the worst blow came before all that, on the night following the meeting. Less than forty-eight E-hours before the election.

* * *

Raschid watched calmly from the sidelines as Kenna oiled onto the big outdoor platform. His eyes swept the audience, making sure his shills were at work, pricking up the vast crowd. Every news livie crew on Dusable was accounted for. Even Yelad's pets had come running when word was leaked a few hours before Kenna's regularly scheduled speech. The talk was that a stunner of a development was about to unfold. The news crews forgot their loyalties, overwhelmed by that headiest of all scents: political bloodshed.

Kenna took up position. The ovation aroused by the shills was deafening. Solon Kenna bowed humbly and raised a weak hand, grinning and begging them to stop . . . "Stop . . . I really don't deserve all this outpouring of love."

The shills hit the button again just as the crowd was starting to believe that they really ought to stop as urged. The ovation was louder than before. Raschid let it go for half an hour, then motioned to let it gradually subside.

Kenna laughed and thanked everyone for such a spontaneous show of support. Then composed his face into a portrait of somber wisdom. He briefly sketched his long career of public service, reminding one and all of the hard fights in their behalf. Then Kenna confessed that he had been overwhelmed by doubts in the course of this campaign. He was getting on in years, he said, and he realized that he might not be able to carry on the banner as Tyrenne.

The crowd was hushed. Beings were beginning to get the drift. A few shouts of "No . . . no . . ." could be heard. Raschid's magic was such that they were truly spontaneous, not the work of shills. Finally, Solon Kenna reached the end. There was a dramatic pause.

"I have been listening most carefully to the views of my opponents," he said at last. "And I have come to the conclusion that only one true voice speaks for us all.

I therefore announce . . . I am withdrawing from the race
. . . and—''

The crowd erupted in fury, but Kenna commanded
them to silence with his august presence.

"And I throw my support to that most worthy of all
beings on Dusable . . .''

On cue, the Dummy walked out on stage to the amazement of the entire planet.

Solon Walsh approached his colleague, tears streaming
from his eyes—it had been Raschid who suggested to
Avri the astringent in the kerchief.

"I give you . . . our new Tyrenne . . . a being for the
new ages . . . Solon Walsh!''

People went mad. Fights erupted. Livie crews smashed
into each other trying to get tighter shots, or sprinting
off for their standups.

But in the middle of all the madness, the perfect picture was on the stage. As soon as the news crews realized
it, they were back to work shooting the image, breaking
heads and standing on fellow beings to get it.

It made a grand, instant campaign poster. Solon Kenna
and Solon Walsh, weeping in joy, their arms flung about
one another in loving unity.

Raschid thought the whole performance had gone well
enough. He had done far better in the past, but all in all,
he had to admit . . . Then his mind did a small, dizzy
slip. When had he done better? With what? Then the roar
of the crowd took him, and he banished the doubts.

The hard part was next. There was still an election to
steal.

Election day dawned to the thunder of Tyrenne Yelad's
shouts of outrage. His eyes were two blood holes from
railing all night at the Judas Solon Walsh. Finally, his
aides got him calmed enough to order the counterattack.

Yelad slammed down at his desk and began pouring
over his illegal options. Confidence quickly returned. He

believed his political arsenal would have made even the
late Eternal Emperor weep.

The steam hissed to a stop. Yelad composed himself
and ordered up a jug of his headiest brew to steady the
nerve for the long day and night ahead.

At that moment a badly frightened aide burst in. Bad
news in the 22nd Ward—one of Yelad's greatest strong-
holds, with one million honest votes in pocket and two
hundred thousand from the grave vaults.

In his fear, the aide told it badly—which meant from
the beginning, each detail drop by drop. Yelad shouted
at him to bottom line it at once. But the being stumbled
so badly that Yelad gritted his teeth and told him to start
anew.

The 22nd Ward was an island, surrounded by factory-
polluted seas. For the working class, which meant all of
the voters, there were only two convenient routes in and
out of the ward, great bridge spans built with a vast hur-
rah and a flurry of mordida twenty years before.

"Yes! Yes! I clottin' know that. Spit it out, you little
drakh butt!"

"Well . . ." the aide wailed. "One of them just collapsed."

"Clot!" was all Yelad could gobble. The voter traffic
would soon make the other bridge impassable. And although there had been no injuries, people might fear to
even chance that one.

Yelad sucked in half his jug of spirits in one go.

The day was not beginning well.

As Yelad tried to gather his wits, Raschid was being
let into the deep, gloomy underground heart of the big
building that housed Dusable's computer balloting system.

The toady ushered him and his three-being team of
techs to a steel vault. The heavy door hung open. Inside
was a snakes' nest of boards and old-fashioned optic wir-
ing.

It was almost too easy. But Raschid knew that in politics, one took it any way it came.

Where earlier there had been two thousand women marching for Kym, election day saw fifteen thousand mothers march out from two wards. Whole gravtrucks of police fled before them.

For three hours they paraded from one ward to the next, gathering beings of all sexes behind banners bearing the likeness of the martyred girl mugger.

Then they all went to vote, sixty thousand of them. Some particularly irate women voted 130 times or more before the polls closed.

Solon Kenna hit the docks and SDT Union hiring halls at dawn. He spread the bribe money so thick and wide the grease could have easily launched a fleet of destroyers, and as he shook each hand and filled each pocket with credits, he looked each being straight in the eye and issued the order for the day.

"Go vote. Go cause trouble."

The masses of workers swarmed out the gate. The voting and fighting raged deep into the night.

Solon Walsh addressed the livie crowds armored in solemn, youthful honesty. But his wrath was so great that even his steely hands shook. The bit of paper with the latest awfulness fluttering in his anger as he shook it before the cameras.

"Yet another betrayal, my fellow citizens. The privy council in its wisdom has just ordered our credits devalued by one half! What does my cowardly opponent, Tyrenne Yelad, have to say to that?"

If any one had looked closely, they would have seen only a few handscrawled words written on it. They were from Raschid, a heavily underlined reminder:

"Don't tell this lie with a smile."

Walsh's stormy brow was a work of art.

* * *

At midday, Yelad's emergency press conference to refute Walsh's charges was canceled. There was more grim news from the 22nd: Huge cracks had been found in the remaining bridge.

No more than seven hundred people from the 22nd voted—which meant that Yelad would also not be able to cast the votes of the dead.

The first of several hundred gravtruck loads of phony voters lumbered into Dusable's capital just after dark. All over the planet Yelad was bringing in similar reinforcements. The beings would be escorted from poll to poll to vote for the Tyrenne, receiving a chit for each vote. The chits were redeemable in cash. There were some seasoned pros on board each of the trucks, beings capable of hitting two to three hundred polling spots before the midnight shutoff. For them, it was very lucrative piecework.

Raschid's force waited in the alley until the first truck passed. They swarmed out, swinging clubs and hurling bottles filled with fiery liquid. The beings on the first truck were dragged off and beaten. The truck was dumped off its gravlifts onto its side. Then it was set on fire—blocking the way with its flaming wreckage.

Not that a barricade was really needed. The other trucks were either quickly overwhelmed, or turned tail to run. There was no pursuit. Raschid had drummed it into every thick skull: stick to detail, no matter what.

Somebody smashed in the strongbox aboard the truck and started handing out the counterfeit voting cards—just one more detail in Raschid's list.

Gillia was a hardened twenty-year veteran of campaign strong-arming and dirty tricks. But he had found himself getting weary of late, and was thinking of retirement. Out of loyalty to Yelad he had decided to stick through one last campaign. Adding weight to that decision was the notion of the experts that this would be the easiest election of them all. Kenna did not stand a chance, so all kinds of opportunities were left for Gillia to do far more skimming than usual. If he used his wits, he would retire almost as rich as a Tyrenne himself.

When Gillia ordered the lead vehicle to turn into the 103rd Ward, he already knew he had been a rosy-butted fool for thinking that way. The word on the street was that all over Dusable, Yelad was taking a tremendous licking. Punishment squads out to do a little lightweight thumping were on the receiving end of their own beatings. Some fights had erupted into full-scale riots. Gillia himself had seen a Yelad ward office in flames—and that was in the first hour of the night's work. Burning barricades and screaming mobs had blocked his entrance into eight wards.

Meanwhile, Yelad's top operators were doing a great deal of screaming on their own. Gillia had never been greeted by such hysteria from the election brass. His poll-riding teams were under tremendous pressure to produce. Snap poll after snap poll showed that the Walsh vote was big and getting bigger. It had to be subverted, and clottin' fast.

Gillia's specialty was seeing that committed voters—committed to the other side—never reached the polls.

As in most places, the elderly and infirm on Dusable tended to vote the ticket. First, after years of backing one party, they were unlikely to change at this stage of the game. Second, they tended to owe their present existence, enfeebled though it might be, to that same ticket. All social welfare, obviously, was under the direct supervision of the local ward captain.

However, it was hard for such beings even to get to the polls. That problem was dealt with using traditional tools. The names of these prized voters were gathered up by the ward captain, who handed out the list to transport teams. On election night vehicles marked with the name of the proper candidate toured the wards, picked up the elderly and the crippled, delivered them to the polls to cast their vote, and then returned them home.

Gillia, and other beings like him, made sure that never happened.

Tonight he had twenty gravcars at his command, all repainted and bearing the name and likeness of Solon Walsh. The game plan was always the same. Spies in the enemy's camp would leak the schedule and names. Gillia would hustle his people out into the appropriate wards. They would go street to street, door-to-door, if necessary, and con the old beings into the gravcars. Then they would dump them fifty or sixty klicks away, stranding them far from their home polling places.

When Gillia's people hit the business center of the 103rd Ward, he issued instructions. The convoy split up and headed for their assigned neighborhoods. Gillia and his two goons continued on alone.

The old being at the first row home he approached greeted him at the door with a confused smile. "Why . . . what are you doing here, young man? I've already done my duty."

Gillia figured she was having him on. He sighed. There were always a few citizens who used any excuse to get out of voting. Oh, well. He would have to bruise her some, just like a legitimate poll rider, or she would be suspicious. He raised a weary arm to strike.

The old being scampered back, remarkably swift for her age. What a lot of drakh. He would have to chase her down.

"Wait," the old woman wailed. "There's been a mistake . . ."

"Right, lady," Gillia growled as he cornered her and got into position to smack. Then he became the startled one as she clawed out a voting card. It was stamped with Walsh's name, and time and date of voting. Aw, clot! The old bugger *had* already cast her ballot.

Gillia hit her anyway. He was too worried to make it

his best shot—just enough to get her on the ground so he could give her a kick in the ribs.

Then, as his boot swung forward, a heavy hand grabbed his collar and he felt himself flailing back. He slammed onto the floor. He tried to roll to avoid the next blow, but he was past it and the roll came out more like a flop. The club caught him in the belly, and air whooshed out.

Gillia fought for breath. A red haze blurred his view. But through it, he could see a grinning young woman standing over him. She had sloping shoulders, a muscular neck, and shapely arms bulging with muscle. Nearby, he heard the old woman's gloating cackle. Above him, the young woman shifted her grip on the club and brought it down.

Just before it hit and pain and blackness descended, he heard his goons outside screaming in terror.

An hour later, Gillia's unconscious body was dumped in a far-off woods, as was every member of his poll-riding team.

Meanwhile, all the gravcars were seized and repainted with Yelad's name and likeness. Raschid's own dirty tricksters spread out through the Tyrenne's own wards.

"Can't let a good move like that go to waste," Raschid had told Avri.

Pavy had been more than happy to supply some of her best mob muscle to the game.

Tyrenne Yelad attacked one hour before the polls closed. Three hundred handpicked goons raided Walsh's headquarters, under orders to break every head, wreck every office, and carry off every document they could find.

The small force outside the building put up a token fight. It was quickly overwhelmed and put to flight. The bonfire team got busy outside stoking up a blaze into which furniture, documents, and anything else flammable would be hurled. A squad hastily assembled a steel ram and smashed through the double doors. A moment later Yelad's goons poured inside.

Raschid laughed as the goons rushed up the stairs. Just before the first wave hit him, he gave the signal. His shock troops leapt out of their hiding places and counterattacked. There were five hundred of them, all just as big, mean, and willing to hurt as Yelad's forces.

Raschid caught the first goon by the club arm. There was a dry snap as he broke it; then he spun to the side and grabbed the next goon by the ear, which he used as a lever to hurl his attacker to the floor. The ear came away in his hand and the being's head gave a bounce on a jutting stair. Raschid hurled the torn-off ear into the startled face of a third brute. As he booted the goon in the crotch and reached for a fourth victim, he saw Yelad's forces buried under the wave of counterattackers.

This was going well. There was nothing Raschid liked better than hands-on electioneering.

Lieutenant Skinner reached the last Walsh polling spot a few minutes before the doors closed. Despite the lateness of the hour, she was in no hurry.

Election night was usually one of Skinner's favorite times. There was always plenty of pleasant hitting to do and heaps of spare mordida about.

This time, however, she was one unmotivated cop. All over, the juice had stopped. She was starting to feel poverty-stricken, and her captain whined that he was no better off. Well, clot him! She was sure he was just looking out for himself. In other wards, her colleagues were moaning over the same misfortune.

So she had hit the streets with no hopes and little oomph. It did not improve her mood any to learn that she was right. Not only was there no mordida, but every citizen was as likely to attack her as to spit in her eye.

Her main job was to greet Yelad's phony voters when they arrived at the polls. She and her six-being team were supposed to hustle them off the gravtrucks, make sure they voted fast and correctly, then load them back on the vehicle to be rushed to the next spot.

Almost no one showed. Skinner got on the horn right away. The first time the shrieking voice on the other side shouted that it was just a mess up, some kind of delay. Skinner said sure and got off. She was not calmed by the hysteria in that voice. The second time, same thing. But, from then on out, all lines were jammed. Skinner realized with a shock that all over Dusable the same thing was happening. Cops like her were making the same panic calls.

Oh, well. She would just duck her head, do her job, and go home and get drunk when the election was over.

During the whole night only a few gravtrucks arrived. But even that was no solace. Because there was a surprise awaiting them at each poll. Joygirls and joyboys were out in force, guarded by so many mob pimps Skinner would have had to have been afflicted with a death wish to interfere. The pleasure sellers would mince up to the mark, throw a little seduction into the air, and the deal would be made. Instead of Yelad, the phony vote would go to Walsh. The payoff, a few sweet minutes in a handy dark place.

There was nothing Skinner could do about it. She didn't have the muscle. After a while, she started getting horny herself. By the time she reached the last stop, she didn't know whether she was too pissed to be horny, or too horny to be pissed.

Her jaw dropped when she saw one of the joyboys working the line of voters. It was her own little lad! Ah, how she had missed him. When she saw his curly locks and soft mouth, all thoughts of anger disappeared.

Lieutenant Skinner fished out her voting card and joined the line.

Clot it! Her vote was going to Walsh.

In the Cairenes—especially on Dusable—there was a puzzling mechanical law that struck every election pe-

riod. No sooner were the polls closed than the main computer would jam up and crash. There it would sit for half
the night while teams of expensive techs were rushed in
to tinker at its works and shake their heads over bitter
caff.

At the appropriate time, there would be huzzahs of
victory from the techs, and the computer would kick in,
counting the votes and spitting out the results.

There was never any suspense in this final act. Yelad
always won.

The Tyrenne huddled in his yawning office with his top
aides. Despite the nightmare that had stalked him all day
and night, Yelad's mood was fairly light. It helped that
he was drunk. It helped still more that the mechanical
law of Dusable elections had cut in right on time. Saved
by a crashing computer! He chortled, took a slug from
the bottle, and growled for his chief registrar to get to it.
The screen lit up on Yelad's desk. *Now* he would see what
he would see.

The way it was supposed to work—clot, the way it
always worked—was that now the real count would begin. The broken-down computer would hum into action.
Its first task was to tally the enemy wards. That would
let Yelad know his opponent's strength. Then he would
have his own vote counted, and the margin of victory
adjusted by the millions of grave votes he had at his command.

He had to be careful. If he cheated too blatantly, the
shrill questioning could wreck the first year of his new
term. This time, however, Yelad was throwing caution
off the roof. Walsh's tactics had him aching for revenge.
He would bury the little clot in a landslide of historic
proportions.

Yelad jumped when he heard his registrar groan. What
the clot?

Walsh's vote was coming in. ''Flooding in'' was a better description. In ward after ward he was sweeping to
victory!

A half hour later Yelad was suddenly sober. He was in deep drakh. Walsh's margin was so great that Yelad would have to vote every dead being in his files. He steeled himself and chugged down half the bottle. Fine! He'd do what was necessary. Hang what happened next. He would still be Tyrenne.

Impatiently he ordered his registrar to start the tally of wards. He settled back for a long night of counting.

The night proved short. One hour later the awful truth began to sink in.

Yelad's vote was nearly nonexistent.

Later, he would figure it out. Somebody had mickied the computer. All across Dusable, every time a committed voter hit the button, it would be recorded instead for Walsh. The official total gave him less than half-a-million votes.

Dusable's dead rested easy in their grave vaults that night.

Yelad had lost.

From that time forward he would be mocked as "Landslide Yelad."

Raschid did not attend Walsh and Kenna's victory party. Instead, he had a very private meeting with Solon Kenna in his offices. It was time to set his price.

The thought came to him as he was watching the election feed on the livie box. It was followed by an overwhelming feeling of urgency. He had to act. Fast.

As he rushed to his hastily arranged meeting with Kenna, the dense clouds that had boiled in his brain for all this time began to thin out, then lift away.

He had passed the Final Test.

Kenna was relieved when Raschid told him what he required: a fast ship, loaded with all the AM2 it could hold, ready for lift within six hours. Kenna thought that no price at all. He figured Raschid would beggar the mordida coffers. Not that it wasn't well worth it. In fact, from his viewpoint, Raschid's payment was so little that even Kenna's crooked soul stung a bit.

"Are you sure," Solon Kenna pressed, "that we can't do anything more?"

"Maybe you can," came the answer. "I'm not sure. But right now, why don't you just stick tight. Enjoy yourself. I'll get back to you."

The Eternal Emperor shook the hand of one singularly happy politician.

CHAPTER TWENTY-FIVE

THE KEY TO the Kingdom looked unimpressive—deliberately so. It was a small moonlet, one of dozens larger and smaller, orbiting around a Jovian planet. The system was notable for only two reasons: it was completely without commercial value, and it was two steps beyond nowhere.

The moonlet had been constructed several centuries before. An asteroid was chosen for its size and worthlessness. Deep space crews were paid to excavate patterns across the asteroid and to install cables in those patterns. The excavations were filled in. The first crew was paid off and informed that their work had been part of a classified Imperial project. Then a second crew was brought in to construct a small underground shelter and, a few klicks away, an underground dock, hidden from line-of-sight to the shelter by a high ridge. Into the shelter went generators, supplies, and several elaborate and undescribed coms. The second crew was paid off. Somehow, as time passed, the beings who had worked on either crew got the idea that the classified project had been a failure, just another unspectacular research pan-out.

Drone tugs moved the asteroid to its chosen location around the gaseous giant and nudged it into orbit. Later Mantis teams, who were not told of the asteroid's existence, were sent in to provide security monitors in the system.

There were four other "keys" scattered around the

universe, their location known only to the Eternal Emperor. They all had the same purpose.

The coms were set to accept only the Eternal Emperor and contained every screening device conceivable, from DNA pattern to pore prints, even to include the specious Bertillon classification. If anyone else entered the shelter, the coms would melt down into incomprehensible slag.

The coms were linked to a ship, somewhere in . . . another space . . . and to the roboticized mining/factory ships around it. On signal, the recommendation from the ship would be changed. Transshipment of AM2 would begin.

The long trains of robot "tankers" could also be controlled from the moonlet. Under "normal" circumstances, such as The Eternal Emperor having died accidentally, they might be routed to the conventional depot worlds. Or, under differing circumstances, elsewhere. To reward the faithful and punish the heathens— or vice versa, depending on what the Emperor decided was the quickest, most expeditious way to regain control.

The Eternal Emperor crept into the system. He was in no hurry whatsoever. He repeatedly consulted the elaborate pickups he had requested be installed in the ship donated by the grateful Kenna. If any of the sensors showed *any* intrusion into the system—a lost mining ship, a drone, or even a wandering yacht—there was only one choice. Instantly abort and move to whichever moonlet was convenient for a secondary command site.

There was nothing reported by any of the out-system sensors. The Emperor chanced an arcing sweep over the system itself. Nothing. Emboldened, he reentered the system and closed on the gaseous giant. All pickups were clean.

He came in on the moonlet on the hemisphere opposite the shelter and nap-of-the-earthed to the dock. Its ports yawned—again, pickups clean—and he landed.

The Emperor suited up, made sure the suit's support mechanisms were loaded, and started for the shelter.

Halfway up that ridge, he muttered under his breath about being too paranoid. It was not easy staying low on a nearly zero-gee world. He had no desire to "pop up" into range if anyone was waiting at the dome, or to punt himself into orbit. Not only would jetting back be embarrassing, but he would be too easy to pick up if he was walking into a trap.

A few hundred meters from the shelter's entrance—just another slide-blocked cave—he stopped. He waited a full six E-hours, watching. Nothing. The way was clear.

The suit's environment system whined, trying to stabilize the temperature and recycle the sweat pouring from the Emperor's body. His fingers unconsciously touched his chest. Under suit, skin, and muscle the bomb waited.

He unsealed his pistol's holster and took a tiny com from his belt. He slid a wand-like probe out. In a rush, he went across the open space to the slide area. The probe was inserted into a nearly invisible hole, and the Emperor touched a button. After a moment, the slide opened. The Emperor could feel the vibration under his boot heels.

He walked into the cavern. The door slid closed behind him. Lights glowed on. He checked a panel. Again, no intrusion. The heaters were on full blast, and atmosphere was being dumped into the shelter. Very good.

He walked to a door, palmed it, and the door slid away. Inside, there was a small bedroom/kitchen/living suite. He closed the door behind him and glanced at another panel. Atmosphere . . . ninety-five percent E-normal. Temperature . . . acceptable. He unsealed his faceplate.

He felt hungry. The Emperor hoped that he had provided adequate rations. He would eat, then activate the com. He walked to the com room entrance—and the world shattered! He was greeted not by gleaming, waiting readouts and signal gear, but by cooled masses of molten metal.

Instantly the signal began, in his brain:

Exposure . . . Trap . . . Discovered . . . Self-destruct! Self-destruct!

Another part of his brain:

No. Wait. Trap not confirmed. Too much time. Cannot recommence program without terminal damage to goal! Return to stand-by! Program override!

The bomb did not go off. Not even when the storeroom door opened and a voice said, "My security operatives were not as sophisticated as they believed."

The Emperor saw a space-suited figure, tall and gaunt. An arm reached up and opened the suit's faceplate. It was Kyes.

Again, the order . . . and again, somehow, the command was overridden.

"I am the only being in this system—besides yourself," Kyes said.

The Emperor found he could think once more. He said nothing, very sure that his voice would crack if he spoke. Kyes waited, then continued.

"Your progression here—and to return to your throne— is clever. It reminds me a bit of an Earth-legend I read. About a human named, I recall, Theseus."

"It could not have been that clever," the Emperor managed.

"Not true. For anyone to look for you, let alone find you, requires beginning with an insane belief: that you did not die. And then incredible resources."

Kyes indicated the destroyed com sets.

"My apologies for the ineptitude of my personnel. Although I am sure other stations besides this one exist. The resumption of the AM2 shipments can still begin— although that is meaningless to me."

The Emperor considered that. The situation was becoming . . . not familiar, but it appeared to be within understanding and possible control. First assumption: Kyes was planning to cut a deal and betray his fellow

conspirators. No. He had said that AM2 was meaningless. Kyes wanted something else.

"You said you and I are the only beings in this system.
To ask the obvious question: What is to prevent me from
simply shooting you and escaping?"

"Why would you do something such as that?" Kyes
asked in astonishment. "Revenge? Hardly a sensible motive, let alone Imperial. Especially considering that our
attempt to . . . alter the chains of power . . . failed."

Failed? Instant analysis: Kyes's previous statement that
"you did not die," and now this. The situation was im-
proving—Kyes had not understood everything.

"Even if you desired to indulge your whim . . ." Kyes
lifted a transmitter from his belt. "Standard vital-signs
transmitter. If it ceases broadcasting, my support team
will move in. I do not think that you could escape their
net."

"You are making some large assumptions, Sr. Kyes. I
have been known to indulge myself on occasion. Privilege of the purple and all that."

"True. At first, when I established where you were
headed, I thought of an ambush—while I remained safely
in the wings. Tranquilizer guns . . . gas . . . whatever.
Instantly immobilize you, hold you in a drugged state
until mind control could be accomplished. But I did not
think any plan I conceived would work. You've slipped
through too many nets in the past.

"Besides . . . if I offered you violence, you would be
almost certain to reject my offer."

"I am listening."

"First, I offer you my complete, personal loyalty and
support. I will do anything—either from within or without—to remove the privy council.

"I am not trying to convince you that my assistance
would in any way decisively ensure the outcome which I
see as inevitable. But I could make their downfall happen
much more rapidly, and probably decrease the amount of
havoc they can wreak as they are destroyed.

"Once your Empire is restored, I offer you my continuing loyalty and support."

"Turning one's coat," the Emperor said, "tends to be habit-forming."

"It will not happen. Not if you fulfill your part of the bargain.

"But that is as may be. You might choose not to be reminded of . . . what has happened by my presence. In which case I accept exile, which in no way will lessen my offer to assist in any way conceivable.

"However, I can offer something still more important. My entire species as your freely consenting—'slaves' is not a correct word. But that is, in essence, what we would be if you can conceive of any slave leaping into chains.

"This, too, is easily achieved."

"Your people," the Emperor observed, "certainly would be welcomed if they chose to become total supporters of my Empire. Not, unless I am missing something . . . easily achieved, as you just said."

"You are wrong."

"Very well then. What, specifically, am I to deliver?" the Emperor asked, although he was suddenly, sickeningly aware of what the answer had to be.

"Life," Kyes said hoarsely, almost stammering. "Immortality. You perhaps understand the tragedy of death. But what if it occurs at a preset, biologically determined time, a time when a being is at the full height of his powers and awareness? The tragedy of our species.

"I want—and I want for my people—eternal life. The same immortality you have.

"I offered to make a bargain. I will better it. I will now guarantee everything I said. As your subject, I ask for this gift."

And Kyes awkwardly knelt.

There was silence—a silence that lasted for years.

"You poor, sad bastard," the Emperor finally said.

Kyes rose. "How can you reject this? How can you ignore my logic? My promises?"

The Emperor chose his words carefully. "Logic . . . promises . . . have nothing to do with it. Listen to what I am saying. *I* am immortal. But—" He tapped his chest. "This body is not. You are asking a gift I *cannot* give. Not to you, not to any other being of any other race or species."

Kyes's eyes were burning lances. "This is the truth?"

"Yes."

And Kyes believed. But his stare continued. Uncomfortable, the Emperor turned away. Again, there was the long silence. The Eternal Emperor reached deep into his bag of tricks.

"Perhaps . . . perhaps there is a compromise. I am willing to make a counteroffer. You help me destroy the privy council, and I will find the resources to commit to a research program, funded and supported as a manhattanproject.

"It might take generations. Such a program—if a solution can be found—will not help you or your generation. But that is the best offer I can make."

He turned back. Kyes had not moved.

"It is unsatisfactory," the Emperor started, "compared to what—" He stopped.

There was no response whatever from the Grb'chev. The Emperor moved out of Kyes's line of sight. Neither Kyes's head nor eyes shifted. The Emperor went to him and moved his hand across Kyes's field of vision. No response.

Perhaps it was the shock, realizing that there was no Holy Grail for Kyes or his species. Perhaps it was less dramatic—he *was* far beyond his time.

Kyes's mouth fell open. Digestive fluids dribbled from it.

The Emperor quickly checked the vital-signs indicator on Kyes's belt. All physical indicators . . . normal.

He snapped his faceplate closed and hurried toward the exit, then turned back.

The idiot that had been Kyes still stood as it had, held erect by the weight of his suit.

"Poor, sad bastard," the Emperor said again.

It was the best epitaph he could manage—and the only one he had time for.

BOOK FOUR

"MORITURI TE SALUTAMUS"

CHAPTER TWENTY-SIX

THE SCHOLARS OF Newton wore a perpetual puzzled expression that an agro-world student once compared to a cow who had just had an inseminator's burly fist jammed up its behind. As the Tribunal neared its opening, Sten saw the puzzled look jump to open, smiling surprise. Kilgour said it was as if the fist had been replaced by the real thing.

Never in its dusty, academic history had the thousands of professors who toiled on the university world been paid so much attention.

When word was purposefully leaked of the events about to unfold, livie crews from all over the Empire raced to Newton to beat the expected privy-council crackdown. Newton's administration was nearly buried by requests for permission to attend, not just from news teams, but from political experts, legal scholars, historians, and the merely curious.

Sten, Alex, and Mahoney scrambled like mad beings to set up a security system to sift through the millions of requests. The task was especially difficult, because the whole idea was to give maximum exposure to the Tribunal's proceedings. They managed to get it all in hand—plus hundreds of other details—before the public opening.

Meanwhile, Dean Blythe, his faculty, and the millions of students who attended the many colleges that made up the university system, were besieged for interviews. No dull fact, boring reaction, or drab bit of color was too

273

lowly for the news-hungry media. For a short time every resident of Newton was a livie star.

The information hunger was particularly intense, because although Sr. Ecu had revealed the general purposes of the Tribunal—sitting in judgment of the privy council—he had kept the nature of the charges secret to all but the judges. Everyone believed the bill of indictment involved the AM2. In other words, conspiracy to defraud. Sr. Ecu could only imagine the surprise when the real charges were announced: Conspiracy to murder.

Sr. Ecu had chosen Newton because of its long history and reputation for impartiality. He had expected, however, tremendous difficulty in getting Dean Blythe to agree to host the Tribunal. Instead, once the security precautions had been detailed, the agreement was quickly reached. It helped that Dean Blythe had been an Imperial general before he had taken up the life of a scholastic. More importantly, one of the first places the privy council had chosen for its budget cuts was Newton. Those cuts had been followed by a host of others as the Imperials trimmed and trimmed to keep the economic ship afloat.

A hefty donation of the AM2 Sten had stolen smoothed the rest of the way.

A huge auditorium was quickly prepared. A long court bench was installed on the stage for the members of the Tribunal. The backstage area was converted into offices for the legal support group. Outside and inside, potential security danger areas were plugged. Teams of guards were assigned to the livie-crew techs responsible for installing communication lines.

Meanwhile the Bhor fighting ships spread out around the Jura System and its capital world of Newton, or began patrolling areas believed most likely for attack routes.

In the midst of all that, the members of the Tribunal and their retinue arrived. Sten and Alex personally greeted each being and assigned the bodyguards who would shadow them from that moment on.

Sr. Ecu had chosen three beings to sit as judges over the privy council. Despite the great danger involved, he had no shortage of volunteer candidates. The depression triggered by the privy council's actions had become so deep that many systems feared for their own survival far more than they did Imperial reprisal.

The three systems he eventually drew from were among the most respected in the Empire—as were the beings who would form the Tribunal.

The first to arrive was Warin, from the great agricultural worlds of Ryania. He was a big, ponderous thinking being whose heavily bone-plated skull hid a three-brain mental system capable of sifting through mountains of conflicting information. Warin was slow and to the point, but he always arrived with plenty of thinking ammunition. He was also completely open-minded as far as the crimes alleged against the privy council.

The second was Rivas, from the distant frontier territory of Jono. Rivas was a slender, quick-witted human, noted for his ability to find middle ground where little existed—an important, much honored skill in the wilds of Jono, where there sometimes seemed more opposing viewpoints than people. He had warned Sr. Ecu that, although he despised the current actions of the privy council, he did not necessarily believe that they were all acting out of selfish motives. His opinion of Kyes, for example, was quite good. His previous dealings with the being had all gone well and had shown Kyes to be honorable.

The final member was perhaps the most respected. Her name was Apus, and she was the Queen Mother of Fernomia. She was very old and cared not a bit that her title carried no royal authority. Her many daughters and granddaughters oversaw the billions of females and few million males who made up the populations of the Fernomia Cluster. Despite her age, her health was excellent, her six spindly legs sturdy, and her mandibles as fluid and flexible as when she had been young. She confessed to Sr. Ecu that she despised the members of the privy council—especially the Kraa twins, who some years earlier had cheated her people out of a fortune in mineral rights—but Sr. Ecu knew that would not affect the Queen Mother's impartial consideration of the evidence.

The three beings were installed in comfortable, well-guarded quarters. Just before the Tribunal was convened, Ecu huddled with the three judges to lay out the rules they would operate under.

It was agreed that he would be the Tribunal referee. It would be his responsibility to see that all evidence was fairly presented and weighed. Any rulings he made could not be overturned. He would also be the public spokes-being for the Tribunal. All queries would be addressed to him, and he alone would be permitted to answer—after consulting with the three judges. It was also agreed that Sr. Ecu would be responsible for gathering evidence and presenting witnesses. The three voted to invest him with authority to swear in court officers to accomplish these things.

Afterward, Sr. Ecu rushed about, dotting the i's and crossing the t's on the final details.

When Sten was summoned to Sr. Ecu's garden quarters, he noted how tired the old diplomat seemed. His sensing tendrils twittered with nervous exhaustion; his color was gray and poor. But Sten had no time to sympathize or comment—Sr. Ecu ordered him to raise his right hand.

Sten did as he was told.

"Do you swear to uphold the integrity of these proceedings and the ancient laws of the Empire under whose sanctity we act?"

Sten swore he did.

"Then, by the authority invested in me I appoint you chief officer of this Tribunal," Sr. Ecu intoned.

Although he had known exactly what was to happen, Sten felt a little intimidated by Sr. Ecu's stern speech. It was also a little comforting that the old diplomat meant every word he was saying. This Tribunal would be no sham.

As he left the garden, Alex and Mahoney were waiting to enter. A few minutes later, they returned, as quiet and humble as he.

In silence, the three started back for their quarters. But as they did so, a small group of guards broke away from the ones posted outside. Sten gaped at them as they took up position around him.

One of them was Cind. Her eyes shone with excitement as she hustled her charges into proper order. Then she drew up before Sten and snapped him a sharp salute.

"Is everything to your satisfaction? Sir!"

"What in the world are you talking about, woman?" Sten grated out.

"Why, this is your bodyguard, sir," Cind said, barely suppressing a grin. "If there are any complaints, please address them to me—the commander of *your* guard."

Sten sputtered he wasn't having any of this. He didn't want a bodyguard, or need a bodyguard. And furthermore . . .

"Sr. Ecu's orders. Sir!" came Cind's response.

Before Sten could argue any further, his two friends burst into laughter.

"Better do as you're told, young Sten," Mahoney admonished.

"Aye, lad," that clot Kilgour said. "Ye're a braw an' noble person, noo. Cannae be riskin't th' life ae th' chief ossifer ae th' court, noo can we?"

As a very happy Cind escorted him back to his rooms, Sten had murder in his heart—and two likely victims chortling nearby.

The opening of the Tribunal was delayed half the morning as thousands of beings converged on the hall. Assigned seats were quickly filled, and the inside temperature soared past the ability of the climate machines to keep control. Outside, thousands of the curious fought to get within seeing and hearing distance of the vid screens and big speakers set up to display the proceedings.

Troops forced wide avenues through the crowds to admit the news livie crews. Their warrior tempers were sorely tested as they pushed and prodded, rather than breaking heads, or simply opening fire. Eventually, order was restored.

A great silence fell as every being craned to get a view of the still-empty stage. It was not just the threat of violence that kept the peace, or anticipation of a one-of-a-kind event in Imperial history.

Above the stage was an immense portrait of the Eternal Emperor. It was a romantic likeness, grandly heroic, of the style favored by the late Tanz Sullamora. Except for the eyes. Sten shivered when he looked at them. They bored straight out, stabbing into the soul of every being.

Sten knew the look. "Well, you puny little being," they seemed to ask. "What have you got to say for yourself?"

The icy grip of that painted glare was broken when Sr. Ecu gave a flip of his tail and skimmed out over the stage. The only sound from the crowd was an unconscious drawing in of breath. Then the three Tribunal judges followed. They took positions at the bench.

There were a few hushed whispers as legal clerks wheeled in carts of documents. Dean Blythe took up his post to the far right. He was to oversee the sanctity of the computer that would serve as the official recorder.

Livie crews dollied in for a series of symbolic tight shots, starting first with Warin, then Rivas, then Queen Mother Apus—and finally Sr. Ecu. The old diplomat waited a few dramatic moments, then spoke.

"The proceedings of this Tribunal are now officially open."

Such a simple sentence, but it brought a gasp from the crowd. Everyone knew that from that moment on, every word uttered was a direct challenge to the privy council's authority.

"We are present to hear evidence concerning grave charges brought against the governing body of this Empire. The fact that these proceedings are being held under armed supervision to protect us from this same body is to have no influence on any member of the Tribunal. All three judges have agreed and sworn to this.

"My first official act of these hearings is to invite the presence of any and all members of the privy council to answer or refute any evidence brought against them.

"This is no empty act on my part. I personally plead with each and every one of them to respond . . .

"Now, for the reading of the bill of indictment:

"Members of the privy council, you have been charged with conspiracy to murder the Eternal Emperor.

"In your absence, a not-guilty plea will automatically—"

The rest was buried in the screaming, shouting reactions from the crowd. It took three more hours to regain control.

By then, there was not much time left before the Tribunal recessed for the day. The only action of real note was that the three judges drew straws to determine who would speak for the privy council, and who for the prosecution.

Queen Mother Apus—who despised the Kraas—ended up their fervent official supporter. Sten was amazed how quickly and ably she took up the task, despite her hatred for the twins, as well as their colleagues. Rivas, who was partial to Sr. Kyes, became the privy council's prosecutor. His voice became instantly tinged with bitter irony whenever a speck of evidence was brought forth against the council.

Sten would have loved nothing more than to become one of the crowd, to witness the events and see justice fairly done, just like any normal being who was fortunate enough to be in this place.

But that, as the Bhor might have said, was not to be his fate. "At the forges of the gods," Otho had once said when deep in his stregghorn, "it is our curse to always be the hammer when they strike."

CHAPTER TWENTY-SEVEN

POYNDEX WAS NOT a being of temperament. Long before, he had put away anger with his childhood toys. He left elation behind with adolescence. In fact, there was not one emotion he did not have under control. Ambition was the only fruit he nourished in this garden of the middle ground. Achieving power was his only pleasure.

So as his colleagues on the privy council raged at the "shocking and spurious allegations" of Sr. Ecu's Tribunal, he knew fear for the first time in his life. He saw the power slipping away.

The instant he saw the liviecast of Sr. Ecu's announcement of the murder charges, he believed it was true. The reaction came from the gut. As he rushed to the hastily called meeting of the council, the surer he became. It became clearer to him as he entered the enormous building the council had constructed as its headquarters. The odd, towering tree that grew up through the central courtyard seemed withered and ailing. For Poyndex, who was not a being taken to symbolic thought, the condition of the rubiginosa still seemed to bode ill.

It just made more sense that the assassination of the Emperor was not the act of a lone madman. A conspiracy was far more likely. And who had the most to gain from such a plot? The answer became all too obvious as he entered the meeting room.

Everyone was in a bellowing rage. The Kraa twins were purple with fury. Lovett kept pounding on the polished meeting table, screaming for bloody action. Malperin was

281

letting loose an odd stream of obscenities at the awful lies being told.

When he saw the violent reaction, Poyndex knew his instincts had been on the mark. He was looking at the beings who killed the Eternal Emperor.

Why else all that outrage? If the charges were false, then it was merely a ploy by their enemies. The council members were all experienced businessbeings who had dealt with such mudslinging all their professional lives.

He also noted their faces when they were in between bellows, gasping for breath. He did not imagine the guilty looks of fear they exchanged. The capper was the Kraa twins. In their anxiety, they immediately switched roles. As they consumed the usual huge quantities of food, the skeletal one stopped her endless trips to the fresher. Instead, the obese one became the twin who was constantly heading off to vomit.

That's when the fear struck him. He had only just achieved his lifelong ambition. As a member of the privy council, Poyndex had reached his dream of great power. He knew he could swiftly consolidate and strengthen it even more as he learned which buttons of manipulation to punch. Poyndex had never had any thoughts of being a great tyrant, a single ruler. He liked staying in the shadows, where it was safer. Also, like Kyes, he had no love of the trappings of office and was content to let his fellow members shine in whatever sun pleased them. Poyndex knew he could get what he wanted far more easily as the being who gave favors, rather than took them.

Before the Tribunal's charges were announced, Poyndex had only just begun to recover from the blow of the loss of his mentor. When Kyes—or the gibbering thing that had been Kyes—was brought back from his mysterious journey, he knew he had lost his main supporter in any contest of wills with the rest of the council.

But, if anything, his colleagues became more dependent on him. They listened closely to his cool advice on all matters, not just those involving the military or intelligence, but on Imperial policy as well. There was no talk of filling Kyes's post with a new council member.

Now that he thought of it, their reaction to what had happened to Kyes was also very odd. They took it quietly—mildly, almost. They asked no real questions and hastily arranged for the poor creature to be cared for in a top-secret military hospital for the insane. Actually, they seemed relieved. Poyndex thought it was because there was one less guilty party who could tell the tale.

As the privy council struggled to come up with a counterattack, Poyndex knew the first thing he had to do was cover his ass. It was apparent, no matter what the outcome, that these beings were doomed. It was not important if they destroyed the Tribunal and its allies. The charges would eventually bring them down.

Poyndex was determined that he would not go down with them. So, as his colleagues debated, he started rummaging through his bag of survival tricks.

The Kraas wanted to fire fleets out in all directions. Every system vaguely involved with the Tribunal would be crushed and garrisoned with Imperial troops. Lovett and Malperin shouted approval. Poyndex waited until some of the steam went out before he spoke.

"I share your outrage," he said. "Although I am not listed by name in these awful lies, I consider an attack on any single member an attack on us all. But we still have to face reality. There simply isn't enough AM2 to accomplish a tenth of what you are saying."

His words were greeted with sober silence. What he said was true. They began narrowing the scope of the operation, bit by bit, Poyndex subtly coaxing them on. Finally it was decided there would only be one target: Newton. A crack fleet would be sent, and all surviving parties—if any—would be hauled back to Prime World for punishment. Malperin cautioned that the troops might not be all that loyal, considering the recent military purges. Poyndex knew that she also was worried that the assassination charge itself would spark a revolt. It was a very guilty statement, one that the others quickly took up. As much as possible, only intensely loyal beings would man the fleet.

Before agreement was reached and the fleet sent, Poyndex raised a purposeful warning flag—for the official record.

"I'm sure, of course, this is what must be done," Poyndex said. "You've argued so persuasively. However, it would be remiss of me not to point out the dangers in this action.

"Some might argue that it would be better to ignore the whole thing. You've already ordered an Empirewide blackout of the proceedings. Continue it. Make no response. Then let them slink away. We could arrest them at our leisure. Also, the attack itself might backblast. Our own allies may become fearful. But I'm sure all of you know these things. I'm only pointing them out so that no little detail might be overlooked."

"Bloody hell on th' allies," one Kraa snarled.

"If we *don't* act, some fools might think those outrageous charges are true," Malperin said.

"Send the fleet," Lovett said.

Poyndex sent the fleet. However, as he was issuing orders all around, he called in his most trusted aides. There was a great deal of ass covering to be done.

Poyndex had to get ahead of events before they ran him down.

CHAPTER TWENTY-EIGHT

IMPERIAL CAPTAIN OF the Guard (Retired) Hosford topped the hill, rested on his staff, and gave himself five solid minutes of wheezing before starting downslope, across the next valley, and up the next ridge. Foothills, he thought. Foothills of the clottin' Himalayas, you ought to add.

Not only did he feel himself too fat and too old for this assignment, but it was a perfectly empty and thankless one.

There had been two things eternal about the Empire. A pistol and a bomb had proven one to be mortal. The other was the Gurkhas.

The Gurkhas were the best soldiers any world had ever produced, human or otherwise. Most people hoped that a species of still-more lethal killers would not appear—or that if they did, they would be as firmly on the side of the Empire as the Gurkhas. The Gurkhas and the Empire were one and the same to the many, many people who had seen them on the livies.

The privy council wanted them back. Both because they wanted absolutely faithful, absolutely incorruptible beings for their bodyguards, and to legitimize their own rule.

Hence Captain Hosford's mission.

Hosford had been—years, lifetime, lifetimes ago, he thought—commander of the Gurkha bodyguard at the Emperor's palace of Arundel. He had been a very promising officer, guaranteed for high rank—as, indeed, was anyone picked for Captain of the Guard.

The assignment was glamorous—and gave its holder no time for a personal life, as Sten had discovered when he had replaced Hosford in the position.

All went well—until Hosford fell in love. Completely, absolutely. So much so that he had covered the walls of his quarters with paintings of Maeve. Maeve never said anything, but Hosford realized the choice was clear. The assignment—or her.

He called in every favor he could to get out. The military powers did not like one of their chosen ones changing the plans they had for him. So the only assignment offered was an exile post on a frontier world. Hosford took it, and Maeve went with him.

Obviously there was no more career for him in the Guard. He resigned his commission, chose not to reenlist when the Tahn wars started, and wandered with Maeve. He had thought that wandering aimless, but he had once plotted his travels and realized that they led, in a perfectly logical pattern, to Earth.

And the Gurkhas.

The Gurkhas who had survived Imperial duty may have been rich, but Nepal was still a very primitive province. It was kept that way by its king, who claimed that his succession ran back to when the mountain gods were born. He must protect Nepal and his people. The country was a sacred place, from the peaks of Dhaulagiri, Annapurna, and Chomolungma to the Gautama Buddha's birthplace in the Lumbini Valley. In practice that meant the Nepalese were actively discouraged from becoming too "civilized." They no longer died of the same diseases, nor was tuberculosis endemic, and lifespan was extended—if not by "civilized" Imperial standards—but it was still a hard, primitive tribal existence. Hosford wanted to help.

He was not permitted to settle in Nepal—no foreigners were allowed in the country except in limited numbers for brief visits. But he and Maeve found a home in Darjeeling, in the nearby province of Gurkhali, once part of a long-fragmented nation called India.

From there, he did what he could. He encouraged education and teachers inside Nepal, assisted any old soldier he could, and helped and found work for the depressed, near-suicidal young men who were rejected from the military.

He and other ex-Gurkha officers were allowed into Nepal twice a year to distribute pension monies, to offer any technical education they could, and to recruit—until six years earlier, when the Emperor had been murdered and the Gurkhas returned home. Every year, Hosford was commissioned by a representative of the privy council to try recruiting once more. Every year he was greeted with smiles and whiskey and told "We serve the Emperor. Only."

The first two years he tried arguing: The Emperor was dead. Were they planning to abandon their military tradition? Their answer was: "No, Captain. We are not foolish. When the Emperor returns, so shall we. But serve this privy council? Never. They are worth less than one yak pubic hair."

Why did he keep returning? The commission was part of it—he left the monies with village heads for their own purposes. But just being in the mountains, being in Nepal, being with the Nepalese was reason enough.

One more year, he groaned. One more trip. One more rejection. This must be the last one. Otherwise his body would be found, years later, dead on some unknown hillside when his heart gave out. This . . . well, no. Perhaps next year. But that would definitely be the last.

Ahead lay the Gurkha Center in the hamlet of Pokhara. Hosford shifted the heavy pack of credits and marched on. He knew what he would see from the next hilltop. The center, and some of his old comrades waiting. Somehow they always knew when he would be there. They would be drawn to as rigid attention as their age permitted. At their head would be ex-Havildar Major Mankajiri Gurung, who, unless he was actually his son, Imperial records said was over 250 years old. Them . . . but that would be all.

Pokhara, in fact, was a confusion of noise, music, and youth. Almost, Hosford estimated, a thousand of them, drawn up in what screaming old men were telling them was a military formation, and if they shamed their clan or Captain Hosford they would be tied up in barrels and rolled into the headwaters of the Sacred Ganges to disappear into the sea.

In front of the assembly stood Mankajiri. He saluted. Hosford returned the salute. He should have waited to ask, but could not.

"These are . . . recruits?" he wondered aloud.

"Such as they are. Mountain wildflowers compared to men of our wars, Captain. But recruits, if they pass your careful eye. Their medical records wait for your examination."

"Why the change?"

"Change? There has been no change."

"But you said you would never serve the privy council."

"Again, no change. These men will serve the Emperor. He is returning. He will need us."

Captain Hosford felt a cold chill down his spine—a chill that had nothing to do with the icy winds blowing down from the nearby mountain tops.

" 'Ow lang wi' the' squawkin't an' squeakin't frae th' Tribunal gae on?" Kilgour wondered.

Mahoney shrugged. "Until every lawyer has his day in the sun, and until every challenge the privy council can come up with now or later is answered."

"Ah hae no plans," Kilgour said grimly, "frae much of a later f'r th' clots. Thae drove me off Edinburgh.

Thae'll be ae accountin' f'r that. Wi' me. Nae wi' a court ae law.''

"Alex. We aren't vigilantes,'' Sten said.

"Ye're intendin't to force us inta th' path ae right-eousness frae somebody's namesake? Nae. Nae. I' this all collapses, an' Ah'm morally cert it shall, thae'll nae gie us a wee home back in Mantis. Morally corrupted, we are, we are.

"Ah'll nae adjust t' ae world where y' need more on ae villain than enow t' authorize the usual.'' Alex drew a thumb across his throat.

"If you're through, Laird Kilgour. We are now sworn officers of a legitimate court,'' Sten said, grinning. "While the lawyers are dicin' and slicin', we have to go out and get some concrete evidence for them to chew over when they get tired of talking about whether the Magna Carta's bridge-building ban might pertain.''

"Ah'm noo through. But Ah'll shut m' trap.''

The three of them studied the screen projections.

"I've been fine-combing,'' Sten started. "Trying to read—or at least read a summary of—everything that's appeared on the privy council, from its establishment to the assassination. I've got another team doing the same thing to the present, looking for possible ancillary crimes.

"But let's start with two specific crimes of blood,'' he said. "First is the murder of Volmer. Why was he iced? We know a pro hit him on an open contract. The contract was let by a crime boss, now dead. The assassin is gone, too. Right?''

"So Chief Haines told me.''

"Do you think she was holding out on you?''

"No.'' All three men were relaxing. This was very familiar to them—the standard plotting session any Mantis Team went through before they opened a mission. The fact that it concerned regicide and high treason was another issue entirely.

"Is she worth talking to again?''

"Probably."

"So somebody's going to Prime," Sten said. "Volmer, one of the privy council, gets killed. Why? Was he passing on the conspiracy against the Emperor? Was he trying a power grab on his own?"

"W' nae hae that enow t' guess."

"No. Input: Just before his murder, the privy council met—on Earth. It's the only time that I can find them meeting away from Prime. At least from the public fiche."

"We need to verify that."

"A visit to Prime, once more," Sten agreed. "I'm not sure we'll find any dirt looking at Volmer's death. But it's worth checking.

"Now. The biggie. The Emperor is taken out by one crazed assassin. Chapelle. A nut-case. Is there any chance that he was a lone lunatic? And that the privy council, already conspiring toward takeover someday, seized the opportunity?"

"Negative," Mahoney said flatly. "They moved too quick. And they're not that bright. Except for maybe Kyes."

"Agreed. I ran through your notes, Ian. You had Chapelle's life day by day—and then he disappeared a month or so before he showed up with a gun. Error on your part? Did you have to get out of town before you found those pieces?"

"Negative again. He vanished. All I had is that he'd been seen in company—twice—with that guy who looked rich and way out of . . . oh for the love of God!" Mahoney exclaimed in sudden exasperation, realizing something.

"It nae hurts," Kilgour said, looking interested, "t' rechew the evidence. Continue on, frae love ae God, Fleet Marshal."

"Rich guy. Control, of course. Which I already thought, not being a total dummy. But I never ran the MO. Crooks use the same modus operandi. So do I, so do you, so does the thug there who isn't pouring. I think it's acceptable to add alk to the equation. My mind's starting to work.''

"Ah." Sten got it, and went to pour Mahoney his requested drink.

"Exactly. Ignore the preliminary drakh for the moment, which would have been: Sullamora ran the wet work end of the conspiracy. Died in the blast. Burble, burble, who cares about whether it was an accident or not. The interesting fact is that Tanz Sullamora was too good to ever meet with somebody who's going to pull the trigger. So there had to be a cutout.

"Control. Projected profile. Please record this."

Sten snapped on a recorder.

"Intelligence professional. Established—clean, classic operation. To find or create a psychopath, steer him in the correct direction, and put him in the right place with the right weapon. Chapelle would have had no connection to the organization itself, nor to any high-level person in that conspiracy."

"Ah'll gie thae," Alex said. Both Sten and Kilgour had their Professional Skeptic hats on. Nothing was true, everything was false—the only way to penetrate any kind of apparat.

"I knew that way back when. Control was always who I wanted. Didn't think things through enough. Problem with having spent the last few years runnin' so'jers instead of spooks like you two clowns.

"Anyway. Professional. First I looked at the Empire. Mercury, Mantis, and ex-both. Nothing."

"Verified . . . or are you being sentimental and protecting the Old Boy's Network?"

"The Emperor," Mahoney said harshly, "was a friend of mine. Erase that from the recording. I didn't fudge on that one."

"Thae's many espionage pros out there hae naught t'do with th' Empire, an' ne'er hae," Kilgour said.

"Exactly. Now. Back to the MO. Little trick of the

trade. You want to run a safehouse, run a drop, have a
team on standby—or anything else nefarious. You don't
find a warehouse in the slum, unless you're an amateur
or a criminal. Find yourself a nice, rich, bohemian, if
possible, neighborhood, where nobody knows or cares
who's coming or going, and pride themselves on minding
their own business.''

''Ah. Rich man—Control—shows up in the slum.
Blows in Chapelle's ear, who always thought he was
meant for greatness. Disappears him—still on Prime, of
course,'' Sten reasoned. ''Control built him, taught him,
armed him . . . in a nice, safe, rich mansion in a nice,
safe, rich suburb. Prime again.''

''Clot Prime,'' Mahoney said. ''Read my lips and listen to what I just said. MO, MO, MO. We all reuse
something that works. Rich . . . rich . . . rich. How
many pros use that as a working tool? Can't be that many,
can there?''

''It's a big clottin' universe,'' Sten said. ''But no.
We're in a little tiny subculture here.''

''I already thought of some names.''

''Fine. You got it, Ian. You're in motion. Question—
curiosity—how will you get him to sing? If you find
him?''

Mahoney sneered.

''Sorry,'' Sten said. ''I'm telling my grandmother how
to suck eggs. Shut the recorder off. Back to my line of
reasoning, such as it is:

''If I were running the conspiracy, I'd want to have the
fewest number of meetings possible. I've got one probably established now—the conference on Earth before
Volmer was killed. Was there a second or third meeting?
More? It seems to me that Sullamora would have informed everyone when he had his ducks—Chapelle, Control, possible opportunity, et cetera—in a row.

''The meeting would not be in an official place. Fear
of bugs, of course. Now, I'm making a big jump. None
of the privy council-types trust each other.''

"Nae a jump. Thae'd be even greater clots than thae be if they did."

"So this meeting, if it occurred, might be on neutral but very clean turf. Question: Did the privy council have any meetings like that?"

"Some lad's headed twa Prime," Alex said. "Suggestion. Amateur plotters clean a'ter themselves. But ne'er think ae then puttin' in ae false trail. Meetin' ae Earth? How wae it arranged? Nae spontaneity, a' course. So Ah'll—pardon, whoe'er goes t' Prime—look for paperwork. I' there's naught, thae was a conspiracy meetin', aye?

"Same wi' any other meetin' a'fore th' Emp' gies slaughtered, pardon, sir."

"Good," Sten agreed. "That's a way in. Anyone else have any sudden flashes? We can leave the backup team in place looking for Sins After the Bang."

"Ah'll pack," Alex said, finishing his drink.

"You will," Sten agreed. "But not for Prime. I'm the one."

"Y're known an' a desir'd target, lad. Dinnae be playin't hero."

"I'm not. Everything on Prime leads through Haines— or could, anyway. Who's she most likely to cooperate with?"

"Ah'll gie y' th' loan ae a mattress manual, Burns' love poems, an' a crook champagne distributor Ah know. But where am Ah headin't twa?"

"Like I said before. We're officers of the court now. But we're understaffed. I'd feel real comfortable with more. Say . . . ten thousand?"

Kilgour considered. "Hae much ae th' AM2 we stole kin Ah use?"

"Beyond what we had to give back to the Bhor . . . what we need for power here and for the Bhor cover fleets . . . whatever it takes. But bargain hard."

"Grannies' wi' eggs once more, lad. I'll gie Otho f'r transp'rtation. Ah hae an idea where I'll look."

"Don't bother Otho. He's busy. I already lined up your ride."

"Ye're smilin' lad. Ah dinnae like thae smile."

"Trust me, Laird Kilgour. You're gonna love it."

Ships flickered into existence, so many minnows swarming to bait around the Jura System. Then, again like minnows, they formed into two fleets and went into parking orbits. Unlike minnows they were not silver, were not uniform, and mostly were not very sleek.

The first fleet landed one ship on Newton. Sten was waiting. Jon Wild, king of the smugglers—or at least their spokesman for this moment—stepped out. Again Sten marveled at his appearance. Not a pirate, not a brawler, Wild looked more like a clerklet or an archivist.

The meeting was very brief—merely a declaration of confederacy. It had taken awhile for Sten's emissary to find Wild, but only moments for the message to be conveyed and understood.

Smugglers needed four things to succeed: Trade laws, transport, cunning, and client prosperity. The privy council had destroyed one and nearly another of those preconditions. No matter how clever a smuggler is, Wild told Sten, if he can't fuel his ship he might as well stay home and farm potatoes. And what boots it if he can find fuel, but his customer has no way of paying for the smuggler's goods?

"So what can you promise me, Sten? Beyond access to the AM2 you seem to have . . . acquired?"

"Not the good old days. The AM2 flow stopped with the Emperor. But with the privy council condemned, they will eventually fall. I find it hard to conceive that *anything* short of complete chaos could be worse than what we have now."

"Smugglers, as a last resort, can live with chaos," Wild mused. "*Somebody* must carry the cargoes. Very well. For intelligence . . . scouting . . . transportation . . . troopships as a last resort . . . you can depend on us. For a time. Until boredom sets in, or those happy anarchists of mine decide to listen to someone else.''

Sten requested Alex's presence when he boarded the ''flagship'' of the second fleet—revenge for Kilgour having stuck him with not only a bodyguard, but an acolyte as well.

He had hoped to surprise Alex.

It did not work very well. Kilgour looked at the projection of the motley throng their ship was closing on and called up the *Jane's* fiche. After glancing at a few entries, he glowered at Sten.

''Y' bastard.''

Alex knew.

''Y'd stick me . . . y'r mate. Y'r wee lifesaver. Th' charmin' an' sophisticated lad whae taught y's all y' ken noo. Y're bent, lad. Y'r proper surname's Campbell!''

''Probably. But do you know a better pilot? Or a group of people better able to keep your potential—and I quote, officers of the court, end quote—under control?''

''M'tongue'd blacken i' Ah agreed wi' y'. An' dinnae be restatin' th' obvious when tha' wee airlock opens.''

Ida was waiting for them. If anything, she had gotten even fatter. She still wore a loose, flowing Gypsy dress, probably with nothing under it, but it was a dress made of the finest fabrics. Tailored—if it was possible to tailor for a blimp. Also, her slangy language had improved—at least a little.

She whooped happily seeing her long-ago Mantis commander and started to buss Kilgour before she remembered their continuing, reason-lost, half-jesting feud. ''You hadda bring him.''

''He gets in trouble without a minder,'' Sten agreed.

''Noo, *thae*'s th' question ae th' hour,'' Alex said.

"Who's th' keeper an' who's th' bairn? I' fact, Ah mean."

Ida led them to her quarters. A bridge suite on a prehistoric ocean ship might have been more luxurious—but that was unlikely. Tapestries. Couches. Tables barely visible under a galaxy of delicacies.

"And it all clears for action in ten seconds," Ida said proudly. "Action stations, and this is a countermissile battery over there—launchers are under the floorboards right now. Over here's an emergency CIC. And the bath becomes a med clearing station.

"We've got Scotch from Earth. Real Scotch. What they call a single-malt. Not that clottin' imitation I read our late and lamented Emperor poured.

"My own lager for you, Kilgour. Not that you'll appreciate it."

Ida Kalderash was a Romany—a Gypsy. The race/culture still existed, and still thrived, living as they did outside conventional society and its rules with a very keen eye for the credit—acquired as an individualistic Rom might see fit. Instead of caravans they used spaceships—for trading, smuggling, or just traveling for adventure and profit. Their customary laws—kris—required them to respect fidelity, their family, and returning favor for favor. Within the Rom. And even then, the customs were hardly commandments.

It was unheard of for a Rom to serve in the military, let alone the supersecret Mantis Teams. How and why Ida ended up on Mantis Section 13, under the command of Lieutenant Sten, was an even bigger and even less answerable puzzler. She had been carried on the rolls as pilot and electronics specialist. She was also their unofficial banker, gambler, and "investment" specialist. At the end of a mission the "investments" would be liquidated, and the team members would be flush enough for truly exotic leaves.

When Mantis 13 had been broken up and Sten transferred to the Imperial Guard, Ida had refused reenlistment and vanished back to her culture.

She had surfaced—in absentia on a fiche—after Sten and Alex had escaped from the Tahn prison at Koldyeze and returned to Prime. The surfacing had been the announcement that she had accessed their pay that had been held while the two were POWs and invested. And invested. She had not explained—but both men became fabulously wealthy. They had been . . . and might be again if the privy council were destroyed and they were no longer fugitives.

Ida had found a unique finale for the announcement: she had turned and hoisted her skirts at them.

As Alex had observed, ''Th' lass still dinnae wear knickers . . .''

''My family will join us for the feast,'' Ida said. ''They're curious to see how much I lied about you two gadje. Don't clot it up, Alex.'' She led them to a sideboard and poured three drinks into crystal goblets. ''To the dead past . . . and a prayer this clottin' present will soon join it.''

Ida had turned somber.

''Your message was welcome, Sten,'' she said.

''I didn't think it would have as large an effect.''

''You expected just me—or me and my vita—my family?''

''That was the best I had hoped for.''

''Times've changed for all of us. You're an admiral. I am now Voivode, chieftain of my band. Other voivodes have been known to listen to me, even if I am a woman.''

''There's more to this many of your people showing up than just you being a heavyweight, Ida. Gypsies, from what I know, what you taught me, don't get together on anything,'' Sten said skeptically.

''No. That is what we are—and there've been terrible tragedies because of this in our past. And another tragedy is on the wind.''

Ida explained. The gypsies may have been outsiders, but they maintained careful intelligence contacts beyond their culture.

"That clottin' council that killed the Emperor's decided that we're lice on the body politic. Mainly 'cause we still have enough AM2 to hold together. They think we've got more'n we actually do—they don't know when a gypsy can't wander, he dies.

"So there'll be an open order on us. Seize our ships. Seize our cargoes. Seize the fuel. What happens to the people on board . . . not mentioned."

"Th' Guard'll nae honor *that*."

"The Guard's changed. Some of them won't. But some of them will. And how many systems think the universe'd be better without us stealin' their chickens, gold, and daughters? Too clottin' many.

"We are not going to wait this time. We are not going to try to turn invisible or hide.

"Your Tribunal's a damn slender reed, Sten. But it's the only one we can see in this clottin' swamp that's risin' up on us.

"So there'll be feasts an' speeches an' debates an' prob'ly a clottin' knifin' or two. Don't mean drakh. You'll end with us swearin' eternal fealty. Or anyway until the privy council's dead meat or you happen to leave the barn unguarded.

"Enough of that." Ida forced herself into cheerfulness. "So I'm takin' this clottin' tub on a recruitin' drive, eh? You housebroke yet?"

"Nae, lass. Tis nae healthy. Drink i' one end, piddle oot th' stern. Keeps th' system on-line."

"You'll fit right in," she said. "Fill the glasses, Admiral. Damn, but I like that! Clottin' gadje Admiral for a barkeep!"

Sten poured. "Don't mind bartending at all, Ida. By the way, two sets of thanks. First for taking care of our money . . . now this."

Ida and Alex drained their glasses. Sten just sipped at his. Ida frowned.

"I can't stay long," he explained. "I've got my own little trip to take."

"And where, Admiral, does it say in the clottin' regs you can't travel with a crawlin' hangover?"

Sten considered. No, it didn't.

And so, yes, he did.

CHAPTER TWENTY-NINE

STEN LANDED ON Prime World with two covers: a livid scar and an Impossible Quest.

The scar was a benign parasite, surgically transplanted onto his face. Nearly two centimeters wide, zigzagging artistically from his scalp line to the corner of his eye and down to his chin, it was part of the "Great Lorenzo" dicta: The best disguise is the simplest, and one that won't blow off in a strong wind. Anyone looking at Sten would see only the horrible scar, no matter how carefully he instructed his mind to be polite. Sten had used versions of the gimmick before, from a alk-ridden nose to partial baldness to a simple, completely shaven head. It worked—almost all the time, at least.

Sten's main concern was that when he extracted from Prime, the parasite might have decided it had found a home everlasting. Kilgour reassured him.

"Dinna fash, lad. I' thae happens, we'll score y' a wee eyepatch an' y' kin join th' pirates."

The Impossible Quest was equally simple. Truth: At the close of the Tahn wars one D'vid Rosemont had appeared on Prime. A flashy, loud-talking, loud-living entrepreneur, he announced his newest business— converting Imperial spacecraft, particularly the tiny, evil tacships, into luxury yachts. Regardless of the inherent absurdity of the premise, Rosemont prospered. For a minute and a half.

Prime's Fraud Squad had taken an interest in Rosemont—his company, yet to produce a single yacht that anyone could find, looked very much like a con game. And then Rosemont vanished, leaving bare bank accounts and a warehouse with three tacships inside. All of that was true.

The harried but friendly—and badly scarred—man appeared on Prime.

False: His name was Elijah Braun. Sten/Braun was credentialed as a private investigator, working for a law firm located on a faraway world between Lost and Nowhere. Rosemont had an heir, who wanted whatever estate existed. Braun knew that the man had not been declared legally dead yet, but the heir was convinced that Rosemont was a victim of foul play, rather than a con who had skated with the swag. Braun was convinced that the heir, already rich, was drug-addled. But a case was a case. Besides, he prattled to the official issuing him his sixty-day visa, it would give him a chance to see Prime, the center of everything and the universe's Most Glamorous World.

"You've seen too many livies, Sr. Braun. Or else you're a history buff. Prime ain't what it was, and it's getting less like it every day."

The official glanced hastily over his shoulder to make sure that his innocent statement had gone unheard. But Sten filed that glance. Unsurprisingly, the privy council's internal security was in full.

Sten noted them everywhere: street cleaners who ignored litter but noted passersby; inept waiters with big ears; clerks who never clerked but listened; block wardens; concierges who asked questions far beyond what was normal. All precautions by the privy council against a largely nonexistent threat. And they were expensive precautions—the council was spending money for all those informers, money it simply did not have.

Sten marveled once again at the odd tendency all too many beings had to want to spy on their neighbor for any reason whatsoever.

None of them thought beyond the moment of what

would surely happen when—not if—the privy council fell. Sten remembered the riots on Heath near the end of the Tahn wars. Not only had the mob ripped anyone in uniform apart, but they had revenged themselves on the Tahn's amateur gestapo in the process.

Not that Sten felt sorry for them. He just wanted his cover to stay intact long enough for him to get in, find what he was looking for, and go home.

He did, however, take a precaution. The current powers did not know everything. Mahoney had told him of a few, very secure, disused safe houses on Prime that might still exist. One at least did. Sten armed himself with a secondary set of false documents that were stashed there.

He then proceeded in his role as Braun. He found an inexpensive hotel, found the landlord of that warehouse, and taped the three hulks inside. He interviewed investors and acquaintances of the vanished Rosemont. He went to the Fraud Squad. They gave him access to their files, and a Visitor's ID.

Braun, over a period of days, professed first bewilderment and then suspicion. He was starting to believe that the heir might be right. Rosemont had not vanished. *Something* had happened to the man. He did have some less-than-palatable acquaintances on the back-alley side of town. Murder, maybe. Suicide? Rosemont, Braun said, had appeared very depressed before he vanished, then turned suddenly cheerful. "He found his back door," suggested a bunco expert, but he gave Braun the names of some friends in Homicide.

Then, timidly, he asked permission to speak to the chief of Homicide. "Y're crackers, an' you're wastin' your—an' her—time. But she's got a policy. Talks to anybody, no matter how loony."

Braun said he was aware that Chief Haines was very busy, especially in these troubled times. So he had prepared a summary of his investigation, complete with a list of questions he would like to ask. He clipped a copy of his Visitor's ID to the fiche, and it went forward.

Sten felt like drakh. He was preparing to use—and possibly jeopardize—a friend and former lover.

He had often wondered about their affair. In one way, it had been the only ''normal'' relationship Sten had experienced. But in another, they had been lovers by circumstance, co-investigating a conspiracy. And their affair had never really ended—Sten had gone off to fight a war, been captured, escaped, and returned to combat. Haines had been drafted into Military Intelligence, and somehow they had never reconnected. He had thought, sometimes, before the privy council made him outlaw, of dropping a line to her, just to see . . . see what, Sten? If there's still a there there?

Probably, he thought, Kilgour was right. Both of them were getting ''morally corrupted''—and getting too moral to soldier successfully in the dirty midnight wars they had grown up in.

Don't get too moral, he prodded himself. Honest spies get trusting and dead. Join the Purity League when this is over if you wish.

He had sent the fiche in to Haines hoping to avoid heart attack city. He hoped she would figure out his intent.

It took two days before he was summoned to her office.

The temperature could have frozen a nova.

''Sr. Braun,'' Haines said. ''I've gone through your fiche, and your questions. Reviewed our own files. Everything my department has suggests you are on a dead end.''

''I might well be,'' Sten said. ''May I record?''

Without waiting for an answer, he put a battered taper—at least its exterior was battered—on her desk and turned it on. Then motioned to her to keep talking.

Haines frowned but continued telling Braun why thinking Rosemont's disappearance was anything other than what it appeared was a blind alley.

Sten had enough. He touched another button on the taper. ''Your bug is suppressed. It's getting fed synthesized chatter.''

Haines came around the desk, almost into an embrace, then stopped herself. "I'm married now," she said very softly. "Happily." That was softer still.

Another world of might-have-been vanished.

"I'm . . . glad for you," Sten said.

Haines managed a smile. "I'm sorry. I must say I've thought about . . . things. As they were. And . . . sorry. At least I can try to lie as well as you do, and let's say that I think of our time together as a lovely moment in the past. Emphasis past."

"Yeah. That's best. I guess, anyway. But who wrote that dialogue? Sounds like a livie."

"Best I could manage. Right off the top. Now," Haines said, trying to be businesslike. "I'd like to be flattered and think you're here to—more livie dialogue—relight the flame. In spite of your being one of the Ten Most Wanted in the Empire. But I think I know better. Dammit."

She turned away for a moment. "That scar?" she asked without turning back.

"Makeup."

"Thank God." She turned back. "Now I'll get angry. I'm getting used."

"Yes."

"First I wondered if I was getting set up. Then I changed my mind."

"Thanks for that much, anyway. But I need help. You were the best contact."

"Sure. Good old Haines. We were pretty good in the sack, so let's see if she'll roll again, just for old times' sake? Let me ask you . . . If I wasn't involved, and you were, would you have gone so far as to pull moonlight on the mattress?"

"I know you're pissed, Lisa. But that's a little—" He broke off, letting it go.

Haines took several deep breaths. "Oh, hell. You're right. But I'm not going to make a career of apology."

And she was in his arms. For a long moment.

"It *was* pretty good, wasn't it?" she asked.

Sten said yes and kissed her again. Finally, she broke away.

"But I wasn't lying. Sam'l is a wonderful man. Probably, to be honest, a little bit more the kind of person I should be with. Not some rogue with a dagger in his arm and murder in his heart. So . . . let's try it as friends. Never tried to be friends with somebody I was in—involved with before. So maybe I can learn something."

Part of Sten wanted to cry. "Sure, Lisa. Friends."

Haines started acting like a cop again. "First, how clean are you?"

"Clean. For at least a few more weeks."

"I gathered," Haines said, tapping the fiche, "that you're running a mission. Your ex-boss have anything to do with it? I thought so. Against the council?"

Sten nodded once more.

"One question—and you'd best not be lying to me. Last time around, after we policed up everyone involved with the late Kai Hakone, there were some bodies in alleys. By Imperial Order. What I'd done is collaborate in a murder conspiracy. I didn't like it then, and I don't like it any better now.

"So if there's what I've heard you call 'wet work,' or 'personal contact' at the end of this . . . don't even ask me."

"No. This is for the Tribunal."

Haines goggled. "Son of a bitch," she said slowly. Of course, in spite of the privy council's blackout, she had heard the Tribunal's announcement of its intent to sit in judgment on the council. "I'm thinking. Yeah. The whole thing—your idea?"

"It was."

"Son of a bitch once more," she said. "I said I wouldn't apologize. But I do. For the last time."

She grinned. "You know . . . maybe in another hundred, hundred and fifty years, if you spend some time in a seminary, you might actually be permitted to join the human race.

"Okay. What do you need?"

Another misunderstanding had been corrected by Alex Kilgour before he left on his recruiting drive. Oddly enough it had minor echoes of what Sten was realizing and saying to Lisa Haines.

Kilgour had informed Sten's bodyguard that for the moment they were no longer needed on their special assignment. They were reassigned to general court security.

Cind had requested an interview with her temporary commanding officer. The first question she had asked Alex was why the change? Had they done something wrong?

"First strike, on y', soldier. Security is security. Y' dinnae need t'know. Sten's got bi'ness ae his own."

"Request reassignment, sir."

"Ae what? Pers'nal backup f'r him?"

"Something like that."

Kilgour growled. "Th' firs' an' only time Ah got involv'd wi' a task, m' Mantis topkick took m' back ae th' barracks. She wailed upon m' melon an' informed me Ah'd best learn t'be a professional ae m' task or go back t' sheep-shaggin'.

"She wae right.

"An' should do th' same t' you.

"But Ah'm sophisticated, noo. I c'd gie th' order— 'So'jer, soldier!'—'n hae done wi' it.

"But Ah'll gie reasons. So gie your head oot ae y'r gonads or where e'er it's lurkin't, an' listen close.

"One, y'r bosses know whae they're doin't. Second, y're complete wrong f'r whae th' boss is doin't. An' dinnae yammer ae me aboot th' longarm an' how y'been studyin't intell'gence. Ah knoo all ae thae already.

"You're wrong f'r th' run because y're too . . . strikin'. You dinnae e'er, e'er, e'er want to be notable i' y'r task is snoopin't ae poopin't. An' y're a so'jer. So'jerin' is a diff'rent discipline thae spookin't.

"But thae's as may be. Last—an' best—reason, y're too clottin' young. Y'believe in things. Y'dinnae ken th' depths ae depravity i' th' spirit. Unless y' grew up bein' nattered ae by Calvinists, ae Ah did. A spook must hae one thing runnin' throo his mind ae all times: Trust nae soul, an' always, always think th' worst ae most selfish ae any an' all.

"A hard an' evil lesson. One y', t'be honest, w'd be best not learnin't.

"Gie y'self back t' th' duties assigned, noo. Ah'll wager thae'll be more'n enow blood t' come. Y'll hae chances t' distinguish y'self ae th' eyes ae y'r superiors or e'en the boss, i' thae's your fancy.

"Dismissed."

Kilgour sighed when she had left. Christ on a pogo stick, he thought. He was starting to sound like a fatherly command sergeant major. Gettin' old, Kilgour. Gettin' old . . .

At first Sten thought going to Prime was nothing more than an ego-damaging, high-hazard bust. He was looking for three things: any more information on the murder-for-hire of the press lord Volmer than Haines had been able to give Mahoney; a paper trail for that first—question mark—meeting of the conspirators on Earth; and whether or not there had been another meeting before Chapelle was put in motion. Plus, as a secondary goal, whether there was anything more on the Chapelle/Control/Sullamora link than was known, in spite of Mahoney's proclamation that it was relatively unimportant.

Thus far, he had done a very good job of getting zeroes. No, Haines had nothing more on Volmer or the "suicide" of the assassin. She frankly admitted that she had not worked the case any further—it was clearly political. These days people had been known to vanish when they started asking uncomfortable questions about politics. She added, however, that she did not think there was anything to collect, at least not until the privy council was deposed and, it was to be hoped, indicted.

Zero One.

As for anything about that meeting on Earth, Sten found a complete vacuum. As far as he could tell, there had been *no* contact between members of the council before they somehow, telephathically, sensed it was time to gather at Sullamora's lodge. At least that was all that was in the open archives and what governmental archives Haines had been able to gingerly pry at. Kilgour had been right—the privy council had been smart enough to destroy or classify whatever memoranda had passed between them but not smart enough to make substitutes. Interesting. Ordinarily that would have been enough for Sten, as an intelligence professional, to take action on. But as an officer of the law, he was trying hard to stay somewhere close to its limits and requirements.

Zero Two.

As for his side quest—he found a mansion that had been rented shortly before Chapelle vanished by a retired colonel general named Suvorov. From some kind of Pioneer Division or Battalion or whatever they called those military things, the estate agent told him. Suvorov was right—the estate agent remembered his dress and credit rating clearly. Solidly built, he thought. Oh yes. A scar on his neck. Don't remember which side. Might I inquire why you're asking, Sr. Braun? Proof that the father my client is looking for is not this man. Thank you for your time.

Big clottin' deal. A smooth operator who used the haunts of the rich to launch his operation. They knew that already. Name—false. Build? Who knew? The scar? Probably as phony as the one Sten was wearing.

Slightly More Than Zero Three. But not much.

The second meeting? He could find no trace of any final parley among the privy council before the assassination other than in their official chambers. He did not think they were dumb enough to plan the death of the Emperor in what they must think to be certainly bugged offices. And were they so skilled that they could set up a conspiracy that ran of itself? Nobody, including Sten, was that good. But where was the evidence?

Zero Four. So far.

Sten wanted Haines to be single, the sky-floating houseboat over the forest to still be there, two bottles of champagne, and the vid disconnected. Oh, yeah. A little general peace without paranoia or goons would go nicely.

He contented himself with one solitary short beer and an equally solitary brood.

He glimmered an idea. But it would, he thought, be in plain view. If the privy council were as paranoid as he thought them to be, he could be strolling into a trap. One set not specifically for Sten, but for anyone with the curiosity of a not particularly bright cat.

It seemed, however, the only and last option.

From first appearances, Hawkthorne had changed very little since Sten and Alex had gone there under deep cover to hire mercenaries for what they called ''The Great Talamein Beatup.'' It still was fairly anarchic—any planet that specialized as a hiring hall for soldiers-for-hire had to have a fairly lax government where the ultimate law was laid down by whoever had the heaviest weapons.

But the mercenaries on Hawkthorne looking for a contract were different from the psychopaths, crooks, opportunists, and would-be kingmakers before.

The Tahn War had changed everything.

Any war produced, in its aftermath, mercenaries. They came from the losing armies, from suddenly stateless soldiers, from the ranks of war criminals, from the bored who wanted to continue experiencing that one insane moment of pure life that was combat, and from those who just could not go back to the farm. Generally they were highly professional. But as peace went on, there was a deterioration in quality. Some got killed, some found their kingdom beyond the clouds, some grew up and realized that that moment of life was surrounded by death, and others drifted on to more stable situations that required only the occasional use of violence.

That had been Hawkthorne before.

The Tahn wars created a new horde of professionals. And the necessary economic cutbacks of peacetime, plus the hamwitted policies of the privy council, had made them potential mercenaries.

Admirals would sign on as ship executive officers. Guard generals would cheerfully command a battalion or even a company. Sergeant majors would wear the blank sleeve of a private without complaining—at least for the moment.

Alex could pick and choose. He did.

Sten dreamed of ten thousand "officers of the court" and hoped for five thousand. Alex could have gotten one hundred thousand. He could afford to be generous.

Money? Nae problem. If the Tribunal failed to start the fall of the privy council, how much was left in the coffers would be completely unimportant once everyone involved bought a fast ticket out of town.

Fuel for combat ships? Kilgour had a "train" full.

He could have enlisted some with a full meal and the promise of regular rations to come.

For some, there was even a more subtle offer, made quietly and in person: If the privy council were toppled, the Imperial military would need restructuring. The corrupt, the incompetent, or those who had bloodied their hands in the purge would be removed. *Some* kind of military would be—had to be—retained. Alex said that frankly he had no idea what it would be. He let the thought dangle.

He stood at the ramp of Ida's flagship and looked down at his army.

From up there, one could see the threadbare uniforms or the shabby termination-of-service civvies some others wore. One could not see the gaunt, hungry faces.

From there, the lines of soldiery and their ships behind them were as rigidly in formation as any Guards unit on formal inspection.

Put 'em in propit dress, he said to himself. Gie 'em a banner to follow, an' lead 'em to a war wi' paper bullets. Thae's happiness.

Kilgour's . . . Killers? Cheap. Kubs? Stupid. Klique? Clack. Kilgour's Keeks? Nae. Jus' a few of 'em were ex-intelligence. Ah. Kilgour's Kilted Kvetchers.

He gave the orders and watched proudly as "his" army, who would never know it, boarded ship for liftoff.

Frae a mo', Ah wae a gen'ral.

An' did y'a like it?

He suddenly had a vision of those soldiers at their fate. Dead slowly or quickly. Bodies shredded beyond reconstruction. Blinded. Crippled. Insane.

Then another vision: He saw all those soldiers wearing a motley of civvies. Bankers, farmers, wives, workmen, tourists in the streets, factories, homes, and pubs of the vast estates Laird Kilgour owned but somehow never got around to asserting his total authority over, back on Edinburgh.

Better. Far better.

Answers y'r wee question, doesn't it, now, he thought. And he ordered the officer of the watch to seal ship and prepare for lift.

No one in the Cult of the Eternal Emperor knew exactly *how* they heard. But suddenly, in a thousand thousand meeting halls on an equal number of worlds, everyone *knew*.

They had been given a great honor.

One of the privy council had become a fertile ground for the True Belief. Not only a ruler, but the being most reputed to be the most intelligent.

Now he had vanished. No explanation was given by anyone. It was not as if Kyes had regularly appeared in vids of the council—But now it was if he had never existed.

The explanation was simple.

The Mighty Kyes had seen the light. As a reward, he had been taken, *in corpore*, to commune with the Holy Spheres, just as the Emperor had.

Kyes, they knew, would not return, any more than the handful of saints who had achieved equal reward. None of them were, after all, the Emperor himself.

This was an event. Kyes would be numbered among the Blessed.

But more importantly, the believers could sense something else:

The time was coming. The Emperor would return soon.

They readied themselves. For what, they did not know. They did not even know if their services would be called for.

But—and let it be so, let us each have a chance to serve, they prayed—they were ready.

"Your pardon."

It was not an apology for intrusion, but a command. Sten looked up at the librarian.

A less likely one he had never seen. Not that librarians fell into physical archetypes. But it was the uncommon one who had a flushed tan from a life mostly spent outside, on foot patrol. Nor did many of them have scarred and callused knuckles. And none wore hard-toed, cushion-soled boots, let alone that telltale sag and wear on the belt that came from a holstered gun.

"Yah?" Sten said.

"You're readin' about the council, right?"

"So? It 'gin th' law? Some kinda new law passed since I got up this morn?" Sten slurred.

The man did not answer. "Please could I see your ID?" Again, a command.

Sten took the ID from his pocket and passed it to the man looming over his terminal. It was not Braun's ID, but the standard, generic phony he had scored from Mahoney's safehouse. According to the card, Sten was a caretaker, hired to mind the closed consulate of a frontier world.

"Janitor, eh?" The security goon passed the card back. "Jus' readin' about th' Lords outa curiosity?"

The Lords. New term.

"Nawp," Sten said. "M'kid wanted to know how th' world worked. Shamed m'self not knowin'. Thought I'd better read up some. Got, well, laid off las' week. So got some time while I'm lookin' f'r a new slot. T'rble, lookin' stupid front a y'r own son."

The man grunted and walked back to the front of the library.

Sten swore bitterly. Very nice indeed when a being could end up in the slammer for going to a library and going through public records. Just a hell of a good government. Be glad you're nonexistent, son of mine, he thought.

Sten had figured the council just might be paranoid enough to put a trace in the libraries. He had found a shop specializing in actor's supplies and purchased the best pancake makeup available. The clerk had glanced at Sten's scar, winced, and not asked any questions. Sten pretended to be embarrassed by having to buy the makeup and also said he was an amateur actor, and he could use a fake mustache in the production he was in. The pitying clerk went along with the pretense and sold him one.

Scar covered, mustache in place—Sten tried to keep from whuffling it as if he were Rykor, or touching it to see if it had come unglued yet—he entered the library.

He was glad he had taken precautions—he had spotted the phony librarian immediately.

Staying with the cheap cover, he had started the search at PRIVY COUNCIL—FUNCTIONS AND DUTIES, beginning when they ascended to total power and staying clear, for the moment, of the time frame he was interested in. Scrolling through the flackery and propaganda wasted a full morning. Then he chanced PRIVY COUNCIL—HISTORY (FROM FORMATION TO PRESENT).

That, evidently, was where the security indicator alarm had been hidden.

He scrolled on, glancing every now and then at the front desk. The goon seemed satisfied.

HISTORY . . . hmm. NG.

Okay. What next?

PRIVY COUNCIL, PICS. ANY PERIOD.

Endless head and shoulders for thumbnails. Group photos at ceremonies. All very official. Very few, Sten noted, of the Kraas. Maybe they knew what they looked like. Almost nothing on Kyes.

Got any other—whoops!

Sten back-scrolled, hoping he had seen what he thought he had.

I have you, he thought fiercely staring at the screen, which showed all five of the councilors hurrying into the entrance of some kind of hall. They were surrounded by security. The pic was rather poorly framed, and Sten saw, in the corner, a cop headed for the camera, an angry look on his face.

So somebody had shot a picture—looked as if he was either a free-lancer or a citizen—of the bastards. The cop was headed for him to try to grab the pic. Good thing the photog was wearing' track shoes or was bigger'n the cop, Sten thought.

Now. What was it?

He read the caption.

Some kind of sporting event. Gravball? Whatever that was. Sten had about as much interest in athletics as he did in watching rocks grow. He had suffered through the obligatory games in the service, rationalizing them as part of the necessary physical conditioning. This was the Rangers against something called the Blues. Teams. The Blues were offworld, the Rangers from Prime. Big match—a hundred thousand people, including privy council to watch . . .

Game played at Lovett Arena.

Oh clottin' really.

Sten did not know how many of the privy council were sports freaks. Not that it mattered. This was the *only* occasion he had been able to find, both in the library and in Haines's records, where the council had assembled on more or less neutral ground to "enjoy" a nonwork-related event.

He noted the date and shut down.

"Clottin' impossible to understand, this politics," he confided to the librarian. "Grab a bite, an' spend the rest of the day readin' sports. Pick up a few coins bettin' at th' bar."

The thug grunted. He didn't care.

Sten could have found a secure com and checked with Haines. He thought it better not to. He probably should have just pulled out and let Haines's police fingers do the rest of the walking. But he was finally on to something. Damned if he was going to let somebody else find the gold from his lead.

He did not eat a midday meal, however. He kept the library's entrance under watch, just in case the goon was *really* looking for brownie points. Nothing.

He came back, deliberately belched in the goon's direction, and went to his terminal.

SPORTS. RANGERS, HISTORY.

Nothing. He jumped ahead to the date of that big match. Blues undefeated three years . . . Rangers won . . . big riots as usual. Nothing. At least nothing he could see that tied the event to any councilman.

He was getting closer.

Lovett Arena.

He was sweaty-palmed. Another tracer, and that goon might not listen to any explanations. How do you winkle in? Try . . . and his fingers touched the keyboard. AM-PHITHEATERS. CURRENT. ENTER.

He was not watching the screen; he kept his eye on the

security man across the huge chamber. The man did not move.

No . . . no . . . damn, but these people on Prime have got a lot of sports palaces. Lovett Arena.

History?

Try it. Built by Lovett's grandsire . . . equipped for every kind of sport conceivable, land, water, or aerial. Lions vs. Christians, Sten wondered. PICS.

He looked at picture after picture, ignoring whatever was in the foreground and what was happening. He was looking at the arena itself.

Clot. If those bastards were going to conspire . . . no. Everything was too open. But wait a minute—that was interesting. ENTIRE ENTRY:

BEHIND THE CHEERS:
How a Stadium Keeps You Fed,
Warm, Safe, and Entertained.

Clottin' poor title.

Parking . . . underground . . . security offices . . . my.

So Lovett's grandfather built himself a private suite, did he? Clottin' awful-looking. Why would anybody hang the heads of dead animals on a wall? Let alone those paintings. But what a wonderful place for a conspiracy to meet. The big game as cover . . . bigwigs like sports, especially if they get private seats . . . privacy.

Sten had proof—enough for him—that there *had* been a final meeting before Chapelle was put into play. How could he get backup, enough to take to the Tribunal? Mucketies needed servants when they played. Were there bartenders who had been around that night? Joygirls? Boys? Maybe barkeeps. But not sex toys—not even the Kraas would be that careless.

What else? He punched out of SPORTS, and took a chance on WHO'S WHO. He entered LOVETT.

His attention was fixed on the screen. Usual plaudits. Educational bg . . . interests . . . entered family banking empire on death of mother . . . Hmm. No entry . . . even in this jerk-off log of him being a sports loon.

Sten's concentration was broken as the library's door banged closed. Damn!

Three uniformed cops entered.

Sten crouched away from the terminal and down an aisle with stacked fiche on either side to a door.

It was locked. His fingers went into a fob pocket and came out with a small tool. Seconds later, the door was unlocked.

He went through the door and relocked it behind him. He heard a shout from the reading room.

Sten, even as he looked for an exit, blinked. This was one hell of a library. Huge vaulted ceiling. Row after row after row of stored fiche, vids, and even books.

He heard fumbling at the door and shouts to get the key. A body thudded against the door.

Sten's fingers curled, and his knife dropped from its sheath inside his forearm into his hand. He ran down into the stacks, loping easily like a tiger looking for an ambush site.

The cops, the security tech in front, got the door open and came into the chamber.

They saw nothing except a couple of robots filing material. They heard nothing. The security man whispered orders: Spread out. Search the whole room.

The cops started to obey perfunctorily. Clot, there they were, wasting time because some clottin' piece of drakh counterspook sees shadows on the wall and wanted them to bust the cops of some private puke. Then the reaction hit them. Maybe private puke—but one who could somehow go through a locked door.

"We'll stay together."

Two of them took out their guns. The third had a truncheon ready.

"You first, hero."

A tiny, lethal-looking projectile gun appeared in the secret policeman's hand.

They went into the tiger's jungle.

Suddenly a tall case teetered and crashed sideways. The teeter gave one cop and the security thug time to flat-dive out of the way. The other two were caught by the heavy case and its cascading contents. The first case brought a second one across from it slamming down. They floundered and shouted. Somebody fired a round that whined up into the library's ceiling and ricocheted wildly.

There was a scuffle as the "tiger's" pads moved him away, deeper into the stacks.

The two went on, leaving their trapped partners to work their own way free.

One of the trapped cops was wedging his way through a snowstorm of papers, his leg still caught under the case, when he heard a quiet thunk . . . and the whiny scratch of somebody trying to take his last breath through a crushed windpipe.

Then there was a sliver of death at his throat. "Scream," Sten ordered. "Real loud."

The cop followed orders.

The scream was still echoing as Sten slit the man's throat, came up, and darted into another row.

The security goon and the surviving policeman ran up. They had a second for a shocked gape at the two corpses and the gouts of blood before shock turned into horror and a metal-bound folio discused in from nowhere, smashing into the cop's forehead. He collapsed bonelessly.

The security man went for the door, backing . . . whirling . . . trying to keep from screeching in horror and running into what he knew would be the tiger's final trap.

A fiche clattered on the floor. He spun—nothing. Then he whirled back, gun hand out. Sten stepped in behind him. The goon went limp as Sten severed his spinal cord. He let the body fall. Two flops and it was a corpse.

Now Sten had all the time in the world.

He found an exit and, nearby, an employee's washroom. He swabbed solvent, and the mustache came off into the disposal; and the makeup was scrubbed clean.

Then he went out the door.

Police gravsleds were howling toward the library. Sten trotted down an alley, then slowed. He strolled onward, glancing curiously as the official units whined past.

Just another citizen of Prime.

CHAPTER THIRTY

"*JOHN STUART MILL*, this is New River Central Control. We have you on-screen. Do you wish landing instructions?"

Mahoney's pilot keyed a mike. "New River Control, this is the *Mill*. Negative on that. Landing permission established at Private Port November Alpha Uniform. Will switch frequencies. Over."

"This is New River. I have your fiche on-screen. Switch to UHF 223.7 for contact with November Alpha Uniform. November Alpha will provide locator only, no control personnel at port. New River Control, clear."

The pilot swiveled his chair. "Five minutes, sir."

Mahoney nodded and keyed the intercom mike to the crew compartment. His ship was a barely camouflaged covert insert craft, renamed for the moment after an old Earth economist. Mahoney thought it a nice addition to the cover he was using.

The screen lit and showed ten beings, armed and wearing Mantis Team tropo-camouflage uniforms. All of them were not only ex-Mantis but soldiers Mahoney had used for missions back when he commanded Mercury Corps.

"We'll be down in about five, Ellen," he told the burly ex-noncom in the compartment.

"We heard, boss. Sure you want us to just stand by? We could have him out by his boot heels in a couple minutes."

"Just stay in a holding pattern. Either he's who I want, in which case he might have more firepower'n we do, or he's not. Do me a favor? You hear shootin', scamper right on in. I'm getting too old for another body reconstruct."

"Yessir. We're ready."

Mahoney reached over the pilot's shoulder and picked up the com mike. "November Alpha Uniform, November Alpha Uniform. This is the *John Stuart Mill*, inbound for landing."

A voice answered. "*Mill*, this is November Alpha. Landing beacon triple-cast, apex two kilometers over field. No winds on field. Land as arranged. Potential client plus two others only. Any other crew remain in ship. Please observe these minimum safety precautions. I will meet you at the main house. Out."

Mahoney clicked the mike twice to indicate that he understood. He grinned at the pilot. "Please, eh? Perhaps he is my boy."

The ship set down in the center of the small, paved field. The port opened, and Mahoney climbed out.

It was hot, dry, and dusty. To one side of the field stretched scrub desert and then low mountains. On the other were vast stretches of white-fenced, very green pastures. The air was very still. Mahoney heard a bird-chirp from a nearby orchard, and, from the pastures, the hiss of irrigation equipment.

He walked up the winding road toward the scatter of buildings. Pasture . . . white fences . . . barns there. Chutes. A breeding establishment? He saw a very old quadruped—an Earth horse, he identified—grazing in a field. No other animals.

He walked past metal-sided sheds, their doors closed and bolted. Stables. Empty. There was a low wall, and a gate standing open.

He entered and walked through an elaborate garden that looked as if it had gone too long without enough maintenance. There were three robot gardeners at work, and a human near them. The man paid him no attention.

Hard times, Mahoney mused. It takes credit to keep a horse ranch going.

He was, however, impressed. He had seen no sign whatever of security devices, guards, or weaponry. But unless he was completely lost, they were there.

A man stood in front of the main entrance, waiting. He was a bit younger than Mahoney. Not as tall. Stocky. He looked as if he worked out on a fairly regular basis. Not an ugly man, not a handsome man. He wore an open-neck shirt, expensively casual pants, and sandals.

"Sr. Gideon," he greeted. "I am Schaemel. Please come in. I have refreshments."

The sprawling house—not quite a mansion—was decorated with heavy furniture made of real wood and leather. The paintings on the walls were old and all of realistic subjects.

"Each year," Schaemel observed, "I manage to forget how hot and dry New River is in late summer. And each year I am reminded. That is a wine-fruit concoction. It is refreshing." He indicated a punch bowl containing ice and a milky liquid. Mahoney made no response.

Schaemel half smiled. He ladled punch into a tumbler and drained it. Mahoney then got a drink for himself.

"So your corporation's getting whipsawed, Sr. Gideon. A hostile takeover on one side, a union organizing on the other, and you think the union's a setup. Everyone's playing dirty and you need an expert. Excellent presentation, by the way."

"Thank you."

"One thing I particularly admire," Schaemel continued, "is your attention to trivia. John Stuart Mill as the name for your yacht, indeed. Perhaps a bit too capitalistic—but nice, regardless."

Mahoney's hand brushed his pants pocket, and, back in the ship, the ALERT light went on.

"I'm very, very glad," Schaemel said, "that it was

you who showed up. I have been waiting for some time for something like this—or something else.

"I certainly never believed the stories of your suicide, Fleet Marshal Mahoney . . . I believe that was your rank when you 'retired.' Spies suicide—not spy-masters."

"You are quick," Mahoney said. "So can we drop the 'Schaemel' drakh, Venloe?"

"I thought that identity was safely buried. But then, I thought *I* was, too."

Mahoney explained: how few real professionals there were; how fewer were not involved with a government, megacorporation, or military; and lastly Venloe's characteristic MO.

Venloe looked chagrined. "And all these years you think you never leave a trail. Tsk. I am ashamed. So how am I to make amends for having engineered the assassination of the Emperor?"

"You assume I'm not here to nail your guts to a tree and chase you around it half a dozen times. The Emperor was also my friend."

"So I have been told. And I have heard stories about you . . . preferring field work on occasion. But if you just wanted me dead, you would not have bothered to introduce yourself before the bangs began. Direct confrontations can produce contusions on both sides—and you are hardly a young hero any more."

"Not correct," Mahoney said, and the easy casualness vanished for a moment. "If I weren't after bigger bastards I well might've shown up and personally cut your heart out."

"Careful, Mahoney. You corrected me on one of my errors, I return the compliment. We do not take things personally in our trade. It can be suicidal.

"But since that is not on the agenda, may we change the subject? You may tell whatever troops you have for backup they can relax."

He walked to a desk and put his hand flat on what

appeared to be a blotter. "My own people are standing down."

He seated himself and indicated that Mahoney do likewise. "I could probably guess what you want. But tell me, anyway. I assume it has something to do with this ludicrous Tribunal I've heard bruited."

"It is. We want you to testify as to the conspiracy. Publicly."

"Me? On the stand? That would be a new experience. Hardly good for my future employability."

"Times don't appear to have been that good, anyway," Mahoney said, looking pointedly out the window at the empty stables.

"The circumstances of my last assignment have forced me to be most careful as to who my employer is. I have turned down some very lush deals because of my supreme egotism in trying for the biggest target of them all."

"Poor lad."

Venloe ignored Mahoney's sarcasm. "Say I agree, however. I stand up in a courtroom and say—say exactly what? That I was hired by one Tanz Sullamora after having performed tasks satisfactorily for him previously? That I located and developed the asset Chapelle and positioned him? And all the details around that? Perhaps. But is that all?"

"Of course not. Sullamora's dead. Nobody gives a clot about him. We want the others. Kyes. Malperin. The Kraas. Lovett."

"Tsk. You want what I cannot give."

"But you will."

"You misunderstand. I *cannot* provide such details. I could testify that it is my moral belief that the rest of the privy council was part of the conspiracy, certainly. But proof? Sullamora never mentioned their names to me. I never met with them, nor with anyone I thought to be their direct representatives. Don't glower, Mahoney.

"I can offer evidence. My presence here. I fled Prime,

of course. But I returned to my home of over twenty years rather than vanish into a new identity and a new part of the universe where I was a complete unknown. Obviously I did not collect my payoff; obviously I have not gone to anyone looking for it. Now, if those bloody-handed idiots on the privy council had any idea that I was Control for that touch, don't you think they would have arranged my disappearance or cooption? More likely the former?''

Mahoney held his poker face. But he did not like what he was hearing.

"So, Mahoney, as I said, I am not your smoking gun, nor do I know where it might be. I will reluctantly offer you a deposition as to my knowledge—but that is all.''

Venloe got himself another tumbler of punch and waved the ladle in Mahoney's direction. Mahoney shook his head, no. Venloe went back to his chair.

"Impasse, is it not? You can kill me . . . try to kill me. But you certainly cannot get out alive. You said you were after bigger bastards—I assume you want to see them gotten.''

"Not quite an impasse,'' Mahoney said. "You are going to pack, and you are going to return with me to Newton. You may be telling the truth, you may be lying. We will find out, for certain.''

"Brainscan? Never. People have been known to die— or to be scrambled—under the cap. If that's the choice, I'd rather fight and conceivably die here.''

"You won't get dead. Or brainburnt. The scan will be done by Rykor. She is—''

"I know of her. The best. But, I confess, somebody wading through my soul gives me shudders.''

"The poor clot who'll do the wading through what you call a soul is the one who'll get the collywobbles.''

"Let me consider,'' Venloe mused. "If I say no, and somehow both of us survive the ensuing . . . discussion, what will happen next? Certainly you will somehow leak the word of my existence to the privy council, expecting them to clean up tracks that are not even there.

"Exactly what they would do. Imbeciles. I do not like this option.

"On the other hand, I go with you. Accept brainscan. Testify. Perhaps your Tribunal will succeed and somehow the forces of''—Venloe's voice oozed sarcasm—"truth, justice, and the Imperial Way magically triumph, and the council falls. Or, what is more likely, their own ineptitude will destroy them.

"In either event, I am quite safe. Protected, in fact. I might not be able to follow my own trade, but I would certainly be kept in the style to which, off and on, I have become accustomed."

Venloe was telling the truth. A political assassin, unless he was killed in the first moments after the assassination or was proven absolutely to be a lone maniac, would be coddled until his death by the state. Whether he talked or not—the hope was that sooner or later he would choose to tell all, even if at that point in time the only beings interested were historians.

Venloe thought, in the hot dry silence. "Very well. I shall assemble my security beings and disarm them. Call for your escort to come in now. They can help carry my luggage to your ship. We have a bargain."

He held out his hand, palm forward.

Mahoney just stared at it. After a moment, Venloe got up and left the room.

Solon Kenna had been in an observatory exactly once before in his life, and that time he had been young, drunk, and lost. Now he found them fascinating—or at least this particular one, on this particular night, looking at this particular projection.

He looked once more at the screen, reassuring himself that delirium tremens had not finally set in.

They were still there, hanging in a parking orbit around Dusable.

Alarms had cacophonied when the fleet was reported. Kenna turned pale and Tyrenne-elect Walsh even paler when told what it probably was and meant. Ships. Many, many ships. Somehow the privy council must have decided that the defeat of Tyrenne Yelad was injurious, and sent the guard.

Dusable's handful of customs patrol ships launched and swept toward the waiting fleet, loudly proclaiming peaceful intent on every band com-able. In the lead ship was Walsh, representing his system.

Kenna had immediately scuttled for shelter. Deep, deep shelter that would rapidly involve plastic surgery and departure.

There was no response.

And no one had ever seen ships like them—although they were clearly of Imperial design.

A ship was boarded.

And then the celebration began.

The ships were robots—robot freighters. Each of them—and the fleet reached out to forever—held enough Anti-Matter Two for one world's full consumption for one year, at maximum peacetime use.

Dusable, in ten years, or fifteen, had never seen that much AM2. And where the clot had it come from?

Kenna crept out of hiding and went to the observatory to verify that Walsh and his crews had not suddenly discovered hallucinogens—and then he realized.

Christ, Christ, Christ, he thought.

That Raschid was connected, he certainly knew. That he was—somewhere—a being of clout was also a given. But that he was—no.

Kenna stood and turned around. He looked up at an old portrait on the wall, part of the dedication plaque of Imperial Observatory Ryan/Berlow/T'lak. The picture was a standard royalty pose of The Eternal Emperor.

It was also, of course, a perfect image of Raschid.

Kenna had heard and even used the old political phrase: "Who was with me before Chicago?"

"I was," he muttered. "I was. We all were."

Times were going to be very, very good for Dusable and Solon Kenna. He guessed that the son of a bitch *was* immortal.

He considered the suddenly changing future and what it might portend, especially for the recently elected Walsh. Next election . . . the hell with it. For now. The next election was not for some years.

He then considered finding a church and praying to any god in particular for giving him, Kenna, the brains to realize what was going on before it went on.

But he brought himself back to reality—and treated himself to a bottle.

Mahoney knew he was in serious trouble.

Rykor came to him in her gravchair, rather than wanting to see him in her chambers or, if matters were very cheery, around the huge, deep saltwater tub that stood in for the frigid arctic waters, crashing storms, and looming icebergs of her home world.

Rykor, from her whiskers to her vast blubber to her flippers, resembled, at least to Mahoney who had so dubbed her, a walrus.

When Sten had come up with the idea of the Tribunal, Mahoney had immediately started finding the tools. One of them was Rykor, formerly one of the Empire's chief psychologists. He found her in bored semiretirement. Liking Sten, having vast if a minority appreciation for Kilgour's sense of humor, liking Mahoney, and—not to be admitted—something beyond the boring sanity of her own race, she had agreed to join in the hunt.

"Well?" Mahoney asked without preliminaries after Rykor's huge gravchair hove into his quarters.

"Quite interesting, this Venloe," Rykor began. "Quite beyond the pale. A *truly* amoral being. I have read of such but never experienced one. My empathy glands remained inactive throughout the entire scan."

Rykor's empathy glands, located near where humans

have tear ducts, automatically responded to the plight or pain of any being under her care. So she seemed to weep while possibly suggesting the most dire fate for a patient.

"What do we have?"

"First, Venloe's health—"

"Hopin' he's dying in convulsions and realizing he'd best stay healthy as a horse, I don't want to hear about his health. I assume excellent. GA."

"I think we—that is, you and I—should prepare an 'Eyes Only' fiche from this scan. His profile is a textbook one and, properly censored and edited, is a valuable contribution to psychology. For you . . . some of the operations he was involved with in the past, you might find interesting and instructive." She whuffled through her whiskers thoughtfully.

"What about the big one?"

"Oh, he is guilty, just as he says. Interesting how precisely he analyzed, with no formal training, Chapelle, and was able to pull his strings without ever an error.

"And Sullamora was Venloe's employer and paymaster. But that is all."

"Nothing? Not one goddamned memo he happened to see over Sullamora's shoulder from the others? Come on, Rykor. Just one thing. The council all got drunk and sang 'We'll be glad when you're dead, you rascal, you.' Anything."

"Nothing. Of course, Ian, realize that this is a Tribunal. His testimony might not be allowed in an exact trial. But I suspect it will be admissible for the Tribunal at least."

Mahoney tried to look cheerful. "Well, it's not what I was hoping, but it'll help. I guess. Have you drained him?"

"Pretty much."

"Hell."

"Don't give up, Ian. You might, indeed, find your smoking gun. Venloe said he gave Sullamora a piece of advice. Not because he cared, you understand, but because he wanted to make sure he got his final payment. He told Sullamore—it was part of a warning for Tanz not to attempt a double cross—that he himself should be careful. Sullamora said something about that not being a factor. He had taken out insurance.''

''Which we shall never find. If he did cover himself, the privy council would have shaken down his estates, his banks, his offices, and his friends looking for it. They would have found it. We won't—if it was there at all.''

''Ian. Cheer up. Perhaps I should tell you a gem of a jest. Alex Kilgour told it to me just after he returned.''

''No. Not only no, but obscenity no. I have heard Kilgour's jokes, thank you. Telling one would only make me feel worse. And if you tell it anyway, I'll—hell.

''Worst thing about being an ex-Fleet Marshal is you can't threaten anybody with courtmartial!''

Trying to find out what happened the night the privy council got sports-happy and decided to attend the Ranger-Blues gravball match was, if not simple, fairly safe. Sten held to his vow that, if possible, he would run the rest of his investigation through Haines.

The first question was to find a suitable secondary cover for asking any questions about anything involving the privy council.

Haines and Sten invented one.

Murder, thankfully, has no statute of limitations. So on the night in question, it seemed that a certain woman had been murdered. The suspect was her mate, who had vanished. He had recently been picked up on another charge, halfway across Prime, and alert police work had found that he was the primary suspect in his mate's murder.

Unfortunately, so the concocted story went on, he had an alibi. He had been working as a temporary barkeep on the night in question—working Lovett's private party.

Haines made the correct calls. Once again, Sten was grateful that she was a hands-on cop—the fact that the chief was working an investigation did not raise eyebrows.

Lovett evidently not only viewed the arena and the decorating of the private suite as an eternal legacy, but its employees as well. The maitre d' for the suite had worked for Lovett for more than thirty years. He was happy to cooperate with the investigation—especially since, being a law-abiding being, he started by exploding the mythical suspect's alibi. Leave it to an amateur, he snorted. He probably could have claimed to have worked any of the prole beerbars in the stadium itself, but not the suite. Long-term-only employees up there, especially on the night in question.

"Are you sure?"

"How could I not be?" the man retorted. "Biggest game in decades, and the privy council itself attends. But I didn't need the usual staff—it was just the six of them. Not even aides or security. So just four people worked the suite that night—me, Mart'nez and Eby behind the bar, Vance runnin' if they'd wanted anything from the kitchen. They weren't eating that night. Not even the Kraas. Excuse me, but that last thing I said—it won't be in the record, will it?"

Haines reassured him. The man said he would be happy to call that murderer a liar in court. Haines said she doubted that would be necessary—there was already enough evidence. She was merely checking any loose ends.

Then she asked, quite casually, "Must have been quite a thrill, being around that much power."

"I didn't think it would be," the maitre d' said. "After all, Lovett's had some parties with important people before. Not one tenth as many as his father, but a few. Even less, now that he's so busy ruling everything. No more'n one or two since—since the Emperor was killed.

"As I said, I thought I was over being impressed. Not true. I wish I weren't so honest, though."

"Why?"

"Oh, if I didn't object to stretchers, I wager I could come up with some snappers about what happened that night, and how maybe one of them asked my advice, or anyway thought I ran the smoothest operation ever.

"But I do—and it didn't. Guess they had something important to talk about. Didn't watch the game much, I saw. And any time any of them wanted a drink, they went over to the serving station themselves.

"At least I got to watch the game on a back-room screen, which surprised me. Usually, big events like this, when Sr. Lovett shows up, I'm so busy running back and forth I have to get it from the vid the next day."

Haines smiled and walked the man out of her office, then went down a few floors to where the poor, harried Sr. Braun had managed to borrow a tiny office, where he was buried in archives, on another empty attempt to prove that Rosemont was no longer among the living.

Sten mused over the information for a moment. "Business. Bloody business. No aides, keep the help in the kitchen. That was the meeting I want."

"Documentation, Sten. No witnesses."

"I'm not sure that's correct. Emphasis—*business* meeting. They leave . . . and probably take their security with them. No cleanup—no *ELINT* cleanup. And the suite's not been used much since then.

"Lisa, friend of mine youth. Do you have four beefy men who'll do you a favor—no violence, only minor law-breaking—and never ever talk about it? It's got to be clean—I don't want any backblast on you. If there's a problem, I'll find my own heavy movers."

Haines smiled. "You aren't a cop who gets promoted if you don't have mentors. Rabbis, we call them. Hell if I know why. And when you get rank, you become a rabbi. I could probably get you half a precinct."

"Good. Four men. I'll get some coveralls made up. Lovett Arena needs help. And good, reliable old APEX Company is coming to the rescue. I'll need a medium gravlighter. Also clean."

"Again, easy. I'll get something from the impound yard."

Sten pulled down and consulted a map. "Okay," he said. "Here's the drill. Two days from now, eight hundred hours, I'll want them—here, at the corner of Imperial and Seventh Avenue. I'll drop them off when we're loaded."

"Two days? Why not now?"

"Because a very dejected Sr. Braun has finished with his investigation and now feels that the Imperial Police were correct. He is returning to his home world to report failure.

"I had two extraction routes. One was if I came out clean, the other if the drakh came down. I'll use the second, since I'll have a bit of a cargo."

"I think I know what you're going after. Why can't the analysis be done here? My techs don't ask questions."

"Lisa, remember what kind of murder we're talking about? Don't trust your people too much. I can't—and won't. And like I said, I'm not willing to leave you holding the bag. Anyway, I'm gone. I've got to look up an old friend."

He gathered his papers quickly.

"Thank you, Lisa."

"Sure. Although I didn't do very much."

"No. You did . . . a great deal. Next time around . . . I'll buy you and Sam'l, it was, your anniversary dinner."

He kissed her briefly, still wanting more, and was gone.

His schedule would be tight: make sure Braun appeared to board the next liner off Prime, contact the liaison with Wild's smugglers, and get a ship down for its cargo. Assuming the cargo would be there.

The manager of Lovett Arena was quite impressed with the polite technician and his crew, especially since there

had been—as best he knew—no complaints about the
business machines provided in Sr. Lovett's suite.

"I would hope not," the technician said. "This is
strictly routine. Our records show APEX installed the
equipment more than five years ago. In a room where
people spill drinks, possibly smoke tabac, and food is
present? How would we look—what would be left of our
reputation—if Sr. Lovett himself tried to use one of our
computers and it crashed on him? We are proud of what
we represent."

The manager was impressed. A service company actually servicing, without ten or twelve outraged screams
and threats of legal action? Especially since he himself
had been unable to find the original contract with APEX.

They stripped the suite bare of anything that went beep
or buzz. Sten almost missed the conference table, then
realized that it contained a simple computer/viewer suitable for reading, reviewing, or revising documents. But
that, and everything else, went onto gravlifts, down into
the bowels of Lovett Arena, onto the gravlighter, and then
vanished.

It was more than a month before the arena's manager
realized that he had been victimized by an exceptionally
clever gang of high-tech thieves.

The machines were carefully loaded onto one of Wild's
ships, sealed against any stray electromagnetic impulse,
and transported to Newton.

Technicians went to work. Sten and Alex hovered in
the background. They may have been somewhat sophisticated technologically, Kilgour especially, but this was
far beyond their level of expertise.

It was almost impossible to erase anything from a
computer. If a file were deleted, its backup would still
exist. If the backup were deleted, the "imprint" would
still be there, at least until something was recorded over
it. Even then, restoration could sometimes succeed.

The computers were first. From them came an aston-

ishing confused burble of various contracts indicating that
Lovett and his friends were hardly straight-arrow businessmen. That information was recorded for possible
later release to civil courts, after and if the council was
toppled. There were no computer phone records.

But that table was it.

Around it, years before, Sullamora had laid down the
law to the other conspirators. At that time, he was the
only one who had hung himself out to dry—contracting
for the murder of the press lord, contracting for Venloe's
services. He put it flatly—all of them were to sign a
''confession.'' It was a card made of indestructible plas.
On it was a formal admission of guilt, a preamble to
assassination. Kyes had been the first to insert the card
into the table's viewer and sign, and the others followed.
Each member of the conspiracy received one card, signed
by all members.

And a technician found it.

The retrieval was spotty, broken by intermittent images of a smiling older couple—someone's parents, possibly, interminably walking past some nondescript
scenery. A homevid?

But it was still there:

WE, THE . . . PRIVY COUNCIL, AFTER DUE CONSIDER
. . . COME TO THE . . . CONCLUSION . . . ETERNAL EM-
PEROR . . . INCREASINGLY AND DANGEROUSLY UNSTA-
BLE . . . DETERMINED TO . . . FOLLOWING . . .
TRADITION . . . STANDING . . . AGAINST TYRANTS . . .
HISTORICAL RIGHT . . . REMOVAL . . . AND HEREBY AU-
THORIZE . . . MOST EXTREME MEASURES . . . DESTRUC-
TION . . . TYRANNICIDE . . . TO ENSURE FREEDOM . . .

The document may have been broken, but it was quite
obvious. And absolutely untouched at the bottom were
the personal marks, the ''signatures'': Kyes. The Kraas.
Tanz Sullamora. Lovett. Malperin.

"I'll probably be able to restore more, sir. There's still some ghosts I haven't ID'd and pulled off the hardware."

Sten was quite happy.

It may have been missing some nonvital screws and springs, but Mahoney—and the Tribunal—had the smoking gun.

CHAPTER THIRTY-ONE

STEN WANTED A little R&R. Badly. He knew he had reason enough to feel brain-, body- and nerve-damaged, but guilt kept whispering in his ear. He ought to be sitting in the back of the courtroom, listening to the careful work of the Tribunal as it moved toward its conclusion.

This was a moment in history. What would he tell his grandchildren? "Yeah, I was around. But was off gettin' drunk and tryin' to get laid, so I can't tell you a whole lot."

Kilgour seized the logical high ground. "Clot th' granbabes y' nae hae, an' likely ne'er sire. Gie y'self off. Thae'll be bloody work t'come. Gore aye up t' our stockin' tops."

Mahoney backed him, telling Sten that he did not think there was any likelihood that the Tribunal would want any evidence submitted of the blown murder run on Earth. "Still, Admiral. I'd prefer you were out of town if they start callin' witnesses. Get going. Enjoy yourself. I'll send if I need you.

"Which will be soon. Not surprisingly, the privy council is planning a response. With moils and toils, they've put together a fleet of their bullyboys. Most loyal, most dedicated, and all that drakh. Translation—those who got their fingers the dirtiest proving their loyalty during the purge.

"When they arrive, we should have a proper welcome. Otho's shaking out a strike element from his ships. He thinks nothing could be finer than to put you on the

337

bridge.'' Mahoney laughed. ''See how fascinatin' a career in the military is? One day a police spy, the next an admiral again.''

Sten kept to himself his feelings about the military in any configuration, retired to his quarters, and thought about his vacation. Go to some tourist town and troll for company? No, he thought not. Not that he was suffering the pangs of lost love—at least he didn't think so. But no, it didn't feel right.

Cities? Not that, either. He had heard the yammer of the ugly throngs on Prime, and right now *any* city reminded him of that.

Stop brooding. Hit the fiche. You'll find something that jumps out at you.

He did.

Rock climbing—the hard way.

It was possible to climb anything using artificial aids—climbing thread, piton guns, chocks, jumars. So, of course, the ''pure'' climbers revolted and climbed with no aids whatsoever.

Sten thought that could be mildly suicidal. He was not *that* depressed. But there was a bit of appealing madness there.

He picked a climb—a vertical needle deep in one of Newton's wilderness areas—and equipped himself with a minor climbing outfit that included enough artificial aids to be able to belay himself as he climbed. He bought a tent and supplies and cursed when he realized he would have to carry a com and a miniwillygun. Most Wanted, remember, boy.

He found Alex and told him he was off. Kilgour, far, far too busy minding security on the Tribunal, barely had time for a farewell grunt and an arm around the shoulders.

Sten found his rented gravcar—and something else. He had forgotten that the word ''solitary'' was banned, at least until the present emergency was over and the council safely in their graves or prison cells. Waiting was his seven-Bhor-strong bodyguard and Cind, equipped similarly to Sten. He thought of protesting, but realized he would lose. If not to them then to Kilgour or Mahoney. It was not worth the battle.

But he issued strict orders.

They were to pitch camp separately from his, at least a quarter klick away. He didn't want their company—sorry to be rude—and he certainly did not want them on the rock with him.

"I don't think the council's assassins—if they have any tailing me, which I don't believe—will go boulder-swarming to make the touch."

The Bhor agreed. Cind just nodded.

"Easy order to follow, Admiral," one Bhor rumbled. "The only record my race has of climbing is when we were chased by streggan."

So Sten's R&R began on a somewhat less than idyllic note. That slightly off-key note continued to sound. The pinnacle was everything it had looked on the vid, punching straight up for almost a thousand meters through the low clouds. It was at the end of a small, rising alpine meadow with its own spring and bone-breakingly cold pond. The meadow was surrounded by the pinnacle's sky-touching big brothers. No one lived in the meadow, except for some small tree-dwelling marsupials, some long-wild bovines, and, Sten thought, a small night-loving predator he never saw.

He pitched his tent, and his bodyguard followed orders, pitching their camp one quarter kilometer, to the exact pace, away, semihidden behind brush on the other side of the pond.

Sten cooked, ate, and went to bed just after dusk. He slept dreamlessly, then rose, collected his climbing pack, and headed for the rock.

For a few hours he lost himself in the rhythm of the climb, the feel of the rock under his palms, and the attention to balance. He wedged a nut into a crack, tied himself off, and dug into his day pack for a snack. He

looked up. Not bad. He was almost 250 meters up.
Maybe he could spot a bivvy site farther up, do a one-
man siege later on, and actually get to the summit before
his vacation ended. He had already spotted at least six
other fascinating routes he wanted to try.

Then he looked down.

Eight faces looked up at him. His bodyguards were
sitting in a semicircle near the base of the pillar, doing
their job. Hell. Climbing was not a spectator sport.

He thought of throwing a piton or shouting something.
Come on, Sten, he told himself. Aren't you being a little
childish? However, he found himself climbing down a
couple of hours before he had planned, and the descent
was not nearly as mind-absorbing as going up had been.

The next day, he tried another route, this one chosen
not just for its interest, but because he did not think there
was an observation point for his damnably faithful bodyguards.

They found one anyway. He forced himself to ignore
them and climbed on. But his concentration, his ability
to lose himself, was . . . not shattered. He still reveled
in what he was doing. But he was . . . aware of other
things.

That night, after he had cooked a rather unimagina-
tive, underspiced curry and eaten solo, he found himself
sleepless. Across the pond, he could see the low flicker
from the Bhor's campsite. They must have found some
dry wood and built a tiny fire. He could almost, but not
quite, hear voices. Almost, but not quite, hear the crystal
chime of a laugh.

Sten swore to himself again. He hunted through his
expedition pack and found a bottle. Then he put his boots
back on and found his way around the pond to the fire-
light. There were only four bodyguards around the fire.
He tapped the bottle against a tree and stepped forward.
Cind and a Bhor came out of the blackness and lowered
their weapons.

"What's wrong?" she snapped, eyes sweeping the night.

"Uh . . . nothing. I . . . just had trouble getting to sleep. I thought . . . if I wasn't intruding . . ."

They welcomed him to their campfire and politely sipped from the bottle of Imperially synthesized "Scotch" Sten had brought along until they could find an excuse to dig out their own supply. Stregg. The Eternal Emperor had once said that stregg was to triple-run moonshine—whatever that meant—as moonshine was to mother's milk.

Regardless, Sten and his bodyguard got royally potted. The quiet alpine meadow was broken by occasional shouts of "by my father's frozen buttocks" and other Bhor toasts. The evening was culminated when three Bhor threw Sten into the pond.

A very juvenile evening, Sten thought confusedly when he woke the next day. Then he hurt too badly to assess the adultness of his situation. He was still in the Bhor camp. His head was pillowed on one Bhor's calf, and another Bhor was using his stomach for a pillow. Sten realized that he was being attacked by lethal air molecules, smashing into his body everywhere.

Cind and a Bhor walked—lopsidedly—into the camp.

"Wake up, you scrots," she snarled. "It's your shift. Oh, Christ, I hurt."

"Hurt quietly then," Sten whimpered. He found the bottle of Scotch that was still unfinished and chanced a swallow. No. No. His stomach tried to climb the distant pillar. He got to his feet. His soles hurt. "I am going to die."

"Do it quietly, then. Sir. Admiral." Turnabout was fair and all that.

By rights, Sten should have proven his ability at command and taken everyone for a five-klick run or something equally Admirally-Heroic. He managed to strip off his coveralls and—clot decency—wade into the pond until the freeze told him that the molecules were not at-

tacking. Then he pulled his coveralls back on and decided
to eat something.

There was no climbing done that day.

But from that point, the R&R became something very
different from Sten's original plans.

One of the Bhor asked about climbing. Sten showed
him some of the tricks on a nearby boulder. Cind had
already taken a basic climbing course, although the
course had specialized in going up the sides of buildings.

And so it went. Climb during the day. Twice he just
went for hill-scrambling around the mountain bases
nearby. At night, they ate communally. Sten moved his
tent into the Bhor campsite.

He spent a lot of time with Cind.

She was easy to talk to. Sten supposed this was some kind
of breach of discipline. What discipline? he asked himself.
You aren't even an admiral any more—technically. Even
if you are, do you want to be? He managed to get Cind to
stop calling him by his rank, and even to drop most of the
"sir's" with which she salted her speech.

He told her about the factory hellworld he had grown
on. He mentioned—briefly—his family. He told her about
Alex Kilgour, and the many, many years they had adven-
tured together.

He did not tell war stories.

Cind, at first, was disappointed. Here was a chance to
learn from the greatest warrior of them all. But she found
herself listening to other tales—of the strange beings he
had encountered, some human, some otherwise, some
friendly, some less than that. Again, there was no gore
to those stories.

The alpine meadow heard, many times, the chime of
crystal.

Cind talked about how strange it had been, growing
up as the daughter of the warrior sect of a jihad-prone
religion, a religion not only shattered by war but one
whose gods had been proven frauds and degenerates. It
had seemed natural to her to gravitate toward the Bhor.

"Although now I wonder sometimes. Was I just going from wanting one kind of belief-shelter"—she used the Talameic word—"to another?"

Sten raised an eyebrow. True or not, it was a sophisticated observation from someone as young as Cind.

He told her about the worlds he had seen. Tropic, arctic, vacuum. The redwoods of Earth. His own world of Smallbridge.

"Perhaps . . . I could show it to you. One day."

"Perhaps," Cind said, smiling very slightly, "I would like to see it. One day."

They did not sleep together. Cind might have gone to Sten's tent, if he had asked. He did not.

A very odd R&R, Sten mused, as his self-alloted vacation time expired and they loaded the gravcar. Not what I expected . . .

But maybe what I needed.

CHAPTER THIRTY-TWO

THE TRIBUNAL WAS nearly ready to announce its decision. After the last witness had been called and the final bit of evidence presented, the judges withdrew to their chamber. Several weeks of backbreaking clerical work followed as they pored over the mounds of testimony.

At first, Sten felt it was a great privilege to be allowed to watch. He, Alex, and Mahoney huddled in the far corner as Sr. Ecu and the three judges debated the relative worth of every detail. As recorder, Dean Blythe oversaw the efforts to officially document the private proceedings for legal history. Sr. Ecu was particularly wary that whatever the outcome, there would be no oversight anyone could use against them.

The judges assumed their roles with a fury. Warin remained totally impartial. Apus, despite her hatred for the Council, was an ardent defender. Sometimes Sten had to shake himself to remember what her true feelings were. One side of him grew angry when she relentlessly hammered away in the privy council's defense. The other side of him admired her for taking her duties so seriously.

Still, it was hard not to get pissed when things like the information he had retrieved from Lovett Arena were dismissed as nothing but rubbish, a trick of science or possibly even planted evidence.

Rivas, on the other hand—who only disagreed with the council for philosophical, not personal, reasons—became their angry tormentor. In public, and even in the privacy of chambers, he shouted down any attempt to weaken the case against the council. Sten did not bother the reasonable side of himself when Rivas went at it. He purely enjoyed the being's constant attacks. It was Rivas who kept pointing things back, talking about how circumstance after circumstance could not be ignored. And he mightily defended the council's secret agreement as proof of opportunity to conspire, if nothing else.

Then, as the weeks lumbered on, Sten's eyes glazed over. Alex and Mahoney were no better. They slipped away whenever possible. Unfortunately, dodging the waiting livie newscasters was worse than boredom. So mostly they stayed and dozed.

But finally it was nearly over. The Tribunal was getting down to the vote. Rivas and Apus had shed their roles as advocates and had joined Warin in impartial consideration. The suspense had Sten's interest stirring again. He leaned forward so that he would not miss a word.

"I don't think we can delay any longer, gentlebeings," Sr. Ecu was saying. "Are you ready for your decision?"

Sten did not hear the answer. Alex had planted an urgent elbow in his ribs. Mahoney was at the door making frantic motions for them to join him outside chambers.

Mahoney wasted no time. As soon as the chamber doors closed behind them he collared Sten and Alex.

"It's Otho," he said. "There's some very strange business at the spaceport. We're wanted. Now, lads."

As they hurried for the spaceport, Mahoney filled them in with what little he knew.

It seemed that they were being blessed with a high-level visit—from Dusable.

"What do those clots want?" was Sten's first reaction.

"Thae's all snakier villains ae any Campbell," was Kilgour's.

"That's all too true," Mahoney said. "But we can't be judging too harshly. We need all the help we can get, no matter how slimy the source."

By help, Mahoney said, he meant that no matter how crooked, Dusable was a recognized governmental body in the Empire—an important body. Not only that, but no mere representatives had been sent. Accordingly to Otho, the newly elected Tyrenne Walsh was on board, as was the president of the Council of Solons, that master of all political thieves, Solon Kenna.

"They are here to officially recognize the Tribunal's proceedings," Mahoney said. "Also, any bill of indictment they may hand down. So they're ready to jump in front of the cameras and announce their stand against the privy council."

Sten did not need a refresher course in politics to know what that meant. When slimy pols like Kenna and Walsh climbed on board, the political winds were definitely blowing in the Tribunal's favor. And when the council's other allies saw that, there was a good chance of many more shifts in the balance.

Only Otho and some of his Bhor troops were at the ship to greet them. The ship had just landed and the ramp run out. He hastily advised Sten that livie crews had been alerted and would soon come crushing in.

"By my mother's long and flowing beard," he growled, "luck is sticking with us. I knew you were lucky the first I met you, my friend." He gave Sten a heavy slap on the back.

Sten noticed that crude as Otho may appear, he was too wise a ruler not to figure out for himself what the sudden support from the Dusable fence sitters would mean for him. No political explanations were needed.

The ship's doors hissed open, but it was long moments before anyone stepped outside. Then Walsh and Kenna emerged, their aides following in an odd straggle. Sten was confused. He expected a typical display of pomp. Maybe it was because the livie crews had not arrived yet. Still, the two pols made a rather drab appearance.

Walsh and Kenna approached—a bit nervously, Sten thought. They almost jumped when Otho growled orders for his troops to draw up to smart attention—at least, as smart as any bowlegged Bhor could be. What was bothering the two? This should be an expected, if a bit puny, honor.

Mahoney stepped forward to greet them. Sten and Alex moved with him. There was a muffled sound inside the ship. Sten was sure it was someone cracking out a command—and he swore he recognized that command. Personally, knew it. He barely noticed as Walsh, Kenna, and their entourage hastily ducked to the sidelines. Sten was too busy gaping.

Squat little men with dark features and proud eyes exited in a precise spear formation. Their royal uniforms glowed with the records of their deeds. Their kukris were held high at a forty-five-degree port arms, light dazzling off the burnished facets of the blades.

Sten knew those men. He had once commanded them.

The Gurkhas! What in hell's name were they doing here? On a ship from Dusable?

Then he saw the answer. He saw it. But he didn't believe it. At first.

The most familiar figure in Sten's, or any other being's life, marched at the apex of the spear line. He towered over the Gurkhas. He looked neither left nor right, but kept those fierce eyes fixed royally ahead.

Sten could not move, speak, or salute. Beside him, he felt the frozen shock of his own companions.

"By my father's frozen buttocks," Otho muttered. "It's Him!"

As it reached them the spears parted and then reformed. Sten found himself staring into those oddly ancient/young eyes. He saw the recognition, and heard his name uttered. Alex jerked as his own name was mentioned after a momentary furrow of those regal brows.

The man turned to Mahoney and gave him a wide, bright grin.

"I'm glad you stuck around, Ian," the Eternal Emperor said.

Mahoney fainted.

CHAPTER THIRTY-THREE

NOT ALL OF the privy council's vengeance fleet was composed of bloody-handed loyalists to the New Regime. Blind obedience cannot make up all of a resume—particularly when the assigned task *must* be accomplished.

Fleet Admiral Fraser, not happy with her orders but as always obedient, commanded the attacking force from the bridge of the Imperial Battleship *Chou Kung*—such as it was. The privy council had stripped AM2 depots bare of their remaining fuel for the fleet. There was enough to get them to Newton, engage . . . and then that stolen AM2 convoy had best have been parked in the Jura System if any of them planned a return journey.

One problem Fraser did not have: her ships were not as undermanned as customary. Would that they were, she thought. The council had ordered all ships brought to full strength. So just as the fuel depots were stripped, so were noncombatant ships and ground stations.

Of course none of the commanders sent their best if they could avoid it. Fraser dreamed of having six months—no, a full E-year before she could beat the new fleet into command unity. Even that long would be a miracle, and Fraser thought wistfully of what she had read about draconian disciplinary methods used on water navies.

And of course there were volunteers. Some eager for action, more because they had chosen to back the council in the purge. If the council fell, these officers could expect no mercy whatsoever from the inevitable courts-martial that would be ordered, courts-martial that, almost certainly, would be empowered to order the ultimate verdicts.

Fraser did what she could as the fleet bored on through nothing, running constant drills and even going to the extreme of ordering some ships' navplots slaved to their division leaders.

She was not pleased—but she felt quietly confident, without underestimating her probable foe. She had carefully analyzed the slaughter of Gregor's 23rd Fleet. It had been skillfully handled, but the tactics were more those of raiders than conventional combat forces. Plus the defenders of the Jura System had a fixed area that must be defended. Fraser planned to bring them to battle well clear of the system. She would divert half her reserves to hit the Jura worlds, Newton being the primary target. She would have to split her forces, but certainly the defenders would have to do the same. Once the rebel units were defeated, Fraser's fleet would land on Newton. At that point, her responsibilities would end—which she was very grateful for.

The orders the grim-faced men in the accompanying troopships had were sealed, but Fraser, if she allowed herself to think about them, knew what they were.

A com officer interrupted the silence on the flag bridge. "Admiral . . . we have an all-freqs broadcast. Source of transmission . . . Newton."

"*All* frequencies?"

"That's affirmative. Including our own TBS and Command nets. Also it's going out on all the commercial lengths we're monitoring."

"Jam it. Except for the Command Net. Ship commanders' eyes only. I have no interest in my sailors seeing any propaganda." An all-frequency cast could only mean that the self-styled Tribunal had reached its verdict.

"We . . . can't."

"*Can't?*" Fraser did not need to say anything more. That was a word that did not exist.

The com officer wilted, then recovered. "No. Broadcast strength's got too much power behind it. Only way to block the transmission is to cut the entire fleet out of external communication."

That was a chance Fraser could not take. "Very well. Scramble as best you can. Patch a clear signal through to my set."

"Yes, ma'am."

Fraser and the other ship COs and division commanders saw what happened clearly. Other screens on other ships showed murky, partial images and speech. But the specific details of what happened were not necessary and, in any event, were quickly word-of-mouthed by any sailor standing duty on a command deck.

The vid showed the inside of the huge auditorium chosen for the Tribunal's hearing. The three solemn-faced judges sat, waiting.

A door behind them slid open, and a Manabi floated out. On either side of the door stood two stocky small humans, wearing combat fatigues and slouch hats, chin straps in place below their lower lips. Both of them were armed with willyguns and long, sheathed knives.

An off-screen voice commented, "All beings witnessing this cast are recommended to record it, as said before."

There was silence. Then the Manabi, Sr. Ecu, spoke.

"This is the final hearing of the Tribunal. However, circumstances have altered intent."

Fraser lifted an eyebrow. That kangaroo court was actually going to find no charges against the privy council? Not that it would matter.

"This is not to say that a verdict has not been reached. It is the finding of this Tribunal that the beings—Srs. Kyes, the Kraas, Lovett, and Malperin—who style themselves as the privy council are indictable.

"This Tribunal finds that a conspiracy for murder was planned and executed by these named beings, as individuals and as a group. We further have found, in accordance with one of the so-called Nuremburg statutes, and so declare their council is a criminal organization.

"Other charges which have been brought up before this Tribunal, up to and including high treason, will not be found on.

"We therefore charge all courts and officers of the law, both Imperial and individual, with the task of bringing the afore-named members of the privy council to a criminal court, to defend themselves against the charges found.

"However, this finding is not the only or the most important purpose of this cast."

Ecu floated to the side and turned to face that door.

It opened.

The Eternal Emperor entered the courtroom.

There may have been pandemonium, or the sound might have been muted. Fraser did not know. Certainly there was a boil of chaos on her own bridge. Eventually she forced order on her own mind, ignoring the shock that all she believed and served was no longer true, and shouted for silence.

And silence there was. Sailors may have stared at their dials and controls—but all that existed was the words that came from that screen.

"I commend the members of this tribunal. The investigators, the clerks, the officials, and the judges. They have proven themselves my Faithful and True Servants, in a time when such loyalty has become a warrant of death.

"They—and others—shall be rewarded.

"Now, we face a common task. To return the Empire to its greatness. It will not be easy.

"But it can—and will—be done.

"The work in front of us must be accomplished. There will not be peace, there will not be order until the Empire stretches as it did before, giving peace, prosperity, and the rule of law throughout the universe.

"I thank those of you who remained loyal, who knew

the privy council spoke out of fear, greed, and hatred, not in my name. But there are others.

"Others who for whatever reason chose to march under the bloody banner of the council. I order you now to stop. Obey no orders from the traitors. Listen to no lies or instructions. If you bear arms—lay them down. You must—and will—follow my orders. You will follow them immediately. There has been enough crime, enough evil.

"I specifically address myself to the misguided beings who are manning Imperial warships, on their way to attack this world and myself.

"You have two hours to obey. All ships of this criminal fleet are ordered to leave star drive and assume parking orbits in the system. No weapons are to be manned. At the end of this time, you are directed to surrender to my designated units.

"You are Imperial soldiers and sailors. You serve me— and you serve the Empire.

"Two hours.

"Any men, units, or ships failing to obey will be declared turncoats and outlaws and hunted down. The penalties for treason are very clear and will be meted with great severity.

"Surrender. Save your lives. Save your honor. Save your Empire."

The screen blanked. An audio came on, saying something about all physical attributes of the man who just spoke—the Eternal Emperor—being cast on a separate channel. Skeptics were invited to compare them with easily available public documents.

Fraser paid no attention. She served the Empire—and now, once more, with a vast relief, the Emperor himself.

"Flag! I want an all-ships link! Captain! On my command, stand by for secondary drive."

"We are going to—" someone on the bridge said.

"Serve the Emperor," Fraser interrupted.

The com officer shot her.

He himself died two seconds later, as Fraser's aide slashed Fraser's weighted baton across the officer's neck.

There were other guns and ceremonial knives out. A blast went wild and disabled the main drive controls. The flag bridge was a melee of mutiny—if that was what it was.

Secondary command centers never went on line—they too were in chaos.

The *Chou Kung* drove on, still under drive.

In miniature, that hysteria and devastation was the entire Imperial fleet as it kilkennied itself.

Some ships obeyed—and were attacked by others still loyal to the council. Other ships tried to continue the mission toward the Jura System. Still others managed to "disappear" into normal space and Yukawa drive. Division commanders snarled com channels, looking for orders, guidance, or agreement.

Then Sten attacked.

The Eternal Emperor had lied about the two hours of grace.

The late Admiral Fraser had correctly analyzed Sten's tactics in the raid on the AM2 convoy. The Bhor, the Rom, and the mercenaries were, indeed, more comfortable in single-ship or small-squadron attacks. She was also correct that the Tribunal's fleet would not be capable of a conventional defense against a conventional attack.

Sten found a third option. He deployed his entire fleet as a slashing cutting-out expedition, coming down on the Imperial units. His orders had been very simple: Attack any ship that is showing signs of fight. Hit them once—hard—and hold full speed. Regroup and reattack. If they go into normal space, go with them. Make sure they're either broadcasting a surrender signal or their main drive is disabled.

"Do not board. Do not close with and destroy. Ignore any ship obeying the Imperial orders.

"This is not a battle to the finish. Otho, I don't want any of your people playing berserker."

"What happens after they're broken?" a mercenary captain had asked.

"Sorry, Captain. There's no time for looting. I say again—no boarding. This whole damn mess is almost over. Let's not get anyone killed unnecessarily."

"What about Imperial survivors?"

"There'll be SAR ships put out. Eventually."

And that was how the battle was fought. Slice through . . . form up . . . hit them again.

Sten fought his ship—a cruiser—and three others. Time blurred. Each combat was different, each combat was the same. He gave his orders through a cold, clear anger.

The Emperor had returned.

Very well. So let's end it.

Eventually there was no one left still firing that was worthwhile shooting back at. Sten came back to himself, staggered with fatigue.

He looked at a chronometer.

The ship-day was nearly ended. He checked the main battlescreen. The scatter of indicators gave no sign that just hours before there had been a fleet to attack. It was, indeed, over.

So much for the nits.

Now for the vermin they had bred from.

CHAPTER THIRTY-FOUR

POYNDEX NOTICED THE tree had lost half its leaves. Like the privy council members who awaited him on the top floor, the rubiginosa seemed to be cowering at the news: The Eternal Emperor was back!

When he saw them huddled in their chairs, he realized that "cowering" was a poor description. Each of them had heard the executioner's song and was dying inside. Malperin looked half a century older. Lovett was a shrunken, pouch-faced little being.

The Kraa twins were the most changed of all. The one who had once waddled about in thick wads of fat had become a baggy, anorexic thing. Her skin drooped disgustingly. The once-thin Kraa had turned herself into a bulging pink ball, skin stretched tight around the new fat.

There was no question on any of their faces that the being who called himself the Eternal Emperor was exactly that.

All four beings leaped on Poyndex as if he were the last lifeboat leaving a hulled ship. He could barely make out the questions in the frightened confusion. "The Eternal Emperor . . ." ". . . What shall we do . . ." ". . . Where can we run . . ." ". . . Should we fight . . ." ". . . Can we fight . . ." On and on. They were working themselves into a suicidal frenzy. They were so hysterically afraid of the Emperor that they were ready to board ships and fling themselves onto his guns with all the troops they could command.

That was not what Poyndex wanted.

He soothed them and sat them down. He put on his saddest, most understanding face. "I think I know how to save you," he said.

They looked up at him, sudden hope in their eyes. Anything would do now. But Poyndex was not after just anything. He believed he had found his way back to power.

"I have not been charged with any crime," he said. "In whatever actions that were taken before I joined you, I had no part. Therefore, it should be no trouble at all for me to personally approach the Emperor."

No one protested, or warned him that it might be certain death, that no matter how blameless he might be, the Emperor was quite capable of killing any being vaguely involved with the privy council. Poyndex smiled to himself at that great showing of concern from his colleagues and friends.

"If you do not object, I'll offer the Emperor a deal."

Poyndex's proposal was simple. The privy council had lost, but they could still cause an enormous amount of damage and shed a great deal of blood. He urged them to retire to the emergency bunker that had been constructed deep under the rubiginosa tree. It was an ideal command center, plugged into every military channel. The bunker itself was constructed to withstand anything up to a direct nuclear explosion. From there they could fight to the death if the Emperor refused the deal.

Poyndex would point all that out to the Emperor. Then he would say that the privy council had no wish to cause so much harm if it could be avoided. In the interest of all the innocent beings of Prime World, they would agree to lay down their arms if granted their lives.

"No prison," the once-fat Kraa snarled. "Me sis couldn't bear the filthy thing."

"I'm not suggesting prison," Poyndex said. "I'm suggesting exile. Under the terms I plan to negotiate, you would be permitted to freely board your private ships and flee to the farthest reaches of the Empire. Beyond the frontiers, if The Emperor he wishes it. And you would be forbidden ever to return.''

''Do you think he'll go for it?'' Lovett whined.

Oh, yes, Poyndex assured. Yes, indeed he will. The Emperor, like Poyndex, was a practical man. Then he told them they ought to proceed instantly to the bunker. There should be no delay—in case the Emperor struck unexpectedly.

Poyndex watched the privy council members hurry off to the fates he had planned for them, like beasts to the butcher.

CHAPTER THIRTY-FIVE

THE KRAAS, ALWAYS aware of that area of the human back between the third and fourth ribs, were the first to correctly analyze the subtext of the Emperor's transmission: "Clottin' Poyndex! Clottin' bassid set us up an' sold us out."

Why not? They would have done the same, had they the chance.

"Shoulda knowed," the now-fat one growled. "Sit here in this clottin' bunker, waitin' an' waitin' an' waitin'. We got no forces in space, th' air, or holdin' the ports."

Their screams of outrage were the loudest it had gotten in the privy council's underground retreat in days. The Kraas had spent the time since Poyndex had left on his "negotiating mission" gorging and purging. Malperin and Lovett found themselves together frequently—but with nothing to say. They might have been a pair of silent ghosts, haunting the cellars below the castle they once ruled from.

The guards and servants learned the art of swiftly and silently following whatever orders they were given and then disappearing into their own quarters.

Then came the announcement, on the special wavelength set aside:

"This is the Eternal Emperor.

"I have been approached by an emissary of the traitorous privy council. They wanted conditional terms for their surrender.

358

"I reject these, in the name of civilization and the Empire itself. There can be no negotiation with murderers.

"I demand immediate, complete, and unconditional surrender.

"Citizens of Prime World—"

At that point the Kraas had begun screaming. No one in the com room heard the details of what else the Emperor ordered. It was nothing surprising: Prime was declared under martial law. All military personnel were to report to their barracks and remain there. Officers and noncommissioned officers were to maintain discipline, but no more. All ships to ground and remain grounded or be fired upon. Police were instructed to keep public order—without violence, if possible. Rioters and looters would be punished . . .

Nothing surprising.

Until the end:

"Imperial forces will be landing on Prime within the hour."

Impossibly, the Kraas' howls became louder.

Trapped . . . clot that . . . out of here.

One of them was on a com to the capital city of Fowler's main port, giving hurried orders to the commander of their "yacht"—a heavily armed ex-cruiser—and its two escorts, ordering preparation for immediate takeoff.

"Why?" Malperin wondered in a monotone. "There is nowhere to run to."

"Clot there ain't! There's allus a back door!"

The other Kraa broke in. "Even if there ain't, damned sure rather go down fightin' than just waitin' f'r th' butcher's hammer!"

And they were gone.

Lovett started to pour a drink. He put the glass down, unfilled, and sat. He stared at Malperin. The silence returned.

* * *

A flotilla of tacships were the first to scream down and across Soward's launch grounds. Other flotillas provided Tac Air over the rest of Prime's ports.

The lead tacship's exec/weapons officer reported three ships, drives active.

"All elements . . . Fairmile Flight . . . Targets as indicated and illuminated . . . Goblin launch . . . *Fire!*"

Non-nuclear medium-range missiles spat out of the tacships' tubes, homing on the Kraas' three ships. Three blasts became a single fireball belching up thousands of feet.

And Mahoney ordered in the fleets.

Sten, as per orders, was the first to bring his in. Destroyers and cruisers hung over Soward and Fowler. He brought his own battleship and its two fellows down onto Prime—flashthought: A bit different than when I skulked out of here last—and behind them the assault transports landed, and armor and troops spilled out.

Kilgour tossed Sten his combat harness, and Sten buckled on the webbing that held the heavy Gurkha kukris and a miniwillygun.

He would command the assault on the council's bunker himself. The Eternal Emperor had given him explicit orders: he wanted the Kraas, Malperin, and Lovett—alive if at all possible. He did not want to see, he added, the work of Sten's Tribunal wasted.

"Admiral." A screen was indicated.

Five armored gravsleds pulled onto the field about three kilometers away. Four were standard squad combat types; the fifth was a command unit.

"Ah think w' flushed some ae them," Kilgour said, mentally plotting their intended destination, that fireball that had been the ready-to-lift ships.

Before Sten could issue orders, a tacship bulleted across the field, scattering area-denial cratering bomblets. The blast flipped two of the sleds out of control, and a third lost power and slammed, nose first, into the smoking, newly dug ditch.

Two were left. Their pilots spun them through 180 degrees, back the way they had come.

But Sten saw that their exit had been sealed, not by Imperial forces or bombing, but by a screaming, boiling mob. Armed and unarmed. Human and alien.

The gravsleds fired into the mob. Beings fell and were shattered. More replaced them.

The squad gravsled was disabled and grounded. Someone, somewhere, had found, stolen, or seized an anti-armor weapon and fired. The blast disintegrated the gravsled—and sent its attackers spinning.

The command sled changed course once more, this time toward the grounded Imperial ships.

It never made it.

Sten saw the flash as a homemade incendiary landed on its top deck and fire poured down into the McLean intakes. The sled shuddered to a halt. Sten saw the rear ramp drop and then—

He *thought* he saw two beings come out: one enormously fat, the other looking like a skeleton wearing a tent. Their hands were upraised, and they were shouting something.

And then the mob poured over them.

Sten turned away from the screen.

"Ah hae i' recorded," Kilgour said. "We'll need ae frame-b'-frame f'r an' ID an' confirm't thae wa' th' Kraas. Thae'll be nae enow lef' f'r th' autopsy."

Sten nodded, still not looking at the screen. "Let's go, Mr. Kilgour. I want the courts to have *somebody* to bring to trial."

The assigned Imperial troops were no better or worse than the rest of the Empire's units Sten had faced lately. It did not matter—Sten had already assumed inexperience and formed his spearhead from the mercenaries.

He assumed they would have to fight their way through the streets of Fowler to the privy council's headquarters—but they did not. The riots and the revenge had already swept through the streets they took: overturned gravcars and -sleds, some burnt-out; improvised barricades; bodies, some uniformed, some not.

Burning and burnt businesses and buildings.

Three times bodies dangling from street lamps.

But nothing they had to stand against.

Surprisingly, there was order, of sorts. Civilians directed traffic as best they could—what little traffic there was. More civilians patrolled the walkways.

The sergeant commanding the combat squad in Sten's assault gravsled stuck his head out of the hatch, shouted a question to one of the civilians, and received an answer.

"Cult a' the Emp, sir. Helpin' pave the way, sir."

Sten thought the cult practiced nonviolence. Perhaps the bruised man he saw being frog-marched by three large women had tripped and fallen downstairs. Or maybe there would be a confession to make later.

He heard the sound of firing as his assault force closed on the council's headquarters.

There were bodies in the mottled brown of the Imperial Guard and riddled gravsleds in front of it. Sten dismounted and was greeted by a sick- and worried-looking captain, a young woman who could not decide whether to cry or swear. It had been the first time she had led a unit into combat—and the first time the unit she had so carefully knitted together took casualties.

She neither cried nor swore—but professionally made a sitrep. The council had guards inside the building—there. Four antitrack launchers sandbagged there and over there. Snipers and rapid-fire weapons upstairs in the building itself. All orders to surrender had been ignored.

Sten thanked her and issued orders. She was to pull her company back. Make sure the area was sealed—nobody out but, more importantly, nobody in. Especially not another lynch mob.

The captain watched in awe as Sten and Kilgour issued a string of orders to their mercenaries and Bhor troops.

You get good, Sten thought, when you're doing it for the fortieth or four hundredth time around and you're armored against seeing your people get killed.

He brought up a company of heavy tracks and used them to bulldoze barricades and smash through the buildings around the headquarters to provide firing positions. Heavy weapons were readied, and fire was opened against the snipers and crew-served guns.

"Th' wee antitrack launchers," Kilgour said. "Ah hae their medicine ready."

He did.

Kilgour had ordered snipers—the best an' y' ken who y'be, dinnae be tryin't t' smoke me—into flanking positions.

As Sten ordered a gravsled to move forward, he sensed Cind moving in close to him. Out of the corner of his eye, he saw her scanning the confusion for hidden danger—danger against him.

The antitrack crews aimed—and were sniped down. More of the council's—soldiers? secret cops? private goons?—ran to replace them.

Willyguns cracked, and the new gunners never made it. A third try . . . and volunteers suddenly got scarce.

"Mister Kilgour?"

Alex shouted orders, and Sten's hand-picked squad doubled into the lowered troop ramp of a heavy track.

"Y' dinnae hae t' be knockin't," Alex ordered the track commander. "An' gie y'self a bit ae coverin't fire. Go!"

The track ground forward, turrets flaming. Its tracks clawed over one of the abandoned antitrack launchers, and then the multiton monster exploded through the entrance of the council's building, into the huge atrium.

The ramp banged down, and Sten and his "arresting officers" came out. He noticed the green-encrusted fountains and what must have been some kind of tall dead tree in the atrium's center. The tank had felled the tree as it slid to a halt before the troops dismounted.

Sten glanced at the small map case he held. "Bunker entrance is . . . over there. Move slow, dammit! Don't end up makin' history by bein' the last one dead."

Good advice, Sten thought. Listen to it. A dead admiral being the last casualty of this . . . war? Revolt? Insurrection? Whatever might rate more than a footnote.

They went down and down, into the bowels below what had been the privy council's proudest construction. Cind and Alex kept close to Sten as they moved from cover to cover like cautious snakes.

There was no need to be careful.

There was no resistance.

Malperin and Lovett were found sitting in a room. They did not seem to hear Sten's orders.

Cind stared at the two beings, at the husks who had once been her rulers. Sten thought he saw pity in her eyes.

Kilgour repeated Sten's orders.

They finally responded to his growls. They stood when Alex told them to, were strip-searched for weapons and suicide devices without protest, then followed the arresting squad back up and out.

It almost seemed, Sten thought, as if they were secretly glad it was all over.

He wondered if their apathy would continue past the moment when the trial began.

CHAPTER THIRTY-SIX

"SIT DOWN, STEN," the Eternal Emperor said. "But pour us both a drink first."

From long habit as former commander of the Emperor's personal guard, Sten knew he was at ease when drink was mentioned. But being "At Ease," and being "at ease" were difficult under the circumstances. It had been many years since he had a shot of stregg with the boss. And in those times, Sten had thought that the word "Eternal" was merely a symbolic title, if he thought of it at all.

He noticed, however, that when the Emperor took his drink, he only gave it an absentminded sip. Sten did the same.

"I won't thank you for all you've done," the Emperor said. "The words would seem silly. At least to me."

Sten wondered what was up. The Emperor, despite his pose of informality, was being damned formal. That usually meant he had a surprise up his sleeve. Sten hoped it did not involve him. He saw the Emperor frown at him slightly, then look at the barely touched stregg in his own hand. The frown vanished, and the Eternal Emperor tossed it back in one swallow. He slid the glass across the table for more. Sten drank his own down and redid the honors. He felt the stregg light its way down and spread out its warmth, but he still felt no more at ease.

He wished like clot he could ask the Emperor how he did it. Where had he been for all those years? What had he done? And why in clot wasn't he dead? No, best not ask. The Emperor was jealous of his secrets.

"The last time we talked together," the Emperor said, "I was doing my damndest to give you a promotion. You turned me down. I hope you aren't planning on making that a habit."

Oh, clot, here it comes. Sten braced himself.

"How does head of Mercury Corps sound?" the Emperor said. "I'll raise its command grade and give you a second star. How does that sound, Admiral?"

"Retired admiral, sir," Sten said, gulping. He had to get it out fast. "And I hate to seem ungrateful and all, but no thanks. Please."

Sten saw the cold look knot the Emperor's brow. Then it eased slightly.

"Why?" It was a one-word command.

"It's like this. I've spent my whole life soldiering. In public service, if you will. I've been rewarded far more than I could have ever dreamed. I was nothing. A Vulcan Delinq. Now, I'm an admiral. And you want to make it with two stars. Thank you, sir. But no thanks.

"I have to start making my own life. Find a place for myself in the civilian world. I was confused before. Maybe I still am. But only a little. Because I'm looking forward to it. It's time for me to start doing the usual, dull human business."

Sten thought of Lisa Haines, and how undull his life might have been if events had not intervened. The whole time he had spoken, he had kept his eyes down. Now he looked up to see the Emperor glaring at him, eyes white steel.

"I'm not doing a good job of this, sir," Sten said. "I'm not explaining very well. It's not something that comes out easy for someone like me."

He said no more. The Emperor would let him know if more was welcome. The glare shut off. The Emperor chugged half his drink, then lifted his legs up on his desk and eased back in his chair.

"I understand," he said. "I'm asking you to make a big sacrifice. Actually, another big sacrifice. But I don't think you realize the situation."

He finished his drink, leaned over, and hooked the bottle with a finger, poured, and shoved the stregg back to Sten. They both drank—and refilled.

"But look at the mess we're in," the Emperor continued as if there had not been a halt. "Beings are starving. Millions have no work. Just about any government you look at is near collapse. Just getting the AM2 to the right places and fast is going to be a nightmare. Much less all the other troubles I see ahead. Now what am I going to do about all this—without any help?"

Sten shook his head. He had no answer.

"So why is it a big surprise when I ask someone like you—with all those years of public service, as you said— to stay with me now? Where else can I get that kind of experience?"

"Yessir," Sten said. "I see your point. But—"

"But me no buts, young Sten," the Eternal Emperor said. "Look. I'm not asking for me. I'm asking for your Empire. How can you refuse? Tell me that. How can you look me in the eye and refuse to help?

"But don't answer yet. Forget Mercury Corps. I have a better idea. I'm making you my chief troubleshooter— with some kind of fancy plenipotentiary sort of title. Help me out with heads of state, tricky negotiations, and any kind of major crisis situation.

"And for your first job, I want you to help me out with the Bhor. I want to do something special for them. They've been my most loyal subjects. They were your idea way back, if I recall."

"Yessir," Sten said.

"So. They're going to have a big celebration in the Lupus Cluster. Honoring my return and all and the victory over those clots who wanted to be my enemy. I want you to go there for me. To the Wolf Worlds. Be my representative at the ceremonies. I can't think of a being they would appreciate more. Can you?''

"Nossir," Sten said. And as he said it, he knew he was doomed.

The Eternal Emperor was right. There was no way he could refuse him this—or the rest that would follow.

The victory celebrations aboard the Bhor fleet lasted all the way back to the Lupus Cluster.

Cind kept a close watch on Sten. He joined in all the toasts and the parties and kept up with his hard-drinking friends, Otho and Kilgour. But in repose, his face became a mask, revealing nothing. She knew him better now. She could sense the thoughts churning through his mind—but what those thoughts were, she had no notion.

Cind saw him jolt up once in the middle of a toast to the Eternal Emperor and look up at the portrait on the ship's banquet compartment wall. He stared at it for a long time, then shook his head and downed his drink. A moment later he was laughing and talking with his friends again.

But Cind would remember that look for a long time—and wonder what was on Sten's mind.

CHAPTER THIRTY-SEVEN

MALPERIN AND LOVETT sat in a cell aboard the Emperor's personal yacht, the *Normandie*. It might have appeared a rather comfortable suite, but the doors were locked and guarded, any conceivable or potential weapons had been removed, and there were sensors monitoring their every breath.

The fog they had been in when Sten captured them had begun to lift.

They had been told they were to be tried. The trial would take place on Newton. They would be offered the finest defense counsels in the Empire, and an adequate time to prepare whatever defense they chose.

Cautiously, mindful of the monitors, the two had begun discussing what they should do, what defense might be offered. They had begun to use circumlocutions as they planned, and, against logic, to whisper.

There had been six of them once—determined to reach for the highest power of all. And, for a moment, they had held it.

Now . . . forget the deaths and forget the cell. Life is to be lived, Malperin said. Lovett managed a small smile.

There was a tap outside, and the compartment door opened.

A man entered. Neither tall nor stocky, he looked to be in good physical shape. He was wearing expensive civilian clothes. He was not an ugly man, not a handsome man.

"Gentlebeings," he said softly. "I have been assigned as your escort and aide for the trial.

"My name is Venloe."

Mahoney stormed into the Eternal Emperor's private office, spewing obscenities. He held a fiche in his shaking hand.

"Lord, Ian. What happened?"

"Some clottin' drakh-head on the *Normandie*! Playing God! 'Prisoners managed to escape cell. Found way to lifecraft. Attempted to enter. Security officer tried to apprehend, but was forced to . . .'

" 'Shot while attemptin' escape!' Christ! Clottin' bastard can't even find an original excuse.

"All that work. Sten'll kill that clottin' moron—but I'll have beaten him to it! Jesus Mary Mother on a gravsled! I'll crucify the clot! Have his guts for a winding sheet." He broke off. "I do not believe this. Clot!"

The Emperor picked up the fiche, put it in a viewer, and scanned the decoded message that had been transmitted in the Empire's personal command code.

He scanned it again, then grunted. "Not good, Ian. Not good at all."

"Not good . . . okay." Mahoney brought himself under control. "You're the boss. How high do we hang this—whoever did this? Not that it matters. What's the spin for damage control?"

The Emperor thought a moment. "None. What happened is what happened. And I'll arrange the proper way to deal with our ambitious gunman. But that's all. No investigation, Mahoney. That's an order." He paused. "So we've lost our war crimes trial. I don't think it matters. There's too much of the privy council's drakh left around for anybody to be much interested in what happened to Malperin and Lovett."

"That's it," Mahoney said incredulously. "Those two just . . . vanished?"

"Something like that. As I said, what happened is what

happened. Pour me a drink, Ian. We'll drink their souls to hell, like Sten's hairy friends say.''

Ian stared at the Emperor, then got up and went to a table, where he found the decanter of stregg.

The Eternal Emperor turned his chair and looked out the window at the once-blasted site of his palace, Arundel. Reconstruction had already begun.

Mahoney could not see his face.

The Eternal Emperor smiled.

About the Authors

CHRIS BUNCH is a Ranger—and Airborne—qualified Vietnam vet, who's written about phenomena as varied as the Hell's Angels, the Rolling Stones, and Ronald Reagan.

ALLAN COLE grew up in the CIA in odd spots like Okinawa, Cyprus, and Taiwan. He's been a professional chef, investigative reporter, and national news editor of a major West Coast daily newspaper. He's won half a dozen writing awards in the process.

BUNCH and COLE, friends since high school, have collaborated on everything from the world's worst porno novel to more film and TV scripts than they care to admit. They stopped counting at one hundred when they suffered the total loss of all bodily hair.

Their cover blown in the Caribbean by angry fans of the Sten series, Bunch and Cole were last seen at Shannon Airport, in the company of drunken Aeroflot pilots. Their suspected destination: The Soviet-Irish Friendship Bar in Leningrad.

Also forthcoming is a trilogy to be published by Crown Books and Ballantine. Their highly praised Vietnam novel, A RECKONING FOR KINGS, is available from Ballantine Books.